Maya Blake's hopes of becoming a writer were born when she picked up her first romance at thirteen. Little did she know her dream would come true! Does she still pinch herself every now and then to make sure it's not a dream? Yes, she does! Feel free to pinch her, too, via Twitter, Facebook or Goodreads! Happy reading!

Clare Connelly was raised in small-town Australia among a family of avid readers. She spent much of her childhood up a tree, Mills & Boon book in hand. Clare is married to her own real-life hero, and they live in a bungalow near the sea with their two children. She is frequently found staring into space—a surefire sign that she's in the world of her characters. She has a penchant for French food and ice-cold champagne, and Mills & Boon novels continue to be her favourite ever books. Writing for Modern is a long-held dream. Clare can be contacted via clareconnelly.com or at her Facebook page.

D0795205

CLAIMING MY HIDDEN SON

MAYA BLAKE

BRIDE BEHIND THE BILLION-DOLLAR VEIL

CLARE CONNELLY

MILLS & BOON

All rights reserved including the right of reproduction
in whole or in part in any form. This edition is published
by arrangement with Harlequin Books S.A.

This is a work of fiction. Names, characters, places, locations
and incidents are purely fictional and bear no relationship to
any real life individuals, living or dead, or to any actual places,
business establishments, locations, events or incidents.
Any resemblance is entirely coincidental.

This book is sold subject to the condition that it shall not,
by way of trade or otherwise, be lent, resold, hired out
or otherwise circulated without the prior consent of the publisher
in any form of binding or cover other than that in which it is published
and without a similar condition including this condition
being imposed on the subsequent purchaser.

® and TM are trademarks owned and used by the trademark owner
and/or its licensee. Trademarks marked with ® are registered with the
United Kingdom Patent Office and/or the Office for Harmonisation
in the Internal Market and in other countries.

First Published in Great Britain 2019
by Mills & Boon, an imprint of HarperCollins*Publishers*
1 London Bridge Street, London, SE1 9GF

Claiming My Hidden Son © 2019 by Maya Blake

Bride Behind the Billion-Dollar Veil © 2019 by Clare Connelly

ISBN: 978-0-263-27364-9

MIX
Paper from
responsible sources
FSC C007454

This book is produced from independently certified FSC™ paper
to ensure responsible forest management.
For more information visit www.harpercollins.co.uk/green.

Printed and bound in Spain
by CPI, Barcelona

CLAIMING MY HIDDEN SON

MAYA BLAKE

PROLOGUE

THE DRUMMING IN my ears was loud. So loud I had the fleeting thought that I was on the verge of suffering a stroke. Of doing myself irreparable harm and comprehensively ending this debacle once and for all.

But that would be too easy.

And the headline…

I could see it now.

*Axios Xenakis Suffers Stroke Due to
Family Pressures!*

They would have no clue as to the unreasonable part, of course. Despite the media outlets lauding the story of the Xenakis near-ruin to phenomenal rise on a regular basis these days, they would be swift to jump on past flaws. Old skeletons would be dragged out of closets. I would be deemed weak. Broken. Not quite up to the task of managing a global conglomerate.

Just like my father.

Just as my grandfather had been falsely labelled after that one risky move that had seen all his hard work whittled away to almost nothing.

He'd had to bear that one misfortune all the way to his grave.

Once a titan of his industry, a simple decision to align himself with the wrong partner had decimated him, leaving the Xenakis name with a stench of failure that had lingered long after his death, causing insidious damage.

Damage that had taken back-breaking hard work to reverse, with my refusal to allow my family name to sink without a trace spurring me to seek daring solutions.

The Xenakis name was no longer one to be ashamed of.

Now it was synonymous with success and innovation—a global conglomerate that *Fortune 500* companies vied to be associated with.

However, the solution being proposed to me now was one set to resurrect the unsavoury ghosts of the past, with their talons of barefaced greed—

'Ax, are you listening? Did you hear what Father said?' asked Neo, my brother.

'Of course I heard it. I'm not deaf,' I replied, with more than a snap to my voice.

'Thank God for that—although you do a great stone statue impression.'

I ignored Neo and fixed my gaze on the man seated behind the large antique desk. My father was studying me with a mixture of regret and apprehension. He knew my precise thoughts on the subject being discussed.

No, not *discussed*.

It was being *thrust* upon me.

'No,' I replied firmly. 'There has to be another way.'

The tension in the room elevated, but this was too serious for me to mince my words. Too serious to let the elephant that always loomed in the room on occasions like this cloud my judgement.

I simply couldn't allow the fact that my grandfather had chosen me as his successor instead of my father to get in the way of this discussion. Nor could I allow the resentment and guilt that had always tainted my relationship with my father to alter my view on what was being proposed.

What was done was done. I'd turned the tides and restored the fortunes of my family. For that even my father couldn't object.

Which was why I was a little surprised when he emphatically shook his head.

'There isn't. Your grandfather was of sound mind when he made the arrangement.'

'Even though he was judged otherwise in other areas?'

Barely fettered bitterness filtered through my voice. The injustices dealt to my grandfather and mentor, the man who taught me everything I know, still burned like acid all these years after his untimely death.

'Now is not the time to reopen old wounds, Axios,' my father said, jaw clenched.

My quiet fury burned even as I accepted his words. 'I agree. Now is the time to discuss ways to get me *out* of this nonsense.'

And it *was* nonsense to expect an arrangement like this to hold water.

'A sweeping agreement where the other party gets to call the shots whenever they like? How come the lawyers haven't ripped this to shreds?' I demanded, striving to keep a tighter rein on my ire.

My father's lips firmed. 'I've spent the last month discussing it with our counsel. We can fight it in court, and probably win, but it'll be a protracted affair. And is now really the time to draw adverse publicity to the company? Or drag your grandfather's name through the mud again for that matter?'

My own lips flattened as again I grimly accepted he was right. With Xenakis Aeronautics poised for its biggest global expansion yet, the timing was far from ideal.

Which was exactly what Yiannis Petras had banked on.

'You mentioned you'd offered him ten million euros and he refused? Let's double the offer,' I suggested.

Neo shook his head. 'I already tried. Petras is hell-bent on Option A or Option B.'

The breath left my lungs in a rush. 'Over my dead body will I go for Option A and hand over twenty-five percent of Xenakis Aeronautics,' I replied coldly. 'Not for the paltry quarter of a million his father bailed Grandpapa out with, while almost crippling him with steep interest repayments!'

The company I'd spent gruelling years saving was now worth several billion euros.

My brother shrugged. 'Then it's Option B. A full and final one hundred million euros, plus marriage to his daughter for minimum term of one year.'

A cold shudder tiptoed down my spine.

Marriage.

To a bride I didn't want and with a connection to a family that had brought mine nothing but misery, pain and near destitution.

During the formative years of my life I witnessed how a fall from grace could turn family members against each other. Clawing my own family out of that quagmire while other factions sneered and expected me to fail had opened my eyes to the true nature of relationships.

Outwardly, the Xenakis were deemed a strong unit now, but the backbiting had never gone away. The barely veiled expectation that everything I'd achieved would be brought down like a pile of loose bricks and that history would repeat itself was a silent challenge I rose to each morning.

While my extended family now enjoyed the fruits of my labour, and even tripped over themselves to remain in my good graces, deep down I knew a simple misstep was all it would take for their frivolous loyalties to falter.

I didn't even blame them.

How could I when my own personal interactions had repeatedly taken the same route? Each liaison I entered into eventually devolved into a disillusioning level of avarice and status-grabbing.

It was why my relationships now had a strict time limit of weeks. A few months, tops. Which made the thought of tying myself to one woman for twelve long months simply...*unthinkable.*

My chest tightened, and the urge to rail at my grandfather for putting me in this position seared me with shame before I suppressed it.

He'd been in an equally impossible position. I knew firsthand what the toll of keeping his family together had cost him—had watched deep grooves etch his grey face once vibrant with laughter and seen his shoulders slump under the heavy burden of loss.

Yes, he should have told me about this Sword of Damocles hanging over my head. But he was gone. Thanks to the ruthless greed of the Petras family. A family hell-bent on extracting another pound of flesh they didn't deserve.

'The hundred million I understand. But why insist on marriage to the daughter?' I asked my brother as his words pierced the fog of my thoughts.

Neo shrugged again. 'Who knows how men like Petras think? Maybe he just wants to offload her. The clout that comes from marrying into the Xenakis family isn't without its benefits,' he mused.

I shuddered, the reminder that, to most people, my family and I were nothing but meal tickets sending a shock of bitterness through me.

'And did you meet this woman I'm to tie myself to?'

He nodded. 'She's...' He stopped and smiled slyly. 'I'll let you judge for yourself.' His gaze left mine to travel over my grey pinstriped suit. 'But I'm thinking you two will hit it off.'

Before I could demand an explanation my father leaned forward. 'Enough, Neo.' My father's gaze swung to me, steel reflected in his eyes. 'We can't delay any longer. Yiannis Petras wants an answer by morning.'

The pressure gripping my nape escalated—the effect of the noose closing round it ramping up my discord. Marriage was the last thing I wanted. To anyone. But especially to a Petras. Both my grandparents and my parents had been strained to breaking point because of the Petras family's actions, with ill-health borne of worry taking my grandmother before her time too.

There had to be another way...

'What's her name?' I asked my father—not because I

cared but because I needed another moment to think. To wrap my head around this insanity.

'Calypso Athena Petras. But I believe she responds to Callie.'

Beside me, Neo smirked again. 'A dramatic name for a dramatic situation!'

I balled my fist and attempted to breathe through the churning in my gut. First they'd forced my grandfather's business into the ground, until he'd broken his family right down the middle by working himself into an early grave. Now this…

'Show me the agreement.' I needed to see it for myself, find a way to assimilate what I'd been committed to.

My father slid the document across the desk. I read it, my fingers clenching as with each paragraph the noose tightened.

Twelve months of my life, starting from the exchange of vows, after which either party would be free to divorce.

Twelve months during which the Petras family who, by a quirk of karma—if you believe in that sort of thing—had fallen on even harder times than they'd condemned my family to would be free to capitalise fully on their new status of wealth and privilege by association.

My lips twisted. I intended to have my lawyers draft divorce papers before I went anywhere near a church.

I exhaled, knowing my subconscious had already accepted the situation.

'Don't overthink it, brother. You're thirty-three next month. This will be over by your thirty-fourth birthday. If you bite the bullet,' Neo offered helpfully.

Slowly, I dragged myself back under control. 'I've worked too hard and too long to restore our family back to where it belongs to lose it to a greedy opportunist. If there's no other way…tell Petras we have a deal.'

My father nodded, relieved, before he sent me another

nervous glance. The kind that announced there was something more equally unsavoury to deliver.

'What now?' My patience was hanging by a thread.

'Besides paying for the wedding, we also need to present the family with a…a dowry of sorts. Petras has asked for Kosima.'

I surged to my feet, uncaring that my chair tipped over. '*Excuse* me?'

My father's face tightened. 'No one has stepped foot on the island since your grandfather passed—'

'That doesn't mean I want to hand it over to the son of the man who caused his death!'

A flash of pain dimmed his eyes. 'We don't know that to be strictly true.'

'Don't we? Did you not see for yourself the pressure he was under? He only started drinking after the problems with Petras started. Is it any wonder his heart failed?'

'Easy, brother,' Neo urged. 'Father is right. The house is rotting away and the land around it is nothing but a pile of weeds and stones.'

But I was beyond reason. Beyond furious at this last damning request.

'Grandpapa loved that island. It belongs to us. I'm not going to hand it over to Petras. Isn't it enough that he's imposing this bilious arrangement on us?'

'Is it enough for you to drag your heels on this last hurdle?' My father parried.

Unable to remain still, I strode to the window of the building that housed the headquarters of Xenakis Aeronautics, the global airline empire I'd headed for almost a decade. For a full minute I watched traffic move back and forth on the busy Athens streets while I grappled with this last condition.

I sensed my brother and father approach. I didn't acknowledge them as they positioned themselves on either side of me and waited.

Waited for the only response that I could conceivably give. The words burned in my throat. Left a trail of ash on my tongue. But it had to be done. I had to honour my grandfather's request, no matter my personal view on it. Or I'd risk everything he'd built. Risk mocking the sacrifice that had taken the ultimate toll.

'Tell Petras he has a deal.'

My father's hand arrived on my shoulder in silent gratitude, after which he exited quietly.

Neo chose more exuberant congratulations, but even then I barely felt him slap my shoulder.

'Think of it this way. For twelve months you'll be free of all the scheming socialites and supermodels who've been falling over themselves to extract a commitment from you. I'll happily carry that burden for you instead.'

'Unless you wish to date one of those supermodels whilst sporting a black eye, I suggest you leave my office immediately,' I growled.

My brother's laughter echoed in my ears long after he'd slammed the door behind him.

But long before the echo died I made another silent vow to myself. Petras and his kin would pay for what they'd done to my family. Before the stipulated year of marriage was out they'd regret tangling with the Xenakis family.

CHAPTER ONE

'SMILE, CALYPSO. IT's the happiest day of your life!'

'Here, let me put some more blusher on your cheeks... you're so pale. Perhaps a bit more shadow for your beautiful eyes...'

Beneath the endless layers of white tulle that some faceless stranger had deemed the perfect wedding gown material and gone to town with my fingers bunched into fists. When the tight clenches didn't help, I bit the tip of my tongue and fought the urge to scream.

But I was past hysteria. *That* unfortunate state had occurred two weeks prior, when my father had informed me just how he'd mapped out the rest of my life. How it was my turn to help restore our family's honour.

Or else.

The cold shivers racing up and down my spine had become familiar in the last month, after a few days spent in denial that my father would truly carry out his intentions.

I'd quickly accepted that he would.

Years of bitterness and humiliation and failure to emulate his ruthless father's dubious acclaim had pushed him over the edge once and for all.

The soft bristles of the blusher brush passed feverishly over my cheeks. The make-up artist determined to transform me into an eager, blushing, starry-eyed bride.

But I was far from eager and a million miles away from starry-eyed.

The only thing they'd got right in this miserable spectacle was the virginal white.

If I'd had a choice that too would have been a lie. At twenty-four I knew, even in my sheltered existence, that being a virgin was a rare phenomenon. At least now I realised why my father had been hell-bent on thwarting my every encounter with the opposite sex. Why he'd ruthlessly vetted my friendships, curtailed my freedom.

I'd believed my choices had been so abruptly limited since the moment my mother fell from grace. Since she returned home the broken prodigal wife and handed my father all the weapons he needed to transform himself from moderately intolerable to fearsome tyrant. I thought I'd been swept along by the merciless broom of wronged party justice, but he'd had a completely different purpose for me.

A purpose which had brought me to this moment.

My wedding day.

The next shudder coagulated in my chin, making it wobble like jelly before I could wrestle my composure back under control.

Luckily the trio of women who'd descended on our house twenty-four hours ago were clucking about pre-wedding nerves, then clucking some more about how understandable my fraught emotions were, considering who my prospective husband was.

Axios Xenakis.

A man I'd never met.

Sure, like everyone in Greece I knew who he was. A wildly successful airline magnate worth billions and head of the influential Xenakis family. A family whose ill fortune, unlike mine, had been reversed due the daring innovation of its young CEO.

It was rumoured that Axios Xenakis was the kind of individual whose projections could cause stock markets to rise or fall. The various articles I'd read about him had boggled my mind—the idea that any one person could wield such power and authority was bewildering. To top it off, Axios Xenakis was drop-dead gorgeous, if a little fierce-looking.

Everything about the man was way too visceral and invasive. Just a simple glance at his image online had evoked the notion that he could see into my soul, glean my deepest desires and use them against me. It was probably why he was often seen in the company of sophisticated heiresses and equally influential A-listers.

Which begged the question—why the Petras family? More specifically, why *me*?

What did a man who dated socialites and heiresses on a regular basis, as was thoroughly documented in the media, have to gain by shackling himself to me?

I knew it had something to do with the supreme smugness my father had been exhibiting in the last several weeks but he had refused to disclose. Somehow, behind the sneers and bitterness whenever the Xenakis name came up over the years, my father had been scheming. And that scheming had included me.

In all my daydreams about attaining my freedom, marriage hadn't featured anywhere. I wanted the freedom to dictate who I socialised with, what I ate, the pleasure to paint my watercolours without fear of recrimination, without judgement… The freedom to live life on *my* terms.

The hope of one day achieving those things had stopped me from succumbing to abject misery.

But not like *this*!

I forced my gaze to the mirror and promptly looked away again. My eyes were desolate pools, my cheeks artificially pink with excess rouge. My lips were turned down, reflecting my despair since learning that I was promised to a stranger. One who'd demanded a wedding within twenty-eight days.

My flat refusal had merely garnered a cold shrug from my father, before he had gone for the jugular—my one weakness.

My mother.

As if summoned by my inner turmoil, the electric whine of a wheelchair disturbed the excited chatter of the stylists. The moment they realised the mother of the bride had entered the bedroom, their attention shifted to her.

Taking advantage of the reprieve, I surreptitiously rubbed

at my cheeks with a tissue, removing a layer of blusher. The icy peach lipstick disappeared with the second swipe across my lips, leaving me even paler than before but thankfully looking less of a lost, wide-eyed freak. Quickly hanging the thick lace veil over my face to hide the alteration, I stood and turned, watching as the women fawned over my mother.

Iona Petras had been stunningly beautiful once upon a time. Growing up, I was in awe of her statuesque beauty, her vivacity and sheer joy for life. Her laughter had lit up my day, her intelligence and love of the arts fuelling my own appreciation for music and painting.

Now, greying and confined, she was still a beautiful woman. But along with her broken body had come a broken spirit no amount of pretending or smiling, or even gaining the elevated position as mother of the bride, soon to marry a man most deemed a demigod, could disguise.

She withstood the stylists' ministrations without complaint, her half-hearted smile only slipping when her eyes met mine. Within them I saw ravaging misery and the sort of unending despair that came with the life sentence she'd imposed on herself by returning when she should have fled.

But, just as I'd had to remain here because of her, I knew my mother had returned home because of me. And somewhere along the line Iona Petras had accepted her fate.

'Leave us, please,' she said to the stylists, her voice surprisingly steely.

The women withdrew. She wheeled herself closer, her face pinched with worry. For the longest minute she stared at me.

'Are you all right?'

I tensed, momentarily panicked that she'd learned what I'd hidden from her for the last few weeks. As much as I'd tried to ignore the ever-growing pain in my abdomen, I couldn't any more. Not only had it become a constant dull ache, it had become a reminder that even health-wise my life wasn't my own. That I might well be succumbing to the very real ailment that had taken my grandmother—

'Callie? Are you ready?'

Realising she was talking about the wedding ceremony, I felt the urge to succumb to hysteria pummel me once again. As did the fierce need to be selfish just this once…to simply flee and let the chips fall where they may.

'Is anyone ever ready to marry a man they've never met?' I asked. 'Please tell me you've found out why he's demanding I do this?' I pleaded.

Eyes a shade darker than my own lapis-lazuli-coloured ones turned mournful as she shook her head. 'No. Your father still refuses to tell me. My guess is that it has something to do with your grandfather and old man Xenakis.' Before I could ask what she meant, she continued, 'Anyway, Yiannis will be looking for me, so I need to be quick.'

She reached inside the stylish designer jacket that matched her lavender gown and produced a thick cream envelope, her fingers shaking as she stared at it.

'What's that?' I asked when she made no move to speak.

Within her gaze came a spark of determination I hadn't seen in years. My heart leapt into my throat as she caught my hand in hers and squeezed it tight.

'My sweet Callie, I know I've brought misery to your life with my actions—'

'No, Mama, you haven't. I promise,' I countered firmly.

She stared at me. 'I'm not sure whether to be proud or to admonish you for being such a good liar. But I know what I've done. My selfishness has locked you in this prison with me when you should be free to pursue what young girls your age ought to be doing.' Her fingers tightened on mine. 'I want you to make me a promise,' she pleaded, her voice husky with unshed tears.

I nodded because…what else could I do? 'Anything you want, Mama.'

She held out the envelope. 'Take this. Hide it in the safest place you can.'

I took it, frowning at the old-fashioned cursive lettering spelling out my name. 'What's this?'

'It's from your grandmother.'

'Yiayia Helena?' A tide of sorrow momentarily washed over me, my heart still missing the grandmother I'd lost a year ago.

My mother nodded. 'She said I'd know when you needed it. And even if I'm wrong…'

She paused, a faraway look in her eyes hinting that she was indulging in all those might-have-beens that sparked my own desperate imagination. When she refocused, her gaze moved dully over my wedding dress.

'Even if this…alliance turns out to be tolerable, it'll help to know you were loved by your grandmother. That should you need her she'll be there for you the way I wasn't.'

I held on tighter to her hand. 'I know you love me, Mama.'

She shook her head, tears brimming her eyes. 'Not the way a mother should love her child, without selfish intentions that end up harming her. I took the wrong turn with you. I left you alone with your father when I should have taken you with me. Maybe if I had—' She stopped, took a deep breath and dabbed at her tears before braving my worried stare again. 'All I ask is that you find a way to forgive me one day.'

'Mama—' I stopped when she gave a wrenching sob.

Her gaze dropped to the envelope in my hand. 'Hang on to that, Callie. And don't hesitate to use it when you need it. Promise me,' she insisted fervently.'

'I… I promise.'

She sniffed, nodded, then abruptly turned the wheelchair and manoeuvred herself out of my bedroom.

Before I could process our conversation I was again surrounded by mindless chatter, unable to breathe or think. The only solid thing in my world became the envelope I clutched tightly in my hand. And when I found that within the endless folds of tulle the designer had fashioned a pocket, I nearly cried with relief as I slipped the envelope into it.

Even without knowing its contents, just knowing it came from my grandmother—the woman who'd helped me stand up to my father's wrath more times than I could count, who'd loved and reassured me on a daily basis during my mother's year-long absence when I was fifteen years old—kept me from crumbling as my father arrived and with a brisk nod offered his stiff arm, ordered me to straighten my spine…and escorted me to my fate.

The chapel was filled to the brim, according to the excited chatter of the household staff, and as my father led me out to a flower-bedecked horse-drawn carriage I got the first indication of what was to come.

Over the last three weeks I'd watched with a sense of surrealism as construction crews and landscapers descended on our little corner of the world to transform the church and surrounding area from a place of rundown dilapidation into its former whitewashed charming glory.

The usually quiet streets of Nicrete, a sleepy village in the south of the island of Skyros, the place generations of the Petras family had called home, buzzed with fashionably dressed strangers—all guests of Axios Xenakis. With the main means of getting on and off the island being by boat, the harbour had become a place of interest in the last few days.

Every hotel and guest house on the island was booked solid. Expensive speedboats and a handful of super-yachts had appeared on the horizon overnight, and now bobbed in the Aegean beneath resplendent sunshine.

Of course the man I was to marry chose to do things differently.

My carriage was halfway between home and the church when the loud, mechanical whine of powerful rotors churned the air. Children shouted in excitement and raced towards the hilltop as three sleek-looking helicopters flew overhead to settle on the newly manicured lawns of the park usually used as recreational grounds for families. Today the whole park had been cordoned off—evidently to receive these helicopters.

Beneath the veil I allowed myself a distasteful moue. But the barrier wasn't enough to hide my father's smug smile as he watched the helicopters. Or his nod of satisfaction as several distinguished-looking men and designer-clad women alighted from the craft.

I averted my face, hoping the ache in my heart and the pain in my belly wouldn't manifest itself in the hysteria I'd been trying to suppress for what seemed like for ever. But I couldn't prevent the words from tumbling from my lips.

'It's not too late, Papa. Whatever this is… Perhaps if you told me why, we can find a way—'

'I have already found a way, child.'

'Don't call me a child—I'm twenty-four years old!'

That pulse of rebellion, which I'd never quite been able to curb, eagerly fanned by Yiayia when she was alive, slipped its leash. She'd never got on well with my father, and in a way standing up to him now, despite the potential fallout for my mother, felt like honouring her memory.

His eyes narrowed. 'If you wanted to help then you should've taken that business degree at university, instead of the useless arts degree you're saddled with.'

'I told you—I'm not interested in a corporate career.'

Nor was I interested in being constantly reminded that I wasn't the son he'd yearned for. The one he'd hoped would help him save Petras Industries, the family company which now teetered on the brink of bankruptcy.

'Ne—and just like your mother you let me down. Once again it has fallen to *me* to find a way. And I have. So now you will smile and do your duty by this family. You will say your vows and marry Xenakis.'

I bit my lip at this reminder of yet another bone of contention between us. I'd fought hard for the right to leave the island to pursue my arts degree, only returning because of my mother. The small art gallery I worked at part-time on Nicrete was a way of keeping my sanity, even as I mourned my wasted degree.

'After that, what then?'

He shrugged. 'After that you will belong to him. But remember that regardless of the new name you're taking on you're still a Petras. If you do anything to bring the family into disrepute you will bear the consequences.'

My heart lurched, my fists balling in pain and frustration—because I knew exactly what my father meant.

The *consequences* being my father's ability to manipulate my mother's guilt and ensure maximum suffering. His constant threats to toss her out with only the clothes on her back, to abandon her to her fate the way she'd briefly abandoned her family. But while my mother had deserted her child and marriage in the name of a doomed love, my father was operating from a place of pure revenge. To him, his wife had humiliated and betrayed him, and he was determined to repay her by keeping her prisoner. Ensuring that at every waking moment she was reminded of her fall from grace and his power over her.

The reason that I'd been roped in as a means to that end was my love for my mother.

Eight years ago, when he'd returned home with my absentee mother after the doctors in Athens had called and informed him that she'd been in a crash, and that the man she'd run away with was dead, he'd laid out new family rules. My mother would stay married to him. She would become a dutiful wife and mother, doing everything in her power to not bring another speck of disgrace to the family. In return he would ensure her medical needs were met, and that she would be given the finest treatment to adjust to her new wheelchair-bound life.

For my part, I would act the devoted daughter...or my mother would suffer.

The horses whinnying as they came to a stop at the steps leading to the church doors dragged me to the present, pushing my heartache aside and replacing it with apprehension.

The last of the guests were entering while organ music piped portentously in the air. In less than an hour I would be married to a man I'd never exchanged a single word with. A man who had somehow fallen in league with my father for reasons I still didn't know.

I glanced at my father, desperate to ask why. His stony profile warned me not to push my luck. Like my heartache, I smothered my rebellion.

My father stepped out of the carriage and held out his hand. Mine shook, and again I was glad for the veil's cover to hide my tear-prickled eyes.

A small part of me was grateful that my father didn't seem in a hurry to march me down the aisle because he was basking in the limelight that momentarily banished the shadow of scandal and humiliation he'd lived under for the past eight years. For once people weren't talking about his wife's infidelity. Or the fact that the woman who'd deserted him had returned in a wheelchair. Or that he'd taken her back just so he could keep her firmly under his thumb in retribution.

Today he was simply the man who'd seemingly bagged one of the most eligible bachelors in the world for his daughter—not the once illustrious but now downtrodden businessman who'd lost the Petras fortune his father had left him.

The doors to the church yawned open, ready to receive their unwilling sacrifice. My footsteps faltered and my father sent me a sharp look. Unable to meet his eyes without setting off the spark of mutiny attempting to rekindle itself inside me, I kept my gaze straight.

I needed to do this for my mother.

I spotted her in the front row, her head held high despite

her fate, and it lent me the strength to put one foot in front of the other. The slight weight of my grandmother's envelope in my pocket helped me ignore the rabid curiosity and speculative whispers of three hundred strangers.

Unfortunately there was only one place left to look. At the towering figure of the man waiting in perfect stillness facing the altar.

He didn't twitch nor fidget. Didn't display any outward signs of being a nervous groom.

His broad back and wide shoulders seemed to go on for ever, and his proud head and unyielding stance announced his power and authority. He didn't speak to the equally tall, commanding figure next to him, as most grooms did with their best man. In fact both men stood as if to military attention, their stance unwavering.

My gaze flicked away from Axios Xenakis, my breath stalling in my throat the closer I approached. Even without seeing his face I sensed a formidable aura—one that forced me again to wonder why he was doing this. What did he have to gain with this alliance?

He could have any woman he wanted. So why me?

And why had several butterflies suddenly taken flight within my belly?

Wild instinct urged me to fan my rebellion to life. *Fight or flight.* Pick one and deal with the consequences later.

But even as the thoughts formed they were discarded.

I had no choice. None whatsoever.

But maybe this man I was marrying would be a little more malleable than my father. Maybe—

He turned. And the feeble little hope died a horrible death.

Eyes the colour of polished gunmetal bored into me as if they were with fierce, merciless hooks. They probed beneath the veil with such force that for a moment I imagined I was naked—that he could see my every weakness and flaw, see to the heart of my deepest desire for freedom.

His lips were pressed into a formidable line, his whole demeanour austere. Axios Xenakis could have been in a boardroom, preparing to strike a deal to make himself another billion euros, not poised before an altar, about to commit himself to a wife he'd never met.

I catalogued his breathtaking features. Wondered if that rugged boxer's jaw ever relaxed—whether the cut-glass sharpness of his cheekbones ever softened in a smile. Did he maintain constant control of those sleek eyebrows so they were permanently brooding? Did his nose ever wrinkle in laughter?

Why was I interested?

I was nothing but part of a transaction to him—one he didn't seem entirely thrilled about, judging by his icy regard. So it didn't matter that the olive vibrancy of his skin drew from me more than a fleeting look, or that he was without a doubt the most strikingly handsome man I'd ever seen.

He was a world removed from the boys I'd sneakily dated at university, before my father had found out and ruthlessly thwarted my chances with them before anything resembling a relationship could form.

Axios Xenakis belonged in a stratosphere of his own. One I was apprehensive about inhabiting.

My footsteps stalled and I heard my father's sharp intake of breath. It was swiftly followed by the tight grip of his hand in warning.

Don't disgrace the family.

Defiance sparked again.

But then I saw my mother's head turn. The ubiquitous misery filmed her eyes, but alongside it was a look so fierce it might have been a reflection from my grandmother's eyes.

It was a look that infused me with courage.

It's up to you, it said. *Do this...or don't.*

My heart thundered. The need to turn around and simply walk away was a wild cyclone churning through me.

At the altar, Axios's eyes never shifted from me, his

stance unchanging in the face of my clear reluctance. It was as if he knew what I'd decide and was simply waiting me out.

And, since I was playing in a game whose rules no one had bothered to apprise me of, there was only one move I could make.

I would play this round, then fight my corner later.

With that firm promise echoing inside me, I stepped up to the altar.

I saw a fleeting disappointment in his eyes before he masked his features. He was *disappointed*? Did that mean he didn't want this?

Wild hope flared within me even as bewilderment mounted. If he didn't want this then there might be room to negotiate. Room to get what I wanted out of this.

Realising I was staring, and that my father had been dispatched and I was now the sole focus of Axios Xenakis' eyes, I hurriedly averted my gaze. But not before acknowledging that up close he was even more electrifying. Perhaps it was the severity of his grey suit. Or the fact that the hand he held out to me screamed a silent command.

The last strains of the hymn trailed away, leaving behind a charged silence. With each second it weighed heavier, pressing down on me.

His hand extended another inch, and heavy expectation thickened the air.

With a deep breath, inevitably I slipped my hand into his—and joined the stranger who was to be my husband.

Almost immediately he released me. But the sensation of his touch lingered, and a sizzling chain reaction I was unprepared for travelled up my arm, flaring wide.

It was enough momentarily to drown out the intonation of the priest's voice as he began the ceremony.

I rallied long enough to murmur the words I'd reluctantly memorised and, when the time came, to pick up the larger of the two platinum wedding bands.

With fingers that still trembled I faced Axios. The impact of his eyes, his towering frame, the much too handsome face momentarily erased the words from my brain.

In silence he held out his left hand, his laser eyes boring into me as he simply...*waited*.

'I take thee...'

'For better or worse...'

'With my body...'

'Love, honour, cherish...'

'Till death...'

With each spoken vow my heart squeezed tighter, the mechanical delivery I'd expected to give morphing into a whispered outpouring wrapped in consternation.

The second I was done he reached for the other ring without taking his eyes off me, again holding out his hand for mine.

And then Axios Xenakis spoke for the first time.

'I, Axios Xenakis, take thee, Calypso Athena Petras...'

The rest of his words were lost to me as the deep, hypnotic cadence of his voice struck like Zeus's thunderbolt into a place I didn't even know existed until that moment.

His voice was...*sexy*. Alluring. Magnetic.

It seemed impossible that a voice could be all those things, and yet I felt every one.

The cold brush of platinum on my skin brought me back to myself just in time to hear the priest announce us as man and wife. To say that my new husband could now kiss me.

I started to turn away. Because this was a far cry from a normal wedding ceremony. And we were far removed from two people in love.

Large, firm hands cupped my shoulders, shocking me into stillness. Unable to stop a cascade of light shivers, I held my breath as he lifted the heavy veil and draped it behind me with unhurried movements. I watched his gaze take in my bound hair, the small headband made of tiny diamonds and pearls that had belonged to Yiayia Helena and the similar necklace adorning my throat.

Had he been anyone else I might have entertained the notion that Axios Xenakis was reluctant to look into the face of the woman he'd just committed himself to. Because when his piercing grey eyes finally settled on me, I caught a momentary confusion, then his eyes widened and his jaw slackened for a split second before he reasserted supreme control.

Any fleeting pleasure I'd felt at gaining some unknown upper hand fled as heat suffused my face at his intense, almost shocked scrutiny.

Admitting that I should have left the make-up artist's work alone didn't help my urge to squirm under his candid regard. But I forced myself to hold his gaze, ignore the consternation in his eyes and the humiliating thud of my heartbeat.

Just when I thought he intended to drag the torture out for ever he slid one finger beneath my chin to nudge my head upward. Caught in the mysterious hypnosis of his gaze, I watched his head descend, so close that heat from his skin singed mine.

I braced myself, my stomach churning with emotions I couldn't name.

I'd been kissed before. Those university colleagues I'd toyed with before my father's bitter reach had scared them away. None of them had elicited this level of shivery anticipation.

His kiss arrived, subtle as a butterfly's wing and powerful as a sledgehammer. Sensation rocked through me like an earthquake, dizzying and terrifying, leaving me with nothing to do but to brace my hands on his chest, anchor myself to reality somehow.

But all that did was compound my situation. Because the solid wall of his chest was like sculpted warm steel, inviting the kind of exploration that had no place in this time and space.

Pull away.

Before I could, he gave a sharp intake of breath. In the next moment I was free of him and he was turning away.

Back to earth with a shaky thud, I fought angry bewilderment even as I strove for composure before our three-hundred-strong audience.

The feeling lingered all through our walk down the aisle, through our stiff poses for pictures and then the ride back up the hill to the crumbling mansion overlooking the harbour—the only home I'd ever known.

The horse and carriage had been swapped for a sleek limousine with darkened windows and a partition that ensured privacy. Beside me Axios maintained a stony silence, one I wasn't inclined to break despite the dark, enigmatic looks he slanted me every now and then.

When it all became too much, I snatched in a breath and faced him. 'Is there something on your mind?'

One eyebrow quirked. 'As conversations go, that's not quite what I expected as our first. But then I'm making many surprising discoveries.'

He wasn't the only one! 'What's that supposed to mean?'

He didn't reply immediately. Then, 'You're not what I was led to expect.'

I couldn't help my lips twisting. 'You are aware of how absurd that sounds, aren't you?'

He stiffened, and I got the notion that once again something about me had surprised him. 'No. Enlighten me,' he replied dryly.

'Not what you were *led to expect*?' The slight screech in my voice warned me that hysteria might be winning but I couldn't stop. 'Let me guess—you thought you were getting some biddable wallflower who would tremble and trip over herself to please you?'

You were trembling minutes ago, when he kissed you.

I ignored the voice and met his gaze.

He'd turned into a pillar of stone. 'Considering the ink

isn't dry on our marriage certificate, perhaps we should strive not to have our first disagreement. Unless you wish to break some sort of record?' he rasped, gunmetal eyes boring into me.

Apart from our marriage, I still didn't know the precise details of the deal between my father and my new husband and it momentarily stalled my response. But the fire burning inside me wouldn't be doused.

'I get the feeling you're just as...*invested* in this thing as my father is, so it bears repeating that you're *not* getting a simpering lackey who will jump through hoops to amuse you.'

His eyes narrowed. 'Your *father*? Not you?'

Short of revealing my ignorance on the matter, I had to prevaricate. 'I'm a Petras—same as he.'

Something that looked very much like contempt flickered through his eyes. 'Consider me forewarned,' he replied cryptically.

Before I could query what he meant the limo was pulling up to the double doors of my family home. Liveried footmen hurried to throw our doors open.

Inside the rarely used but hastily refurbished ballroom guests drank champagne and feasted on canapés and my father gave a painfully false speech. I only managed to sit through it by reaching into my pocket and clutching the envelope within.

The moment the speeches were done Axios was swarmed upon by fawning acquaintances, eager to engage the great man in conversation. I told myself that my primary emotion was relief as the stylists, also roped into acting as my attendants, rushed to straighten my veil and train, twitching and tweaking until they were satisfied that I'd been restored to their vision of bridal beauty.

But just when I thought I'd have a moment's reprieve Axios's gaze zeroed in on me, his eyes falling to the barely touched food on the plate that lay next to my untouched glass of champagne.

One brow rose. 'Not in the mood for celebrating? Or are you trying to make some sort of point by not eating?'

I couldn't eat—not when the inkling was deepening that Axios Xenakis was far from a willing participant in this devilish deal. And if that was the case, what had I let myself in for?

I pushed the anxious thought away and let my gaze fall on his equally full plate. 'You should talk.'

He lifted his champagne and took a healthy gulp. 'Unlike you, this occasion isn't one I feel inclined to celebrate.'

My breath caught, but before I could ask him to elaborate, he continued.

'And in the interest of clarity let me warn you that neither you nor your father have any cards left to play. Should you feel inclined to make *more* demands.'

Christos, what exactly had my father done?

But even as the question burned fire boiled in my blood. 'Are you threatening my family? Because if you are, please know that I will fight you with everything I've got.'

His lips twisted at my fierce tone. 'What a fiery temper you have. I wonder what other surprises you're hiding beneath those unfortunate layers of... What *is* that material?'

As much as I hated my wedding dress, his remark sparked irritation. 'It's called tulle. And you should know. You paid for it, after all.'

The barest hint of a sardonic smile lifted his sensual lips. 'Writing a cheque for it doesn't mean I pay attention to every single detail of a woman's wardrobe. I have better things to do than concern myself with the name of the fabric that comprises a wedding gown.'

'But this is *your* wedding too,' I taunted, knowing my mockery would aggravate.

Something about this towering hunk of a man, who'd made it clear that this was the last place he wanted to be, riled me on a visceral level, firing up a need to dig beneath his formidable exterior.

'Isn't it supposed to be one of the momentous occasions of your life?'

Every trace of humour disappeared. Piercing grey eyes pinned me in place, and the tension vibrating from him was so thick I could almost touch it.

'Momentous occasions are highly anticipated and satisfactorily celebrated. You'd have to be delusional or deliberately blind to imagine I'm in such a state, Calypso Petras.'

The way he said my name, with drawling, mocking intonation, fired my blood. Along with other sensations I couldn't quite name.

'It's Calypso Xenakis now—or have you already forgotten?' I fired back, taking secret pleasure in seeing the irritated flare of his nostrils.

'I have not forgotten,' he answered with taut iciness.

'If this is such an ordeal for you, then why all this?' I waved my hand at the obscenely lavish banquet displayed along one long wall, the champagne tower brimming with expensive golden bubbles, the caviar-laden trays being circulated, and the designer-clad guests, shamelessly indulging their appetites.

'Because your father insisted,' he replied, his voice colder than an arctic vortex. 'As *you* well know.'

I opened my mouth to tell him for once and for all that none of this made sense to me because no one had bothered to consult me about my own wedding.

The sight of my mother's face, staring at me from one table away, pain and misery etched beneath her smile, dried the words in my throat.

For whatever reason fate had tangled the Xenakises and the Petrases in an acrimonious weave and my mother and I were caught in the middle. I could no more extricate myself than I could turn my back on her.

A tiny, tortured sound whistled through the air and I realised it came from my own throat—a manifestation of that hysteria that just wouldn't die down. I stood abruptly, knowing I had to get away before I did something regrettable.

Like climb on top of the lavishly decorated lonely high table, set apart from everyone else to showcase the newly married couple in all their glory, and scream at the top of my lungs.

That just wouldn't do. Because while I might have acquired a new surname, it was dawning on me that until I learned the true nature of what I was embroiled in I would be wise to keep a firm hold of my feelings.

And an even firmer hold of my wits.

CHAPTER TWO

MONEY MAKES THE world spin.

I swallowed my champagne, careful not to choke on it as I dispassionately observed the guests indulging in the revelry of my sham of a wedding.

Money had made this happen, and in the exact time frame I'd requested it.

Money had put that smug smile on Yiannis Petras's face.

Money had made the family, decimated by my grandfather's fall from grace, rally together for the sake of enjoying the rejuvenated fruits of my labour.

I'd seen first-hand how the lack of it could cause backbiting and untold strain. Ostensibly solid marriages crumbled under the threat of diminished wealth and influence. I'd seen it in my parents' marriage. It was why I'd never have freely chosen this route for myself.

My gaze shifted to my brand-new wife.

Had money influenced her agreement to this fiasco?

Was she getting a cut of the hundred million euros?

Of course she was. Had she not proclaimed herself a true Petras?

For those seconds as she'd hesitated at the altar I'd entertained the notion that she shared my reluctance, had imagined the merest hint of resistance in her eyes.

Her words had put me straight.

A cursory investigation had revealed that while she'd graduated from Skypos University with a major in Arts, she'd done nothing with her degree for the last two years. Her father's daughter through and through, sitting back and taking the easy route to riches.

So what if outwardly she wasn't what I expected?

I snorted under my breath at this colossal understatement. Calypso Petras...*ochi*, make that Calypso Xenakis...was beyond a surprise. She was a punch to my solar plexus, one it was taking an irritatingly long time to wrestle under control.

Even now my senses still reeled from what I'd uncovered beneath her veil. She was far from the drab little mouse I'd assumed.

'I believe there's a rule somewhere that states you shouldn't scowl on your wedding day.'

I resisted the urge to grind my teeth and faced my brother. 'You think this is funny?'

'This whole circus? No. I believe that ring on your finger and the look on your face makes it all too real.' Neo affected a mocking shudder intended to rile me further.

It worked.

'I'm talking about your implication that my… Calypso.' *Thee mou*, why did her name sound so…erotic?

Neo's eyes widened before glinting with keen speculation. 'If I recall, I didn't give you any specifics.'

There was a reason Neo was president of marketing at Xenakis Aeronautics. He could sell hay to a farmer.

My fingers tightened around my glass. 'You deliberately let me to think she was…unremarkable.'

She was quite the opposite. Hers was the confounding kind of beauty one couldn't place a finger on. The kind that made you stare for much longer than was polite.

Neo shrugged. 'No, I didn't. And don't blame me for the dire state of your mind, brother,' he answered.

The low heat burning through my blood intensified. And while I wanted to attribute it to this conversation, I knew I couldn't. Ever since I'd pulled that hideous veil off her face and uncovered the woman I'd agreed to marry a different irritation had lodged itself deep inside me. One I wasn't quite ready to examine.

But that wasn't to say I was ready to let Neo off the hook for…

For what?

Making obfuscating observations about Calypso Petras

that had made me dismiss her from my mind, only to be knocked off-kilter by her appearance?

Granted, she still wasn't my type. Her eyes were too large…much too *distracting*. They were the type of turquoise-blue that made you question their authenticity. Framed with long eyelashes that begged the same question. And then there were her lips. Full and sensual, with a natural bruised rose hue, and deeply alluring despite the absence of gloss.

The dichotomy of fully made-up eyes and bare lips had absorbed my attention for much too long at that altar. And it had irritated me even further that since our arrival at the reception those lips had been buried beneath a hideous layer of frosty peach.

But it hadn't stopped me puzzling over why the two aspects of her initial appearance had been so at odds with each other. Or why she'd seemed…startled by our very brief kiss on the altar.

False innocence wrapped around her true character? A character that contained more than a little fire.

My mind flicked to other hints I'd glimpsed over the last few hours. While I was yet to discover what lay beneath the layers of the wedding gown, there were more than enough hints to authenticate her voluptuousness.

Yet to discover…

The peculiar buzz that had been ignited during that fleeting kiss notched up a fraction, the fact that the brief contact still lingered on my lips drawing another frown.

'Your new wife is looking a little…unhappy. Perhaps you should see about fixing that?'

About to state that I had nothing to fix, that her happiness was none of my concern, I found my gaze flicked to the table. Despite the picture of poise she was trying to project she looked pale, her eyes flitting nervously. A quick scrutiny of our guests showed she was the object of several stares and blatant whispers.

A helpless prey in a jungle of predators.

My feet moved almost of their own accord, the niggling urge to reverse that look on her face irritating me even as I moved towards her, effectively silencing the whispers with quelling stares.

Regardless of how this union had come about, rumours couldn't be allowed to run rife. This was how undermining started.

As I neared, silence fell. Her gaze shifted, met mine. Her chin lifted, a wisp of bewilderment and skittishness evaporating and her eyes flashing with defiance.

For some absurd reason it sparked something to life inside me. Something I fully intended to ignore.

Defiance or bewilderment, the deed was done. She and her family had capitalised on an agreement made under duress and bagged themselves a windfall. She should be celebrating.

Instead I caught another trace of apprehension as I stopped beside her chair. Eyes growing wide, she looked up at me. The graceful line of her neck—another alluring feature that seemed to demand attention—rippled as she swallowed.

Thee mou, if this was an act then she was a good actress!

Aware of our audience, and a burning need to find out, I held out my hand to her. 'The traditional first dance is coming up, I believe.' The earlier we could get this spectacle out of the way, the quicker I could resume my life.

Her gaze darted to the dance floor, her reluctance clear. 'Is that…really necessary?'

Something about her reluctance and her whole demeanour grated. She was behaving as if I was contaminated!

'Enough with this pretence. That wide-eyed innocent thing will only work for so long. Give it up, Calypso.'

She offered me her hand, but the eyes that met mine as she stood sparkled with renewed fire. 'No one calls me Calypso. My name is Callie,' she stated firmly.

I attempted to ignore the slim fingers in mine, the smooth softness of her palm and the way it kicked to life something inside me as I led her to the middle of the dance floor.

'I'm your new husband—surely I don't fall under the category of *no one*?' I curled my arm around her waist, a singular need to press her close escalating inside me as the band struck up a waltz.

She stiffened. 'Are you insinuating that you're *special*?'

For some reason my lips quirked. 'By your tone, I'm guessing I'm not. Not even special enough for you to grant me the simple gift of addressing you as I please?'

Her lips firmed again, drawing my attention to their plumpness. Reminding me of that all too fleeting taste of them.

'And what am I to call *you*? Other than *stranger* or *husband*?'

For some reason the fiery huskiness of her voice drew another smile. A puzzle in itself, since humour was the last emotion I should have been experiencing. I was in this situation because of money and shameless greed.

'Call me Axios. Or Ax, as most people do. I doubt we will reach the stage of coining terms of endearment.'

'On that I think we're agreed,' she replied, her gaze fixed somewhere over my shoulder.

Another scrabble of irritation threatened to rise, but I suppressed it when I noticed that once again, beneath the show of sharp claws, she was trembling, her wide eyes a little too bright. As if she was holding on to her composure by a thread.

'Is something wrong?' I asked. Again I questioned my need to know. Or care.

'What could possibly be wrong?'

She didn't bother to meet my gaze. If anything, she attempted to detach herself, which ought to have been impossible, considering how close we were dancing. But I was learning that my new wife had several…interesting facets.

'It is polite to look at me when you address me.'

She maintained her stance for another few seconds, then her blue eyes rose to mine. The urge to stare into them, to commit every fleck and expression to memory, charged through me, this time bringing a wave of heat to my groin.

I inhaled slowly, forcing myself to ignore that unsettling sensation and address her as I would any acquaintance.

Even though she wasn't.

Even though she'd taken my name and we were effectively bound together for twelve long months.

'This thing will go smoother if we attempt to be civil with one another. Don't you agree?'

'I'm not a puppet. I cannot act a certain way on command.'

'But you *can* dispense with that little-girl-lost look. And I find it curious that you would choose to refer to puppets. Perhaps you're familiar with knowing exactly which strings to tug to get what you want?'

Unlike me, she didn't attempt to disguise her frown. 'What are you talking about?'

'This whole scheme, orchestrated by you and your family, has gone off without a hitch. Feel free to stop acting now.'

She inhaled sharply, her eyes darting to the guests dancing around us. 'Please keep your voice down.'

'Afraid you'll be found out? Are you really so blind to the fact that every single guest is speculating wildly about how two people who've never met are now married?'

Her plump lips pressed together for a moment. 'I can't control what other people think. But I do care about perpetuating unfounded rumours.'

'Do you, *yineka mou*?'

Her blue eyes shadowed and her gaze quickly flicked away. 'Can you not call me that, please?'

'Why not? Are you not my wife?'

The more the term fell from my lips the deeper it bored

into me, as if rooting for a place to settle. Of course the search would be futile, because this was far from what I wanted.

The strain and stress of trying to save his failing company while keeping his family and his marriage together had driven my grandfather into an early grave, his spirit broken long before the heart attack that had suddenly taken him. It was the same stress that had nearly broken my own father, forcing him to step down after a mere two years as CEO.

I didn't intend to weigh myself down with similar baggage.

I refocused on Calypso, attempting to ignore the effect of her soft curves against my body as she asked, 'So, what happens after this?'

'"This"?'

'After we're done here,' she elaborated.

Unbidden, my thoughts flew ahead. To when the evening would turn exclusive and intimate. When wedding euphoria traditionally took on another, more carnal dimension.

A traditions I *wouldn't* be indulging in.

'Do you plan on getting back into your helicopter and leaving me here?'

The carefully disguised hope in her voice threw me back to that day in my father's office a month ago, when an agreement that bore all the hallmarks of blackmail had crash-landed into my life and threatened the Xenakis name and business. Did she really think she and her family could take financial advantage and then sail off into the sunset?

The silent vow I'd taken that day to ensure neither Calypso nor her father escaped unscathed resurged as I looked down into her face. A face struggling for composure and a body twitching nervously beneath my hand.

I pulled her closer, steadied her at her slight stumble, and lowered my lips to her ear.

'It's our wedding night, *matia mou*. How would it look if we didn't stay under the same roof? Sleep in the same bed?'

My lips brushed the delicate shell of her ear and she shivered. A moment later wide, alluring eyes sought mine.

'Sleep in the same bed? But you don't even know me. What…what's the rush?'

I opened my mouth to tell her there was no rush. That giving her my name was the final payment she and her family would extract from me. Instead I shrugged, noting absently that a part of me was enjoying this a little too much.

'Other than ensuring there will be nothing to be held over my head when the whim takes your father? Are you suggesting a period of getting to know one another before we decide if we must consummate this marriage?'

She gave a little start. '*If?* Don't you mean *when*?' she whispered fiercely, her eyes wider, searching.

Again the words to answer, to state that this dance was as close as we would get for the duration of our agreement, remained unsaid on the tip of my tongue. If she believed I would further compound this debacle by gracing her bed, so be it. She would discover differently later.

Absurdly, the pleasure in that thought of delivering disappointment never arrived. Instead I was unarmed by a disturbing throbbing in my groin, by the temptation to take a different approach. To gather her closer, breathe in the alluring perfume that clung to her silken skin.

I did just that, nudging her close with a firm clasp on her lower back. And heard her sharp intake of breath.

Pulling back, I glanced at her pale face. 'Are you all right?'

Her swift nod assured me that she was lying, and the wild darting of her gaze confirmed that belief.

'Calypso?'

'I… I'm fine. Just a little headache. That's all.'

I frowned. 'Then why are you touching your stomach?'

Her hand quickly relocated from her midriff to my shoulder, her smile little more than a grimace. 'It's nothing, I assure you.'

About to refute that assurance, I was forestalled by the end of the music and the applause that followed. And then by the arrival of Iona Petras.

My introduction to Calypso's mother, along with everyone else in the Petras clan, had been stiff and perfunctory, with no disguising exactly what this bloodless transaction was.

Everyone except Calypso.

'May I have a private moment with my daughter?' the older woman asked, although I got the feeling it was more an order than a request, giving me a momentary glimpse of where Calypso had inherited her quiet fire.

My fingers started to tighten on Calypso's waist, as a peculiar reluctance to let her go assailed me. I strenuously denied it and released her. 'By all means.'

A silent conversation passed between mother and daughter before Calypso held out her hand. Without so much as a glance my way, they exited the ballroom.

A fine irritant, like a tiny pebble in my shoe, stayed with me throughout all my inane conversations with people I didn't know and another five-minute ribbing from Neo. By the time my father approached I had the notion that my jaw would crack from being ground so tight.

'Am I mistaken or do you two seem to be getting along?' my father asked.

'You are mistaken,' I quipped, unwilling to admit how that dance and the feel of Calypso in my arms had fired up my blood.

He grimaced. 'I was hoping this would be less of an ordeal for you if you got along.'

'I said I'd do what needs to be done. And I will.'

Despite that small, startling flame of anticipation burning inside me.

Despite the fact that I'd completely dismissed any occurrence of a wedding night until exactly five minutes ago.

That sensation of her slender back beneath my hand…

that pulse beating at her throat… The shivers she couldn't control.

The fire of anticipation flared higher, resisting every attempt to dampen it down.

But did I need to?

This abhorrent agreement hadn't, thankfully, included a stipulation for consummation. But would it be a true marriage without it?

Enough!

Wrestling with myself over this was beneath me. Everything Yiannis Petras had asked for had been delivered. They would get nothing more from me.

That declaration lasted until my new wife walked back into the room and attempted to dismiss me with a vacant smile, even while her eyes challenged me.

Something locked into place inside me.

A challenge that needed answering.

Without stopping to question the wisdom of doing it, I crossed the wide room to where she stood. Took the hand loosely fisted by her side and brushed my lips over her knuckles.

Satisfaction sizzled through me when her breath caught. 'Say your goodbyes, Calypso. It's time to leave.'

'So what now?' I cringed inwardly at the nerves in my voice.

The helicopter ride—my first—from Nicrete to Agistros, the large island apparently owned entirely by Axios, had been breathtaking and exhilarating, and thankfully had not required much conversation. Largely because Axios had piloted the aircraft and I'd felt too nervous to disturb him, even if there'd been anything to talk about.

My mind was still a jumble after our charged snippets of conversation and that little slip on the dance floor, when he pulled me close and the ache in my belly manifested itself, and my last unsettling conversation with my mother.

But most of all it was the look in Axios's eyes before he'd

whisked me away from the reception and down to the waiting helicopter that kept my heart banging against my ribs.

That look was far too unsettling and electrifying for me to rest easy.

Especially not after landing on a dedicated cliff-side helipad on this island that boasted its own dormant volcano and a jaw-dropping villa that seemed almost too beautiful to be real.

I thought it was the setting sun that leant it that fairy tale look and made the unevenly staggered storeys seem to go on for ever. But every single facet of it turned out to be real, from the blush-hued stone, the towering arched windows, the rooftop infinity pool that seemed to blend into the sky and the endless reception rooms and bedroom suites, each holding priceless ancient works of art interspersed with the work of new cutting-edge artists whose work I loved.

Every jaw-dropping fact I'd read about Axios Xenakis had seemed amplified the moment he'd stepped out of the helicopter, and his aura was intensifying with each second as he walked me around Villa Almyra, exuding flawless power and authority.

Now, standing in the luxury sitting room adjoining what I assumed to be the master bedroom, I couldn't hold my words back.

He didn't answer for the longest time. He shrugged off the bespoke jacket he'd worn for the wedding ceremony. Then strolled over to the extensive drinks cabinet.

'Would you like a drink?' he asked.

About to refuse, I stopped. It would buy me time to ease my nerves. 'Mineral water, thanks.'

He poured my drink, then a single malt whisky into a crystal glass, handing mine to me before taking his time to savour his first sip.

The feeling that he was waiting, biding his time for… *something* threatened to overwhelm me, even while my senses skittered with alien excitement. Slowly it grew hotter, more dangerous.

His gaze raked over my wedding dress for a charged few seconds. 'Now we do whatever you want. It's *your* wedding night after all,' he drawled.

I got the feeling he was testing me. For what, I didn't know. And I wasn't sure I was ready to find out.

'The modern art pieces all over the house. Did you pick them yourself?'

His eyes widened fractionally, as if I'd surprised him. 'Yes,' he bit out. Then, on a softer note, 'Good art rarely loses its value.'

A layer of my nerves eased as I nodded. 'And pieces from emerging talent only appreciate with time.'

He strolled to the massive fireplace in the living room and leaned one muscular shoulder against the mantel. 'Masterpieces from the greats are all well and good, but modern art has its place too. They should be appreciated side by side.'

Just as he had placed them all over the house. I took a sip of water, settling deeper into my seat. 'I agree. Does that theme echo in all your properties?'

'Yes, it does.'

Before I could express pleasure in the thought, the gleam in his eyes arrested me.

'Is this how you wish to spend your wedding night, Calypso? Discussing art?'

The nerves rushed back and my hand trembled. 'What if it is?'

'Then I suggest you might want to be in more comfortable attire than that gown?'

Again, his eyes raked me, sending heat spiralling through me.

'Is this a ploy that usually works for you?'

One corner of his mouth lifted before his eyes darkened. 'Like you, I've never been married, so we both find ourselves in strange waters. Either way, the dress is going to have to come off one way or the other.'

'And if you don't like what is underneath…?' I dared. 'Will you send me back?'

His eyes narrowed. 'Is that what you're hoping for?'

Was it? I could have sworn my answer would be yes until actually faced with the question. But the word stuck in my throat, refusing to emerge as he sauntered towards me, taking a moment to discard the crystal tumbler so both his hands were free to capture my shoulders when he stopped in front of me.

'What I'm hoping for is that you will stop dishing out those enigmatic smiles and tell me what you meant earlier,' I said.

He frowned. 'You've lost me,' he drawled.

'When you said *if* we were to consummate this marriage? Are you incapable of doing so? If so perhaps you should get one of your staff to show me where I'm to sleep.'

His eyebrows rose. 'If I didn't know better I'd think you just issued me a challenge,' he drawled, in a voice that ruffled the tight nerves beneath my skin.

His scent filled my nostrils, his calm breathing propelling my attention to his sculpted chest, to the pulse beating steadily at his throat. To the magnificent vitality of his skin and the sheer animalistic aura breaching my tightly controlled space. Screaming at me to notice his masculinity. And not just to notice. He drew me with a power I'd never known before. I didn't just want to breathe him in. I wanted to touch. Explore. Taste.

That sensation was so strong I stepped back, eager to diffuse it.

The hands that held me stemmed my movement, and hard on the heels of my immobility came the realisation that I wanted to stay right where I was. But I didn't want him to know that.

'Well? *Are* you?' I taunted.

A mysterious smile tilted one corner of his lips before his hands slid down to my elbows. 'It should be easy enough to prove, *matia mou*.'

Just like that I was hit with the reality that this was my wedding night. That I was all but taunting him into…*possessing* me.

The thought sent a shiver through me. Coupled with something else. Something way too close to the forbidden desire that had coursed through me when I'd allowed myself to dream of this day some time in the dim and distant future, when I was out from under my father's thumb and free to have a boyfriend. A lover. A *husband*.

But how could that be? The man I'd imagined bore no resemblance to this formidable man, who wore arrogance and power as if it were a second skin. *Theos*, even his frown was attention-absorbing.

'Are you cold?' he asked.

I shook my head. Like everything else in this stunning villa, the temperature was perfect, blending with the early summer breeze.

'Then what's wrong?' he rasped, his eyes turning speculative again, as they had when I almost gave myself away on the dance floor.

The pain had thankfully receded, but other questions loomed just as large. The subject of my virginity and how that would factor into things, for one.

I pushed it away, seizing on another pressing need. 'I want you to tell me exactly what your agreement with my father is.'

One eyebrow rose. 'Isn't that a case of shutting the barn door after the horse has bolted? What's the point of rehashing the subject?'

It was time to come clean. 'I… I may have let you operate under the assumption that I know what's going on.'

Surprise flickered through his eyes before they narrowed. 'Are you saying you don't?'

'Not the exact details, no.'

Scepticism flared. 'You expect me to believe that? When you walked willingly by his side up the aisle?'

'Tell me you've never done something against your will and I'll call you a liar,' I replied.

The flare of his nostrils confirmed what I suspected—that this marriage was as much without his approval as it was without mine.

'Assuming it was solely your father who pushed for this, what steps did you take to stop him?'

None. Because my protests, like everything else, had fallen on deaf ears. I didn't say the words out loud, his timely reminder that, despite the promise I'd made, my mother's fate was in my father's hands, stilling my tongue. My hesitation gave Axios the answer he needed.

'I didn't, and the details don't matter. We are where we are. But I know there's an agreement between you. I simply want you to spell it out for me so I know what I'm dealing with.'

He stared at me, his measuring gaze weighted. I shouldn't have been relieved, even a little pleased to see the cynicism fade a little, but I was.

'Maybe he didn't tell you. How very like Petras to want to keep the spoils all for himself,' he muttered almost absently, before dropping his hands from my arms to say abruptly, 'Under an agreement signed between your grandfather and mine, Yiannis Petras, or any appointed representative after his death, can collect on a debt owed by my family. Your father wanted twenty-five percent of my company or the cash equivalent. We settled on one hundred million euros. And you.'

I couldn't hide my gasp at the confirmation that I'd been sold like a chattel.

Again, his cynicism receded. 'He really didn't tell you? Are you saying you're a victim in this?' he breathed.

The label smarted. 'I'm not a victim. But, no, he didn't tell me.'

Jaw gritted, he shoved a hand through his hair. 'So you don't know that under the terms of the agreement he'll also receive the deeds to Kosima?'

'What is Kosima?'

A bleak expression darkened his face. Whatever Kosima was, it held an emotional attachment for him.

'It's the private island where my grandfather was born. It was his favourite place on earth. Your grandfather knew that when he and my grandfather struck their unholy agreement. I assume he passed the information on to your father.'

My heart lurched with guilt, and for a wild moment I wanted to ease his pain. 'And my father demanded it as part of the agreement?'

Again his lips twisted, before his gaze slanted over me from head to toe. 'Of course. Just as he demanded that I marry *you*.'

This time my heart lurched for a different reason. He truly hadn't wanted this marriage—was entangled in it against his will just as I was.

About to stress that I had known absolutely nothing about this, that my father's avaricious demands were nothing to do with me, I heard that stern warning from my father slam into my brain. I didn't doubt that he would make my mother's life even more of a living hell than it was now.

The realisation that nothing had changed, that nothing *would* change, settled on me like a heavy, claustrophobic cloak.

'Why did you go through with it?' I asked. When he frowned, I hurried to add, 'You obviously hate what my family has done to you, so why…?'

My disjointed thoughts rumbled to a halt, my insides twisting with dread. A caged lion was an unpredictable creature, and from the first moment I'd set eyes on him I'd felt his banked fury.

Now I knew why.

His eyes blazed grey fire at me. 'You think I didn't try to find a way that didn't involve tying myself down for twelve months or handing over a multi-million-euro pay-out your father has done *nothing* to earn?' he sliced at me.

My breath caught. 'Why twelve months? Why not three...or even six?'

His mouth tightened. 'Ask your father. He had the power to nullify some or all aspects of this agreement. He chose not to. And he counted on me not fighting this in court because adverse publicity is the last thing my company needs right now. Your grandfather was an unreasonable man who my own grandfather had the misfortune of partnering with.'

'I know they started the airline business together, but—'

'Your grandfather wasn't interested in an airline business. He wanted to invest in boats, despite knowing next to nothing about them,' he spat out the words. 'But because they were tied together my grandfather was forced to work twice as hard to maintain both arms of the business. The only way Petras would agree to dissolve the partnership was to leave without taking his quarter-of-a-million-dollar share of the business immediately. If he had done so he would've bankrupted the company. But that didn't stop him from demanding crippling interest on the loan, and an agreement promising a percentage of Xenakis Aeronautics should he or any other Petras need a future bail-out. But even then, it was too late. My grandfather had spread himself too thin, trying to maintain two suffering businesses, but he was too proud to declare bankruptcy. The strain broke his marriage and his family, and after my grandmother died his heart just...gave up.'

My heart twisted at the anguish in his voice. 'I...'

What could I say? *I'm sorry*? Would Axios even believe me? What did it matter? My father had cunningly used the past against him. Against both of us.

'I didn't know any of this.'

His jaw rippled. 'My grandfather was my mentor. He taught me everything I know. But he withheld the extent of how bad things were until it was too late. Until I had to watch him wither away.'

After an age of losing himself in the bleak past, his eyes zeroed in on me.

'Why? If you didn't know all this, why present yourself to me at that altar like a sacrificial lamb?'

The cynicism was back full force. 'I'm not a lamb!'

One corner of his mouth lifted. 'No, I'm learning that my initial impression was mistaken. But I still want to know why,' he pressed with quiet force.

How could I tell him without speaking of the very thing I'd done all this to avoid? If my father had managed to pressure a powerful man like Axios Xenakis to do his will, what would he do to my mother if he found out I'd been divulging family secrets?

'Perhaps I had something to gain too,' I responded truthfully, knowing how it would be viewed.

True to form, his eyes slowly hardened, and that disappointment I'd briefly spotted at the altar flashed across his face.

As one of his hands slowly rose to cup my face, it seemed he wanted to delve deeper, perhaps even attempt to understand how we had become caught in this tangled web. But then he slowly withdrew, his demeanour resigned, even a little weary.

An urge to soothe him spiked through me. I managed to curb it, barely managing not to fidget under his piercing scrutiny.

'Did the agreement stipulate that we needed to…to consummate the marriage?' I asked.

He froze, and a sizzling, electrifying look entered his eyes. I got the feeling that he'd been waiting for this…that somehow coming to this point was what that sense of heightened expectancy had been all about.

'Not specifically, no.'

'But you don't know that it won't be held against you… against us…further down the line?'

He gave an indolent shrug even while his eyes continued to pin me in place. 'He's *your* father, Calypso. You tell me.'

I couldn't rule it out. And I suspected Axios knew that.

'Maybe he will. Maybe he won't. But I can't take the risk.'

With my mother's words echoing in my heart, my hunger for freedom grew with every second.

He took a slow, steady step towards me. His hands at his sides, he simply stared down at me, his only movement the deep rise and fall of his chest.

'What does that mean, Calypso?' he queried softly.

'It means I want there to be no room for misunderstanding later.'

Slowly, his hand rose again, his knuckles grazing my cheek. My shiver made his eyes darken.

'I need to hear the words, so there's no misunderstanding now.'

Heat suffused my face, as if chasing his touch. But his gaze wouldn't release me. Not until the words trembling on my lips fell free.

'I want to consummate this agreement. I want you to… take me.'

The full force of the words powered through me, shaking me from head to foot. Dear God, this wasn't how I'd imagined losing my virginity. None of this was how I'd dreamed it. So why did my insides twist themselves with… *excitement*?

For the longest time he simply stared at me, a myriad of emotions crossing his face. Eventually that dark gleam returned in full force, his presence filling the room as he turned his hand and brushed a thumb over my lips.

'Are you sure you don't wish to discuss…art?'

The thickness of his voice displaced any levity his words

attempted. And it drove home that this was happening. My wedding night. No, it wasn't the one I'd dreamed about, but really, if life was fair, would my father have tossed me in as part of a hundred-million-euro deal?

That thought was buried beneath the turbulent need climbing through me as he dragged his digit back and forth over my lip.

'I'm sure,' I answered, in a voice that sounded nothing like mine.

He tilted my gaze to his, making a gruff sound at whatever it was he saw on my face. His head started to lower—just as the other delicate subject raced to the forefront of my mind.

Tell him. He's going to find out soon enough.

'There's something you should know.'

One eyebrow rose in silent question.

'I'm a virgin.'

His fingers froze beneath my chin, his whole body turning to marble. 'What did you say?'

I swallowed the knot in my throat, praying the shivers would stop coursing through my body. 'I've never done… never been with a—'

A curse fell from his lips, raw and stunned. 'Why?'

Finally—*finally*—that burst of hysteria filtered through. 'You're asking why your wife is a virgin? Isn't that an odd question?'

'*Ne*—and it is precisely why I want to know why a twenty-four-year-old who looks the way you do is still untouched.'

Heat flowed through me. 'Looks the way I do…?'

The faintest colour washed his cheekbones. 'You must be aware of your beauty, Calypso,' he rasped, and his deep, husky voice set fire to my belly.

I blushed at the raw intensity in his words that reached into a secret part of me and took control of it. Hot tingles raced over my skin, warming me from the inside, tighten-

ing low in my belly and hardening my nipples. A gasp tore
from my throat. His gaze dropped to my parted lips, his
eyes darkening with each charged second that ticked by.

Then his eyes narrowed. 'Surely Petras didn't keep you
under lock and key simply for this possibility?' Incredulity
racked his voice.

Pain lashed through me, because the same thought had
occurred to me. My father might not have visited the ultimate indignity upon me by spelling it out in black and white,
but by thwarting all my previous attempts at a relationship
he'd ensured his deal would be sweetened with my virginity. Another indication as to how little he cared for me.

Despite the anguish racking me, I raised my chin, pride
insisting I did not confirm his suspicion. 'Does it not occur
to you that I've simply not met anyone interesting enough?'

Shrewd grey eyes conducted a slow scrutiny. 'Your pulse
is racing. Your face is flushed. I don't need a crystal ball
to tell me you're excited. It is safe to say that, regardless of
why you've remained untouched before, you're definitely
interested now, Calypso.'

I silently cursed my body for betraying me but I wasn't
ready to be cowed yet. 'You want me to bolster your ego
by admitting I find you attractive?'

His head went back, as if he was surprised by the question. Of course he did. Good looks. Power. Influence. All
attributes that made him irresistible to women. The stunning parade of women he'd purportedly dated was evidence
that his effect on the opposite sex was woven into his DNA.

A sexy, arrogant smile curved his lips. 'I don't need you
to *tell* me, *matia mou*. I *know* you do.'

My gasp was swallowed by the simple act of his head
swooping down and his mouth sealing mine in a hot, savage
possession that snatched the breath from my lungs. If that
kiss in the church had been spine-tingling, this complete
mastery was nothing short of earth-shattering.

The bold sweep of his tongue over my sensitive lower lip

fired electricity in every cell. When he followed that with the lightest graze of his teeth, in another clever tasting, a tiny hunger-filled sound left my throat.

Axios muttered something beneath his breath before the fingers capturing my chin moved to my lower back, tugging me closer, until the hard column of his body was plastered against mine and the wide stance of his powerful legs cradled me. Until the hot brand of his manhood was unmistakably imprinted against my belly, in a searing promise of what was in store.

His lips devoured mine with unapologetic hunger. And when one hand grasped mine and redirected it to his chest I gave in to the heady desire and explored him. Tensile muscle overlaid by his expensive cotton shirt was warm and inviting, and after a tentative caress, I sighed and gave in to *more*. The ultra-masculine line of his shoulder and neck drew my fingers, and that mysterious hunger built up into something that both terrified and thrilled me.

He made a gruff sound when my fingers brushed his warm, supple throat. It was enough to startle me. Enough to remind me that I didn't really know what I was doing. That, while I understood the mechanics of sex, I wasn't well-versed in its nuances.

Nerves dulled by the fire of arousal resurged, breaking free by way of a helpless whimper.

He raised his head and stared at me for the longest time before catching my hand in his. 'Come,' he commanded huskily.

I snatched in a much-needed breath. We both knew where we stood—that we were products of my father's machinations—surely we were going into this with our eyes open, in the knowledge that this was a one-time thing…weren't we?

Molten grey eyes watched me. When I slid my hand into his, he led me to some wide, imposing double doors. With casual strength he pushed them open to reveal the most magnificent bedroom I'd ever seen. While it bore unashamed signs of masculinity, the Mediterranean blue hues of the furniture blended with solid wood and gold-trimmed furnishings in the kind of design afforded only to the rich and influential.

But of course the centrepiece of the huge space was the bed. Emperor-sized, with four solid posts, its only softening effect was the muslin curtains currently tied back with neat ribbons.

Axios released me long enough to toss away extraneous pillows and pull back the luxury spread before he recaptured me. This time both hands went to my waist, his gaze dropping down to where he held me. He muttered something under his breath that I couldn't quite catch and when our gazes reconnected flames danced in the dark grey depths.

My knees weakened and I lifted my hands to rest them on his shoulders. He drew me closer while his hands searched along my spine, located the zip to my dress and firmly drew it down.

The dress gaped and he drew in a harsh breath, his gaze trailing over my exposed skin to linger on my barely covered breasts. Through the silk his hands branded my skin, making me squirm with a need to feel them without any barrier. As if he heard my silent wish, he took hold of the straps and eased them down my arms. The material pooled at my feet, leaving me in the scrap of lace panties and matching strapless bra.

One expert flick and the bra was loosened. Instinctively, I moved to catch it. Moved to delay this exquisite madness unfurling inside me.

Axios caught my hand, drew it firmly back to his shoulder. 'I want to see you, Calypso. I want to see everything.'

Unable to stand the raw fire in his eyes, I fixed my eyes on his chest. On the buttons hiding that steel and muscle from me. Again he read my wants with ease.

'Take my shirt off, *yineka mou.*'

Yineka mou. My wife.

Why did my insides dance giddily each time he called me that? Especially when we both knew this was an enforced, transient thing?

'Don't keep me waiting.'

The husky nudge brought me back to him. With fingers that had given up being anywhere near steady, I reached for his sleekly knotted tie, tugged it free and released his top shirt button. It was simpler to avoid his eyes as I concentrated on my task, but halfway down, when my fingers brushed his abs, he hissed under his breath.

Impatience etched on his face, he took hold of the expensive cotton and pulled the shirt apart. That raw display of strength tossed another log onto the flames building inside me. By the time he lifted me free of my wedding gown and took the few steps to the bed I'd lost the ability to breathe.

Riveted, I watched him shrug off the shirt, followed by his other clothing, before prowling to the bed. With the ease of a maestro he caught me to him, his fingers sliding up my nape and into my hair to release the three pins that secured the thick strands. His eyes raked my body as he slowly trailed his fingers through my hair. The effect was hot and hypnotising, the need to melt into him surging high.

So when he settled his expert lips over mine all I could do was moan and hold on, shudder in shocking delight when his chest grazed my hardened nipples.

But soon even that grew insufficient. Tentatively I parted my lips, in anticipation of the next decadent sweep of his tongue. When it grazed mine the zap of electricity convulsed my whole body.

Axios tore his lips from mine, incredulous eyes burning into me. 'You truly *are* innocent…' he muttered.

Mercifully, he didn't require an answer, or he was too impatient. After another searing kiss, in which his tongue breached my lips and brazenly slicked over mine, he trailed his lips over my throat.

Each pathway he claimed over my skin sent a pulse

straight between my legs, plumping and heating my core until I thought I would explode. Large hands moulded my breasts, his fingers torturing the peaks. I cried out, my senses threatening to splinter.

The feeling of delving into another dimension, one where only pure pleasure existed, swelled through me, drawing me into a place of wonder. A place where I could give expression to what I was experiencing.

'That's...so amazing. How is this feeling possible?'

Had I said that out loud? Axios momentarily froze, but I was too caught up in bliss to find out why. Then his caresses continued, his mouth pressing kisses on my midriff, my belly, along the line of my panties.

When he tugged them down, my breath stalled.

He parted my thighs, trailed kisses up one inner thigh, then another.

'Your stubble feels...incredible.'

Again I felt him still.

'Am I doing something wrong? Please...'

Long fingers grazed the swollen nub, sending feverish pleasure racing through my body. Without him close to anchor me I grabbed hold of the sheets. Anything to keep me from disintegrating beneath the force of pleasure ramping through me.

Except that force tripled when his mouth settled with fierce intent on my feminine core. Brazenly, he tasted me with a connoisseur's expertise, teasing and torturing and dragging me to the brink of madness.

Until a new tightness took hold of me.

'Ah...it's too much... I... I can't take it...'

'Yes, you can,' he declared huskily.

His lips went back to wreaking their magic, to piling on that enchantment, until I simply...blew apart.

Bliss such as I'd never known suffused my body, convulsions rippling over me before sucking me under. I was aware of the cries falling from my lips, was aware that

Axios had returned to my side, and I gripped him blindly, needing something solid to hang on to.

When he moved away I started to protest before I could stop myself. His kiss settled me for the few moments while he left the bed. The sound of foil ripping barely impinged upon my enchanted calm, my senses only sparking to life when he resumed his overwhelming presence between my thighs.

The intensity of the eyes locked on mine was almost too much to bear. I sought relief elsewhere. But there was none to be found in the wide expanse of his shoulders, the ripped contours of the chest I suddenly yearned to explore with my mouth, or… *Theos mou*…the fearsomely impressive evidence of his maleness.

The tiniest whimper slipped free. And while it brought an arrogant little twitch to his lips, there was also a slight softening of his fierce regard.

'Look at me, Calypso.'

The low command brought my gaze back to his. To the lock of hair grazing his eyebrow that I yearned to brush back. The slightly swollen sensual lips I wanted to kiss.

'Do you want this?' he asked.

The thought of stopping now was unthinkable. 'Yes,' I answered.

He gripped one thigh, parting me with unwavering intent.

The first shallow thrust stilled my breath. The second threw me back to that dimension where only sensation reigned.

Apprehensively, I exhaled. Axios moved his powerful body, withdrawing before penetrating me. Once. Twice.

On the third glide the sting was replaced by a different, jaw-dropping sensation, one that dragged me deeper into that dimension.

'You're…so deep. It feels…incredible.'

Above me, Axios hissed, his fingers digging into my

thigh as he held himself, still and throbbing, inside me. The sensation was indescribable. But...

'Why aren't you moving? Do *I* need to? Maybe if I roll my hips...'

Tentatively I experimented, then cried out as pleasure rained over me.

'That was...sensational. I want to... Would you mind if I did it again?'

'No. I wouldn't,' he said thickly, then met my next thrust with an even more powerful one.

What the hell was happening?

I stared down at Calypso. Her eyes were shut in unbound pleasure.

My fraying control took another hit, the feeling that this little witch with her wide streak of innocence that had turned out not to be a clever trick was responsible for my curious state driving confusion through me.

The giving and taking of carnal pleasure was far from new to me but this...

I wanted to tell her to open her eyes. To centre her to me. To—

'Why are you stopping? Please don't stop. I want more.'

Her husky, innocent plea ramped up my arousal, the enormity of what was happening lending a savage edge to my hunger I'd never experienced before.

But just to be sure she was right there with me I leaned closer, flicked my tongue over her nipple. 'Do you like this, Calypso?'

Short blunt nails dug into my back. 'Yes!'

'And this?' I pulled the tight bud into my mouth, suckling her sweet flesh with fervour.

'*Ne.* That... You do that so well. I never want it to end.'

Theos. Did she not know what she was doing? That this kind of uncensored commentary could drive a man over the edge?

But she wasn't doing it with another man. She was doing it with *me*. The man she was bound to for the next twelve months.

Her husband.

Knowing I was her first shouldn't be sending such primitive satisfaction through my blood. And yet it was, settling deep inside me with such definitive force it threw up a shock of bewilderment.

I was thankful to avoid examining it in that moment. Because the utter nirvana of taking her, hearing her unfettered pleasure, was creating an unstoppable chain reaction inside me. One that kept me thrusting into her snug heat, my pulse racing to dangerous levels as her delicious lips parted and another torrent of words ran freely.

'*Glykó ouranó*... I'm on fire... What you're doing to me... Please... I need... I *need*...'

My teeth gritted as I hung on to control with my fingertips. As her sweet body arched beneath mine and her head thrashed on the pillow.

'You need to let go, Calypso.' I sounded barely coherent to my own ears.

With a sharp cry she gave herself over to her bliss, her sweet convulsions triggering mine. The depth of my climax left me gasping, the stars exploding across my vision unending.

Leached of all power and control, I collapsed onto the pillows, stunned by the sorcery I'd just experienced. A unique experience I wanted to relive again. Immediately.

Soft arms curved around my waist and I reached for her before I could stop myself—before I could question the wisdom of lingering when I normally exited. Pulling her into me when I normally distanced myself.

I will. In a moment.

Once I'd gathered myself. Once this experience had been dissected and slotted into its proper place.

I would have fought any future attempt by Yiannis Petras to further line his pocket, but Calypso's way of sealing all avenues had been…better. Pleasurable, even.

Or foolish?

I tensed, unwilling to accept that perhaps I could have found another way. Not succumbed to this bewitchment so readily.

So draw a line under it. Leave!

Her soft breathing feathered over my jaw. Sleep was stealing over her slightly flushed face. The urge to join her whispered over me—another wave of temptation that lingered for far too long, making me close my eyes for several minutes before common sense prevailed.

So what if the sex was sublime? It was just sex. Come tomorrow my life would resume its normal course. This whole day would be behind me.

I'd done my duty. Had ensured Petras would no longer be a threat to my family. For now the night was still young. There was no rush to go anywhere…

Except temptation was ten times stronger when I woke in the early hours of the morning. In the murky light of dawn I caught the faintest glimpse of the slippery slope my grandfather had been led down by another Petras.

A road I couldn't risk.

I put words to definitive action by rising and leaving the bed, gathering my clothes and walking out of the master bedroom.

Because my business with my wife was over.

CHAPTER THREE

MY TRANSITION FROM sleep to wakefulness was abrupt, bracing in the way that fundamental change manifested itself. Confirmation that I hadn't dreamt any of it registered in unknown muscles throbbing with new vigour. The sheets also bore evidence of what had happened, and confirmed that Axios had left some time in the night.

Had he chosen to sleep somewhere else? Or had his helicopter taken off during one of the brief stretches of time when I'd fallen asleep?

Although my agitated thoughts wanted to latch on to the fact that it was the sex that had driven him away, intuition suggested otherwise. Axios might not have wanted to experience the depth of chemistry that blazed between us but he'd been caught up too. Maybe a little bit too much?

Because I was reeling from the wildness of our coming together, the sheer abandonment that still rocked me to my core. The sheets might have cooled in his absence but his possession still remained. As did my growing consternation.

Last night my decision had seemed so clear-cut. Close all avenues by which my father could further interfere in my life. But the experience had been nothing like clear-cut. The experience of sleeping with Axios had been…unparalleled.

And now he was gone.

I refused to allow the dull thudding of my heart to dictate my disappointment. Whatever my future held, it was time for action.

About to get out of bed, I paused as my last conversation with my mother replayed one more time.

'You will know very quickly if this is the right choice for you. If it isn't, don't be like me. Don't accept it as inevitable. Do what is right for you.'

'What are you talking about, Mama?'

'Find your own happiness, Callie. Don't let your father's

actions dictate the rest of your life. Your grandmother said the same thing to me on my wedding day and I didn't listen.'

'*I don't think I have a choice. You... Papa—*'

'*Forget about me! There's nothing your father can do that will hurt me any more. Knowing you're unhappy because of me will break my heart. Promise me you'll put yourself first.*'

'*Mama—*'

'*Promise me, Callie!*'

My promise weighed heavy on my heart as I rose from the bed. For a moment I swayed in place, my limbs weak with recollection and my body heating after every little wanton act of last night.

But, lips firmed, I approached what I hoped was the bathroom. There, further signs that this was Axios's domain were everywhere—from the luxury male products to the thick dark robe hanging next to the shower.

Trying not to let the intimacy of his belongings get to me, I quickly showered. Thankful for the voluminous towel that covered me from chest to ankle, I was contemplating the less than palatable thought of wearing my wedding dress again when a soft knock broke into my thoughts.

I cleared my throat. 'Come in.'

One of the younger staff members who helped manage the villa entered with a shy smile. She'd been introduced to me last night, when my senses had been grappling with unfolding events.

With a strained smile, I pulled the robe closer around me and returned her greeting.

Her gaze passed quickly over my towel. 'May I assist you with anything, *kyria*?'

'If you could direct me to where my belongings are, I'd appreciate it.'

'Of course. This way, please.'

Expecting her to leave the room, I was surprised when she crossed to the opposite side and opened another door.

I followed her through a short hallway into another impressive suite, complete with living room, bathroom and dressing room.

An adjoining suite.

'I came to ask if you would like some breakfast, Kyria Xenakis?'

The title added another layer of shock to my system and it took me a few seconds to answer with a question of my own. 'Um…is Kyrios Xenakis still here?'

She nodded. 'Yes. But he will be leaving soon. So if you wish to—'

'Yes, I would very much like to. Can you wait for me to get dressed?'

Her eyes widened a touch, probably at the request. But I didn't care. I needed answers. Needed to know how he intended the next twelve months to proceed. And, if necessary, insist on taking back control of my life.

My father had shown me that he cared nothing about me except as a pawn to further his needs. Regardless of my commitment to Axios, I didn't intend to be pushed around any more.

That affirmation anchored deep as I concentrated on getting dressed.

The small suitcase that had accompanied me when I left Nicrete was empty, its contents sitting on a lonely shelf in the vast dressing room. But those weren't the only contents of the large, opulent space. Rack upon rack of clothes were displayed in fashion seasons, with matching shoes arranged by colour, height and style.

Awestruck, I stared. It was by far the most extensive collection I'd seen outside a clothes store. Simply because I didn't know who the clothes in the closets belonged to, I fished out a simple shirt dress from my own belongings, added comfortable flats and caught my hair in a ponytail.

The maid led me down the stairs and through several halls before stopping at a set of double doors.

'He's in there,' she said softly. Then melted away.

The faint sound of clinking cutlery reached my ears as I paused to take a fortifying breath. But, aware that no amount of deep breathing could prepare me for the morning after last night, I pushed the door open.

He was seated at the head of a long, exquisitely laid table. Impeccably dressed in formal business attire, minus the jacket, with the sun streaming down on him.

I almost lost my footing at the sheer visceral impact of his masculinity. It really was unfair how attractive Axios Xenakis was. How the simple act of caressing his bottom lip with his forefinger, his brow furrowed in concentration, could spark fire low in my belly.

You're not here to ogle him.

Fists tightening at the reminder, I approached where he sat. 'We need to talk.'

He took his time to look up from the tablet propped up neatly next to his plate, to power it down with a flick of his finger before cool grey eyes tracked over me from head to toe and back again.

'*Kalimera*, Calypso. Sit down—have something to eat.'

His even tones threw me. He wasn't behaving like a man who'd left his marriage bed after bedding his virgin wife. In fact, he seemed far too confident. Far too...*together* for my liking.

When I didn't immediately obey he rose, his gaze resting on me as he pulled out a chair and...waited.

I sat, because hysteria would achieve nothing. What I intended to say to him could be said standing or sitting. Besides, this close, the potent mix of his warm body and his aftershave was making my head swim. Reminding me of what it had been like to stroke that warm body, to cling to it as fevered bliss overtook me.

'What's on your mind?' he enquired as he poured exquisite-smelling coffee into my cup, then nudged platters containing sliced meats, toast and cheeses towards me.

Cool. He was far too cool.

Something was going on here. I probed his face and saw the slight tension in his jaw. The banked emotion in his eyes. I might have known Axios for less than twenty-four hours, but I'd quickly deciphered that his eyes gave him away. Right now, they were far too shrewd.

My heart jumped into my throat.

'My father may have put us both in this position, but there's no reason why we should remain like this.' Relief welled as my voice emerged strong and steady.

His nod of agreement stunned me. 'You're right,' he said.

'I am?'

He shrugged. 'The agreement states that we should be married for a year minimum—not that we need to be in each other's pocket. Of course that's not to say it's cart blanche for you to do as you please.'

'What does *that* mean?'

'It means that for the time being Agistros is yours to enjoy. We will revisit our circumstances again when I return in a few weeks.'

His announcement was still resonating inside me when he rose from the table and strode, his head proud, shoulders stiff, towards the door.

'When you return? Where will you be?'

He paused, his tall, imposing body swivelling towards where I sat, frozen. 'In Athens, where my business is, and where I intend to stay for the foreseeable future.'

Despite sensing this had been coming, I found the announcement took me by surprise. 'You're leaving me here on my own?'

Theos—could I sound any more alarmed?

He gave a curt, unfeeling nod. 'It is the best decision.'

I pushed my chair back and stood, feeling a yearning spiralling inside that wouldn't be silenced. A yearning to know that his condemnation of my father meant that he was different. That, despite tarring me with the same brush as my parent, he wouldn't punish me too.

'Why can't I live in Athens too?' *With you.*

It would be the perfect place finally to put my art degree to good use. To start a career.

His hardening features broadcasted his displeasure at that question even before he spoke. 'Why force us to endure one another when we don't have to?'

'I'm perfectly happy living on my own. I can rent a flat, get a job in an art gallery—'

The twist of his lips reminded me again of how hot his kisses could be. 'What's the point of staging an elaborate wedding to fool the world if my wife immediately moves into an apartment?'

'Then why did you do it?' I challenged.

'Your father timed his strike to perfection—because my company needs stability now more than ever.'

Invisible walls closed in on me. 'So this is a *business* decision?'

His jaw clenched. '*Everything* that has transpired between us has been based on a business decision.'

Even last night?

My heart lurched and I was glad I was sitting down. 'There has to be another way.'

'There is. You stay here, in our purportedly happy home. You'll want for nothing. Your every wish will be catered for. Buy as much art as you wish to—or even make it if you want.'

Yesterday the promise of freedom from this nightmare would have brought boundless relief. Today, all I felt was… trapped.

'I can't. I can't live like that.'

The words were uttered more for myself than for him. Born from my deep desire never to fall under another's command the way my father had forced me to live under his.

'How long am I to stay in this gilded *prison*?'

His eyes darkened. 'If this is a prison, *yineka mou*, it is not of my making. I tried for months to make your father listen to reason. *He* caused this situation, not me. If you want a way out of this, then find one.'

With that, he walked out, leaving my insides cold as ice.

Axios's words echoed through the long days and nights that followed his departure from Agistros. Long after the days in the luxurious paradise had begun to stretch in brain-numbing monotony.

My new husband, having made his feelings clear about our forced marriage, didn't bother to come home. The stunning villa had indeed become my prison, and its elegant walls and priceless furnishings closed in on me more with every day that dragged by.

And the more my world became narrow, the louder my mother's words and the contents of my grandmother's letter clamoured.

By the end of the second week dejection had me in a constricting hold. But alongside it was the discomfort in my abdomen, which wouldn't let up. Telling myself it was a psychosomatic reaction to my current situation began to feel hollow when I knew my grandmother had felt similar symptoms in the year before her death.

Then the housekeeper informed me one sun-drenched morning that Axios had left a message to say that he would be away on business in New York for another ten days. It seemed like the ominous catalyst I needed.

In the privacy of my suite, I quickly considered and discarded the things I wouldn't need. My large hobo bag was big enough to hold the most crucial essentials, and the small stash of cash I'd saved from my allowance was more than enough to see me through the first few days of my unknown adventure.

After that…

My heart lurched as I attempted to hold down my breakfast the next morning. I took my time, ensuring I was well-sustained before I left the table. Aware of the housekeeper's keen eye, I calmly drank another cup of tea, then helped myself to fruit before drawing back my chair.

'Agatha, I'm thinking of visiting friends. I'm not sure how long I'll be. A few days—maybe longer.'

Surprise lit the housekeeper's eyes. 'But Kyrios Xenakis said you were to stay here—'

'Kyrios Xenakis isn't here. And he's not coming back for ten days. I seriously doubt he'll miss my absence in the meantime.' I slapped on a smile to take the sting out of my words.

She gave a wary nod. 'When do you wish to leave? I'll tell Spiros to ready the boat.'

'Don't bother. I'll grab a water taxi from the harbour. The walk down will do me good.'

Disapproval filmed her eyes. '*Kyria*, I don't think that's a good idea.'

One of the few facts I'd learned about my absent husband was that he was far wealthier than I'd imagined. The members of the Xenakis dynasty basked in the sort of wealth that required bodyguards and well-orchestrated security for them to travel. Exactly the sort of attention I didn't need.

'I appreciate your concern, but it's not necessary, Agatha. Thank you.'

I walked away before she could respond. And, since I wasn't entirely sure she wouldn't alert Axios at the very first opportunity, I rushed up to my suite, grabbed my bag and hurried back down.

Two hours later I stepped up to the sales counter at the airport on the mainland. 'One-way ticket to Switzerland, please.'

The attendant eyed me for what seemed like for ever before issuing my ticket. But if I thought that was nerve-racking, discovering what my grandmother had left for me once I arrived at the Swiss bank left me shamelessly sobbing in a cold and grey bank vault.

And then everything that had gone before paled in comparison to the fear that gripped my heart when I sat before a Swiss doctor three days later.

Dr Trudeau, a short, grey-haired physician with kind eyes, peered at me over his rimless glasses, gentle fingers tapping the file in front of him before he sighed.

'Miss Petras, I have good news and bad news. Although I'm not entirely sure how welcome the good news will be once I explain what I believe is happening with you. I'm so sorry.'

CHAPTER FOUR

One year later

THE TURQUOISE WATERS of the Pacific were so blindingly beautiful they brought tears to my eyes. Or perhaps it was the stinging salt from the spray.

It definitely wasn't because today was my first wedding anniversary.

No. Most certainly not that.

On the list of the most forgettable things to happen to me in the last year, my hastily arranged wedding and the shockingly cold ceremony was right at the top. Not to mention the trapped groom who couldn't wait to walk away from me. The man I now had the dubious pleasure of calling my husband.

My heart leapt into my throat even as I pushed Axios's image away. He would need to be dealt with soon.

But not just yet.

I lifted my face to the blazing sun, willed it to pierce through my desolation and touch my wounded soul. I needed brightness and mirth, sunshine and positivity. If only for a little while longer... It might all be gone soon, slipping through my fingers like mercury.

Gripping the railing of the sleek sailboat transporting me from an exclusive Bora Bora resort to the adjoining uninhabited island where I'd ordered my picnic, I mentally went through my list from bottom to top.

Number five: Take control of my life. *Check.*

Contrary to my fears, walking away hadn't doomed me or my mother. My monthly phone calls reassured me that she was fine. My father, now a hundred million euros richer, was engrossed in yet another business venture. Better still, he hadn't challenged any of the terms of the contract he'd made with Axios.

Number four: Do something worthwhile with my painting. *Check.*

The past year had been frightening in some ways but immensely fulfilling in the exploration of my talent. I was still basking in the knowledge that I could have had a career if fate hadn't pushed me down a different path.

Number three: Accept that my condition might not have a happy ending and that my prognosis might follow my grandmother's. *Check.*

It had been a difficult acceptance, often pitted with tears and heartache and grief for all the things I might never have. For what this would do to those I love.

Number two: Cherish my precious gift for as long as I can. *Check. Check. Check.*

The last item on my list filled me with equal parts desolation and trepidation. But it needed to be done.

Number one: Hand over my precious gift to Axios Xenakis.

As if that gift knew he was in my thoughts, a soft cry rippled through the sun-drenched breeze, followed by a sharper one, demanding attention.

Smiling, I turned from the railing and crossed the deck to the shaded lounge. There, lying amongst the cushions, was the reason for my heartbeat. The reason I needed to keep fighting for my unknown future.

'Are you awake, my precious boy?'

At the sound of my voice Andreos Xenakis kicked his plump legs, his arms joining in his giddy response as his searching eyes found mine. For an instant my breath caught. The similarity between the piercing grey eyes of father and son was so visceral, I froze.

Another insistent cry had me reaching for him. His warm, solid weight in my arms quieted the worst of my trepidation, and soon even that evaporated beneath the sheer joy of cradling him, feeding him, doing such mundane things as changing his nappy and handing him his favourite toy, basking in his sweet babbling while I enjoyed the stunning view and just...*being.*

Pushing away the terrifying news the doctor had given me that day in Switzerland and the choice I'd had to make, I breathed in relief when the boat slowed and a staff member approached with a courteous smile.

'We're here, miss. Your picnic is set up for you on the shore.'

Whatever the future held, I would deal with it.

After all, I'd dealt with so much this past year.

Except the future had found me before I was ready. And it came in the form of a solitary figure with furious gunmetal eyes and a gladiator stance, waiting with crossed arms on the jetty as the sailboat returned to the exclusive resort.

My heart leapt into my throat, my breath strangled to nothing as I watched the figure grow larger, more broody, more formidable.

More everything.

He'd grown harder. Edgier. Or perhaps that was all imagined. A product of those feverishly erotic dreams that frequently plagued me.

Whatever... The man who watched me in silent condemnation as the boat gently butted the wooden planks on the jetty had zero mercy in him. And when his gaze shifted to Andreos and widened with chilled shock I had the distinct notion that I'd played this wrong.

I'd been too selfish.

Taken too much time for myself.

Too much time with my son.

'Axios.'

He didn't respond to my whispered utterance of his name. He couldn't take his eyes off Andreos. His strong throat moved in a swallow and his pallor increased as several expressions charged through his eyes.

Shock. Amazement. Utter fury.

'What are you doing here?' I asked.

Finally eyes the colour of a dark arctic night clashed with mine. 'What am I *doing* here?' he asked with icy incredulity. 'This is what you have to say to me after the stunt you have pulled?'

My insides shook but I forced myself to hold his gaze. 'You'll want to discuss this, I'm sure, but can it wait till—?'

'I'll *want to discuss this*? Are you for real?'

A drowsy Andreos stirred in my arms, his senses picking up on the frenetic emotions charging through the air.

'Miss, would you like us to—?'

'Leave us.' Axios's tone was deep. Implacable.

I wasn't in the least bit surprised when the staff hurried away.

'How did you find me?'

It seemed a monumental feat for him to drag his gaze from Andreos.

'Through an act of sheer coincidence. The owner of this resort happens to be a business acquaintance of mine. He was on a rare tour of his property when he spotted you. Had he not chosen to take his yearly tour this last week…' He stopped, shaking his head as if grappling with the sheer serendipity of the occurrence that had led him to me.

My chalet was on the beach, and I made the short walk to the gorgeous timber-clad structure aware of his every step behind me.

'I intended to come back—I promise.'

'You *promise*? Why should I take your word on anything? You told the staff you were visiting friends when all along you intended to abscond from our marriage. And now you're hiding in a resort on the other side of the world under a false name. Not to mention you seem to have had a child during that time. I am assuming the child is yours?'

'Of course he his. Who else's would he be?'

He went as rigid as an ice statue, and what little colour

had flowed back into his face on the walk from jetty to chalet receded momentarily before fury reddened his haughty cheekbones once more.

'So I can add infidelity to your sins?'

'Infid—? What are you talking about?' Shock made my voice screech.

Andreos whimpered as I laid him down in his cot, and then went back to sound sleep.

'We used contraception on our wedding night, as I recall,' he rasped with icy condemnation.

'Well, I wasn't on birth control. I never have been. And, while I'm not an expert, I'm sure there's a caution that states that condoms aren't one hundred percent foolproof.'

'And I'm suddenly to accept that the protection that has never failed me before suddenly malfunctioned with *you*?'

I wasn't sure why the reference to other lovers drilled such angst through me. His lovers, past or present, were of no consequence to me. I had no hold over him, nor did he over me, when it came right down to it. All that had brought us together was my father's greed and manipulation.

'I don't know what to say to make you believe me but I know the truth, Axios. Andreos is yours.'

Piercing eyes locked on mine for the better part of a minute. 'If he's mine, why have you hidden him from me for the better part of a year?'

His voice had changed, turned grittier, and he even looked a little shaken as his gaze swung again to Andreos. He started to walk towards the cot as if compelled, then stopped, shook his head.

'Why is he here on the other side of the world when he should be in Greece, with his family?'

It would have been so easy to blurt out everything that had happened to me since that dreaded visit to the doctor in Switzerland. and the urgent summons to hear my diagnosis three gut-churning days later, when it had been confirmed that there was indeed a growth in my cervix.

But I was also told I was pregnant, and that any further exploration, even an initial biopsy to ascertain its malignancy or benignity, would jeopardise my baby.

I could have told him about the latest scans I had in my suitcase, taken by Dr Trudeau in Switzerland, and his recommendation to take action.

But if Axios's presence here wasn't warning enough that the time I'd bought for myself was over, the look in his eyes said I wouldn't escape scot-free.

Nevertheless, I wasn't the same woman he'd married. Harrowing decisions made in the cold grip of fear had a way of changing a person.

'Why does it matter to you, anyway? I thought you would be glad to see the back of me for ever.'

A ferocious light glinted in his eyes for a heart-stopping second before he took a step towards me. 'You married a Xenakis, Calypso. You think simply packing your bag and walking out through the door is the end of it? That you simply had to hightail it to the other end of the world for your marriage vows to cease to have meaning?'

I stemmed my panic as his words rankled. 'Our vows had *meaning*? I could've sworn you challenged me to find a way to make them *stop* having meaning.'

His eyes narrowed. 'You think *this* was the answer?'

'It was *my* way!'

'Perhaps I should've added an addendum that finding a way needed to involve discretion and consideration. Nothing that would throw a spotlight on me or my family. My mistake. Tell me, Calypso, do you think disappearing off the face of the earth for over a year screams discretion or consideration?'

I shrugged with a carelessness I didn't feel. 'You didn't stick around long enough to hash out another course of action. I did what was best.'

'What was best for *you*, you mean?'

My senses wanted to scream *yes!* Caution warned me to

remain calm. To talk this through as rationally as the tower of formidable fury in front of me would allow.

'You still haven't told me why you're here.'

He made another sound of incredulity. 'Because you're my wife! Because the whispers need to cease. Because you will not jeopardise everything I've worked for. And that's just for starters.'

'Ah, *now* we're getting to the bottom of it. You're here because of what my absence is doing to your business? Is that it, Axios?'

With lightning speed warm fingers curled over my nape. His hold wasn't threatening, simply holding me in place so that whatever point he needed to make would be accurately delivered.

'While no one would dare say it to my face, rumours of my wife fleeing our marital home has caused ripples in my life. The kind I can do without. So make no mistake: I intend to remedy that. Whatever point you intended to make, it ends now.'

Each word contained a deadly promise—an intention to have his way that stoked the rebellion that had gone dormant in the last year back to life.

'Believe it or not, my walking out had absolutely nothing to do with you.'

'Enlighten me, then, *matia mou*. What was it all about?' The soft cadence of his voice didn't fool me.

'What could possibly have driven you from the life of luxury and abundance your father battled for so cunningly?'

The mention of my father brought my goals back into focus. Reminded me why I hadn't been able to stomach staying under Axios's roof for one more day. That feeling of a loss of control. Of suffocation. Of not being able to live my life on my own terms. My choices being taken away from me without so much as a by your leave...

'I'm not my father,' I stressed, with every cell in my body.

'No, you're not. But while I was prepared to give you

the benefit of the doubt before, your actions have led me to form a different opinion about you. So whatever your reasons were, tell me now.'

'Or what?'

He didn't speak for the longest moment. Then his attention shifted to the cot where Andreos slept, lost in baby dreams. My heart tripped over itself as I watched Axios's face. Watched him speculate with that clever mind financial analysts rhapsodised over.

'Is he the reason?'

'What do you mean?'

His jaw rippled. 'If there was an indiscretion, I urge you to confess it now rather than later.'

His words shouldn't have scraped my emotions. Considering what my mother had done, and the fall-out and gossip that had followed, I knew all too well how assumptions were made, judgements passed without verification. But the reality that he suspected Andreos wasn't his lanced a soft spot in my heart.

A fierce need to protect my child's honour ploughed through me. 'We may not have known each other before we met at the altar, but you should know that I would rather cut off my own arm before attempting to lie about my child's parentage. Whether you're willing to accept it or not, he's yours.'

If I'd expected my fervour to melt his coldness, I was sorely disappointed.

'Your vigorous defence of your child is admirable. But, as you said, we were virtual strangers before we came together. If you want me to believe you, tell me where you've been. Every single thing you've done in the past year. Then perhaps I'll consider believing you.'

The list reeled through my head.

Finding the bank account in Switzerland my grandmother had left in my name.

Seeing the private doctor who'd treated me.

Getting the results and feeling the soul-wrecking fear that my fate would echo my grandmother's.

Making the choice I had to make.

Andreos's arrival.

Saying the fervent prayers for *more*. One more day. One week. One month.

One year.

I couldn't tell Axios any of that. Even the simple joy of rediscovering my love of painting and finding the shops and galleries I'd sold my watercolours to seemed too sacred, too private to share with the man who looked at me with rancour and suspicion. Whose every breath seemed like a silent pledge to uncover my secrets.

My life. Lived on my terms.

That was what I'd sworn to myself that rainy afternoon in my hotel room after leaving Dr Trudeau's office. For the most part, it had been.

Axios's arrival had simply shortened the time I'd given myself before checking off the last item on my list.

'You'll consider believing me after you've triple-checked everything I say?'

The unapologetic gleam in his eyes told me he intended to do exactly that. Tear through every new, unconditional friendship I'd formed along the way, every haven I'd sought refuge in.

My stomach churned at the thought of Axios finding out the true state of my health and exploiting it the way my father had done with my mother. It was that terrible thought more than anything else that cemented my decision to keep my secret.

If he found out my condition, he would wonder if the state of my health affected my suitability as a mother. Unlike my mother, my flaws weren't outward. For the precious time being, I could hang on to that.

As for when I couldn't...

'All you need to know is that Andreos is yours and I'm prepared to return to Greece. If that's what you want?'

His nostrils flared and his gaze raked my face for long sizzling seconds before his lips twisted. 'Oh, yes, wife. The time has most definitely come for that. And whatever it is that you're keeping from me, rest assured, I'll find out.'

With that he stepped back.

Thinking he was going to leave me to grapple with the turmoil his unexpected arrival had caused, I watched, my heart speeding like a freight train, as he headed to the cot where Andreos slept.

Silence disturbed only by the slow stirring of the ceiling fan throbbed in the room as Axios stared down at the son he hadn't accepted was his. His jaw clenched tight and his throat moved convulsively as he watched the rise and fall of the baby's chest.

He remained frozen for so long I feared he'd take root there. When he turned abruptly and tugged a sleek phone from his pocket my senses tripped.

'What are you doing?'

Eyes the colour of a stormy sky met mine as he hit a number and lifted the handset to his ear. 'Getting the answers I need.'

The sharp orders he gave in Greek when the phone was answered didn't surprise me. The irony that the one truth I'd told him was the one he was having a hard time accepting wasn't lost on me. But, conversely, I understood. I too had wondered why fate would choose to lay both joy and sorrow on me in one fell swoop, leaving me with a choice that had seemed both simple and terrifying.

After all, my actions pointed to behaviour that would've left *me* suspicious too. And, considering what my own mother had done for the sake of freedom and love—an act that was an open secret in Nicrete—I didn't blame Axios for wanting to verify that the baby he'd helped create was truly his.

When he was done making an appointment for his private doctor to visit his home in Athens the moment he returned, to take DNA samples for a paternity test, he hung up, his piercing regard staying on me as he tucked his phone away.

I ignored the blatant challenge and asked the question more important to me. 'Is it going to hurt him?'

For the most fleeting second the charged look in his eyes dissipated. 'No. I'm told all it requires is a swab from his cheek.'

I nodded. 'Very well, then.'

He frowned, my easy acquiescence seemingly throwing him. But his face returned to its formidable hauteur in moments, and his strides were purposeful as he strode to the house phone and picked it up.

Before he dialled he turned to me. 'Is the child okay to travel on a plane?'

'The *child's* name is Andreos. And I'd thank you not to make any plans without discussing them with me first.'

A muscle ticked in his jaw. 'Why? Did you not tell me that you intended to return to Greece?'

'Yes, I did.'

'When exactly were you proposing to do that? When he was a year old? When he was five or perhaps ten?' he grated out.

The cold embrace of knowing that time wasn't on my side stalled my answer for several seconds. 'I was thinking days—not months or years. My booking at this resort is only for a week. I was going to fly back to Athens from here.'

His lips flattened. 'I don't plan on leaving you behind, Calypso. My good faith where you're concerned is gone. When I fly out of here in three hours you and the child will be by my side. And that state will continue until such time as you choose to come completely clean about your actions for the past year or I furnish myself with the information.'

After that, there really wasn't much more to say.

Moments after Axios left my suite the head concierge arrived with instructions to get as many staff as I needed to help me pack. I almost laughed, considering my meagre belongings and everything Andreos needed could fit in one small suitcase.

I dismissed the staff and was done with my packing in twenty minutes. The rest of the time I spent sitting beside Andreos's cot, hoping against hope that my time with him going forward would be just as peaceful as the past precious months had been. Because I didn't intend to be separated from him for a second. Time was too precious. Too special. And I would fight for every moment.

As if aware he was at the centre of my thoughts, he stirred and woke, his face remaining solemn for a few seconds before a toothless smile creased his chubby face. Blinking back the tears of joy that just looking at him prompted, I scooped him up and cradled him close.

By the time Axios knocked on the door we were both ready.

After another taut spell of staring at Andreos with turbulent eyes, he eyed the single suitcase with grating consternation. 'This is all you have?'

'I believe in travelling light.'

His expression darkened. 'What about safety equipment for the baby? A car seat?'

'I find it easier to hire what I require as and when I need it. And, before you disparage my methods, I research and make sure everything I use is of the highest safety standard.'

His gaze remained on me for another second before he nodded at the porter.

My suitcase was quickly stowed on a sleek private boat. Within minutes my last sanctuary had become a dot on the horizon.

I'd forgotten just how ruthlessly efficient Axios Xenakis could be. I received another rude reminder when, upon our arrival at the jetty, a smiling courier presented me with a gleaming state-of-the-art buggy and car seat combo, already assembled.

I braced my hand on Andreos's back, tugged him closer to where he nestled snugly in his papoose. 'That won't be necessary. The airline I'm flying with will have all the equipment I need.'

Axios stepped forward and took hold of the pushchair. 'You think I'm going to let you out of my sight now I've found you?'

'But I have a ticket—'

'And I have a private jet.'

Of course he did.

I'd blocked so many things out of my mind for the sake of pure survival. But the world had kept on turning. Axios had remained a powerful mogul with looks that weakened women's knees. And, as a billionaire who commanded an airline empire, didn't it stand to reason he'd possess his own plane?

A short SUV ride later we arrived at the private area of the airport, where an obscenely large aircraft bearing the unique Xenakis family logo stood gleaming resplendently beneath the French Polynesian sun.

'So what's it to be? Athens or Agistros?' he asked silkily.

I stared at him in surprise. 'You're giving me a *choice*?' It was more than he had the last time. More than my father ever had. Not that I planned on reading anything into it.

He shrugged. 'The location doesn't matter. Whichever you choose will be home. *For all of us*,' he added succinctly.

I chose Athens.

A mere twenty-four hours later we drove through the imposing gates of Axios's jaw-dropping villa. A different set of staff greeted us, and an even more opulent set of adjoining master suites had been readied for the prodigal wife's return.

I was standing in the middle of cream and gold opulence when I felt his presence behind me. Not wanting to look into those hypnotising eyes, I kept still, my precious bundle safely tucked in my arms.

My skin beginning to tingle wildly, I snatched in a breath and held it when his mouth brushed over the shell of my ear and he said, in a low, deep whisper, 'Welcome home, *yineka mou*. And rest assured that this time you will not get away from me that easily.'

CHAPTER FIVE

MY SON.

I have a son.

My chest squeezed tight. The emotions tumbling through me were…indescribable.

Back on Bora Bora everything inside me had prompted me to accept Calypso at her word—accept that the child was mine. Only I'd made the mistake before of thinking I could manage her, that she was a victim when she was anything but. She was cunning. Intelligent and resourceful enough to disappear without a trace for a whole year.

And apparently to take what is mine with her.

The result of the paternity test spelled out in stark indelible ink confirmed that, in this at least, Calypso had spoken the truth. But swiftly on the heels of that knowledge came a mystifying mix of searing fury and heady delight—the former for what I'd been deprived of and the latter for the astounding gift I hadn't even realised I wanted.

My son.

She kept him from me. Deliberately. Chose to leave my home and have my baby on her own, with no care as to what my feelings were in the matter. Why? Because I'd left her on Agistros? In the lap of the kind of luxury most people only dreamed about?

But did you give her any choice?

I swallowed the bite of guilt as my eyes locked on the paper.

Andreos.

Even as a part of my brain tested the name out and accepted that it fitted him my fingers were shaking with the enormity of everything I'd missed. Things I'd never have thought would matter suddenly assumed colossal importance.

His first cry.

His first smile.

His first laugh…

Did babies his age laugh? I'd been robbed of the opportunity to find out for myself.

I tossed the document away and stood. Sudden weakness in my legs stopped me from moving. One hand braced on the polished wood surface, I sucked in a deep breath, attempted to bring myself under control.

Control was essential. Over my erratic emotions. Over my wayward wife and over the belief that she should take such actions without consequence. To deprive me of my own flesh and blood…

Why?

The deeply visceral need to know straightened my spine.

I found her in the smallest living room—the room farthest from my study and the one she seemed to have commandeered for herself and Andreos since her return. He lay on a mat on the floor, his fists and legs pumping with abandon as Calypso crouched over him. A few toys were strewn nearby, momentarily forgotten as mother and son indulged in a staring game of some sort. One that amused Andreos…*my son.*

So babies his age did smile. They also returned their mother's stare with rapt attention until they were tickled, then dissolved into heaps of laughter.

Something stirred raw and powerful within me as I stared into the eyes that had seemed familiar to me from the start, even as I cautioned myself against full acceptance. The feeling intensified as I watched Calypso's utter devotion, saw the bond between mother and son, the unit I'd been excluded from.

The unit I wanted to belong to—

Sensing my presence, Calypso's gaze flew to mine, then immediately shadowed.

Theos mou, was I really that frightful?

'You can be.'

I dismissed the uncanny sound of Neo's voice in my head.

Too bad. I'd given her four days to settle in. Four days of swimming in the uncharted waters of her re-entry into my life with a son...*my son*...in tow.

It took me but a moment to summon Sophia, one of several household staff who'd been infatuated with Andreos since his arrival.

To Calypso, I said, 'We need to talk. Come with me. Sophia will look after Andreos.'

Her clear reluctance lasted for the moment it took for her to spot the piece of paper clutched in my fist. Then she slowly rose.

About to head back to my study, I changed my mind and headed up the stairs.

'Where are we going?'

The hint of nervousness in her voice rankled further.

'Where we won't be disturbed,' I replied as evenly as I could manage.

'But...'

I stopped and turned. 'Do you have a problem with being alone with me?'

The faintest flush crept into her cheeks, but her head remained high, her gaze bold. 'Of course not.'

Truth be told, perhaps my suite wasn't the best choice. Amongst everything I'd imagined might happen when I finally located my wayward wife, discovering that the chemistry that had set us aflame on our wedding night still blazed with unrelenting power was the last thing I'd expected.

The fact that I couldn't look at the curve of her delicate jaw without imagining trailing my lips over her smooth skin, tasting the vitality of the pulse that beat at her throat or palming her now even more ample breasts was an unwelcome annoyance that nevertheless didn't stop my mind from wandering where it shouldn't.

Did unfettered pleasure still overtake her in that sizzling, unique way it had during our one coming together? Did she go out of her head with unbridled passion at the merest touch? If so, just who had been stoking that particular flame in her year-long absence?

It took every ounce of control I had to contain my searing jealousy at the thought. Answers to those questions would come later. *This* was too important.

Without stopping to further examine the wisdom of the venue, I made my way into the room.

She followed, making a point to avoid looking at the bed as she passed through into the private living room. From my position before the fireplace I watched her take a seat and neatly fold her hands in her lap. Had her pulse not been racing in her throat I would have been fooled by her complete serenity.

'He's mine.'

Just saying the words dragged earth-shaking emotion through me, robbing me of my next breath. That a small bundle could do that—

'I told you he was.'

There was a new defiance in her demeanour, a quiet, fiery strength that had been there a year ago but had matured now.

'I've never lied to you.'

'Then what do you call *this*?' I tossed the report on the coffee table.

She paled a little, her throat moving in another swallow. And why did I find that simple evidence that she felt *something* so riveting?

'You were always going to know your son, Axios. I simply took a little time before informing you.'

Rejection seared deep. 'No. I should've been informed the moment you found out you were carrying my child.'

'Why? So we could discuss it like a *loving married couple*? Or so you could treat it as another *business* transaction, like our arranged marriage? I'm sure you'll forgive me for choosing neither option, since the former was a farce and the latter was unpalatable.'

The accusation scored a direct hit, making my neck heat with another trace of guilt. Over the last year I'd gone over everything that had happened in those twenty-four hours. Accepted that perhaps I could've handled things differently. But was this the price I had to pay for it?

'I had a right to know, Calypso.' My voice emerged much gruffer than I'd intended. And deep inside me something like sorrow turned over.

Her lashes swept down, but not before I spotted the sea of turmoil swelling in the blue depths. My nape tightened and my instincts blared with the notion that she was hiding something.

'What if I told you that I didn't know what I wanted?' she asked.

A white-hot knife sliced through me at the thought that it would have decimated me had she taken a different route than bearing my son.

'Calypso…'

Her name sounded thick on my tongue. I waited until she raised her gaze to mine.

'Yes?'

'Regardless of this…disagreement between us, you will have my gratitude for choosing to carry our son for ever.'

Her eyes widened in stunned surprise. 'Um…you're welcome,' she murmured.

Once again her gaze swept away from mine—a small gesture that disturbed and confounded me. And then that defiant bolt of blue clashed with mine and absurd anticipation simmered in my gut.

'He's here now. Can we not put what has gone on in the past behind us and move on?'

'Certainly we can. As soon as you tell me what I want to know I'll take great strides to put it all behind me.'

Again that mutinous look took her over, sparking my own need to tangle with it. To stoke her fire until we both burned.

'Are you prepared to do that, Calypso?'

For several moments she held my gaze. Breath stalled, I awaited an answer…*one* answer…to quell the questions teeming inside me. But then that unnerving serenity settled on her face again.

'It's not important—'

'*Not important?* You leave my home under cover of a blatant falsehood, then you disappear for a year, during which time you bear my son, and you think your absence isn't *important*?'

'Careful, Axios, or I'll be inclined to wonder whether you actually missed the wife you bothered with for less than a day before walking away.'

I sucked in a stunned breath. A year ago she'd warned me that she wouldn't be biddable. Discovering she was innocent had clouded that warning. But this kitten had well and truly developed claws. Sharp ones. I was tempted to test them. Intellectually and…yes…*physically*.

Unbidden, heat throbbed deep in my groin, stirring desires I'd believed were long dead until one glimpse of my wayward wife from a jetty in Bora Bora had fiercely reawakened them.

That unholy union of sexual tension and unanswered questions propelled me to where she sat, cloaked in secrets that mocked me.

Her slight tensing when I crouched in front of her unsettled me further, despite the fact that I should've been satisfied to see that she wasn't wholly indifferent to me.

'You want to know about the inconvenience your absence caused, Calypso?'

She remained silent.

'Some newspaper hack got wind that my wife wasn't in Agistros, enjoying her first weeks of marital bliss. Nor was she with friends, as she'd led everyone to believe. To all intents and purposes she seemed to have fallen off the face of the earth.'

A delicate frown creased her brows. 'Why would that be of interest to anyone? Especially when you intended to banish me to Agistros for the duration of our arrangement anyway?'

'You're my wife. Everything you do is news. And appearing to have deserted your marriage was definitely newsworthy.'

She blinked. '*Appearing* to have?'

'I have an outstanding PR team who've had to work tirelessly to put a lid on this.'

There was no hint of remorse on her sun-kissed face. Instead she looked irritated. 'If you've managed to somehow spin my absence to suit our narrative then there's no problem, is there?'

I allowed myself a small smile, one her gaze clung to with wary eyes. 'You would like that, wouldn't you? To escape every unpleasant fall-out from your actions?'

'You don't have the first idea of what I want, Axios.'

My name on her lips sent a punch of heat through me. Thinking back, I couldn't recollect her ever saying it before Bora Bora. Not when she'd spat fire at me, not when she'd confessed her untouched state, and not when she'd been in the complete grip of passion. Certainly not when she'd asked me to take her with me to Athens.

There had been far too many times over the last year when I'd regretted not doing so—not because of that infernal hunger that had long outstayed its welcome, but simply because it would have curtailed her actions.

But the past was the past. There was still the future to deal with. And my new reality.

My son.

'For the sake of probability, and if I were in the mood to grant wishes, what exactly would you want, *matia mou*?'

Wariness made her hesitate, but slowly defiance laced

with something else pushed through. 'I'd want a divorce. As soon as possible.'

Stunned disbelief rose in me like a monumental wave I'd once ridden on the North Shore, and then just as swiftly crashed on the beach of her sheer audacity and shock. It was all so very dramatic.

I couldn't help it. I laughed.

Her pert little nose quivered as she inhaled sharply. 'What's so funny?'

Affront and defiance flushed her skin a sweet pink, drawing my attention to her alluring features. My wife was now all woman. An arrestingly feminine woman who'd just demanded...*a divorce.*

'Why you, my dear, and your continued ability to surprise me.'

'I'm glad you're amused. But I'm deadly serious. I want a divorce.'

Humour evaporated as abruptly as it had arrived. Leaning forward, I grasped her upper arms and fought not to be distracted by her smooth supple skin or the need to caress her and reacquaint myself with her.

My once sound argument about staying away from her had backfired spectacularly. I'd left her on Agistros thinking that she'd be safe and I'd be saved from temptation. Look how that had turned out.

Even with sex off the table I should have kept her close. I could have prevented her fleeing. Instead I'd borne the subtle snipes of those who had been quick to point out my failure. Quick to compare me to my grandfather and test me to see whether I'd crack under the same pressure.

With Calypso gone I'd experienced a taste of what he'd gone through—sometimes even with members of my own family.

Now she was back...and asking for a divorce.

'We seem to have veered a little off-track to be indulging in hypotheticals. You'll recall that, according to the agreement, this marriage needs to last at least twelve months.'

'Yes, I remember.'

'Twelve *ongoing* months. Not twelve absentee months.'

She swallowed and my fingers moved, some compulsion driving me to glide my fingers up her neck, trace the colour flowing back into her cheeks. She made a sound under her breath, bearing a hint of those she'd made on our wedding night.

Before I could revel in it she pulled back abruptly. My hands dropped back to her arms.

'My father hasn't contested the agreement,' she said.

'So you took the time to check on his activities?' Disgruntlement rumbled through me at the thought.

Her flush gave me my answer. 'What are you saying, Axios?'

'I'm saying the clock stopped the moment you walked out. But, fortunately for you, your father is no longer in the picture. For one thing he can't prove that you've been an absentee wife—unless you apprised him of your intentions?'

'No, I didn't,' she muttered, her eyes not quite meeting mine.

I'd long suspected that while she might have avoided contact with her father, her mother was a different story. But Iona Petras had remained resolutely closed-lipped about the whereabouts of her daughter.

'Good—then the ball, as they say, is in my court.'

She met my gaze boldly, read my clear intent and gasped. 'You mean you have the power to give me a divorce but…?' Her voice dried up, a telling little shiver racing through her body.

'But I won't, sweet Calypso. Not until a few things are set straight.'

'What things?'

'For starters, my PR company didn't make *all* the problems go away. While I frustrated the news media enough to make them chase other headlines, my competitors and my business partners were another story. Your absence fuelled enough rumours about instability to stall my latest deal.'

A peculiar expression that resembled hurt crossed her face. 'So this is about stocks and shares again?'

The disparaging note in her voice grated. 'Why? Did you want it to be something more?'

She stiffened. 'No.'

Her firm, swift denial rankled, but again I dismissed it. 'There will be no divorce. Not until I'm completely satisfied that there will be no permanent fall-out from your actions. And not until we've thoroughly discussed the impact this will have on Andreos.'

She stiffened. 'Does it occur to you that I might be doing this for him? That this arrangement might not be the best environment for him?'

'Then we will strive to make it so. You'll get your divorce, if you wish it. It could be as early as a month from now or it could be the year you were supposed to give me. In that time, wherever I go, you and my son will go also. He will be your priority. But when called upon you will be at my side at public functions and you will play the role of a devoted wife. And you will do all of that without the smallest hint that there's dissent between us.'

Her sweet, stubborn chin lifted in a clear defiance. 'And if I don't? What's to stop me giving the newspapers what they want? Telling them the true state of this so-called marriage?'

Why did her rebellion fire me up so readily? In truth, very few people got to display such attitude towards me. Neo tried me at the best of times, but even he knew when to back down. The rest of my family fell in line, because ultimately I held the purse strings.

But it seemed my errant wife's fiery spirit turned me on. Made me want to burn in the fire of it.

I caught her chin in my hand, my thumb moving almost

of its own volition to slide over the dark rose swell of her lower lip. She shivered, this time unable to disguise her arousal. I intensified the caress, a little too eager to see how far she was truly affected. Blue eyes held mine for another handful of seconds before they dropped. But her breathing grew more erratic, her pulse hammering against the silken skin of her throat.

I held still, my groin rudely awakening as the little eddy of lust whipped faster, threatened to turn into a cyclone.

'You really wish to defy me? You think that now you and your family have received what they want they can simply sit back and enjoy the spoils of their ill-gotten gains? Do you think that I will let you get away with it?'

She glared blue fire at me. 'I won't be ordered about, Axios. I won't be dictated to like one of your minions!'

'I would never mistake you for a minion. But a little hell-cat, intent on sinking her claws into me? Definitely.'

For a charged moment she returned my stare. Then her gaze dropped to my lips.

A sort of madness took over. A breathless second later our lips met in a fiery clash, the hot little gasp she gave granting me access to the sharp tongue that seemed intent on creating havoc with my mood and my libido.

Caught in the grip of hunger, I slicked my tongue against hers, took hold of one hip to hold her in place. She attempted to smother her moan, attempted not to squirm with the arousal I could already sense. I needed more. Needed confirmation of…*something*. Something that bore a hint of the torrid dreams that had plagued me almost nightly for a solid year. Something to take away the disarming hollowness that had resided in me since I'd got the call in New York that my wife had fled Agistros.

My teeth grazed the tip of her tongue when it attempted to issue a challenge. This time she couldn't hold back her moan. Couldn't stop herself from straining against me, from gasping her need.

And when she did I took. Savoured. Then devoured.

Her moans fuelled my desire, and the scramble of her hands over my chest, then around to my back facilitated the urgent need to lay her on the sofa so I could slide over her, to once again experience the heady sensation of having Calypso beneath me.

Her nails dug in deeper as I lowered myself over her, felt the heavy swell of her breasts press again my chest. The recollection that she'd borne my child, that she still nurtured him, was a powerful aphrodisiac that charged through me and hardened me in the most profoundly carnal way.

Could I get any more primitive?

Yes, my senses screamed.

The deepening urge to claim and keep what was mine thundered harder through me, drawing me away from the naked temptation of her lips to the seductive smoothness of her throat, her vibrant pulse, the exquisite valley between her breasts.

It took but a moment to slide the thin sleeve of her sundress off her shoulder, to release the front clasp and nudge aside the cup of her bra to bare her delicious flesh to my ravenous gaze. To mould the plump mound in anticipation of drawing that stiff, rosy peak into my mouth.

Beneath me, Calypso's breath caught. Her eyes turned a dark blue with the same fiery lust that was causing carnage wit in me, then snapped to mine and stayed there.

Slowly, with an ultra-feminine arching of her back that held me deeply enthralled, she offered herself to me, somehow turning the tables on me. Because for all that this was supposed to be a punitive lesson, a way to remind her who held the power now, after her actions had swung the tide to my advantage, I was caught in a vortex of desire so voracious I couldn't have stopped even if I'd wanted to.

So I lowered my head and with a powerless groan sucked the bud into my mouth.

Savage hunger exploded inside me, all my senses lost as

her fingers locked in my hair and held me to my delightful task.

'Oh... *Theos mou*,' she gasped.

The memory of our one night together, of her unreserved responsiveness and the unique way she'd expressed her pleasure, sharpened my hunger, sparking a desire to relive that experience. I slid one hand beneath her body, urged her even closer. She answered by arching higher, offering more of herself to me.

'Tell me what you're feeling,' I urged thickly, aware that my voice was hoarse, barely intelligible.

She froze, the eyes that had rolled shut mere seconds ago flying open.

Watching her, I lazily caught that peak between my teeth, felt a carnal shudder unravel through her. 'You taste exquisite.'

Arousal and denial warred in her face, and then her fingers flew from my hair as small but effective hands pushed at my shoulders. 'No! Stop!'

For a moment I considered a different tactic. Negotiation. Talking her round to my way of thinking. Satisfying this need that dogged us both. But hadn't my family and I given the Petrases enough in this lifetime? This was supposed to be the time to extract *my* pound of flesh after what they'd done to my grandfather. Besides, sex was what had led us here in the first place. Was I really going to fall into the well of temptation I'd counselled myself against a year ago when I should be dealing with the reality of my son?

The reminder was enough to propel me off her and across the room. Even then it took several control-gathering breaths to master my raging libido. It didn't help that her reflection in the window showed her naked breasts for another handful of seconds before she righted her clothes.

When she was done, she rose. She didn't approach—which was a good thing, because I wasn't sure I wouldn't have given in to the urge to finish what we'd started.

'Axios…'

I gritted my teeth, the discovery that my name on her lips was its own special brand of hell driving my fingers through my hair.

This had gone on long enough. 'This is no longer purely business, Calypso. I want to know my son.'

I caught another expression on her face—one that sent a different type of emotion charging through me.

I turned around, wanting to verify it more accurately, but whatever it was had gone, her face a composed mask.

'Of course. I won't stand in the way of that.'

Why didn't that agreement satisfy me?

Why did that hollowness still remain?

'Good. Then we shelve discussion of divorce until further notice.'

That gruff, shaken tone was gone. It was almost as if that little display of emotion over his son had never happened. As if the wild little tumble on the sofa less than five minutes ago was already a distant memory.

But, no…there were tell-tale signs. Signs I didn't want to notice. Like how deliciously tousled his dark, luxuriously wavy hair was now, courtesy of my restless fingers. How colour still rose in his chiselled cheekbones.

And that definitive bulge behind his fly—

With a willpower that threatened to sap the last of my composure I averted my gaze from the pillar of temptation he represented, and reminded myself why we were here in the first place. Dear heaven. I needed to be done with this before the desire I'd believed eroded by distance and absence made a complete fool of me.

'I need your word, Calypso.'

The implacable demand centred my thoughts. Reminded me that this wasn't over. Contrary to what I'd believed, twelve months of living apart from him had done nothing to lessen my sentence. I was back to square one, with a child to think about.

A child Axios fully intended to claim.

'Where exactly does Andreos feature in your grand plan?' I asked, belatedly focusing on the most precious thing in my life. On safeguarding his welfare before I embarked on fighting for my survival.

Axios's head went back, as if the question offended him. 'He is my son. He will be brought up under our care with the full benefit of the Xenakis name at his disposal for as long as he needs it.'

Through all of this I'd held on to the secret fear that Andreos might suffer. Over the past year I'd meticulously researched the Xenakis dynasty, with Andreos's needs at the forefront of my mind.

Outwardly, they appeared a close unit—but, as with most super-wealthy and influential families, rumours of acrimony abounded. Once or twice it had been rumoured that Axios's status as CEO had been challenged by a daring cousin or uncle. None had succeeded, of course.

'You give me your word that you'll protect Andreos, no matter what?'

'Of course. I vow it.' His voice was deep and solemn and immediate.

Relief weakened my knees, and for some absurd reason I wanted to throw my arms around him. 'Thank you.'

His frown deepened, speculation narrowing his eyes. I turned away before he could read my anxiety. Now wasn't the time to think about my precarious health…about the tough road ahead. About the battle my grandmother had fought against cervical cancer and eventually lost.

And it certainly wasn't the time to dwell on the fact that the pain in my abdomen remained, its presence edging into my consciousness with each passing day.

'Possible cancer… Prognosis uncertain if you choose to keep your baby…'

Dr Trudeau's words broke free from the vault I'd kept them in. Along with the frighteningly easy decision I'd made to keep my baby for as long as I could instead of chasing risky surgery. The tearful gratitude for every day Andreos had nestled in my womb, growing despite the unknown threat to his life and mine.

And his sweet cry the moment he was born.

I'd learned quickly that for my son's sake I needed to compartmentalise. His keen intelligence and sensitivity, even at such a tender age, had focused me on giving him my very best—always. But giving him my best included fighting to remain in his life. Even if I had to temporarily entrust him to Axios in order to do so.

'Do you agree?' Axios pressed, his gaze probing mercilessly.

'I'll give you what you want on one condition. Take it or leave it.'

After a moment he jerked his head in command for me to continue.

'I'll stay until your precious deal is done. On condition that you don't attempt to interfere in my relationship with my son.'

'What gives you the impression that I'd wish to do anything of the sort?'

My shrug fell short of full efficiency under his heavy frown. 'It's been known to happen.'

'Who? Your father?'

I could have denied it, kept up the years-long pretence. But time was too precious to waste on falsehoods. So I nodded. 'Yes.'

Axios moved towards me, his frown a dark cloud. 'What did he do to you?'

I hesitated now, because on the flipside I didn't want to bare my all to him. The desire to continue living on my own terms hadn't diminished an iota since my return to Greece. And even if I intended to agree to Axios's demands

I would always keep one small corner of my life free from his interference.

'He manipulated every relationship I ever had in some way. I don't want that to happen with Andreos.'

The grey gaze boring into mine stated blatantly that he wanted more. Mine declared I'd given him all I intended to.

'I've seen you with Andreos. He thrives under your care. I'd be a fool to jeopardise that.'

Before I could breathe my relief he stepped closer, bringing that bristling magnificence into touching distance. I balled fingers that tingled with the need to feel his vibrant skin under my touch again.

'You have my word I will not interfere. Will you give me yours?'

Again I was mildly stunned that it was a question rather than a declaration. But the searing reminder that giving in to one emotion around Axios was simply the gateway to a flood of other sensations I needed to keep a tight leash on, had me swallowing the desire.

'I will stay for as long as it takes to give you what you need,' I offered.

He accepted it with a simple nod, as if it was nothing to celebrate. And perhaps in the grand scheme of things it wasn't. We were picking up where we'd left off with the added inconvenience of needing to put out more fires than he'd initially anticipated.

After several skin-tingling moments during which he simply stared at me, as if probing beneath my defences to read my secrets, I twisted away, eager to escape those all-seeing eyes.

'I need to get back to Andreos.'

'We're not quite done, Calypso.'

About to ask what else we needed to talk about, I felt my tight throat close even further when he stepped closer. His scent curled around me, reminding me of what had happened on the sofa a short while ago. Had things really got out of hand so quickly? My body still hummed with unspent energy, and my heart hadn't quite settled into its steady cadence.

'I'll come with you to visit my son.'

The throb of possessiveness in his voice sent my senses flaring wide with warning. What exactly that warning was refused to surface as we left his suite.

As it turned out it wasn't necessary to return to the ground floor. Sophia was carefully navigating the stairs, with a sleepy Andreos in her arms. We followed her as she entered the opposite wing of the villa, where a nursery had been set up by a team of designers on the first day of my return.

Seeing us, she smiled. 'We played for a while, but I think he's ready for his nap, *kyria*,' she said softly.

The sight of Andreos fighting a losing battle to stay awake drew a smile from my heart. Handing him over to Sophia even for such a short while had made my heart ache. I knew it would be a million times worse when I had to leave, but somehow I trusted Axios with his care. Sophia's clear devotion to him was an added bonus.

I reached out for him but Axios stepped forward.

'Do you mind?' The demand was gruff but gentle.

In stunned surprise I nodded. Still smiling, Sophia handed son over to father and discreetly melted away.

The sight of Axios holding his son for the first time shouldn't have brought a thick lump to my throat. The sight of his strong, powerful arms carefully cradling my baby, his throat moving in a convulsive swallow, shouldn't have fired a soul-deep yearning through my body. A yearning for things to be different. For fate not to be so cruel.

Why? Did I wish for things to be different between Axios and I?

Absolutely not.

As for other yearnings—hadn't I already been granted more than enough? I'd prayed for a healthy son and been given the child of my heart. I'd prayed for a little more time and had enjoyed almost four beautiful months.

But the thought of leaving him, even to fight for my health—

'What's wrong?'

I jumped, my gaze rising to see Axios watching me.

'Am I holding him wrong?'

The touch of uncertainty in his voice caught a warm spot inside me and loosened another smile from me as I approached, unable to stop myself from reaching out, kissing Andreos's forehead and cheek, breathing in his sweet and innocent scent.

'No, you're not doing anything wrong.'

Grey eyes so very similar to his son's dropped to the now sleeping Andreos, and his chest slowly expanded in a long breath before he headed over to the brand-new, state-of-the-art cot set out for our baby.

With the utmost care he transferred Andreos from his arms to the cot, barely eliciting any protest from him. Arms thrown up beside his head in angelic abandon, Andreos slept on as his father draped a soft cotton blanket over him, drew a gentle finger down his cheek and straightened.

Still smiling, I glanced over at Axios—and my heart leapt into my throat. Gone was the gentle look he'd bestowed on his son. In its place was a bleak visage full of loss and yearning that made me gasp. Made that pulse of guilt rise again.

The sound drew his attention to me. When he took hold of my arm and steered me out of earshot I tried to think past the naked tingles his touch brought. To think how I could contain the relentless waves of turbulent emotion bent on consuming us.

'I'd like answers to a few questions, Calypso. If you feel so inclined?' he rasped.

Seeing no way to avoid it without collapsing the agreement I'd struck, I nodded.

His hand dropped to my wrist. 'We'll discuss this further over lunch.'

Lunch was an extensive selection of *meze* fit for a small banquet—not the intimate setting for two laid out on one of the three sun-splashed terraces.

Axios must have spotted my surprise as he pulled out my chair because he shrugged. 'I didn't know your preferences so I instructed the chef to prepare a large selection.'

'Oh…thank you.'

His gaze rested on me as he lowered himself into his own chair. 'Again, you sound surprised. Believe it or not I want things to go as smoothly as possible for both of us.'

The knowledge that this included simple things such as what I ate widened the warm pool swelling inside me. Even cautioning myself that it was foolish to entertain such a sensation didn't do anything to stem it as I helped myself to pitta bread and tzatziki, feta cheese and chickpea salad and succulent vine leaves stuffed with lamb and cucumber.

'Where was Andreos born?'

His deep voice throbbed with one simple emotion—a hunger to know. And for the very first time since my decision to live life on my terms, twelve long months ago, I experienced a deep stirring of guilt.

But along with that came a timely warning not to divulge everything. Knowledge was power to men like Axios. Men like my father. And every precious uninterrupted moment with my son was as vital to me as the breath in my lungs.

Although in the past four days since my return, Axios had seemed a little more…malleable. While the man who'd laid down the law and walked away from me in Agistros still lurked in there somewhere, this Axios tended to ask more and command less.

But still I carefully selected the bits of information that wouldn't connect too many dots for him and replied, 'He was born in a small clinic in Kenya, where I was volunteering. He came a week early, but there were no complications and the birth was relatively easy.'

He didn't answer. Not immediately. The glass of red wine he was drinking with his meal remained cradled in his hand and his expression reflective and almost...yearning as he stared into the middle distance.

'I would've liked to be there,' he rasped. 'Very much.'

The warm pool inside me grew hotter, turning into a jet of feeling spiralling high with emotions I needed to wrestle under control before they got out of hand.

But even as the warning hit hard I was opening my mouth, uttering words I shouldn't. 'One of the nurses filmed the birth...if you'd like to see it?'

What are you doing sharing your most precious moments with him?

He's Andreos's father.

Axios inhaled sharply, the glass discarded as he stared fiercely at me. 'You have a video?'

I jerked out a nod. 'Yes. Would you—?'

'Yes.' The word was bullet-sharp, and the cadence of his breathing altered as his gaze bored into me. 'Yes. Very much,' he repeated.

For the longest time we remained frozen, our gazes locked in a silent exchange I didn't want to examine or define. Soon it morphed into something else. Something equally intimate. Twice as dangerous.

Perhaps it was in the molten depths of his eyes, or in the not so secret wish to relive what had happened upstairs ramping up that ever-present chemistry. Whatever it was, we'd brought it alive on that sofa and now it sat between us, a writhing wire ready to sizzle and electrify and burn at the smallest hint of weakening.

Forcing my brain back on track didn't help. Hadn't we been discussing childbirth? The product of what had happened in a bedroom the last time we were both present in one.

'I'll let you have the recording after lunch,' I blurted, then picked up my water glass and drank simply to distract myself.

From the corner of my eye I watched him lounge back in his seat, although his body still held that coil of tension that never dissipated.

After a moment he picked up his glass and drained it. '*Efkharisto*,' he murmured. 'Now, on to other things. Arrangements are being made to equip you with a new wardrobe. My mother tells me the things you left behind are hopelessly out of date.'

I frowned, the change of subject from the soul-stirring miracle of Andreos's birth to the mundanity of high fashion throwing me for a few seconds. 'I don't need a new wardrobe.'

'Perhaps not—but might I suggest you let the stylists come anyway? Who knows? You might find something you like for our first engagement on Saturday,' he replied.

The last tendrils of yearning had left his voice, to be replaced by the cadence I knew best. One of powerful mogul. Master of all he surveyed. Despite the pleasant heat of the sun a cool breeze whispered over my skin, bringing me harshly back to earth.

'What's happening on Saturday?'

'It's been four days since you returned. It's time we presented you properly to the world. My mother has organised a party in your honour. She was unwell when we married last year, and couldn't make it to the ceremony. She's anxious to meet you. And, of course, she's yet to meet her grandson. Call this a belated welcome, if you will, but several business acquaintances will be there, so it's imperative that everything goes smoothly.'

'Is it really necessary to parade me before your friends and family?'

'I think it's best to put the rumours to rest once and for all. Then we can concentrate on our son.'

While his attention to Andreos warmed my heart, the prospect of being paraded before his family and business didn't. 'And how do you propose we do that? Is there a storyline I need to follow, chapter and verse?'

He smiled as if the thought of playing out a role so publicly was water off his back. 'Leave that to me,' he stated cryptically. 'All I require from you is to present a picture-perfect image of loving wife and mother. I trust I can count on you to do that?'

For the sake of uninterrupted bonding with my son I would go to hell and back. 'Yes.'

Perhaps my agreement was too quick. Perhaps the depth of feeling behind it was too revealing. Whatever, his gaze grew contemplative, stayed fixed on me.

And when he walked away, moments after the meal was done, I got the distinct feeling there were more bumps and curves on this peculiar road I'd taken than I'd initially realised.

CHAPTER SIX

A PRE-PARTY FAMILY MIXER.

A harmless-sounding statement until you were confronted by the full might of the formidable Xenakis clan.

The gathering had been deceptive. Over the course of two hours they'd trickled in—some by car, others by boat. And Axios's formidable-looking brother Neo, looking a little distracted and a lot harassed, had come by sleek helicopter, with the iconic Xenakis Aeronautics logo emblazoned on its side.

Inexorably the trickle became a stream, and then a torrent. By four p.m. the largest salon in the villa, the surrounding terrace and the perfectly manicured lawn were overflowing with aunts, uncles, cousins and distant offshoots—some from as far afield as Australia and New Zealand.

Fascinatingly, despite the low buzz of tension surrounding their interactions, there were no overt signs of dissent.

Perhaps because I was their main focus.

I didn't want to admit it, but the six-hour makeover session I'd endured earlier in the day boosted my confidence now, as impeccably dressed men and couture-clad women approached the place where I stood next to Axios, with a wide-eyed Andreos nestled in my arms.

My hair had been brought back to shoulder-length, layered and trimmed into loose stylish waves that gleamed with new vitality. And the rails upon rails of new clothes hanging in the closets of my vast dressing room, complete with matching accessories and priceless jewellery, were the *pièce de résistance*.

After months of wearing flats and tie-dye sundresses, and ponytailing my hair, the transformation took a little getting used to. While the teardrop diamond necklace glittering just as bright as the pristine white linen shift dress and tan platform shoes were making me feel intensely aware of the kind of circles I'd married into.

The most striking of the women within those intimidating circles was Electra Xenakis—Axios's mother.

Her hair was a distinctive grey, which had been used to enhance her beauty rather than been dyed away, and it framed an angular face, highlighting superb cheekbones and the striking grey eyes she'd passed on to her sons. Tall and slender, with a ramrod-straight posture, she was formidable—until she gave a rare smile. Then warmth radiated from her every pore, and the icy grey palazzo pants and matching top she wore were suddenly not so severe.

On meeting Andreos she dissolved into hearty tears. And that unfettered display of love for her grandchild thawed the cold knot of apprehension inside me, easing my anguish at the thought of a permanent separation from my child.

The distance I'd needed to get my composure back after handing Andreos over to his grandmother lasted mere minutes before I sensed a presence beside me. It wasn't as visceral and all-encompassing as Axios's, but it demanded attention nevertheless.

I glanced up to find Neo Xenakis standing before me.

'I never quite got the chance to welcome you into the family last year.' His tone was measured, his eyes just as probing as his brother's.

'I guess the circumstances weren't exactly…conducive,' I replied.

'*Ochi*, they weren't. But your disappearing act didn't help matters, I expect?'

I stiffened. 'I had my reasons,' I replied.

Without answering, he dropped his gaze to the contents of the crystal tumbler he clutched. 'Whatever they were, I hope it was worth keeping a father from his child?'

Again his tone was more appraising than censorious, as if he was attempting to understand my motives. Again my guilt resurfaced. And this time brushing it away wasn't easy.

Before I could formulate a response, a deeper and more visceral voice asked, 'Is everything all right?'

For me not to have sensed his arrival spoke volumes of the kind of magnetism the Xenakis men possessed. And now Axios had arrived next to me the force of their presence had doubled. Their sole focus was on me, but one set of grey eyes was vastly more potent than the other, sending my composure into free fall.

I took a long, steadying breath to reply, 'We're fine.'

Axios's gaze slid from mine to his brother, a clear question in his eyes.

Neo's expression clouded for a moment, then he shrugged. 'Like your wife said, we're fine. No need to go Neanderthal on me.'

Before either of us could enquire what he meant, he excused himself and struck out for the large gazebo on the south side of the garden, currently decked out with fairy lights and free of guests.

'Is he okay?' I felt compelled to ask.

Axios's gaze stayed on him long enough to see his brother lift a phone to his ear before he turned to me. 'His issues aren't mine to disclose, but Neo is touchy on the subject of babies. Like the rest of the family, news about his nephew's existence surprised him. But, since Andreos is single-handedly winning everyone over, I suspect the circumstances of his arrival will be forgiven soon.'

Had he deliberately excluded himself from that statement? Unwilling for him to see the bite of anguish that distinction brought, I turned my gaze to where the majority of the Xenakis clan had now gathered, choosing to see the bright side.

Andreos was indeed holding centre stage, tucked into his favourite blanket and nestled lovingly within his grandmother's arms. The absolute devotion on the older woman's face eased my heartache, but in the next moment the sudden thought that my own mother hadn't met my son hit me with tornado-strength force.

'What is it?' Axios asked, the eyes that hadn't left my face since his brother's disappearance narrowing.

The fleeting thought to shrug off his question came and went, and I couldn't help the small shaft of pain that came with it. 'My parents haven't met him yet.'

His face tightened, the mention of Yiannis Petras drawing a reaction I would have preferred to leave out of the already fraught atmosphere. I held my breath, ready to fight my corner.

'We can arrange a visit for your mother later…if you wish?'

Surprised by that response, I blinked. 'I do. Thank you.'

After another minute of assessing scrutiny he nodded. 'Whatever your reasons for fleeing Agistros, I accept that I could've handled our last meeting a little better,' he said, his voice a deep rasp.

My lips were parted in shock when another wave of Xenakises wandered over. Axios's droll look and almost-smile told me he'd seen my shock at his apology.

I managed to get my emotions under control beneath his family's probing glances, watching their silent musing as to what had transpired with Axios's stray wife. I was grateful for their circumspection because, as baptisms of fire went, it could have been worse.

It was with far more trepidation that I contemplated my extensive closet three hours after everyone had disappeared into their various guest rooms and private homes to get ready for the main event. The knock on the door barely snagged my attention. Absent-mindedly I responded, my fingers toying with the tie of my bathrobe as I contemplated the stunning array of clothes.

'As much as you seem to enjoy simply staring at them, you do actually have to pick an outfit to wear for the party, you know?' Ax drawled, his deep tone more amused than I'd ever heard him.

I jumped and turned around, barely able to hold back a gasp at the sight of him, standing a few feet away, wearing half of a bespoke tuxedo. His pristine snow-white shirt was half buttoned, but neatly tucked into his tailored trousers, and his bowtie was strung around his neck.

The intimate knowledge of what resided beneath his clothes dried my mouth as I stared, slack-jawed, several superlatives crowding my brain.

Debonair. Breathtaking. Insanely gorgeous.

Slowly the silence thickened and he raised one sleek eyebrow. 'Can I help with anything?'

The hand I waved over my shoulder at the closet was irritatingly fluttery. 'I can't decide what to wear. Meeting your family was one thing... This is a different ballgame.'

His gaze travelled from the top of my hair, which still held its earlier style, thanks to the expertise of the stylist, then lingered at the belt holding my robe closed, before moving to my bare feet. Each spot his eyes touched triggered fiery awareness.

'You handled my family admirably and won them over with Andreos. Even Neo—and he's a handful at the best of times,' he added dryly. 'You'll excel just as well tonight.'

The deeply spoken reassurance made my heart lurch. To hide its effect I scrambled for something else to concentrate on, and spotted his dangling sleeves and the cufflinks in his hand.

'Do you need help with those?' I asked, even though assisting him would involve stepping closer, breathing in the intoxicating scent that clung to him and never failed to send my senses haywire.

He held out his arms. 'If you wouldn't mind?'

Breath held, in the hope that it would mitigate the erotic chaos stirring to life inside me, I reached for the two halves of his shirtsleeve in one hand and held out the other for the cufflinks. The tips of his fingers brushed my palm as he handed them over, and every inch of my skin responded as if set alight.

Intensely aware that my nipples were hardening, and that a pulse had started throbbing between my thighs, I hurried to finish my task, my own fingers brushing the inside of his wrist in the process.

Axios inhaled sharply, an incoherent sound rumbling from his chest.

Could we not even exchange a common courtesy without feeling as if the world was about to burst into flames?

Evidently not.

Which was probably all the warning I needed to keep my distance. Never to repeat what had happened on his sofa.

'*Efkharisto,*' he murmured, his voice deep and thick.

His eyes were molten, as heated as that needy place between my legs. Unable to withstand his gaze, for fear I'd give myself away, I turned to face the rack of clothes. Of course my senses leaped high when he stepped next to me, then took another step closer to the open closet.

To my shaky memory this was perhaps the first time I'd been this close without having his laser eyes on me. The opportunity to give in to the urge to stare was too hard to resist.

The breadth and packed strength of his shoulders.

The vibrancy of his lustrous hair.

The sharp, mouthwatering angle of his freshly shaved jaw.

Too busy fighting the way every inch of Axios triggered this unwanted but unstoppable reaction, I didn't notice he'd made a selection until he pivoted, the momentary gaping of his shirt delivering one final punch of his sheer magnetism before he drawled, 'You'll look beautiful in any one of these gowns. But this one will do, I think.'

Heat engulfed my face as I reached out and snatched the gown from his hand, hastily stepping back. 'I...thanks.'

'You need help with the zip?' he asked, in a voice thicker than before.

Aware of the dangerous waters I was treading, I shook my head. 'I think I'll manage. Thanks.'

He hesitated for a stomach-churning moment, then nodded. 'I'll return in fifteen minutes. We will go downstairs together, if you wish.'

I nodded my thanks.

Contrary to his stealthy arrival, I was conscious of Ax's departure for the simple reason that he seemed to take the very air out of the room with him, leaving me breathless as I shrugged off the robe and slipped the gown over my head.

Barely paying attention to the design, I zipped it up and stepped into the heels that had been helpfully paired with the dress, spritzed perfume on my neck and wrists, and was adding the finishing touches to my make-up when his knock came.

Very much aware of the silk clinging to my hips and breasts, I prayed my body wouldn't give me away as I opened the door.

For the longest time he simply stared at me. 'Beautiful,' he finally stated, and the sizzling gleam in his eyes only lent him a more dangerous air, rendering all my efforts for composure useless as I accepted there was no level this man couldn't reach in the drop-dead gorgeous stakes.

'Thank you,' I replied, my voice a husky mess.

He held out his arm. I took it, and was still in a semi-daze when we exited the limo at the entrance to the six-star luxury hotel in the middle of Athens where the party was being held.

The moment Ax and I stepped into the ballroom silence fell over the guests, every eye fixed on me.

'I don't know whether to smile or scowl. What's *de rigueur* these days?' I murmured.

'Just ignore them. That's what I do when I feel out of place.'

I laughed, mostly to hide his unabated effect on me. Besides, I couldn't help it, because picturing Axios as a fish out of water was like attempting to imagine what the landscape inside a black hole looked like.

'Something funny?'

'You wouldn't look out of place amongst a clutch of nuns in a prayer circle.'

He smiled, and just like that my body went into free fall, breaking one tension while ratcheting up another. And as I was crashing down, towards some unknown destination, it struck me that this was the first time I'd seen any semblance of a smile from the man I called my husband.

'An unusual compliment, I think, but thank you all the same,' he said.

'You should've told me the whole of Athens would be here tonight,' I said, a little desperate to maintain a disgruntled distance from him.

He lowered his head even closer to murmur in my ear, 'Put your claws away, *pethi mou*. You look much too beautiful to pick a fight.'

'I'm sure we can find something to fight about if we look hard enough.'

Was I really that desperate to start a fight? Simply to stop this unruly attraction in its tracks?

His amusement disappeared, to be replaced with the unwavering regard that never failed to trigger mini-earthquakes inside me. My breath snagged in my throat as he stepped closer, until there was nothing but a whisper of space between us. To anyone observing us we'd look as if we were sharing an intimate moment. But I knew what was coming even before he spoke.

'Keep tossing those little challenges at me, Calypso, and I'll delight in picking you up on one.'

The electric promise in those words sent a bolt through me. It lingered through all the introductions to influential individuals, A-list celebrities and even more of the Xenakis clan and it slowly began to re-energise, that spark of rebellion re-ignited.

For some reason I *wanted* to challenge him.

So when I found a moment's reprieve I looked up from my untouched glass of champagne into his face. 'Do you know what I think, Axios?'

A simple but effective hitch of his brow commanded me to continue.

'I don't think you will pick me up on any challenge. I don't think you'll do anything to risk this reputation you're bent on protecting.'

'Are you brave enough to test your theory, I wonder?' he asked, and something untamed pulsed beneath his civil exterior. Something that made the glass in my hand tremble wildly.

His gaze dropped to it before returning to my face. With a wicked smile he raised one imperious hand and traced his knuckles down my heated cheek.

'Pick your battles with care, Calypso. You look stunning in this dress—every eye in the room keeps returning to you time and again, and I'm the envy of every man here. You should be celebrating that, not picking a fight with your husband.'

With that, he leaned even closer, replaced his hand with his mouth for the briefest of moments…

And then he walked off.

Leaving me shaking with a cascade of emotions.

The only reason I felt out of sorts was because that little incident in my dressing room had thrown me—shown me a different side to Axios that had intensified the illicit yearning inside me. And while standing next to Axios wreaked havoc with my equilibrium, watching him, the most prominent man in the room, walking away left me with a yawing hollow in the pit of my stomach.

Did I really want him? Or was I just terrified by the knowledge that the only eyes I wanted on me were his, not the guests' who kept coming up to me, some blatantly questioning why the great Axios Xenakis had tied himself down to *me*.

I shook my head, hoping to clear it of these confusing thoughts.

'I hope you're not shaking your head because you wish to deny me your company?'

I attempted to control my bewildering thoughts before turning towards another one of Ax's cousins.

At my blank look he said, 'I'm Stavros. We met earlier.'

I nodded, attempted to smile. 'Hello.'

His smile was reserved, but genuine. I found myself wishing for another smile. One that was edged in sizzling grey. I was really losing it.

'Having fun?'

I shrugged. 'I'm in a room full of some of the most powerful people on earth, sipping champagne and enjoying the status of hostess with the mostest. What's not to love?'

As with most of the Xenakis clan, his expression grew speculative. 'You sound…distressed. Is everything all right?'

About to answer, I looked across the room to where Ax had been talking to the trade minister moments ago. He was staring directly at me, as if he could see to the heart of my jumbled emotions.

That he could do that from across the room panicked me and irked me. Nevertheless, I had to hold on to what was important. And that was Andreos. Regardless of my personal situation, I couldn't afford for anything to jeopardise my time with my child.

With a deep breath, I forced a smile and turned to Stavros. 'I'm absolutely fine, Stavros. Sorry if I sounded a little off. Chalk it up to missing my baby.'

'Ah, a little separation anxiety, *ne*? As the father of young children, I remember that state well, too.'

'Yes… Speaking of which, would you mind excusing me? I'd like to call and check on him.'

This time Stavros's smile was a little tight. 'Of course. But I hope you'll honour me with a dance when you return?'

For some reason his request made me glance at Ax. He was once again engrossed in conversation with a clutch of men who were no doubt hanging on his every word.

That spark of rebellion returned and I answered Stavros's smile. 'Maybe. We'll see…'

Excusing myself, I wove through the crowd, my pinned-on smile beginning to fray a little more at the edges every time I was stopped by a well-meaning guest wishing to very *belatedly* congratulate me on my marriage and Andreos's birth, while subtly probing for cracks in my demeanour.

True to his word, Axios had taken care of all the speculation and chosen the most direct explanation for my absence.

'My wife wished to have a peaceful pregnancy and took the time she needed to safely deliver our son.'

Only the most daring would choose to probe my absence after that.

All evening I'd watched him hold court, effortlessly exuding power and charm over hardcore businessmen and moguls I'd only read about in the newspapers.

And while the wedding last year and the family gathering earlier had already shown me his authority and charisma, watching him speak to and mingle with some of the most influential people in the world truly rammed home to me the almost frightening power he wielded.

He was a powerful man whom my father had managed to bend to his will. A man whose reputation I'd put in jeopardy with my disappearing act.

Had I been fooling myself by striking a deal with him?

Enough! Running rings around my decisions was futile.

I stepped out onto the thankfully empty terrace of the grand hotel ballroom and called Sophia. Reassured that all was well, my thoughts flew as they often did when I thought of Andreos to the battle that awaited me. To the fear that my time with him would be cut short.

My hand dropped to linger over my stomach, to the dull ache residing deep inside...

'Are you all right?' Axios demanded with a gravel-rough voice.

I jumped and whirled around, hastily dropping my hand when his gaze moved to it. 'You're spying on me now?'

He sauntered towards me. 'I came to check on you because I didn't want you to feel neglected. And I haven't forgotten that you fled your marriage after one day and didn't return for a year,' he returned with sizzling fire.

'Because you were happy to leave me alone on your island without a care for what *I* wanted. Have you forgotten that? Did it even occur to you that I might want a different life for myself other than what *you* chose for me?'

For the longest time he didn't reply. Then, 'That was an error in judgement. One I regret,' he intoned solemnly.

The unequivocal apology had the same effect as the one earlier. My jaw dropped. 'You...do?'

'*Ne,*' he drawled.

For another charged moment he stared at me. Then his gaze dropped to my phone.

Almost dazedly I stared at it. 'You can stand down your spies. I was simply calling Sophia to check on my son.'

A deeply possessive look glinted in his eyes. 'He's *our* son, *pethi mou*. Yours and mine and no one else's.'

The very idea of Andreos being anyone else's child but Axios's was so profoundly impossible I almost laughed out loud. And then that notion faded under the weight of the electrified atmosphere crackling between us. The feeling of being caught on the edge of a lightning storm that never quite went away.

It didn't take a genius to see that Axios was in an equally edgy mood.

Attempting to dissipate it, I waved the phone at him.

'He's fine, by the way. According to Sophia, he went down without a fuss.'

Axios shrugged. 'He's almost four months old. I believe that as long as he's warm and well fed he has very little to worry about.'

'It's a little more complicated than that. He needs love and laughter. He's also at the stage where he'll really start recognising his mother's absence.'

Bleakness flashed across his face, momentarily slashing my insides. 'What about his father's? And whose fault is it that I'm not fully equipped with that information, Calypso?' His voice throbbed with raw emotion.

'Axios—'

His hand slashed through the air a split-second before he closed the gap between us and settled his hands on my shoulders. 'I want to move on from this. But there are questions you still haven't answered.'

My heart dipped. 'Like what?'

'What's the big secret about your whereabouts? I hunted for you high and low. My investigators visited Nicrete— discreetly, of course, since I had to protect my family from untoward gossip. The general consensus there was that Calypso Petras was far too level-headed, far too considerate to have made such a selfish move. At least without assistance or coercion of some sort. Perhaps from a source no one had considered.'

'What source?'

His tension heightened, his whole body seemingly caught in a live electric feed. 'You tell me.'

'Maybe a secret admirer? Perhaps even another man?' I taunted.

A fierce little muscle ticked in his jaw. 'Was it? Considering you were a virgin, I wasn't inclined to think you would jump into another man's bed that easily. Tell me I wasn't wrong,' he bit out.

He hadn't thought the worst of me.

The idea of it left me nonplussed for several seconds, considering he still had no idea of my whereabouts for the past year. Considering he had to have overheard some of the blatant whispers at the party.

'Why the interrogation? I thought you were all about keeping up appearances? Convincing the world that my absence was a well-orchestrated plan?'

'That's been taken care of. The results will be evident soon enough. Let's discuss us,' he said, then immediately frowned as if he hadn't expected to say that.

Perhaps he hadn't. After all, wasn't he the man who'd never engaged in a relationship that lasted more than a few weeks?

'*Us?* Are you sure? You seem as surprised by that word falling from your lips as I am to hear it.'

For the longest time he stared at me. Then he shrugged. 'Only a fool stays on a course that's doomed. Perhaps I'm embracing new changes. Attempting to be…different.'

My heart lurched, even as I tamped down fruitless hope. All this meant nothing. Not if my prognosis was as dire as my senses screamed that they were. Not if this marriage was ticking down to dissolution.

'Can we not do this here? I'd like to go back in.'

'Why? So Stavros can succeed at working his angle?'

I blinked in surprise. 'What are you talking about?'

He edged me back a step, following me so we were wedged against the stone balustrade. 'Just a heads-up. His marriage is on the rocks. He's attempting to raise his stature by undermining my authority every chance he gets—chances which, unfortunately for him, haven't been readily available. I'd rather not see you be his pawn,' he breathed, his voice absolutely lethal while being so soft.

Too late, I accepted that the fire inside me was building out of control. His body surged closer, reminding me in vivid detail of the hard-packed, streamlined definition of muscle beneath his bespoke suit. And the fact that his body could render me speechless with very little effort.

'You can stand down. I can take care of myself.'

'*Ne*, I'm beginning to see that,' he murmured, and again there was the barest hint of grudging acceptance in his eyes.

But I didn't get the chance to explore the discovery because his head slowly lowered.

Hot, sensual and commanding, his lips slanted over mine. With a gasp that was way too husky and way too revealing I threw up my hands. Somewhere in the back of my head I was aware that I'd dropped my phone. But it didn't seem to matter, because his tongue was delving between my lips, seeking entrance I was helpless to deny.

He tasted me with a brazenness that struck a match to the desire that had been straining to be freed after that episode on his sofa. With effortless ease he set it ablaze between one snatched breath and the next.

His tongue stroked mine with a possessiveness that took control of my whole body, so that when one hand slid from my shoulder and down my back to draw me into sizzling contact it felt as if I was made of warm, pliant dough, ready to mould myself to any shape of his bidding.

When his other hand angled my head to deepen the kiss it was all I could do to slide my own hands around his neck. To hold on tightly as the dizzying journey zipped like a rollercoaster ride I never wanted to end.

With a helpless moan, I parted my lips wider, strained onto my toes the better to absorb more of the experience.

Ax made a gruff sound that disintegrated beneath our frenzied kiss. His hold intensified until we were plastered together from chest to thigh. Until the unmistakable imprint of his thick, aroused manhood blazed hot and potent against my belly.

My fingers convulsed in his hair as the memory of him inside me, possessing me, surged into life. Feverish need pooled between my thighs, hunger prising another moan from my throat.

Before it could be anywhere near sated Ax was pulling away, his gaze searingly possessive as it moved from my damp and tingling mouth to my eyes.

'Now that we've shown the world how hot we still are for each other, will you come inside with me and dance with your husband?' he asked, his tone husky but firm.

Did he really want to dance with me or had he kissed me just for show?

The eyes burning into mine seemed to be attempting to read me just as hard as I was trying to reading him.

What was he looking for?

What was *I* looking for?

My scrambling senses flailed, and I was aghast at how easily and completely he'd overtaken my senses. How even now, with a few snatched breaths, I still couldn't think beyond the need to experience that kiss all over again. Yearning for more than just a kiss.

Realising he was awaiting a response, I scrambled the appropriate words together. 'Yes. If I must.'

He swooped down to pick up my discarded phone, then linked his fingers with mine before tugging me after him.

The crowd parted at our re-entrance, and some of the gazes I met were alight with the knowledge of what we'd been doing out on the balcony.

Being mired in my confused emotions saved me feeling embarrassment at those looks. It also made me pliant enough to survive half of the slow waltz with Axios before my senses began to return.

The reality of finding myself plastered to my husband once more, with the effects of that kiss still lingering in the form of my peaked nipples and erratic breathing, made me glance wildly around, avoiding his gaze as I tried to gather my shredded composure.

'Look at me, Calypso,' he instructed gruffly.

Almost helplessly I met his gaze.

His expression was studiously neutral but his eyes glinted with residual emotion. 'What just happened is nothing to be ashamed of,' he said gruffly. 'In fact, some might think it…fortunate that we're compatible in some ways.'

I wanted to laugh, because he was oh, so savvy about such things. While I continued to flounder.

'Don't you think it's a touch…*needy* to feel you have to be the centre of everyone's attention?' I asked.

The arrogant smile he slanted down at me said he didn't care one way or the other what people thought.

'I don't wish to be the centre of everyone's attention. Just yours,' he drawled.

For the sake of our audience, I sternly reminded myself, even as my insides lurched and jumped with misguided giddiness.

To mitigate that sensation I pressed my lips together and swayed in his arms, hoping the music would soothe my ragged nerves and spirit the rest of this infernal night away.

But, as fate had shown me time and again, hopes and dreams belonged in fairy tales. Axios danced me through three more tunes before conceding the fourth to the mayor.

Thereafter, quickly reclaimed by my so-called doting husband, we moved from group to group, his hand firm on my waist and his piercing grey eyes smiling down at me through each introduction.

His acting skills were exceptional. Our guests lapped up every soft caress, indulgently smiling at my every recounting of why I'd been away as if it was a true Greek love story.

We stopped within every circle long enough to project an image of cordiality before moving on. And I regurgitated the practised story of my absence until I feared I was blue in the face. Until I was ready to scream the truth to the whole world.

Perhaps his shark-like instincts sensed my frazzling composure. Because Ax turned to me as I impatiently waved away another offer of champagne and started to open my clutch.

'What is it?' he asked.

Remembering he had possession of my phone, I looked at him. 'Can I have my phone back? I want to check on Andreos.'

His gaze rested on my face for several beats. Thinking he wasn't going to answer, I was surprised when he turned to the business acquaintances he'd been talking to.

'It's time for us to take our leave. My beloved cannot bear to be away from our son for long, and I find that I'm not far behind her in that sentiment.'

Indulgent laughter followed, quick goodbyes were said, and before I knew it we were heading out to the waiting limo.

Settled into the back seat, I found my senses once again crowded with the sight and sound of Axios. My inability to dismiss him.

'I could've gone home on my own. You didn't need to leave with me.'

One sleek eyebrow spiked. 'You wanted me to stay there and reverse the effect of everything we've achieved this evening?' he replied.

'You seem to be a master at convincing everyone that the moon is made of caviar. I'm sure they'll believe whatever you tell them.'

He gave a low, deep laugh. Which drained away as his eyes latched to my face. 'Perhaps I do have this unique gift you speak of, but I also meant what I said. I've missed months of my son's life. I don't intend to miss any more.'

'For how long?'

His whole body froze. 'Excuse me?'

'How long do you think this phase of yours will last?'

'You have lost me…'

A thought that had been niggling me despite his assertion rose to the fore. 'You didn't want this marriage and we never got around to discussing children. We're only here because a condom failed at the crucial juncture.'

'And you think those circumstances beyond my control preclude me from assuming my mantle of responsibility towards my son? Did it you?'

'I… It's different.'

'How?' he challenged.

'I love him! I would do anything for him. While you…'

'What? Speak your mind, *glikia mou*.'

'You just want to show off your virility.'

After several tense seconds he settled back in his seat. 'You're right. I do want to show him off. He is my son, after all. As for showing off my virility—again, the evidence is there for all to see. But, while you're wrong if you think you're the only one invested in Andreos's existence, I'm aware that only time will prove what I say to you. So I guess the ball's in your court on that one.'

'How so?'

'You're the one who's in a hurry to leave. You say you were always going to come back? I'm choosing to believe you. If you want to ensure my devotion to my son is as strong as yours, then you need to rethink the urgency of your divorce demands, do you not, *pethi mou*?'

Despite his silky tone his eyes bored into mine in the dark interior of the car, and the notion that he was attempting to see right into my soul assailed me.

The thick lump wedged in my throat stalled my answer. Because *time* was the one commodity I might not have.

CHAPTER SEVEN

THE LIMO SWEEPING through the gates of his Athens mansion drew from me a breath of relief. But I soon realised I wasn't going to be set free from Ax's presence when he trailed me up the stairs to the door of Andreos's room.

I hesitated before the doors—partly because I didn't want to bring charged tension into Andreos's presence and partly because a tiny part of me wanted space to dissect everything that had happened this evening. But the greater part of me wanted to keep my son all to myself. Just for a little while.

A sharp cry from within dissipated every thought.

As Ax held the door open for me I entered the room in time to see Sophia lifting Andreos from his changing mat.

She stopped and smiled when she saw us. 'Good evening, Kyria Xenakis. You're just in time for Andreos's midnight feed. Would you like me to warm the bottle for you?'

I waved her away and Ax strode forward to take Andreos from her arms. 'Go to bed, Sophia. I'll take care of it.'

With a smiling nod, the young girl retreated to the adjoining bedroom, shutting the door behind her.

Ax adjusted his hold on Andreos, his strong hands lifting him aloft so they were face to face. My breath caught and, recalling his words in the car, I watched father and son stare at each other, one expression showing unabashed curiosity while the other probed with raw intensity as Axios absorbed his son's every expression as if hoarding it for his memory.

A little ashamed at questioning his motives in the car, I bit my lip as something settled inside me. No matter our personal angst, Axios cared for his son. Perhaps in time he'd love him almost as much as I did.

In that moment I wanted to tell him he would have years of special moments like this if I didn't manage to defuse the time bomb ticking inside me, but the words remained locked tight in my throat, the need not to have this time diluted with unwelcome outside influence stilling my tongue as I joined them.

Sensing another presence, Andreos turned towards me, his chubby arms windmilling as he babbled in delight. Then delight turned into familiar irritation as hunger kicked in and he whimpered his displeasure.

'Someone is impatient for his feed,' Ax mused, before his gaze dropped pointedly to my chest.

A fierce blush suffused my face. My breasts had been growing heavier in the last couple of hours. Even without the need to feed him myself I would have needed to express some milk before going to bed.

Expecting Ax to hand him over, I watched in surprise when he headed to the antique rocking chair I used for feeding Andreos. 'You're staying?'

'Unless you have an objection?' he asked, and I realised it was a genuine query.

About to say yes, I stunned myself by shaking my head.

A look flitted across his face faster than I could decipher it before he nodded. Once I was seated in the chair, which I'd discovered had been in his family for generations, Ax handed Andreos over. Then he started to move towards the adjacent sofa.

'Um…' I said.

He turned immediately. 'What is it?'

'Can you help me with my dress?'

Piercing grey eyes darkened a fraction as they moved to the halter neck of my dress. He gave a brisk nod, and in one deft move freed the fastening.

I caught the front before I was completely exposed, but there was no hiding from Ax's focused attention as I positioned Andreos on my lap.

He latched on with greedy enthusiasm, one fist planted firmly on my breast while both chubby legs jerked up to wrap around the forearm of the hand I'd laid on his plump belly to steady him.

The familiar action tugged at my heartstrings and drew a smile.

'Does he always do that?' Ax rasped, his voice gruff with emotion.

For a precious few seconds I'd forgotten he was there, watching my every move, absorbing his son's routine. Now my gaze met his and I nodded shakily, strangely overcome to be sharing this little snippet of time with the man who'd helped create my precious son.

'Since he was two and a half months old. I think it's his way of telling me to stay put. He'll let me go when he's satisfied.'

Ax lounged back in his seat and crossed his legs, a curious, heart-stopping little smile playing at his sensuous lips. 'He's a Xenakis. He knows what he wants.'

That display of unabashed male pride would have been unbecoming from any other man. From Ax it was a solid statement acknowledging his progeny. Progeny that would be completely his if I lost my fight.

The lance of pain to my heart made my breath catch.

'What is it?' Ax asked sharply. 'Does it cause you pain?'

My gaze flew to his and I had to swallow before I could answer. 'The breastfeeding? No, it doesn't.'

His narrowed gaze moved from Andreos and back to me. 'Then what is it?'

I flailed internally as I tried to find a plausible response. 'I was just remembering our conversation in the car. Perhaps I was…a little harsh.'

One brow quirked, but it was minus the mockery I'd become used to. *'Perhaps?'*

'Okay, I was. I… I don't want us to butt heads over Andreos.'

His hands spread in a manner that suggested a truce. 'Neither do I, Calypso.'

As milestones went, this was another sizeable one in an evening filled with small earthquakes of surprise. My breath caught. Andreos whimpered. I looked down to find eyes so much his father's wide and curious upon me. Reading my every expression just as intently as his father probed beneath my skin.

'Maybe we should discuss this further later?'

'I agree,' Ax responded, then proceeded to watch me with hawk-like intensity all through the feed.

When I transferred Andreos to my other breast Ax's gaze tracked my blush after dropping once to my nipple. But this time my self-consciousness was reduced. The natural act of providing sustenance for my baby was one I realised I didn't mind sharing with his father.

Just as abruptly as he'd wrapped his sweet limbs around my arm Andreos dropped his legs and he detached with a loud plop.

Ax rose and sauntered over, wordlessly securing my dress as I sat Andreos on my lap and rubbed his back. I was rewarded with a loud burp three minutes later.

With a gentle caress of his son's head, Ax stepped away. 'I have a few phone calls to make. I'll meet you in my suite when you're done here.'

The reminder that our suites were interconnecting and the memory of what had happened in his sent a pulse of electricity through me as I watched him walk away.

His icy indifference had receded. Something had happened on that balcony tonight. The realisation that Ax didn't tar me with the same brush as my father had eased something in me.

I was pondering the new path this might lead to as I laid a sleepy Andreos back in his cot and then entered the suite forty-five minutes later.

Both the living room and bedroom in Ax's suite were empty. Entering my own suite, I crossed to the dressing room, quickly undressed, then slid on my night slip before throwing a matching silk gown over it.

I was brushing my hair at my dressing table when Ax walked in, both hands in his pockets.

He paused in the doorway, his eyes holding a skin-tingling expression and resting on me for a long moment before he prowled forward. He stopped behind me and I waited, my breath locked in my throat as one hand reached out, tugged the brush from me and slowly dragged it through my hair.

For a full minute he said nothing, and the hypnotic sensation of his movements flooded my system with torrid lust.

'You'll be pleased to know our strategy worked,' he drawled eventually. 'My family and friends believe we are happily reunited. I expect my business partners to fall in line by morning.'

Something shook inside me. The easy way he laid his hand on me was a stronger warning that things were shifting. That the conversation on the balcony had indeed sparked much more than a rebellion and the need to answer it in both of us.

Before I could heed the warning he nudged me to my feet, slid his hand down my arm to link with my fingers. 'Come with me.'

Even the imperious tone had altered, become less…autocratic.

I followed him into his living room.

There, on a wide screen, he'd set up the video I'd given him. 'Ax…?'

'I haven't had a chance to watch this yet. Or perhaps I was putting it off,' he said, with a hint of vulnerability in his voice that stunned me enough to take the seat next to him when he settled on the plush sofa.

'You want to watch it now?' I asked.

His eyes met mine, held me in place. 'Yes,' he stated simply.

With a flick of his finger on the remote the video came to life. The simple but clean walls of the hospital room in Kenya came into view before the camera swung over the machines to rest on my heavily pregnant form.

My breath strangled into nothing as the uniquely intimate and life-changing event unfolded on the screen, tugging at the very heart of me.

Beside me Ax caught his breath audibly as he watched a contraction hit me, and the hand that still held mine tightened. This footage had been taken about ten minutes before Andreos's birth. Ax watched every frame without taking his gaze off the screen, his whole body rapt as Andreos was laid in my arms for the first time. He watched me kiss his wrinkled forehead, heard me murmur, 'My little miracle,' as tears of joy spilled down my face.

His throat moved in a swallow when the video ended, and he immediately hit 'rewind' and watched it all over again.

Then his gaze shifted to me.

'Ax...'

He shook his head, raised my hand to his mouth, gently kissed the back of it. 'It was a magnificent birth.'

Deep inside me something *essential* melted, pulling me into a dangerous spell I wasn't entirely certain I wanted to fight. Emotion clogging my throat, I smiled.

'He's a beautiful boy,' he rasped, a throb of deep pride in his voice.

I blinked unbidden tears away. 'Yes. He is.'

'As beautiful as his mother.'

As my breath caught all over again, his thumb rubbed across my knuckles.

'Again you have my thanks—especially since you had to go through that alone.'

'I'd do anything for him,' I replied, and I knew the fervent well of my emotion had registered with him.

For the longest time he simply stared, then his gaze returned to the screen, his vision going a little hazy. 'The reality of him—' He stopped. 'He may be an unexpected arrival in my life, but I want the chance to do right by him. To do things differently—'

Again he stopped, prompting questions I couldn't halt.

'Differently from what? Your father? I noticed your stiff interaction at the wedding, then again at the family mixer, and assumed *I* was to blame.'

He shook his head. 'Our issues go back a little further. I was still a teenager when my grandfather announced that I was to be his successor. In his eyes my father didn't have what it took to make the tougher decisions.' A muscle ticked in his jaw as his lips firmed. 'My father disagreed. He attempted to prove my grandfather wrong.'

I frowned. 'How?'

'My grandfather temporarily handed him the reins of the company. Six months later my father suffered a breakdown brought on by extreme stress. He didn't take the prognosis well.'

'What did he do?'

'He believed my grandfather had humiliated him. And when my grandfather made it known that he'd seen me as his successor all along, my father…didn't take it well. His resentment festered irreparably.' His lips twisted. 'Which, in a nutshell, is the story of my whole family.'

'But you all seem so…*united*—give or take the odd vibe or two.'

He shrugged cynically. 'Self-interest, especially where wealth is concerned, has a way of binding even the most dissenting individuals. My father may not like the status quo but he's had to accept it.'

'Is there no way to repair your relationship?'

A hint of bleakness came and went in his eyes within a heartbeat. 'We've accepted our strengths and our weaknesses. My father may resent me for seemingly usurping him, but he doesn't want the role.'

'You offered it to him?'

His lips thinned. 'A few years ago I suggested a partnership. He refused.'

'He wanted all or nothing?'

His lips twisted. 'Don't we all?'

Pain lashed me. 'Not all of us. Our fathers, maybe.'

Grey eyes met mine and a moment of affinity lingered between us, threatening to burrow into vulnerable places.

I cleared my throat. 'Is that why you're determined to try with Andreos?'

He'd said on the balcony that he was attempting to be different. The part of me that wasn't terrified of what the future held desperately craved to see that difference.

The question took him aback, and a naked yearning blanketed his features before he mastered it. 'Is it wrong to wish for a better outcome with my son than that between my father and I?' he rasped.

Again, a deep, sacred sensation pulled at me. Harder. Stronger. Making it impossible to breathe.

Despite the danger of falling under the silken spell he was weaving, I laid my hand on his arm. 'No, it's not.'

His gaze dropped to my hand. Silence charged with electricity filled the room as something flashed in his eyes. Primal and fierce. The video and our conversation had done something to him. Shifted the dynamic.

I was tempted to run. To hide from it. But I was just as determined not to regress.

'So…where do we go from here? After tonight, I mean?'

His eyes dropped to my lips, then moved back up to seize mine.

'Now we consolidate on what we've started,' he murmured huskily.

I wanted to ask for clarity. Wanted to ask whether he meant us or the larger world. But his fingers wound tighter around mine, his free hand rising to slide into my hair, dragging over my scalp in a wickedly evocative move that snatched the air from my lungs and hardened my nipples into aroused peaks.

Those penetrating eyes tracked my every reaction, his nostrils flaring when he caught the visible signs of my agitated state.

'And how do you propose to do that?' I asked.

'By making things real both inside and outside of the marriage bed,' he stated, his voice deep and sure.

Lightning-hot excitement charged through me, the need to experience this altered Axios overwhelming me. Would the change he wanted with his son manifest itself with me too, even in the short time I might have?

Only one way to find out.

I tugged myself free and stood to my feet.

Mutiny flashed in his eyes.

When he started to reach for me, I held up a hand. 'If you want me to change my mind convince me that you're worth it,' I said.

Then I fled.

I went after her like a beast possessed.

She was mine.

My wife.

All evening I'd caught tantalising glimpses of her. The way she moved, the thoughtful way she responded to strangers' rabid curiosity, even accommodating Stavros…

I'd run the gamut from telling myself I didn't care about all the facets of herself she was revealing to feeling a determination to pin her down and extract every last secret from her.

But that video…

Her father was in possession of a hundred million euros. My name could have commanded an entire wing in a plush private hospital. And yet Calypso had chosen to deliver our son in a state-run hospital in Kenya with third-rate equipment. And, not only that, she'd done all that with an inner strength that shone through the footage, surrounded by people who had clearly held her in high regard.

She'd spent some of the past year volunteering. I couldn't name a single member of my family who would devote their time to charity unless it came with a tax write-off or a star-studded gala where they could show off their diamonds.

And besides the awe-inspiring act of giving birth, the most striking thing about Calypso Xenakis was the determination I'd seen on her face in that video.

It had sparked something inside me. A need for...*more*.

That intoxicating little incident on the sofa this afternoon, compounded by the kiss on the balcony this evening and watching her nurse our son, was what had finally fully awakened the primitive beast inside me. The video was evidence of her strength and resilience, despite my less than stellar behaviour last year.

Even confessing the true relationship between myself and my father—a subject I'd never discussed with another living soul—had felt...liberating. That we were both products of our circumstances had triggered an affinity in us that had in turn laid out a different way to approach what had been thrust on us.

Perhaps it didn't need to be finite.

That admission to do things differently this time had surprisingly settled deep inside me.

The Calypso I'd married had possessed a banked fire.

The woman who'd returned from her mysterious absence was flame and grit.

Heat I was unashamedly drawn to. Grit I wanted to explore.

Both characteristics drove me after her.

I arrived in the suite just as she was entering her own bedroom. I stopped her with the simple act of capturing her delicate wrist. The electricity of contact simply reaffirmed my decision.

She waited, one eyebrow elevated.

Theos mou, did she know how alluring she was, with her blue eyes daring me even as her agitated breathing announced that she wasn't unaffected by this insane chemistry?

'I want you, Calypso. And unless I'm wildly off-base you want me too.'

'That's it? Surely you have better negotiating skills than that, Axios?' she taunted.

The breathless sound of my name on her lips escalated the heat pounding through my bloodstream. I wanted to kiss her. To prove with deeds instead of words how combustible this thing between us was.

'You're not the same woman I left on Agistros last year. I see that now.'

More than that, she had the power to walk away again if she chose.

The strange sensation of being on slippery ground forced me into further speech, even as I questioned the wisdom of the route I was taking.

'Come to my bed—not because of our agreement or because of your ultimatum. Do it because you want to. Because we can make each other feel things we've never experienced before.'

Her lips parted in a soft gasp. 'You… I do that to you?'

I couldn't help the hoarse laughter that was ejected from my throat. I dropped her wrist and removed myself several mind-clearing paces away.

'Barely two hours ago, I was close to saying to hell with propriety and taking you on that balcony. What do *you* think?'

Despite the heat flaming up her face her shoulders went back, accepting her power over me. It was all I could do to remain standing where I was and not stride across the room to demonstrate just how much the hunger inside me lashed through her too.

But this was too important.

I wasn't an animal, and she needed to grant me clear acknowledgement of her desire before it would work. But it *was* going to work. There were no viable alternatives to allay this…this insane *craving* inside me save for the highly unsatisfactory avenue of self-pleasure, which I wasn't willing to consider any more.

'I'm a man with healthy appetites, Calypso. And I haven't had sex since our wedding night. Do you know that?'

She gave another gasp, this time a heated one that went straight to my groin. She backed against the door, as if putting distance between herself and the live wire of desire lashing us would work.

Eyes wide, she lifted her chin in further challenge. 'How do I know that's true?'

Frustration threatened to erupt. I tamped it down. 'I don't make a habit of lying, *yineka mou*. Regardless of how we came together, I took a vow I intend to honour until I'm no longer bound by it. But if you don't believe me I can give you the number of a top investigator and you can discover the truth for yourself.'

'Even if I believe you, maybe you didn't seek another woman's bed because you didn't want to jeopardise your precious deal.'

She was really good at pushing my buttons. And the curious thing was that I preferred this version of Calypso to the one who'd glided down the aisle a little over a year ago.

I shrugged off my tuxedo, watched her gaze cling to my torso before another blush pinkened her smooth skin. 'Whatever my reason for staying celibate, I wish it to end now.'

'Because you decree it?'

'Because you're woman enough to admit you want me too. Because *when* you come to my bed it'll be because your needs are as strong as mine and you're not ashamed to give in to them.'

Tossing the jacket aside, I gave in to the urge and re-

turned to her, my senses jumping at the promise of decadent friction when she swallowed but stayed her ground.
And then, because I wasn't above playing dirty to get my
way, I unbuttoned one shirt stud. Then another.

Brazenly, I revelled in the tremor that went through her
lush frame as her eyes followed my undressing with abashed
appreciation. A layer of femininity which might have been
there all along or I might have missed called to the beast
in me.

'I want to lay you on my bed…make you cry out my
name in climax.'

Her eyelashes fluttered before sweeping down. That tell-
tale sign that she was hiding something nearly derailed me.
It certainly froze me in place, congealing my insides with
the knowledge that, far from being a forward-thinking man,
some things were sacred to me.

'Tell me what you're thinking.'

She remained silent for far too long. In real time it was
probably a handful of seconds. But it was enough to unnerve
me. Enough that when she deigned to lift those hypnotising
eyes to mine all that remained in me was a frenzied roar.

I watched her lips move but didn't hear the words she
uttered. Her eyes grew wider, possibly at my expression.
She started to step back.

I closed the gap between us and tugged her to me. With
her heavy magnificent breasts pressed against my chest all I
wanted was to lose myself in her. To slay this terrible *need*.

Her nostrils quivered as she inhaled rapidly. Against my
chest her hands fluttered, and a trembling I wanted to believe had nothing to do with sex seized her.

'Axios…'

'I said I want to be different, Calypso. Take this leap
with me?'

But even as her eyes widened at my words she hesitated,
her lower lip caught between her teeth, taunting me with
the prospect of unaccustomed denial.

And all the while my insides churned with emotions I didn't want to examine.

All the while delicate tremors filtered through her body and her breathing grew more erratic with her undeniable arousal.

I was on the very edge of my sanity when Calypso's fingers whispered over the button above my navel, toyed with the stud for a second before fluttering away again. Eyes that refused to meet mine remained fixed on my chest.

She released her lip and I fought the urge to lean down and bite the plump, wet curve.

Before her wicked hands could further wreck me, I caught them in one hand. 'Calypso, look at me.'

After an eternity her lashes lifted. Dark blue hypnotic pools pulled me in, threatening to drown me.

'Say the words. I want to hear them,' I pressed, aware that my voice was a gravel-rough mess.

She inhaled. 'I'll take the leap with you. For now.'

I had to hand it to her—she knew how to time her negotiations to maximum effect. But I'd given my word and I wouldn't go back on it. Besides, the earlier we excised this fever from our systems the earlier we could start the extrication process.

The earlier I could return to my life as I knew and preferred it.

The punch of satisfaction I expected never arrived.
More...

'For now?' I repeated, dismissing the hollow echo of the words.

I steeped myself deeper in the moment. Revelled in the fingers gripping my shirt as if the small scrap of cotton would ground her. She swallowed again, then gave a nod.

I crooked a finger under her chin and nudged her head upward. 'Tell me, *pethi mou*,' I insisted.

'I want you,' she whispered.

The breathy little sound washed over my chin and throat,

making something frenzied and untamed leap inside me, filling me with the prospect of what 'more' could mean.

'More...' I pressed, wanting irrevocable confirmation that she wanted this.

Her chin lifted, her eyes gleaming boldly. 'I want to be in your bed. I want you to take me.'

I slid my hand up her delicate spine to tangle in her hair. To grip it and keep her attention on me. 'I want to make you mine again. Tell me you want that.'

Her fists bunched, a breathy little sound escaping her throat as she swayed closer. 'I want to be yours.'

Like over a breached dam, a torrent swelled inside me. Removing her silk dress was as simple as catching the fragile material and ripping it off her body.

She gasped, staring down at the tattered fabric at her feet before attempting to glare at me. 'I don't believe you did that.'

A smile caught me unawares. 'I didn't think you were that attached to it. If so, I'll buy you a dozen more,' I vowed thickly. Because the sight of her body, displaying changes after bearing my son in the form of slightly thicker hips, a rounded softness in her belly and, best of all, the heaviness of her breasts, had intensified the throbbing in my groin.

I was barely aware of sinking to my knees, framing her lush hips and pulling her to me. I welcomed the fingers clenching tight into my hair as my lips found the sensitive flesh below her navel and brazenly tasted her creamy skin. When she sagged against the door I went lower, removing her panties before catching one leg and throwing it over my shoulder so I could find the heart of her, the true feminine core that called to me with the strength of a dozen sirens.

'Ax!'

Her sweet cry urged me on, her taste a drug surging with unstoppable force through my bloodstream. I didn't relent until she was splintering in my arms, her moans music to my ears. Only then did I scoop her up and carry her to my bed to begin all over again.

Her head rolled on the pillow, her hair fanning out in a dark silken halo as her lips parted on hot little gasps as I rediscovered every delightful inch of her body.

'*Omorfi…*'

The word tumbled unbidden from my lips as I caught one pearled nipple in my mouth. And she *was* beautiful, with a certain indefinable layer of femininity and strength adding to her allure.

'When you glided up that aisle like an obedient wraith I had no idea you were hiding this…this steel and sensuality beneath that frothy gown.'

Her eyes widened in dazed surprise. 'Was that why you left the next morning? Because I wasn't what you expected?'

It was my turn to be stunned. To ponder how events had unfolded through her eyes. But now wasn't the time to admit I'd been unnerved then too. Just as I was now.

'No. My delivery wasn't great, but I believed leaving was best. However, *this*…' I slid a hand down her ribcage, revelled in her unfettered response '…was certainly a surprise.'

And the fact that she was even more responsive now threatened to annihilate my self-control completely.

Before I was entirely consumed I reached for a condom, donned it and accepted the enthralling welcome of her parted thighs. I slanted my lips over hers, unwilling to leave any feast unsatisfied as I entered her in one deep, glorifying thrust.

Pleasure detonated in a shower of fireworks as I seated myself deep within her. Felt her tighten around me, drawing me deeper. When she sought to shatter me further with needy whimpers and greedy hands I tore my lips from hers, gritted my teeth in an effort to make this last.

But of course the next layer of sweet torture waited in the wings. With her mouth free, and the nirvana of a higher plane of pleasure waiting, I watched her slide into

that unique dimension, that place where her unfiltered pleasure rippled from her alluring lips.

'My God, you're so big. *So* deep. I feel every inch of
you…'

A muted roar rumbled up my throat as her words threatened to completely unravel me.

Her nails sank into my back, ripping away another layer
of control. And just like on that night I'd never been able to
put out of my mind I realised she was unaware of herself,
that pleasure had transported her into another dimension.

'Shall I roll my hips like that first time? That was incredible.'

'Calypso…' I wasn't sure whether saying her name was
warning or encouragement. Either way, she didn't respond.
She continued her mind-altering commentary. Commentary
that fired a white-hot blaze inside me alongside the fiery
one already raging from possessing her.

I stared down into her stunning, unguarded face as I
pushed in and out of her, racing both of us towards that
special peak.

Another man would have taken advantage of the situation, prised secrets from her subconscious while she was in
this state. But that was an invasion my conscience wouldn't
let me stomach for longer than a nanosecond.

So I refocused on the words tumbling from her lips,
revelled in them for another reason altogether. Because
they turned me on. Because no other woman had brought
this unique, exquisite surprise to my bed. Because hearing
her vocalise her pleasure charged mine in a way I'd never
thought possible.

Increasing the tempo of my thrusts, I lowered my body
to hers, drew her tighter against me. 'Wrap your legs around
my waist, *omorfia mou*.'

With gratifying speed, she complied.

'Now, tell me more,' I growled in her ear. 'Tell me everything you're feeling.'

Whether she heard me or not, I didn't know, but the words spilled out.

Unmanned by her unfiltered longing, I kissed the corner of her luscious mouth and groaned when she chased mine when I withdrew.

'Kiss me. Please kiss me.'

'Say my name, *matia mou*. Say my name and I'll kiss you.'

'Axios,' she moaned. 'Kiss me, *please*, Axios.'

Unable to resist the sultry demand, I kissed her again. Felt her tighten around me in response and gritted my teeth to keep myself on that dizzying plateau for one more second. She was eroding every ounce of my willpower, pushing me towards the zenith long before I was ready.

And there was little I could do to stop it.

Especially not when my mind was already flying to the next time, to the next position.

She would be on top. Yes, she would ride me, her heavy breasts high and proud, while those unfettered words fell from her lips. The image was so potent, so vivid, I lost the ability to think straight.

My unguarded growl in response to that scenario pushed her higher. Her nails dug into my shoulders, her head thrashing on the pillow.

'Let go, Calypso. Now!'

The command set her free. With a sharp, sweet cry, she dissolved into uncontrollable convulsions, her body writhing beneath mine in innocently uncoordinated movements that finally shattered my control.

With a roar torn from deep within I succumbed to exquisite, untrammelled bliss. Time ceased to matter. I was aware I'd collapsed on top of her, one propped arm the only thing stopping me from crushing her. But her own arms were wrapped tight around me, as if holding me together.

The singular, searing thought that I wanted to remain

here *indefinitely* charged through my daze, forcing me to move. Forcing sanity back into this madness.

But even as I gathered her to me after my return from the bathroom she was unravelling me again, the hand on my chest reaching deeper as she turned her face to me.

'Ax?'

'Hmm?' Unfamiliar dread clenched my gut, escalating the notion that somewhere along the line I'd fallen under her mercy and her whim.

Her breath fluttered out in an almost reverent exhalation as her eyes lifted to mine. 'You're the only man I've ever been with. I just thought you should know.'

That gift, freely given when it could have been withheld in light of our circumstances, punched and winded me. The notion that opening up to her had possibly earned me this unsettled me even more.

Questions and wants and needs surged higher than before, racing to the tip of my tongue before circumspection halted them. I wanted more from her. But did I have more to give to her and to Andreos?

I pushed back the dismaying sensation.

She was staying...for now.

That unsettling little addendum would be tackled later. After much-needed regrouping.

'*Efkharisto.*'

The word emerged deeper, graver than I'd expected. I did nothing to offset it. Nothing but accept that things *had* to be different.

Nothing I'd seen of the marriages around me had fuelled a need to embroil myself in one—not when they strained so easily and threatened to break at the smallest hint of adversity.

But, in the hypothetical scenarios where marriage *had* crossed my mind, I'd known that unshaken faithfulness and stalwart support would be the cornerstone of its success. Not the kind of marriage held together by financial worth—the kind my grandfather had struggled to hold on to and ended up paying dearly for.

That reminder cooled my jets long enough to let in rational thought. Long enough to know that Calypso and I needed a base of trust from which to operate.

Which meant getting her to open up about her secrets…

I decided to come at it from a different angle. 'Are you ready to tell me why you chose to leave Greece?'

Her eyes shadowed and her lashes swept down. But before I could catch her chin and redirect her attention on me she lifted her gaze, her eyes boldly meeting mine with a resolution I wasn't sure whether to welcome or battle.

'Okay.'

Relief stunned me. 'Okay?'

She nodded. 'I want whatever time we have remaining to be peaceful.'

I forced my teeth not to grit at the reminder of a timescale. 'Good.'

A touch of nerves edged her features. When she went to move out of my arms, I caught her back. 'It would please me if you stayed right here for this.'

CHAPTER EIGHT

HE WAS UNRAVELLING ME with his low-voiced requests. With this side of him that hinted at the kind of man I'd dreamed of calling husband and father to my child. The kind of man who asked me to take a leap even when I knew that ultimately my path might lie elsewhere.

Tell him.

Maybe this could all turn out differently.

You could have more nights like this, far into the future.

But what if the worst happened? I couldn't put Andreos through that.

Besides, while Ax had readily agreed to my stipulation… for now…he'd given me no insight as to what would happen beyond that.

But I'd bought myself a little more time—and, *Theos mou*, I wanted to experience this again. And again. Without angst or acrimony.

Even now, with my limbs weak from their physical and emotional expenditure, hunger was slowly gathering force, anticipation adding fuel to a fire which didn't seem in a hurry to burn itself out. And if all it took was a simple re-counting of my year, where was the harm?

I pushed away the voice urging caution and when I opened my mouth the words that tumbled out surprised even me.

'My grandmother was a feminists' feminist. She hated every aspect of a patriarchy that dictated what she could and couldn't do. She especially hated it when my grandfather died and everyone expected her to remarry because she had a young daughter to care for.'

I caught the edge of Ax's puzzled frown and couldn't help the smile that tugged at my lips.

'She never did remarry, but after she lost her house she was forced to live with my parents. I grew up in the shadows of her rebellion. She urged me to stand my ground. To question everything.'

His frown cleared, a droll look entering his grey eyes. 'Ah. I see.'

'Needless to say she butted heads with my father almost on a daily basis.'

Ax tensed. Not wanting the mood tarnished, I passed my hand over his chest—a soothing gesture that worked with Andreos but might not work with his father. My breath caught when he exhaled after a handful of seconds.

'Anyway, I found out on my wedding day that she'd left me an envelope. My mother was to give it to me when she thought I needed it.'

A trace of regret flashed across his face. 'She thought you'd need it the day you married me.'

It wasn't a question, more of an acceptance of how things had turned out.

I shrugged. 'Besides my father, none of us knew much about you. What little I knew before we met at the altar I found out online,' I said, recognising but unable to stop the hint of censure in my tone.

The regret in his eyes deepened as he nodded. 'I accept that. So your father really kept you in the dark about everything?'

'Yes. And it wasn't anything new. He did that most of my life.'

'Why?'

The whisper of family shame slithered over my skin. 'Surely you've heard the rumours?'

'I prefer facts to rumours,' he stated.

I didn't bother to ask what he'd heard. I wanted this discussion over as quickly as possible.

'My mother left home when I was fifteen. She'd met another man and was planning on leaving my father. But they were involved in an accident. The man died. My mother survived—obviously—but she suffered a spine injury and… Well, you've seen her. My father brought her back home and promised to take care of her—under certain conditions.'

The hand that had been lazily trailing through my hair froze. 'It seems your father makes a habit of using people's misfortunes against them.'

I couldn't deny that truth. And when Ax used his hold to gently propel my gaze up to his I couldn't hide it from him.

Whatever he saw in my face made him exhale again. 'I used to think that was an encompassing Petras family trait,' he murmured.

'*Used* to?' Did that mean he'd changed his mind? That he *wasn't* tarring me with the same brush as my father any more?

He continued to stare at me for a long stretch. 'You're nothing like him. You have a formidable inner strength that he doesn't—clearly inherited from your grandmother,' he said.

The low, gruff words opened up a fountain of emotion inside me that stopped my breath, especially when he brushed his lips over mine, as if wanting to seal the words in.

Getting carried away would have been so easy, but I forced myself to pull back. 'Anyway, I moved from under my father's thumb to under yours without any intermission—'

He stiffened, his face growing a shade paler. 'Under my thumb? I made you feel like that?'

I shrugged. 'You dictated where I would live. How I would live. Without giving me a say. So when you told me to find a way… I did.'

His jaw tightened and after a moment he nodded. 'I don't blame you for staging a rebellion. I would have in your shoes too. Perhaps not with anonymity but…that's understandable considering my reaction to our marriage.'

Tears prickled my eyes, threatening to spill at the thought that he was seeing things from my side. 'Anyway, my grandmother's letter left details of a Swiss bank account in my name. I went to Switzerland to see what it was all about. She'd left me the means to live under a new identity if I chose. There was also a box with some of her things in it.'

'That's how you were able to live without detection for a year?' he said.

I nodded. 'I think she meant me to use it more as a way to rebel against my father than a way—'

'For you to escape your new husband?' he finished with terse amusement.

'Either way, it seemed like a sign.'

A touch of hardness entered his eyes. 'Leaving your husband tearing his hair out for a year.'

'You weren't my husband. You especially weren't interested in being one the morning after the wedding. You married me to save your precious company, so don't pretend my absence caused you any personal slight or even—heaven forbid—any *anxiety*!'

'You carried my name. You were supposed to be under my care. Believe me, your disappearance was punishment enough—especially when I was left imagining the worst,' he rasped in a raw tone.

Plastered to him as I was, I felt the shudder that shook his frame, and his set jaw and the flash of bleakness in his eyes spoke to a vulnerability I'd never have imagined him capable of until tonight.

I stopped breathing, because… No, I hadn't quite thought about it. 'It wasn't just our forced marriage, Axios. My father was threatening my mother too.'

Fury flashed in his eyes. 'What?'

'He wanted to keep me in line through her. But she made me promise I wouldn't stay if I was unhappy. It all got a bit too much.'

'Did he carry out his threat?'

I shook my head. 'I'm guessing he was too busy playing with his windfall.'

The monthly phone calls with my mother had assured me she was okay, and had been all the wind beneath my wings I'd needed to stay away.

He bit out a tight curse and threw an arm over his forehead. 'Your father has a lot to answer for, but he's saved himself a trouncing by leaving your mother alone,' he growled. After a moment, his gaze pierced mine again. 'My investigators eventually traced your flight from Greece to Switzerland and assured me that my wife had simply chosen to run away of her own accord. At least now I know how you managed to avoid detection after you left Geneva, but perhaps you'd be so kind as to finish telling me where you went?'

The pulse of anguish still underlined his anger, but knowing it wasn't directed at me made it easier to finish my re-telling.

'I took a train to Strasbourg and then wandered through Europe for a time before heading to South-East Asia. After that I made my way through Africa.'

All the while keeping in touch with Dr Trudeau and praying for my baby's continued health.

'When did you know you were pregnant with Andreos?' he rasped.

My stomach hollowed out in remembrance, and it took every ounce of self-control not to show how that fateful day still affected me. How the possibility that I would never meet my child had left me broken and sobbing for one day straight, until the fervent prayers had begun.

'I found out early. In Switzerland.'

He waited, his gaze imploring me for more. But I had nothing more to give. Nothing that wouldn't see the precious time I had left with Andreos compromised.

And it would be. It was clear Axios was deeply possessive and protective of his son. Over the past few days I'd learned just how meticulous and all-powerful he could be. I couldn't afford for the time I had with my baby to be compromised.

Or, on the flipside, he simply wouldn't care.

Pain snaked through me, dulling my heartbeat. No, he was better off not knowing.

'Why Kenya?' he asked, tugging me back to the present.

'Because I was seven months pregnant when I got there. Because I loved it there and knew I wouldn't be able to travel. I chose to stay and have Andreos there.'

Again, he lapsed into contemplative silence, those piercing grey eyes pinning me to the bed. Then, 'Thank you for telling me,' he said simply. Gruffly.

Tears prickled. To hide them, I lowered my head until our lips were a whisper apart. He didn't protest. His eyes simply went molten and his hard body stirred beneath mine as I closed the gap and helped myself to the magic of his kiss.

He allowed my exploration for a minute. Allowed the tentative probe and the slide of my tongue against his in a deeper kiss while the hand around my waist moved in a slow caress up and down my back, until he boldly cupped my bottom and brought me into brazen contact with his impressive arousal.

Then he flipped me over and took complete control, effectively emptying my brain of everything but the naked desire snaking through my body, setting me alight with a need so acute all I could do was let it wholly consume me.

Nevertheless, his warning ricocheted in my head long after our bodies had cooled. Long after his deep, steady breathing indicated sleep.

Because telling myself I didn't care what my actions had caused Axios after I took up the fight for my health, that I wasn't important enough to cause a ripple in his existence, didn't quite ring true in my head. I cared. Even if marrying him and taking his name had been a transaction dictated by my father for financial gain, our coming together had produced a son. And that mattered. Whether I liked it or not, Axios mattered to me. More than perhaps was wise.

The intensifying ache inside that reminded me I might have less time than I imagined added to the turmoil churning inside me, keeping me awake as dawn approached. Eventually mental exhaustion won out, and I fell into a sleep fuelled with pleasure and pain, blissful happiness and acute sadness.

Thankfully I was in a state of happiness when I resurfaced from sleep to the sound of a cooing baby.

'*Kalimera*, my angel,' I murmured, my drowsy awakening made all the better by my sweet baby's enthusiastic babble and the innocent smell of his freshly bathed body.

Eyes still closed, I felt my heart bursting with a joy that widened my smile.

'He's been very patient as he waited for his mama to wake, but I fear that state is about to be over,' drawled the deep, masculine voice of my baby's father.

My eyes flew open, the reminder of where I was and what had transpired last night fracturing my smile as I encountered the arresting image of a rudely vibrant Axios, one hand propping up his head and the other resting lightly on his son's stomach.

Andreos, his curious gaze switching between his father's face, mine, and just about every bright object it could touch upon, wriggled with impatience and babbled some more before letting out a cry that signalled he was well and truly done with waiting to be fed.

My lungs flattened with surprise and an unexpectedly sharp yearning as Ax shifted onto his back, lifted his son and held him aloft, a drop-dead gorgeous smile breaking out on his face as father and son stared at each other.

'You've made it this far, *o moro mou*. Give it another half-minute and you will be rewarded, hmm?' he teased.

I sat up, unable to help my blush and self-consciousness at the reminder that I was naked under the sheets.

After anointing his son's forehead with a gentle kiss, Axios turned to watch me sit up and arrange the pillows around me in preparation to feed an increasingly impatient Andreos.

When I was settled, Axios handed him over. And, just like last night, he didn't seem in a hurry to leave. In fact, he settled back on his pillow, his gaze unashamedly fixed on me as I settled our son at my breast.

Sunlight streamed through the partially opened curtain, bathing the parts of Axios I could see in mouthwatering relief—mainly his very naked, very chiselled torso. The effort it took to drag my gaze away and avoid the incisive eyes was depressingly monumental.

'I… What time is it?'

'It's a little after nine,' he answered, reaching out to caress his son's bare, plump foot. 'You were out of it when the monitor signalled that Andreos was awake. Sophia was about to give him a bottle, but I thought I'd bring him to you instead.'

I nodded, my throat clogging at the picture of togetherness and domestic bliss his words painted. Before I could stop myself, might-have-beens crowded my heart and I stared down at Andreos, painfully aware of Ax's presence in the pictures that filled my mind.

A little desperately, I reminded myself that this was all temporary. A short stretch of time to enjoy with my son before—

'Calypso?'

I blinked, unable to stop myself from being compelled to meet his gaze.

His eyes narrowed and he waited a beat before asking, 'What's wrong?'

I shook my head. 'It's nothing. I'm just a little tired, that's all.'

His shuttered gaze said he knew I was being evasive.

But he let it go. 'Not too tired to spend a few hours out of the city, I hope?'

Surprised, I stared at him. 'Out of the city?'

He nodded. 'I thought we could fly to Agistros for the afternoon. Agatha will organise a picnic for us and we'll spend a little time by the water.'

'Why?' I blurted.

He tensed slightly. 'On the rare occasion that I find myself with free time, I wish to spend it with our son. With you. I thought you might enjoy it. Am I wrong?'

I flushed. 'I… No.'

I'd planned nothing except spending a lazy day with Andreos. But the thought that Axios had plans, that he wanted to include us, kicked a wild little thrill into my bloodstream. A *dangerous* thrill. One I needed to nip in the bud sooner rather than later.

'I was planning on heading down to the beach here, but one beach is as good as any other, I suppose.'

A sly smile tilted one corner of his lip. 'I beg to differ. The beaches on Agistros rival the best in the world.'

My cheeky need to tease grew irresistible. 'According to *you*.'

His smile widened. 'Since I own it, my opinion is the only one that counts.'

The statement was so unapologetically arrogant I laughed. The sound seemed to arrest him, his eyes turning that molten shade that sent heat pulsing through my blood as we stared at each other.

'I believe this is the first time I've heard you laugh,' he rasped, his gaze raking over my face to settle brazenly on my mouth, almost effortlessly calling up another blush that suffused my face. 'I like it.'

Without warning his hand rose, his fingers trailing down one hot cheek and along my jaw before dropping down to recapture his son's foot.

Something heavy and urgent and profound shifted inside me. The thought that I didn't know this facet of the man I'd married and that I wanted to hit me square in the midriff, before flaring a deep yearning towards all the dark corners of my heart.

My smile felt frayed around the edges as I fought to maintain my composure, fought not to blurt out another prayer for things I didn't deserve.

I'd been given so much already.

Gloom wormed through my heart, the fear of what lay ahead and of fighting an uphill battle I might not win casting shadows over the gift of another day.

I was still struggling to banish it when a knock came on the door.

'Ah, right on time,' he murmured.

With another heart-stopping smile Axios launched himself out of bed. Naked and gladiator-like in all his glory, he walked across the suite, stopping long enough to pull on a dark dressing robe before heading for the door.

He returned a minute later, wheeling a solid silver trolley loaded with breakfast dishes. Bypassing his side of the bed, he stopped the trolley close to me before hitching up a thigh and settling himself next to me.

I tried and failed not to watch him pour coffee for himself, tea for me, and lift a large, succulent bowl of ripe strawberries.

He waited until I'd put Andreos over my shoulder and begun rubbing his back to elicit a burp before he shifted closer. Dipping one end of a strawberry into a bowl of rich cream, he leaned forward and then held the plump fruit against my lip.

'Taste.' His voice was deep, low. Hypnotising.

I leaned forward, parted my lips and took the offering. He watched me chew with the kind of rapt attention that could wreak havoc with a woman's sensibilities. Only after I'd swallowed did he help himself to a piece—minus the cream.

He alternated between feeding me and himself until the

bowl was empty, and then he set about piling more food on a plate.

'I can't eat all that,' I protested as I laid a very satisfied Andreos down beside me.

Axios shrugged, setting the tray in my lap. 'Our son is very demanding. And I get the feeling that state is only going to get more challenging. You'll need all the advantages you can get.'

About to tell him there was nothing I was anticipating more, the words stuck in my throat, and a bolt of heartache clenched my heart in a merciless vice.

Thankfully Axios was in the process of lifting a newspaper from a side pocket of the trolley, granting me a scant few seconds to get my emotions under control before he straightened and flicked the paper open.

Then a different sort of tension assailed me.

Seeing the pictures gracing the front page, I felt my gut twist. While I'd known we'd be under scrutiny last night, it hadn't occurred to me that we'd actually make front-page news.

The first picture had been taken when we'd first entered the ballroom. With our heads close together, Ax's masculine cheek almost touching mine, it hinted at an edgy intimacy between us that was almost too private.

From the look on Axios's face, he didn't feel the same.

He turned the page and my insides churned faster. There were more pictures, including some of us on the balcony, his hand splayed on my back, right before he pulled me in for that toe-curling kiss.

Axios stared at the pictures with something close to smug satisfaction.

'Did you know we were being photographed?' I asked, biting into a piece of ham-layered toast and concentrating on stirring my tea so I wouldn't have to look at the picture. At how the sight of Axios in a tuxedo continued to wreak havoc with my equilibrium. Nor face the fact that a very large part of me was wondering what true intimacy with this man whose name I'd taken would feel like.

He shrugged. 'I suspected we might be.'

That he was very much okay with it—had perhaps even wanted us to be photographed—was evident.

'And has it achieved what you meant it to?' I needed the reminder that this was all for a reason. For a definitive purpose which *didn't* include getting carried away with fairy tales.

With a flick of his fingers he folded the paper and picked up his coffee. 'If you mean are my business partners back on board, then, yes. But let's not rest on our laurels just yet,' he said.

Did that mean more socialising? More moments like those on the balcony? And why didn't that fill me with horror? Why was my belly tingling with thrilling anticipation?

Questions and sensations stayed with me through a quick shower and lingered while I chose a bikini set, pulled a floaty spaghetti-strap sundress over it and slipped my feet into stylish wedge shoes.

Stepping out to join Axios and Andreos two hours later, on the landscaped lawn that led to the helipad, I noticed we were flying in a different, larger chopper.

Axios caught my questioning look. 'This one is more insulated. To better protect Andreos's delicate eardrums,' he said, casting an indulgent glance at the baby nestled high in the crook of his arm.

Of course he *would* have a special helicopter that catered for babies!

With the sensation of having woken up in an alternative universe from which I couldn't escape, I walked beside him to the aircraft.

The trip, unlike last time, flew by, and before I knew it we were skimming the beaches of Agistros, the azure waters of the island sparkling in the sunlight.

The villa was just as breathtaking as it had been a year

ago, and this time, without deep trepidation blinding me, I was better able to appreciate it. Granted, there were other equally precarious emotions simmering beneath my skin, but just for today I let the dazed dream wash over me, revelling in simply *being* as Axios stepped out of the helicopter, reached to help me out and took control of Andreos's travel seat.

Expecting tension, in light of the way I'd departed the villa the last time, I breathed a sigh of relief when the staff, headed by Agatha, spilled out with welcoming smiles. It was obvious that news of Andreos had travelled as they cooed over him.

When Agatha carried him off to the kitchen to supervise the picnic preparation, I drifted into the living room with Axios.

Dressed in the most casual attire I'd seen him in so far—high-spec cargo trousers and a navy rugby shirt—he nevertheless still looked as if he'd stepped straight off the cover of a magazine.

To keep myself from shamelessly ogling him, I drifted over to the set of framed photos on one of the many antique cabinets gracing the room. There was a slightly faded one of an old man, his distinguished and distinctive features announcing him as Theodore Xenakis. Ax's grandfather. The man who'd been forced under duress to make an agreement that had changed lives—including mine.

Perhaps it wasn't the best choice of subject matter to bring up on what was meant to be a lazy day by the beach. But after hearing Axios open up about his father, I wanted to know more. Yearned to learn what had formed the man whose name I bore.

Once we'd made our way down to a private beach, tucked into the most stunning bay I'd ever seen in my life, I found myself asking, 'Did your grandfather ever live here on Agistros?'

He stiffened, but his tension eased almost immediately. 'In the latter part of his life, yes.'

There was more to that statement. 'Why? I mean, I've seen your family. I know you're dispersed all over Athens, and on several family-owned islands. I also know that Agistros belongs to you. So why did he live here? Did he need care?'

For the longest time I thought he wouldn't answer. When he did reply, his tone was low. Deep. As if remembering was painful.

'Before his company fell on hard times my grandfather invested in real estate and gifted islands to every family member. Neo has an island twenty miles from here.'

At the mention of his brother it was my turn to stiffen. 'I don't think Neo likes me.'

Ax's eyes glinted, a hard kind of amusement shifting in their depths. 'He's going through a…a situation.'

'A "situation"?'

'Something's been taken from him that he wasn't quite ready to part with,' he said cryptically.

I frowned. 'Someone's stolen from him?'

'In a manner of speaking.'

Recalling our conversation, I frowned. 'A woman?'

Again, dark amusement twisted Ax's lips. 'Yes. And a formidable one, I hear.'

Realising he wasn't going to elaborate, I pressed gently, 'So…about your grandfather…?'

A trace of bleakness whispered across his face. 'He left Kosima, his favourite island, for many reasons. But mainly because the strain of trying to save his company took a toll on his family, especially my grandmother. After she died we didn't deem it wise for him to remain on Kosima by himself. So he came to stay here.'

I wanted to probe deeper, find out why the once booming Xenakis empire had swan-dived to the brink of bankruptcy three years before his grandfather had died. But I held my tongue because I suspected my own family had had a hand in the Xenakis family's misfortune. Also, that flash of bleakness resonated inside me, his pain echoing mine.

Not wanting the day ruined by revisiting the animosity between our families, I stared at the stunning horizon, a different urge overtaking me. 'I wish I could paint this,' I murmured, almost to myself.

Ax turned to me. 'When was the last time you painted?'

Unsurprised that he knew of my passion, I answered, 'All through my pregnancy, and a short while after Andreos was born.'

'Why didn't you pursue your painting before?'

I shrugged. 'There wasn't much call for it on Nicrete.'

His silence was contemplative. 'You wanted to do something with it in Athens. Do you still want to?' he asked, a trace of guilt in his voice.

Not if I don't have much time left.

'Perhaps not full-time but…yes.'

'I would like to see you paint.'

Something melted inside me and I couldn't help my gasp. 'You would?'

He gave an abrupt nod. 'If you would allow it…very much.'

Again something tugged inside me, harder this time—a feeling of my world tilting, making me sway towards him.

To counteract it before I did something supremely unwise, I tugged my dress over my head. 'I'm going for a swim.'

With every step from sand to sea I felt his gaze burn into my skin, heating me up from the inside out. Thigh-deep, I dived into the cool, exquisite water, hoping it would wash away the discordant emotions zinging through me.

This really shouldn't be difficult. All we had to do was exist in the same space until I was absolutely certain Andreos would be safe and cared for, before I returned to Dr Trudeau in Switzerland to face my fate.

All I had to do was prevent myself from falling under Ax's spell. Surely it wasn't that hard?

Yes, it is. I feel more for him with every passing minute!

The weight of that verdict was so disturbing I didn't sense his presence until the second before he wrapped a strong arm around my waist.

His hair was slicked back, throwing the sharp, majestic angles of his face into stunning relief. Droplets of water sparkled on his face, a particularly tempting one clinging to his upper lip, evoking in me a wild need to lick it off.

'Andreos!' I protested.

'He's fine,' he said with hard gruffness as he pulled me closer, tangled my legs with his.

I looked over and sure enough our son was well-insulated by plump pillows, shaded by a large umbrella, happily playing with his rattle.

'Calypso…'

My name was a thick demand I couldn't resist. And when he pulled me into his arms and slanted his sensual lips across mine I gave in, my conflicting thoughts melting away under the heat of mounting passion.

Afterwards we returned and spread out on the blankets. A trace of trepidation returned, tingeing the closeness wrapping itself around us, a closeness I wanted to hang on to despite the uncertainty lurking in the future.

Because this version of Axios, who wanted to see me paint, who had opened up about his grandfather, was a version who could so easily worm his way into my heart.

On the Monday morning after our first trip to Agistros I arrived downstairs to find six high-spec easels and an assortment of expensive paints and brushes. Stunned, I blinked away tears as Axios presented them to me.

'You…you shouldn't have.'

He shook his head. 'You've denied your passion long

enough,' he said. 'A year longer than necessary because of me,' he added heavily.

Next he organised special transportation for my mother to visit. Having not seen each other for a year, our reunion was tearful, her joy over her grandson boundless.

Seeing her, reassuring myself that she was all right despite the pain still clouding her eyes, lifted a weight off my shoulders. And that melting sensation returned full force when Axios set out to charm her—a ploy that worked to dissipate the lingering tension between them once and for all.

From my father I heard nothing. And, frankly, it didn't overly bother me.

After that our lives fell into a pattern.

Weekdays were spent at the villa in Athens, with at least three evenings of the week spent at one social engagement or another, which inevitably made front-page news, while Saturday and Sunday were spent on Agistros.

It was almost idyllic—the only fly in the ointment Dr Trudeau's increasingly urgent emails and the knowledge that now I was assured of Ax's complete devotion to our son I had no cause to put my health issues on hold.

It was on one weekend a few weeks later, in the place we'd now designated our picnic spot, when he glanced over at me as he reclined on a shaded lounger with a sleepy Andreos dozing on his bare chest. Father and son were besotted with each other, the growing bond between them a source of untold joy to me.

'I'm flying to Bangkok on Tuesday for business.'

Since he never discussed his business arrangements with me I met his gaze in surprise, unwilling to expose the sharp sting that had arrived and lodged in my midriff. 'Okay...'

'You and Andreos can come with me.'

The swiftness with which the sting eased was dismaying—and a little terrifying. Enough to trigger a waspish response. 'Is that a question or a command?'

The flash of flint in his eyes stunned me. Hard on its

heels came the realisation that I much preferred his blinding smiles. The sexy growls when he was aroused. Even his sometimes mocking tones.

Theos, I'd fallen into a highly dangerous state of lust, complacency, and a host of other things I didn't want to name. One in particular had been gaining momentum, clamouring for attention I was too afraid to give it. It was there when I woke. It blanketed me before I fell asleep and teased my dreams. It was there now, pulsing beneath my skin as Ax's gaze locked on mine and another blinding smile made an appearance.

'It's whichever you find easiest to comply with.'

For some absurd reason my heart flipped over even as I wondered whether he was asking me along because the thought of being separated from us for any length of time was disagreeable to him or because of appearances.

His expression was mostly unreadable, but there was something there. A touch of apprehension I'd never seen before. And, though it was highly unwise to latch on to it, I found myself leaning towards it, indulging myself in the idea that he *cared* whether I agreed or not.

'How long is this trip going to last?'

'It's to finalise a new airline deal I've been working on for a year. It's been challenging at times, so I expect both sides will want to celebrate after the deed is done. Prepare to stay for the better part of a week. Did you travel to Thailand on your trip?' he asked, but his almost flippant query didn't fool me for one second.

Axios was a master at subtle inquisition. Over the past weeks he'd dropped several questions unexpectedly.

'No. My coin-flip landed in favour of Indonesia instead of Thailand, so I went to Bali.'

'Then this will be your chance to explore another country,' he replied smoothly, despite the trace of tension in the air.

Andreos chose that moment to make his displeasure at

the charged atmosphere known. Axios absently soothed a hand down his small back, but his eyes remained fixed on me.

When I reached for him Ax handed him over. Then he stayed sitting, his elbows resting on his knees.

'Will you come with me?' he asked, his eyes boring into mine.

And because that undeniable yearning for *more* wouldn't stop—because I craved this...*togetherness* more than I craved my next breath—I answered, 'Yes.'

CHAPTER NINE

TIME IS RUNNING OUT…

The unnerving sensation that time was slipping through my fingers had arrived like a thief in the night and stayed like an unwanted guest, permeating my every interaction with Calypso. I couldn't put my finger on *why* and nor did I have a clear-cut solution.

The sensation left me off-kilter and scowling as I climbed the steps into my plane two days later.

A lot of things I'd believed to be cut and dried had become nebulous in the past few weeks. The idea of marriage…of *staying* married, for instance…didn't evoke the same amount of resistance it had done a year or even a month ago. As for being a father…

Thoughts of Andreos immediately soothed a fraction of the chaos inside me. My son's existence had brought a deeper purpose to my life I wouldn't have believed possible had I not experienced it for myself. The chance to pass on my heritage to him, to teach him about the sacrifices his grandfather had made filled a bleak corner of my soul.

As for his mother…

The warmth I'd enjoyed with her over the past few weeks, watching her joy in painting and simply basking in the unit she and Andreos presented had subtly altered, leaving me with more questions than answers. Even more acute was the feeling of exposure after revealing so much of myself and the anguish her family's actions had caused mine.

Yes, but only one member of her family…not all of them…

My chest twinged with another sting of guilt. I'd learned from my grandfather's mistakes, applied his good mentoring to my life and avoided the bad. Shouldn't the same apply to Calypso? Especially when she'd been caught in the same web of greed as I had?

The urge to hash this out with her grew stronger. And

yet the fear of repeating the mistakes of last year, driving her away, stopped me.

It didn't help that over the last day or so she'd seemed under the weather, thereby curtailing any serious conversation I'd felt inclined to have or my reaching for that final resort of last resorts—tugging her into my arms in the dark of night and letting the mindless bliss of having her melt every fractious thought away.

Harmony and unstinting passion—it was a combination I would never have associated with her a few weeks ago, but I now craved to have it back.

My gaze fell on her as I entered the living area of the plane. She was chatting to one of the attendants, her alluring smile sparking heat in my bloodstream as she nodded to whatever was being said.

Unable to help myself, I let my gaze trail over her. The cream form-fitting jumpsuit caressed her luscious body from shoulder to ankle, its emphasis of her supple behind and lush breasts drying my mouth and reminding me that it had been three long days since I'd had the pleasure of her body.

The attendant departed, and as Calypso turned to sit I noticed the top buttons securing the front were left undone to reveal her impressive cleavage. My groin stirred harder and it was all I could do not to give a bad-tempered, frustrated groan.

I approached, dropping into the seat opposite her. She held Andreos like a buffer, her gaze stubbornly avoiding mine even though she was aware of my presence.

'The silent treatment isn't going to work where we're headed. You do know that, don't you?'

The blue eyes that finally deigned to meet mine were shadowed, her face still showing a hint of the paleness that raised an entirely new set of ruffled emotions inside me.

'Don't worry, Axios. I'll put on the appropriate performance when needed.'

Even her voice had lost a trace of that passionate lustre that fired up my blood.

'Are you all right?' The words were pulled from a deep, *needy* part of me.

Her eyes widened, then she nodded abruptly and her gaze dropped to Andreos. 'I'm fine. Just a slight…stomach ache.'

The unsettling sensation deepened, the niggling feeling that I was missing something escalating. 'Did you take anything for it? I'll get the attendant to bring you—'

She shook her head hastily when I reached for the intercom button, but I didn't miss the shadow that crossed her face, the knuckles that whitened in her lap.

'It's… I'm fine, Ax. I think I'll go and lie down with Andreos for a while after we take off.'

True to her word, the moment we reached cruising altitude she unbuckled herself, rose, and headed to the back of the plane with Andreos.

The urge to follow, to demand answers to the teeming questions ricocheting in my brain, was so strong I clenched my gut against the power of it.

I stayed put, forcing rationality over impulse. I had business to take care of, conference calls to make. And yet somewhere on that endless to-do list the looming issue of our agreement ticked louder.

An agreement I'd lately found myself re-examining with growing dissatisfaction.

Restlessness drove me to my feet. At the bar, I poured myself a cognac and tossed it back, hoping the bracing heat would knock some sense into me. All it did was emphasise the expanding hollow inside me and quicken this alien need demanding satisfaction.

Setting the glass down, I started to walk back to my seat—and then, unsurprised, I found myself moving towards the back of the plane.

After my soft knock elicited no response I turned the

door handle. Lamps were dimmed, the window shades drawn, but still I saw them. Both asleep.

One with small, chubby arms thrown above his head in innocent abandon.

My son. My world.

The other curled on her side with one arm braced protectively over Andreos and the other draped over her belly.

My wife.

But not for much longer. Unless I took steps to do something about it.

Resolution slid home like a key in a lock I didn't even realise needed opening. Now I did—now the possibility of *more* beckoned with a promise I didn't want to deny.

Shaking out a light throw, I tucked it over both of them, then stepped back.

Calypso made a distressed sound in her sleep, an anxious twitch marring her brow for a second before it smoothed out and her breathing grew steady.

Was her stomach still bothering her? I frowned as that niggling returned.

My hand clenched over the door handle.

Were her secrets disturbing her sleep? Could that be the last stumbling block I needed to overcome to make this marriage real? If so, could I live with it?

The breath locked in my lungs was released, along with the bracing realisation that, regardless of what the secret was, it needn't get in our way. If she was prepared not to let it.

Very much aware that several things hung in the balance, I stepped out, shut the door behind me and returned to the living room. But through all my strategising and counter-strategising my resolution simply deepened.

My grandfather had sacrificed and nearly lost everything in his dealings with one Petras.

But perhaps it was time to draw a line underneath all that, let acrimony stay in the past where it belonged.

Perhaps it was time to strike yet another bargain.

A more permanent one.

Thailand was magical.

Or as magical as a place could be when I knew that dark shadows crept ever closer. Knew that my stolen time was rapidly dwindling away.

It marred my ability to enjoy fully the sheer magnificence of our tropical paradise except on canvas, with the paints Axios had supplied me with, which conversely helped in keeping my true state under wraps for a little longer.

The discomfort in my abdomen which he had erroneously assumed was my period kept him from the jaw-droppingly stunning master suite of our Bangkok villa at night. And when we were required to make an appearance together at one of the many events marking the successful merger of Xenakis Aeronautics and a major Thai-owned airline he was painfully solicitous, showering me with the kind of attention that made the tabloid headlines screech with joy.

The kind that made my heart swell with a foolish longing that I knew would make the inevitable break all the more agonising.

The kind he'd showered me with over the last few weeks but that now came with a speculative look in his eyes. As if he was trying to solve a puzzle. As if he was trying to make our situation *work*.

But my guilt at the subterfuge was nothing compared to the grief tearing my heart to shreds at the thought of leaving Andreos.

When, after four days in Bangkok, Axios announced that we were relocating to Kamala in Phuket for the remaining three days, for a delayed honeymoon, I knew I couldn't hide from my feelings any longer.

I was in love with Axios.

Even knowing he didn't feel the same couldn't diminish the knowledge that I'd been falling since that night on the balcony. Since I'd agreed to *for now*. But, contrarily, accepting my true feelings meant I couldn't in good conscience burden him or my precious baby with the battle ahead.

I was in love with my husband. And to spare him our marriage had to end.

Tucked inside the bamboo shelter of a rainforest shower, I gave in to the silent sobs tearing my heart to pieces, letting the warm spray wash my tears away. When I was wrung out, I carefully disguised the tell-tale signs of my distress with subtle make-up before leaving the suite.

In bare feet and a floaty white dress that whispered softly around my body, I approached the sound of infant giggles, a deep, sexy voice and the playful splash of water.

Axios was enjoying a lazy swim with Andreos. And, as much as I wanted to stop and frame the beautiful picture father and son made, so I could carry it in my heart, I knew my emotions were far too close to the surface to risk detection.

Instead I made my way past the pool and through the glass hallway that led to another stunning wing of the multi-tiered luxury villa. To the special place I'd discovered on our arrival.

The suspended treehouse was accessed by a heavy plank and rope bridge from the second level of the villa and a broad ladder from the level below. I took the walkway, enjoying the swaying movement that made me feel as if I was dancing on air, and entered the wide space laid out with polished wooden floors, wide rectangular windows and a roped-off platform that gave magnificent views of the Andaman Sea and the Bay of Bengal.

A riot of vivid colour brush-stroked the horizon, signalling the approach of night. Silently awed, and my breath held, I watched the colours settle into breathtaking layers of a purple and orange sunset.

I wasn't sure how long I stood there, lost in my turbulent thoughts, selfishly praying for things I couldn't have. And even when I sensed Axios's approach I didn't turn around, didn't give in to the raw need to fill my senses with the sight and sound of him.

Instead I gripped the rope barrier until my knuckles shrieked with just a fraction of the pain shredding my insides.

Whether he sensed my mood or not, Axios didn't speak either. But when he stopped behind me I felt the intensity of his presence. And when he slid an arm around my waist and engulfed me in the poignant scents of father and son I couldn't help the scalding tears that prickled my eyes.

With a soft moan I sagged into his hold, and the three of us stood on the platform, staring at the horizon as the bright orange ball of the sun dipped into the sea and a blanket of stars started to fill the sky.

'Come,' he said eventually, his voice low and deep. 'The chef is almost done preparing dinner. Let's go put our son to bed, hmm?'

Throat tight with locked emotion, I nodded, making sure to avoid his probing gaze as we made our back into the villa. After putting a dozing Andreos in his cot, we retraced our steps to the open terrace, where a candlelit dinner had been laid out.

There, Axios pulled out a chair and I sat, my stomach in knots and my heart bleeding, as I looked at the face of the man I was hopelessly in love with.

The man I could never have.

Theos mou, she was gorgeous.

The breath that had stalled in my lungs fought to emerge as I watched candlelight dance over her face and throat. Even the veil of melancholy shrouding her didn't detract from the captivating mix of fire and calm I wanted to experience for a very long time.

For ever.

Our three-course dinner had passed in stilted conversation, and our appetites had been non-existent. She'd refused dessert and I'd downed my aromatic espresso in one go.

But it was time.

Business pressures had forced this conversation to the back burner for the last four days. It was time to lay my cards on the table.

'About the divorce you requested: I would like to renegotiate…'

A vice tightened my sternum when wild panic flared in her eyes. The hand resting on the table began to tremble and she snatched it away, tucking it into her lap as she exhaled sharply. 'What do you mean, "renegotiate"? You gave me your word!'

For the first time I felt a visceral need to take it all back, to smash it to pieces and rebuild something new, something lasting from the rubble created from greed and blind lust. Because there was something more here. This…*distance* between us had cemented my belief that this wasn't just sex. That I'd fallen deeper, farther than even my imagination could fathom. Perhaps even into that dimension where Calypso could exist.

The thought of that ending…of never experiencing it or her at some point in the future…twisted in something close to agony inside me.

The state was further evidenced by the quiet panic this very argument was fuelling inside me—the fine trembles coursing through my body, taunting me with the possibility that this might be the one deal that eluded me. That my actions last year and since finding her on Bora Bora might have doomed me in her eyes. The very thought that I might fail where I'd succeeded at everything else. Everything that mattered…

No.

'I know what I promised, but I no longer think it's—'

'No!'

She surged to her feet, and the trembling in her hand

seemed transmitted to her body as eyes steeped in turmoil centred on mine. But when she spoke her voice was firm, the most resolute I'd ever heard her. And that only twisted the knife in deeper. Because I sensed a dynamic shift in her the like of which I'd never experienced before.

She seemed to falter for a moment, her hand sliding to her stomach, before she shook her head. 'You made a promise, Axios, and I'm going to have to insist you deliver on that promise.'

That gesture...

'Tell me why, Calypso. Give me a reason why you won't even hear me out,' I challenged, feeling the ground slip away beneath my feet even as I rose and faced her across the dinner table.

'Why?' he grated again when words failed to emerge from my strangled throat in time to answer his question.

His features were changing from a determined sort of cajoling to frighteningly resolute.

'Are you pregnant?' he added hoarsely, and there was a blaze of what looked like hope in his eyes as they dropped to my stomach.

'What? No, I'm not pregnant,' I blurted, dropping my hand.

Was that disappointment on his face?

'Can we take a breath and discuss this rationally?' he asked.

The desire to do just that—to let him talk me into dreaming about an impossible future—was so heart-wrenchingly tempting it took the sharp bite of my nails into my palm to stop agreement spilling from my lips.

'No. I'm all talked out, Axios. All I want now is action. For you to stick to your word and…and let me go.'

His grey eyes went molten for a handful of seconds before his jaw clenched tight. 'Why? We've proved in the last few weeks that we're completely compatible. As parents to Andreos. And in the bedroom.'

Desperately, I shook my head. 'We…we can love Andreos as much together as apart. As for the bedroom…it's just sex. Basing a marriage on it is delusional.'

'I beg to differ. The kind of compatibility we have is unique. Don't be so dismissive of it. Besides, how would you know? I'm the only lover you've ever had,' he tossed in arrogantly.

And he would be the only one for me. 'That still doesn't mean I want to give up everything for the sake of—'

A throat clearing on the edge of the terrace interrupted me. Sophia, now Andreos's official nanny, had travelled with us to Thailand, and she looked supremely nervous.

'What is it?' Axios demanded.

'There's a call from Switzerland for Kyria Xenakis. They say they've been trying to reach you.'

I felt the blood draining from my face as Axios frowned. *Dr Trudeau, tired of waiting for me to contact him.*

'Tell them I'll call back tomorrow,' I said hastily.

The second Sophia hurried away, Axios's gaze sharpened on me. 'Why are you getting a call from Switzerland?'

'I still have business there,' I replied, hoping he'd let it go.

For a terse moment I thought he'd push, but then he sighed. 'What were you going to say before? For the sake of what, Calypso?'

For the sake of unrequited love.

Mercifully, the words remained locked deep inside me, the only hint spilling out in my strained voice as I fought to remain upright, to fight for this vital chance to do this on my own terms.

'I can't—I don't *want* anything long-term. I want to be free.'

To fight for the chance to return whole. Even to dream of starting again with a clean slate.

Hope dried up as Ax's face turned ashen, his eyes darkening with something raw and potent. Something I wasn't sure I wanted to decipher, because it resembled the helpless yearning inside me.

But that couldn't be. Axios not only hated what my father had done to him, he despised what my family had done to his grandfather. I was the last person he could be contemplating hitching himself to for the long term. Which meant that whatever his proposal was it still had an end date. That even if Dr Trudeau had a sliver of hope for me I might not have a chance with Ax.

Nonetheless, temptation buffeted me until I had to hold on to the edge of the table to keep from falling into it.

'Free to live your life? What about our *son*, Calypso?' he demanded scathingly, his voice ragged. 'Do you intend to drag him along on another freedom jaunt? Are you so blinkered to his needs that you would rip him from me to satisfy your own needs?'

'Of course not!'

The searing denial was the final thread holding my emotions together. I felt the hot slide of tears and could do nothing to stop it. So I stood there, my world going into one final free fall, and set the words I despised but *needed* to say spilling free.

'He…he's happy in Athens. He's a Xenakis. You love him. He belongs with you. You can…' *Keep him. Love him. The way I might not be able to.*

The final words dried in my throat, the final selfless act of handing over my precious son unwilling to be given voice. But still he *knew*.

Knew and condemned me absolutely for it.

Brows clamped in horror, he stared at me. 'Are you—?' He stopped, shook his head in abject disbelief. 'You're leaving him behind? Your quest for freedom is so great that you intend to completely abandon your son?'

His voice was bleak, his eyes pools of bewilderment.

'Or it is something else, Calypso? Is it me? Have I

not proved I can be a good husband, provide for you and our son?'

There was my chance. Say no and this would be over. Tell him he'd failed me and it would be done. But I couldn't. Because even if he didn't love me, he hadn't failed me.

'Please, Axios—'

'Please what?' he asked urgently, stalking around the table towards me. 'Make it easier for you to walk away from your child? From me?'

His chest rose and fell in uncharacteristic agitation, his eyes dark, dismal.

'I watched my grandfather's world crumble around him. You want me to let you do the same to mine?' he rasped jaggedly.

I squeezed my eyes shut. 'Please don't say that.'

'Why not?' he demanded, his expression hardening. 'You want easy? Let me make it simple for you. Take one step out through the front door and you will never set eyes on Andreos again. I will make it my mission to erase your name from his life. It will be as if you never even existed.'

Choked tears clogged my throat and my world turned inside out with sorrow.

'You would do that? Really?'

He hesitated, one hand rising to glide roughly over his mouth and jaw before he shook his head. 'Make me understand, Calypso. What could possibly be out there that you won't get with me? What could be more important to you than to care for our child? To watch him grow and thrive under our care?'

I pressed my lips together, the agony of keeping the naked truth locked inside me so it wouldn't stain Andreos killing me. 'My...my freedom. I want what I've wanted for as long as I can remember, Axios. I want to be free.'

For the longest time he simply stared in stark disbelief. Then his breath shuddered out. And with it the last of the bewilderment in his eyes. Now he saw how set I was on bringing this to an end, his jaw clenched in tight resolution.

'Is that your final decision?' he grated.

My balled fist rose from the table, rested on my abdomen and the possible time bomb ticking inside me. 'Yes. It is.'

'Very well. You'll hear from my lawyers before the week is out.'

My breath strangled to nothing. *It was over. Just like that?*

'Axios—'

'No!' His hand slashed through the air. 'There's no room for bargaining.'

And in that moment, presented with his bleak verdict, I felt the words simply tumble out. 'I'm sick, Axios. I have a lump…in my cervix.'

He froze, his eyes widening with shock as he stumbled back a step. 'What?' he whispered, his face ashen.

'I suspected it last year—a few weeks before we married. The doctor in Switzerland who confirmed I was pregnant also confirmed the presence of the lump. My…my grandmother died of cervical cancer—'

'Why have you waited this long for treatment?' he railed.

'Andreos. I wanted to make sure he was safe. And loved.'

He went even paler, his eyes growing pools of horror and disbelief. 'You've known this…you've carried this for a year…and you didn't tell me?' he rasped, almost to himself as he gripped his nape with a shaky hand. 'Why? Because you were testing me? Because I let you down? Because you don't trust me?'

No! Because I love you. Because I can't let you both watch me die.

'Because I didn't want to put Andreos through what might happen. He was a miracle, Ax. I couldn't…didn't know if I could carry him to term, but once I knew I was pregnant I knew I had to *try*.'

'You found out about the lump the same day you found out you were carrying Andreos?' he asked, his voice still stark.

I nodded. 'I just... I couldn't lose him, Ax. I couldn't risk a biopsy to find out whether my prognosis was the same as my grandmother's. But I agreed to frequent scans that wouldn't harm the baby. When the first one showed that the pregnancy was stopping the lump from growing—'

'You chose to stay pregnant,' he finished, awed disbelief in his voice.

I sniffed back tears and nodded again. 'You see, Andreos was a miracle in so many ways. Conceiving him bought me time, and once he was born... I just couldn't let him go.'

'But the lump is still there. It's causing you pain, isn't it?' he asked, even though the knowledge blazed in his eyes. 'That's why you touch your stomach. That's why you were unwell on the plane. And the timing of your return... That was your plan all along—to hand over Andreos and go off and fight this on your own?'

'Yes,' I answered simply. 'I've had one scan since Andreos was born. It showed a small growth rate. But it's... it's time for further tests. Axios, I watched my grandmother suffer in the last months of her life. I can't...*won't* put Andreos through that if that's what I'm facing. I *have* to leave. I would prefer it if you didn't fight me. But...what you said... about erasing me from his life—'

Axios cursed and shoved both hands through his hair. 'That was an idle threat. You'll always be his mother and he'll know you as such. He'll know your courage and what you did for him,' he intoned in a low, solemn voice.

At my sob of relief his lips firmed and he stared at me for an age. 'Andreos,' he said heavily, with a finality that struck real fear into me. 'He's the only reason you're doing this.'

It was a statement—as if he already knew the answer. He took a step back. Then another. Until an unpassable chasm yawned between us.

'Very well. If you've made your choice then so be it.'

I'd expected this to come, but still I stood in utter shock as Axios blazed one last searing look at me, then turned and stalked away.

Shock turned into numbing self-protection when, upon waking up alone in the master suite the next day, I learned from Sophia that Ax had left. That he'd left instructions for Andreos and I to return to Athens alone.

As if the staff knew things had changed drastically, from the moment we walked through the front door of the Athens villa the atmosphere seemed altered. The only one who thankfully remained oblivious was Andreos. Having mastered the art of rolling over, he was now determined to conquer sitting up in record time, and thus provided the only source of delight in the house.

In a bid to make the most of whatever time I had with him, before Ax returned, I all but banished poor Sophia as I greedily devoured every precious second.

Two days turned to three.

Then four.

And then came the news from the housekeeper that Ax was expected mid-afternoon.

The urge to delay my exit, to see his face one last time, pummelled me. But, knowing I couldn't delay the inevitable, I booked my flight to Switzerland. The bag I'd hastily packed while Andreos napped stood like a silent omen at the foot of my bed.

'The car's waiting, *kyria*,' Sophia informed me, her face wreathed in worry.

Unchecked tears streamed down my face as I leaned down and brushed my lips over Andreos' plump cheek. 'Promise me you'll look after him?' I managed through a clogged throat.

Sophia's anxious gaze searched mine. 'I… I promise. But, *kyria*—'

I shook my head, knowing I'd break down if this was prolonged. 'That's good enough for me. Thank you, Sophia.'

Bag in hand, I hurried out, flew down the stairs to the waiting car. Blind with tears, I didn't register his presence until the car was pulling away.

'I will allow those tears for now, *pethi mou*. But for what comes next I'll need that formidable resilience I've come to know and adore.'

CHAPTER TEN

'AXIOS! WHAT…WHAT are you doing here?'

His face was as gaunt and ashen as the last time I'd seen it. But in his eyes purpose and determination blazed in place of horrified anguish.

Even so, the sight of him shook me, his presence unearthing a cascade of emotions through me.

When he didn't answer, when all he seemed to want was to absorb every inch of my face, I tried again. 'I thought you'd gone…that I'd never see you again.'

His chest heaved in a mighty exhalation. 'I had to go,' he replied gruffly.

Despair and disappointment slashed me wide open. 'Oh. I understand.'

He gave a grating self-deprecating laugh that was chopped off halfway through. '*Do* you? Do you understand how utterly useless and powerless I felt? How I had to walk away because I knew I'd failed you again?'

'What? Why would you—?'

'We will dissect that later. But for now…' my breath caught as his thumb brushed away my tears, '…it's tearing me apart to see these tears,' he grated roughly.

Which only made them fall harder.

'Andreos… Leaving him…that's tearing *me* apart.'

'Just Andreos?'

The question was deep and low. But heavy with unspoken emotions.

I lifted my gaze to find him watching me with hawk-like intensity, his eyes burning with a new light. One that made my insides leap.

'Ax…'

Before I could answer his hand seized mine, his eyes steadfast on me.

'Will you give me the chance to make things right, Ca-

lypso? Trust me just for a little while?' he demanded with
a hoarse plea.

About to answer, I paused as we pulled up at the private airstrip and stopped next to his plane. 'Axios, where
are we going?'

He alighted and held out his hand. I slid out of the car,
still in a daze, and didn't resist when he pulled me close.

'You've lived in fear for over a year, while bearing and
caring for our son. You've loved him unconditionally when
you could've taken a different option without judgement.
But you don't need to be alone in this. You never need to
be alone again,' he vowed.

The depth of his words made my heart pound with tentative hope. That hope turned to shock when I spotted the
middle-aged man standing at the door of the plane.

'Dr Trudeau...what are you...? What's he doing here?'
I asked Ax.

'He's here to help. As are the others.'

Taking my hand, he led me onto the plane. And my shock
tripled.

'Mama?' Seated amongst three other distinguished-looking men was my mother. When she smiled tremulously
and held out her arms a broken sob ripped through me as I
rushed forward and threw myself into her embrace.

'Your husband rightly felt that you should be surrounded
by those you love in your time of need.'

Did that include him?

Fearing I'd give myself away if I looked his way, I kept
my gaze on my mother.

'You should've told us, Callie.'

I shook my head. 'I couldn't risk not having Andreos.'

And that seemed to settle the matter with her. She nodded, then looked over my head. I didn't need the signal to
know that Ax was approaching.

'Let me introduce you, Calypso.'

Swiping my hand across my cheek, I composed myself

and stood. Besides Dr Trudeau, the three men were all doctors too, specialising in everything to do with the cervix.

'Your mother has been instrumental in providing details about your grandmother's condition. With your permission, we'll head to Dr Trudeau's clinic and start the tests.'

I gasped, my gaze finding Ax's. 'That's what you've been doing the last three days? Rounding up specialists?'

He nodded, that blaze burning brighter in his eyes. 'You are far too important, *yineka mou*. I'm leaving nothing to chance.'

I swayed. He caught me, held me tight.

After pinning me with his gaze for several seconds, he glanced around. 'We're about to take off,' he said. 'I would like to talk to my wife in private, so I trust you can all amuse yourselves?' At their agreement, he turned to me. 'Calypso?'

I nodded, a million hopes and dreams cascading through my brain as I followed him into the master suite.

He waited long enough for me to be seated and buckled in before stalking over to the drinks cabinet. Dazedly, I watched him pour a glass of cognac, grimace, and pour a thimbleful into a second glass. Walking over, he handed the smaller drink to me.

'A small sip won't hurt,' he stated gruffly, almost pleadingly.

With another befuddled nod I accepted it, took the tiniest sip and shuddered my way through swallowing it down. As the spirit warmed my insides, another sensation filtered through. But the joy bubbling beneath my skin fizzled out when Axios sank onto his knees before me.

'Was it just about Andreos?' he asked starkly. 'Were you leaving only because of him or did I feature anywhere in your thoughts?'

'Ax—'

'I know I didn't give you the wedding of your dreams, or make the time after that palatable. But did I drive you away completely, Calypso?'

There was a layer of self-loathing in his voice that propelled me to grip his hand. 'I just didn't want to burden you—'

'Burden me? You're my *wife*!'

'One who was a stranger when we exchanged vows! I didn't know how…what you would do…'

'What I would *do*? What other option was there besides seeking medical—' His curse ranged through the room. 'Did you think I'd exploit you the way your father did your mother?'

'I didn't know then.'

For an eternity he simply stared at me. '*Then?* Does that mean you know different now?' he asked, his voice awash with hope and his eyes alight with a peculiar kind of desperation that tore through me.

I didn't realise my nails were digging into the sofa until he set his hand on mine, stilling my agitation. I wanted to cling to him. *Theos* did I want to. But the fear of fanning false hope, triggering another torrent of might-have-beens that would further shatter my heart, stopped me.

Discarding his drink, he took both my hands in his. 'Tell me, please, if I have a chance with you. No matter what happens I intend to stay and fight this thing along with you. But after that—'

I pressed a hand to his lips. 'We might not have a future,' I whispered. 'It wasn't just about Andreos. I didn't want to put *you* through that.'

His fingers tightened around mine, and when his eyes fused with mine, I felt the live wire of his desperation.

'That's why you tried to leave me again this time?'

Suspecting I wouldn't be able to speak around the lump in my throat, I nodded.

A hoarse breath shuddered out of him. 'I never thought I'd be so relieved at such a reason for being dumped.'

He stopped abruptly, caught my face between his hands and blazed me a look so intense my insides melted.

'I love you, Calypso. I fell in love with your defiance in Bora Bora. Fell in love with you when I saw your love for our son. I adored your strength when I watched that video. Watching you paint, seeing your talent…awed me. Despite the odds, you have fought and continue to fight for what you want. One day our son will grow up to learn what an inspiration you are. He'll watch you and know he has the best mother in the world.'

The tears came free and unchecked. 'Oh, Ax…'

'Getting the call that you'd gone the morning after our wedding altered something inside me. I wasn't ready to admit it, but I knew I'd failed you. That I'd failed myself. Your agreeing to take a leap with me felt like a second chance. And with every breath I vow to make it worth your while.'

'Was…was this what you were going to tell me in Thailand?'

'Yes. I knew I was in love with you. I planned on begging you to give our marriage a chance. But—'

'But I chopped you off at the knees before you could lay out everything my own heart and soul wanted to tell you. That I loved you and would've given anything to remain your wife.'

He froze. 'Say that again, please?' he begged.

'I love you, too, Ax. Even before the possibility of Andreos and the possibility of love I was drawn to you. Something inside me made me put *you* at the top of my bucket list. I was always going to come back, even if only for a short time, because my heart knew I belonged to you. And these last few weeks have felt like a heaven I didn't want to leave. I may have been devastated when you left me the morning after our wedding, but watching you leave me in Thailand…'

He closed his eyes for a single moment. 'I knew I was making a mistake even before I got on the helicopter after our wedding night. But when I left this time I knew I was coming straight back. That nothing would stop me. Because you're my heart, *pethi mou*. My very soul.'

To cement that vow he slanted his lips over mine, kissed me until we were both breathless.

'Tell me again,' I commanded.

His eyes burned with feeling. 'I love you. With all that I am and everything in between.'

He kissed me again as the plane sped down the runway and soared into the sky.

When I broke away to look out of the window, he gently caught my chin in his hand. 'What is it?'

'Andreos.'

A warm smile split Ax's face. 'He has Sophia and a dozen other staff curled around his plump little fingers. They will take care of him until we send for him in the morning. He's our little miracle and we will fight this thing together. All three of us. For now, you will let me take care of you. You will allow me the privilege of helping to make you better. Please, my love?'

I nodded, but still hesitated. 'What if it's too late? What if they can't…?'

He slid his thumb across my lips, silencing my doubts. 'Whatever happens we face it together. For better or worse, you have me for life. I will never leave your side and I will never fail you again.'

His words unfurled my joy. This time I wasn't alone. I had my precious baby and the husband of my heart. I intended to fight with everything I had for the chance to ensure my days were blessed with nothing but love, health and happiness.

At cruising altitude, Axios swung me into his arms and strolled to the bed. I curled my arms around his neck and looked into molten eyes blazing with love.

'I love you, Calypso,' he said again, as if saying the words filled him with as much happiness as it filled my heart.

'*Se agapo*, Axios.

EPILOGUE

A year later

'WHAT ARE YOU DOING?'

'Starting on your payback,' Axios drawled, striding across the master bedroom in Agistros to lay me down on the king-sized bed before trailing his lips over my shoulder to the sensitive area beneath my earlobe.

'What?' I gasped, delightful shivers running through me at the wickedness he evoked.

'You owe me a full pregnancy experience. I can't think of a better time to start than now. I want to experience it all—from morning sickness to the moment our baby enters the world.'

I made a face. 'Morning sickness isn't very sexy.'

He dropped a kiss on the corner of my mouth. 'Perhaps not. But I made you a promise to be here for the good as well as the bad, *eros mou*. So I will be on hand to hold your hair when you throw up. To massage your feet when the weight of our child tires you. And everything you need in between. If that's what you want too?' he asked, hope brimming in his voice.

I curled my arms around his neck. 'More than anything in the world.'

The operation to remove what had turned out to be a benign lump in my cervix six months ago had been a resounding success, with every trace of it gone and quarterly scans showing it hadn't returned.

Today Dr Trudeau had given us the all-clear to try for another baby—a statement Axios seemed determined to capitalise on immediately. And with a doting grandmother to help care for Andreos, in the form of my mother, life couldn't have been better. Her decision to leave my father hadn't been easy, but I'd supported her. Yiannis Petras hadn't resisted for long, busy as he was with frittering away his millions on one bad investment after another.

Ax groaned. 'Don't cry. It rips me up when you do.'

I laughed tremulously. 'Oh, God, then prepare yourself. Because I'm very hormonal during pregnancy.'

'Hmm, I will have to think of ways to counteract that.'

'What did you have in mind?'

'Why, endless seduction, of course. I can think of nothing better than making love to my beautiful wife while she nurtures our baby in her womb.'

More tears flowed. With another groan, he sealed his lips to mine—most likely to distract me. It worked. Within minutes I was naked and gasping, lost in the arms of my true love.

And when, at the height of feeling, he looked deep into my eyes and whispered, 'I love you, Calypso,' he went one better and kissed my tears away.

The power of him moving inside me, possibly planting his seed inside me, triggered fresh tears.

I was still emotional when our breaths cooled. When he pulled me close and whispered in my ear.

'Our adventure is only just beginning, *eros mou*. And I couldn't have wished for a better partner at my side to experience it all but you, Calypso Xenakis.'

'Nor I, you, my love,' I returned, with every ounce of the love I held in my heart.

* * * * *

BRIDE
BEHIND THE
BILLION-DOLLAR
VEIL

CLARE CONNELLY

For Penny Jordan,
whose beautiful, sensual, romantic Mills & Boon novels
have given me hours and hours of romance-reading
pleasure, not to mention a certainty that
dreams really can come true.

PROLOGUE

Twelve years ago

'LISTEN TO ME.'

Thanos looked up at his brother, barely able to see him through the fog of rage and disbelief that shrouded his every thought and feeling.

'We will get it back.'

Thanos gripped the pen in his hand, returning his attention to the imperious black line at the bottom of the contract. A contract for the sale of Petó, the company their grandfather, Nicholas Stathakis, had built from the ground up. The company Thanos had learned to operate at his grandfather's knee. The company that meant everything to him.

'No.' He dropped the pen to the boardroom table, extending to his full six and a half feet, striding across the room with a ramrod-straight back.

He knew his half-brother was watching him, and he knew Leonidas was feeling the same sense of outrage and disbelief. Only Leonidas was somehow better at processing this. He was calm, outwardly, even as their world crumbled around them, whereas Thanos wanted to torch the building on his way out.

He braced his palms on the floor-to-ceiling glass, looking out on downtown Athens. All of this they had once commanded.

All of this, their father had destroyed.

'We will get it back, Thanos,' Leo repeated, with urgency. 'But we must sell it for now.'

Nausea split Thanos's side. Sell it? Sell the jewel in their grandfather's business empire? Because their father had tied the company to the mafia?

Thanos ground his teeth together, locking his jaw intently. He wanted to say there was another way. He wanted to fix this. To make it better. And suddenly he was eight years old again, watching his mother walk away. He was eight years old and knowing himself to be the instrument of a family's breakdown. He was eight years old and everything in this world was his fault. But this was so much worse.

Nicholas had trusted Thanos with Petó, and he'd been careless. He'd trusted Dion Stathakis—their father—when he should have seen what was happening right beneath his nose.

What could he do now?

'I cannot bear to think of someone else running his business.' Thanos's voice cracked with the strength of his emotions.

'Do you think I can?' Leonidas growled, and Thanos turned to face his brother then, their eyes meeting with complete understanding. This situation was wrong. Wrong in every way.

Leonidas softened his expression a little. 'But this is the best possibility we could have hoped for. Kosta Carinedes wants Petó. His plan to fold it into his own logistics empire are sound, so too the rebranding he envisages. Petó will live on, Thanos, and it will continue to prosper.'

Thanos's stomach clenched. 'But not by our hands.'

'No.' Leonidas's eyes glittered in acknowledgement of that.

'I will not live in a world where this company is not mine, Leonidas. One day, one way or another, Petó will be ours again.'

Leonidas nodded slowly but Thanos wasn't satisfied. 'Swear it to me, Leo. Swear to me now that we will right this wrong—and all our father's wrongs—even if it takes us the rest of our lives.'

Leonidas expelled a soft, low breath. 'I swear it. But you must sign the contract now.'

Thanos nodded, knowing his brother to be correct. Still, he glared at the paper as though it were a writhing tangle of snakes at his feet. He lifted the pen with difficulty and hovered it over the page, his perennial tan paled to straw in that moment.

He scrawled his name on the page and silently swore to himself, once more, that this wasn't the end.

This wasn't over—not by a long shot. Petó was a part of his blood and his DNA, and it always would be.

CHAPTER ONE

ALICE TOOK A full ten seconds to remember who she was and what she was doing. For a moment, the appearance of one man had managed to skittle everything from her mind: her job, her responsibilities; the mountain of medical bills she had in her handbag waiting for her to wade through at lunch time; the credit card that was almost maxed, and the fact this temp position would be finishing in two weeks, meaning she'd yet again need to find a job; her mother's worsening condition and Alice's inability to find a proper long-term solution for her care. Every second of every day those considerations pursued her, but for a moment, with the sound of the elevator doors opening to the top floor of the glass and steel monolith that was Stathakis Towers, she found the chatter of her mind was silenced and all she could do was stare.

Her almond-shaped brown eyes tracked his progress across the office, her pulse hammering her body from the inside out, the closer he came to her desk.

Thanos Stathakis was here. In his office. In Manhattan.

Despite the fact she'd temped for the man for five months, she hadn't once laid eyes on him, outside the endless stream of photos that littered the Internet. Photos of him invariably in a state of undress, relaxed, surrounded by a bevy of supermodels and actresses, partying, drinking, living the kind of life Alice could barely imagine.

The kind of life her father had also adored. The thought should have been sobering, but it wasn't. She was almost mesmerised by the sight of him in the flesh.

Thanos Stathakis wasn't just a man.

He was a legend.

His success in business was renowned—alongside his brother, he'd turned a crumbling business into an empire once more, like a powerful phoenix rising from the ashes of scandal and failure. But it was more than that. Thanos Stathakis was unlike anyone she'd ever known—in person, it was easy to see why the world's media was obsessed with him.

If there was a mould for tall, dark and handsome then Thanos had certainly broken it. He was broad-shouldered, slim-hipped, with strength and charisma in every long stride of his powerful legs. Unlike the photographs she'd seen of him, he wore a suit now, navy blue with a crisp white shirt that only served to emphasise the depth of his tan. His eyes were caramel-coloured and rimmed in thick, curling black lashes, so he looked almost as though he'd worked overtime with a mascara wand. He was the very image of the billionaire magnate she knew him to be, with the exception of his hair, which was somehow wild and untamed, as though he'd stepped straight off a speedboat on the Riviera and into the doors of this Manhattan monolith.

She stared at him because she couldn't help it, and even when his eyes jerked to hers, she didn't look away. Not for several long, compelling seconds.

His lips curled in what could have been a smile, or could have been derision, and then he stopped close enough to her desk for Alice to hold her breath.

'You're the temp?'

It was enough to jolt her back into the present—and who she was to him. The temp! As if she hadn't been keeping his life running seamlessly these past five months, since his regular assistant had been on leave.

'Alice, yes.'

'Alice.' He nodded, as if it didn't matter, and in a way that made her absolutely certain he'd have forgotten her name again in an instant.

Except he didn't turn and walk away. He continued to stare at her in a way that set her pulse racing, so she had to forcibly remind herself that he generally occupied himself with glamorous models, that there would be nothing in her somewhat plain face to cause him to stare like this. No, he must have another reason for looking into her eyes as though he'd seen her before.

He blinked then, like severing a thread, his dark lashes closing against his cheeks, forming perfect fans for the briefest of seconds before he opened his eyes and speared her with his intent gaze.

'Print the file on P & A Industries. I have a meeting in ten minutes.'

He spun on his heel and stalked towards the office to her left—an office she'd only been into once or twice since taking up this role. It was his office, and he hadn't been in New York the whole time she'd been at Stathakis Corp.

It was the final straw in rousing Alice back to reality.

Years ago, she'd looked at another man with that same deer-in-the-headlights sense of drowning and she'd come to regret it hugely. She'd fallen for Clinton's practised flirtation, hook, line, and sinker, and learned a valuable lesson—she wouldn't fall for another man's easy charms, ever again. And Thanos Stathakis was not in the realm of Clinton. Thanos was…bigger and somehow more dangerous.

She had no business staring at him as though he were the second coming.

She pushed back from her desk, following behind him. 'A meeting, sir?'

He opened the door, moving into the enormous space without turning the lights on, so it was Alice who flicked the switch and brought the overheads to life.

Like the rest of the building, this large room had a Scandinavian feel, with light timber furniture, pale walls and a cream carpet. The artwork was minimalist, the light fittings modern and striking. His desk sat against one wall with a state-of-the-art computer atop it and a piece of expensive art behind it; across the room, framed perfectly by floor-to-ceiling windows that showcased an incredible view of Manhattan, was a boardroom table large enough to accommodate twenty-two people.

'Mmm…' He made a noise of agreement, shrugging out of his jacket and placing it carelessly across the back of his chair. The movement only served to highlight the breadth of his shoulders and arms that looked to have been sculpted by God's own hand. Her lips parted and she stared—she knew she was staring but almost for the first time in Alice's life her self-control was nowhere to be seen.

'You know,' he drawled with a sinful smile pulling at those impossibly strong lips. 'That thing where people come to the same place at the same time to discuss a pre-arranged schedule of topics?'

She blinked, embarrassment shifting through her, and she was glad then that she didn't blush easily. 'I know what a meeting is,' she said softly, the fact he was teasing her setting off a thousand fires in the depth of her soul. 'I just meant it's not in your diary.'

Something flashed in his expression—triumph? Wariness?—and then he nodded curtly. 'It was arranged this morning. Kosta Carinedes happens to be in New York so I thought it was a good opportunity to…see him.'

Alice nodded. 'Fine. How many people will be at the meeting?' She was already slipping back into her professional groove, thinking of how quickly she could alert the catering team to send up refreshments, how many copies of documents she'd need to print.

'Just him and me. And you,' he added, as an afterthought. 'In case I need anything throughout.'

She nodded. 'I'll have the kitchen send up some sandwiches—'

'That won't be necessary. Just coffee. Strong and black.'

Alice nodded again. She remembered the handover notes that had been left for her, which described in detail how Thanos Stathakis liked to take his coffee.

'Fine.'

'You'll print the file?'

She nodded. 'Yes, sir.'

She was almost at the door when his voice stilled her. 'Alice?'

She spun around to face him once more, catching a slight frown on those sculpted lips. 'I don't like being called "sir".'

'I'm sorry, si—'

'Thanos,' he insisted.

'Thanos.' His name was bewitching on her lips. She said it and immediately wanted to say it again and again. She said it mentally as she printed the files he'd requested, and as she made a pot of Greek coffee, carrying it carefully into his office. He was on the phone when she entered. She busied herself arranging the documents in place, trying to ignore the sensation of heat that travelled the length of her spine as he hurled words in his native Greek, the words like a sunset after a storm, impossibly bright and intriguing.

She retreated from his office without noticing the way

his eyes followed her, scooping up her laptop and a bottle of water, before making her way to the boardroom table.

When she entered this time, he was no longer on the phone. 'My brother sometimes thinks I cannot tie my shoes without him,' he said, but the words were tinged with amusement. He stood, stretching his arms over his head, yawning and smothering it with his hand.

This was a man who was supremely confident. How Alice envied him that! She had worked hard to appear strong and put-together, to look as though she'd outgrown the wounds of her past, but she knew she came across as cold and aloof most of the time, even when that strength came out of a need to protect a too vulnerable heart.

It seemed unlikely Thanos had ever felt a hint of self-doubt in his life.

Except it wasn't just confidence that oozed out of him. It was determination. She felt it emanating from him in waves and it held her in her spot for a moment, even as she knew she should go back to her own desk, to be waiting for Kosta Carinedes when he arrived.

'Is there anything I should know before this meeting?' she heard herself asking instead, reluctant to take herself from his office.

'No. It is a simple matter. He has something I want; I intend to buy it back today.'

The words were clipped, his expression business-like. 'I anticipate the meeting will conclude quickly enough.'

'Fine.' Alice checked everything was in order and without looking in Thanos's direction—perhaps out of fear that she might not easily be able to look away again—she returned to her own desk.

Not five minutes later, the lift doors pinged open and a man emerged. Older than Alice had expected, with a lined face and a kind smile, his hair was greying, his body a little stooped, dressed in a suit that looked bespoke with expensive leather shoes.

'Stathakis?' he said as he approached Alice's desk.

'This way, sir.' She stood, gesturing towards Thanos's office. At the door, she knocked twice and then pushed it inwards, stepping back to allow the older Greek man to precede her.

From her vantage point, she saw the way Thanos's body momentarily tensed and the determination she'd observed moments earlier was back, a palpable force in the room.

Kosta spoke first, in Greek, and Thanos returned the greeting in their native tongue before switching to English.

'Alice, my assistant, doesn't speak Greek.'

Kosta threw a look over his shoulder and then shrugged. 'Perhaps you can tell me why I have been summoned here?'

Even that was a telling statement. Thanos Stathakis had the power to summon just about anyone to his office, and it was a power he had flexed this morning.

'You don't know?'

Kosta shrugged his shoulders. 'I presume it has something to do with P & A?'

Thanos's stare was direct. 'Yes.' He gestured towards the table. 'Please, take a seat.'

The old man hesitated for a moment and then did as he'd been bid, moving to a chair on one side of the table and settling himself into it. Alice watched as he lifted the coffee to his lips, sipping it, then returning the cup to the saucer at the same time Thanos took a seat at the head of the table.

'You've received my offer?' That confidence was back, brimming and blinding. Alice stared covertly at Thanos as she settled herself at the end of the boardroom table, flipping her laptop open and pulling up a blank Word document to take notes.

'My lawyer advised me of it,' the older man remarked with another shrug of his shoulders, in what Alice was recognising as a trademark gesture.

'And?'

Kosta expelled a soft breath. 'Did my silence not answer your question?'

Alice jerked her gaze to Thanos on autopilot. He didn't visibly react to Kosta's question. 'Silence can mean many things.'

Kosta's lips compressed. 'Not in this instance.'

'You want to sell.' It was a question and yet Thanos delivered it more as a statement, one that was laced with iron.

'To the right buyer, yes.' Kosta took another sip of his coffee.

Alice hovered her hands over the keyboard.

'You are aware that your business contains part of my business?'

Kosta's eyes narrowed. 'I bought Petó from you and your brother many years ago. Whatever claim you had to it transferred to me on that day.'

From where Alice was sitting, she had a full view of the table. She saw the way Thanos moved his hand to beneath the table, and the way he squeezed his fist so tight his knuckles glowed white.

'But you must dispose of your business,' Thanos said slowly, carefully, with no hint of emotion in the words.

'Why must I?'

'Because you are not married, you have no children, no grandchildren, and because P & A is a family company. You will not list it publicly, nor would you wish it to be broken up and sold off after your death.'

Alice bit down on her lip, sympathy for the older man rushing through her. How strange it must be to have someone refer to your mortality in such a cavalier fashion!

'The fate of my company is not your concern.'

Thanos's eyes narrowed and Alice's heart gave a little lurch. As handsome as he was at any time, like this—formidable and businesslike—he was impossibly fascinating.

Thanos held Kosta's gaze for a long moment, a muscle jerking in his jaw that only Alice was in a position to see. 'Your profit has been down these past two years.'

'It's a tough economy.'

'No, it isn't,' Thanos pushed ruthlessly. 'You're losing market share and you don't know how to get it back.'

Kosta's eyes glinted. 'You think I came here to be lectured?'

Thanos didn't apologise, nor did he back down. 'I'm not telling you anything you don't already know. If you do not act now, your once great business will fade away into insignificance. Thousands of people will lose their jobs. All because you are too stubborn to see what you must do.'

Kosta's rejection of that assertion was obvious. '*My* business. *My* problem.'

At this, Thanos straightened in his chair, his expression like flint. 'I might have agreed to sell Petó to you, but I never stopped thinking of it as mine. You rolled it into your business, which means I care about your business too. Sell me P & A and I will ensure your legacy is safe.'

Kosta let out a laugh of disbelief that had Alice slipping her gaze to focus on the older man's face. 'You think I would trust you with my company?'

'Why should you not?' It was a banal enough question, but Alice heard the undertone of steel and looked to Thanos once more. A tight smile was cracking his face but waves of anger were shifting off his frame.

'Because you are your father's son, and I will not have my family's legacy dragged through the mud.'

Alice sucked in a sharp breath, surprised at how offended she was by the scathing indictment. Thanos turned to face her, the noise apparently drawing his attention, and when their eyes locked, sympathy exploded inside her.

'I know you are not like him,' Kosta hastened to add, an apology inherent in the words. 'You are different. But the potential for scandal is the same.'

Thanos dipped his head forward, so Alice couldn't see how he reacted to this explanation.

'I cannot open my paper without seeing your photo,' Kosta continued. 'You drink too much, party too much, sleep with any woman who moves. Your reputation as the playboy prince of Europe is almost too mild for your excessive lifestyle.'

Thanos lifted his head, his face like a mask of iron. 'And what is my lifestyle to do with this? Do you think it affects my ability to run your company?'

'I think there is no one better than you,' Kosta contradicted. 'You have a head for business that I have always admired. Even when you were still a boy, following after your grandfather, watching him as though he were an idol brought to life, you had more nous than he and I in our little fingers.'

Alice wondered if Thanos felt pride then, if the compliment did anything to soften his response.

'I learned from the best,' Thanos conceded, finally.

'Yes. Nicholas was one of the best men I have ever known.' Kosta leaned forward, bracing his elbows on the table. 'I always respected him. Liked him. What your father did—'

That same muscle twisted in Thanos's cheek as he ground his teeth together. 'Is not relevant. I made my peace with it a long time ago.'

'Did you?' Kosta's look showed disbelief, but he didn't pursue that line of questioning. He sipped his coffee.

'Your grandfather and I were from a different genera-
tion. Things were different. Our parents, and us, we val-
ued family. Old-fashioned morals. We liked things to be
respectable. A handshake was as good as a contract.' Kosta
shook his head and Alice saw a spark of longing in his
eyes. 'The world is different now. Perhaps I am a relic,
with no place in it.' His eyes narrowed. 'But if you think
I'm going to see my company fall into the hands of a man
who regards womanising as a sport, then you know nothing about what this business means.'

Thanos held Kosta's gaze across the table. Neither man
faltered and Alice felt as if she was intruding on a deeply
personal moment.

'No one will work harder for P & A than I will,' Thanos promised, at length.

'That may be so,' Kosta agreed. 'But I will not sell it
to you.'

Alice swept her eyes shut for a moment, more invested
in the outcome of this meeting than she would have thought
possible.

'I don't intend to take no for an answer.'

'You don't like to hear no from anyone. It's part of why
you've been so successful in repairing the damage your
father did. But that does not change my answer. I will not
sell P & A to a man like you, Thanos Stathakis. Not for
twice what you're offering; not for anything. Not until
you've grown up.'

Alice flicked through the pile of bills, a half-eaten sandwich to her left. Her credit card had very little available
cash on it—it wouldn't come close to paying off her mother's latest hospitalisation.

Her heart squeezed as she remembered the sight of her
mother being rushed through the corridors, the blood clot

threatening her life, panic surging through Alice as she knew how close they were to the end.

But Jane Smart had defied all odds and survived—she remained in a coma, but she remained.

Alice flipped over to another bill, nausea filling her. It was too much. How could she ever manage to cover this?

She was so engrossed in her finances that she didn't hear the door to Thanos's office click open, nor did she hear his approach until he was practically on top of her.

Self-consciously, she laid her hand over the bills, aware that it barely covered the bright red paper demanding immediate payment.

'Did you need something, sir?'

He didn't correct her use of the formal title now. He was brooding. Thinking. Even more determined since Kosta had walked out of the office. 'What did you think of Kosta Carinedes?'

Alice was surprised by the question. She sat back in her chair a little, momentarily forgetting about her bills, and her lunch. 'In what way?'

'In any way. Did you perceive he was serious in his reasons for not wanting to sell to me?'

Alice captured her lower lip with her teeth, gnawing on it thoughtfully. 'I can't see why he would lie,' she said finally.

'No, nor can I. After all, the price I've offered is above the market rate of the company. He's a fool to walk away from it.'

'Perhaps he doesn't really want to sell?'

'He knows he must.' He shook his head, dragging a hand through his hair, throwing it into even greater disarray. 'He's just being stubborn.'

Alice nodded, turning back to her desk thoughtfully. After all, the older man had raised a valid point. Thanos had a reputation for seducing women left, right and centre. He was rarely without a date on his arm, and it didn't seem to be the same woman for long. He partied non-stop, but what did that matter? Everything he touched in a commercial sense turned to gold. Surely that was more important when it came to handing a business over?

'Maybe he'll change his mind,' she offered, lifting her gaze back to his face. He was staring out of the window, his expression unreadable.

'I don't think so.'

'Then you'll just have to change it for him,' she said quietly, turning back to the bills, flicking to the next one with a frown on her face, unaware of the way his eyes swivelled to follow her.

Thanos regarded this mild-mannered assistant thoughtfully. She was plain-spoken and unaffected. Unlike most of the women he dealt with, she wasn't going out of her way to flatter and please him. She was acting as though she barely noticed he was a man. It was unusual for him to come across a woman who didn't respond in a certain way.

And it was fascinating.

She was pretty, he supposed, in an understated way—though she also went to very little effort with her appearance. Her suit was old and boxy, hiding any curves she might have beneath too much fabric. Her hair was silky and luscious, long, he suspected, though it was impossible to know as she wore it pinned in a sensible, low bun at the nape of her neck. In fact, everything about her was sensible. Plain. Businesslike.

His eyes dropped lower, to hands that were sorting through a pile of papers—red, with *OVERDUE* marked at the top. And despite his own monumental problems, curiosity lifted inside him.

'What are you doing?' he asked.

She looked at him with a slight frown on her face, almost as though she thought he might have left.

'I'm catching up on some personal business. It's my lunch break.'

He looked at his watch. 'It's the end of the day.'

'I didn't have time to have it any earlier.' She said it as though she was worried he might be cross with her, as if she feared recriminations. That was unnecessary. Though she was only a temp, and he hadn't been to the New York office for almost a year, Thanos knew that Alice worked harder than most of the permanent executive support team. Her security card was frequently the last one swiped out at the end of the evening, and oftentimes the first one to appear on the staff list.

She worked long hours and, though his workload was nothing if not exhausting, she'd somehow managed to keep his business and personal life running like a well-oiled machine.

If he needed his jet fuelled up, he emailed Alice. Gifts organised, Alice. Anything done with his apartments? Alice. She oversaw all aspects of his life and yet they were only today meeting for the first time.

And he knew nothing about her.

Why did that bother him? He couldn't have said. Stathakis Corp employed thirty thousand people globally. One woman shouldn't have interested him like this.

And yet, he found himself propping his hip on the edge of her desk, and looking at the bills with more interest. She shuffled them self-consciously.

So he knew one thing about her.

She was a poor money manager. She had to be, given what the temp rates were for an executive assistant at this level. Sure, there was agency commission to come out of her salary packet, but regardless of that, her rate was generous.

'Did you need anything else, sir?'

She spoke without looking at him, but he detected a faint tremble in her fingertips as she filed the bills under some other papers, pointedly reaching for her sandwich.

He straightened, with a frown. 'No.' As he moved towards the door, his frown didn't ease.

'How long do you expect to be in New York?'

Her question caught him off-guard. Thanos never liked to be anywhere for long. He'd arrived in Manhattan a day earlier anticipating his business here would be wrapped up within twenty-four hours. Now he paused, with no idea when he'd be able to get out of town.

'I have no idea.'

Silence for a moment and then, 'So I'll see you tomorrow?'

He turned back to face her, and there was no warmth in her expression. In fact, he couldn't have said if she'd asked the question with curiosity or apprehension, but both sparked a ridiculous urge to laugh.

Instead, he nodded stiffly. 'Yes. Goodnight, Alice.'

CHAPTER TWO

'WHAT YOU NEED is to get married, Thanos.'

Leonidas's words came to Thanos as if through a thousand galaxies—crackly and distant. He jerked out of bed, completely naked, and strode through his penthouse apartment.

His brother's statement was exploding through his brain, like stardust and gold. He reached for the crystal decanter of Scotch and poured himself a generous measure, moving towards the grand piano and tapping a key lightly. Manhattan glistened beneath him, all shimmering lights and elaborate dreams.

This was the first time in years he'd been alone in this city. Usually, he called one of his past lovers—of which there were many here in the city—and enjoyed a night of unbridled, no-strings passion.

But the meeting with Kosta had left him inexplicably dissatisfied.

Thanos was a master at keeping his personal life separate from his private life. The fact he had a well-documented and active bachelor lifestyle was neither here nor there. He knew he was, unequivocally, the right person to take over P & A.

And beyond that, Petó deserved to come home.

'I know it's out of left field but have you actually passed out?' Leonidas's words were filled with humour.

Thanos sipped his Scotch slowly, his eyes moving from one high rise to another. When he eventually spoke, it was with a sardonic drawl. 'I understand that you're in the heady bliss of being a newly-wed but I think we can safely say marriage is the last thing on my mind.' In fact, the very idea turned his blood cold. One week after his mother had dumped him on Dion Stathakis's doorstep, throwing a traumatised little boy into the home as one might a cat into a flock of pigeons, Thanos had sworn to Leonidas that he'd never be stupid enough to fall in love or get married.

He'd been eight and miserable, his heart broken, his soul crushed—looking back, he could see now that he'd also been terrified. His mother, the woman who'd raised him, the only family he'd ever known, had told him she couldn't 'do this' any more, and dropped him like a sack of potatoes.

His father had made it abundantly clear he didn't want Thanos, that he was raising him out of duty. When Dion's own marriage had crumbled because of Thanos's unexpected arrival, a large part of Thanos's heart had been sealed closed—he knew it would never open again.

Was it any wonder Thanos viewed relationships and commitment as something best avoided?

'I don't mean a *real* marriage,' Leonidas explained with mock simplicity.

Beyond the window, dusk was falling, the night sky turning an inky black, no stars to be seen in the brightness cast by the vibrant city. Thanos cradled his drink in the palm of his hand.

'Kosta has given you the solution; you're just not listening. He won't accept any offer you make because you're a walking tabloid headline. This isn't just a top five hundred company he's selling. It's his *family* empire.'

'It's *our* family empire too.'

'He bought Petó a long time ago. I doubt he continues to consider it as a distinct entity from P & A.'

'And nor do I. I am not attempting to separate Petó from the fold. I am willing to take on his business as well.'

'Yes, I get that. But he's not willing to sell to us. Not given your…predilection for headline-grabbing behaviour.'

Thanos stiffened, the criticism sitting uneasily around his shoulders now. He'd never felt uncomfortable about his lifestyle before; he'd never had any reason to. But hearing first Kosta and then his brother cast aspersions on the way he lived was filling Thanos with a sense of impatience. 'My social life is no impediment to my running Stathakis,' he heard himself point out coldly.

'True, but neither of us could do anything worse than our father did to trash our family name, right?'

Thanos winced, sympathy for his brother at the forefront of his mind. Years had passed since that awful day when Leonidas's young family had been murdered as a vendetta against their father but even now that Leonidas was married with a beautiful little girl who was growing *way* too fast, Thanos still felt sorrow for what had been lost.

'You and I are nothing like our father.'

'I know.' Leonidas and Thanos were quiet for a moment, their point of difference from Dion Stathakis one of sheer determination. Both men had sworn, many years earlier, even before his criminal prosecution, that they would never emulate his lifestyle. They had always admired their grandfather and followed much more closely in Nicholas's footsteps.

'So show Kosta he's wrong about you,' Leonidas continued, his voice insistent. 'He thinks you're just some

debauched tycoon, with more money and sex appeal than
sense—'

'So? Even if that were accurate—' and he didn't want
to contemplate how many threads of truth there were to
that observation '—I'm the best man to turn that company
around and make sure it continues to thrive in the twenty-
first century. No one will care for the business as I will;
you know that.'

'Yes,' Leonidas conceded softly.

'So what? Because I happen to like sex and the tabloids
happen to like me, he thinks I'm not qualified?'

'He wants more than just a business deal,' Leonidas
said gently. 'The company's his legacy. It's not just a business to him—it's a way of life, and it's his birthright. He
wants to protect that.'

Thanos had no difficulties relating to Kosta's desires
on that score. His own life had been devoid of the kind of
parents most people grew up with. His mother had abandoned him and his father had taken him in reluctantly,
but there had been grandparents and what wouldn't Thanos have done for them? What wouldn't he have done in
their honour?

Wasn't it because of them that Leonidas and Thanos
had worked tirelessly for the better part of a decade to restore Stathakis Corp to the behemoth it had been before
their father's fall from grace? To restore, in part, the Stathakis name?

And wasn't it largely what drove him now? A desire to
bring home Petó, an important and missing piece of the
puzzle that was their empire? They'd diversified in their
restructure, buying up tech companies, new economy in-
vestments to shore up the old. But still, he'd never forgotten
the promise he'd made to himself on the day they'd signed
the contracts. He had hated selling Petó, the transport com-

pany his grandfather had been so proud of, the company that had enabled all their later successes. It meant *everything* to Thanos, and clearly it meant everything to Kosta.

So Thanos just had to show Kosta that the legacy was safe in his hands.

If only Kosta could see that the best way to preserve what his grandparents had built was to sell the company to a man who would have the skills, acumen and motivation to take the whole enterprise to the next level.

'You are a fool if you don't simply tick this box for Kosta and move on. Get married and he will sell it to you in an instant.'

Thanos threw his Scotch back, his brother's suggestion making an infuriating kind of sense, despite his determination never to marry.

'Putting aside for the moment the fact that he's going to see through this play in an instant, who would I even marry if I were to go through with it?'

Leonidas laughed. 'There must be hundreds of women you've slept with. Choose the one you like the best.'

'I don't like any of them enough to marry. And I don't generally go back for repeat performances.'

Leonidas's sigh came down the phone line. 'If you want the company, you're going to have to make your peace with this. It's the only way.'

'It's crazy.'

'No, it's actually very sensible.'

'I cannot simply marry some random woman.'

'Why not?'

'Because I'd be doing it purely for commercial gain.'

'So? Find someone who would be marrying you for their own commercial gain. Or have you forgotten what you're worth?'

'It's completely unscrupulous.'

'Why?'

'To fake a marriage to fool an old man?'

Leonidas was quiet a moment. 'Do you not think the end justifies the means?'

Thanos ground his teeth together. He could accept many things in life, but not losing Petó.

Besides, Leonidas was right—Kosta had all but drawn a map for Thanos as to how he could succeed in the purchase.

Settle down. Stop being so wild. At least appear to have become a family man.

So perhaps his brother had a point.

Marriage.

He might hate the idea of getting married, but a wedding like this—with each partner knowing it was purely mercenary? If he was clear on that point from the outset?

If there was an escape route always within reach?

So that no matter what happened he would know there was a definite termination point established, a date when the marriage would end and his life could go back to normal?

Perhaps that kind of marriage wouldn't be so bad. A marriage, in name only. But to whom?

Alice disconnected the call with wobbly fingers and stared at her office wall. Tears that she rarely allowed herself to give into cloyed at her throat, so she had to press the heel of her palm to her eyes to stop from crying.

Bankruptcy.

The word hung in the air like a thousand little arrows, pointed at her soul. How could it have come to this? No matter how hard she worked, she could never get ahead, and now her credit-card company was demanding she close her accounts, settling her debts in full, or they'd commence bankruptcy proceedings.

She clamped her teeth down on her lip, trying to stave off an actual sob, trying to see some kind of light, somewhere, at the end of this tunnel. There had to be something she could sell, something she could do.

Except, there wasn't. She'd hawked everything of value over the years, reluctantly parting with anything they could make money from, including the diamond earrings her mother had loved so much—a gift from Alice's father, when they'd first met.

She hadn't been able to go to college, she couldn't get a job that paid more than this one, and no reputable bank would touch her with a barge pole in terms of a loan. She knew what her credit rating was.

She let out a guttural noise of impatience and stood, pacing across the office, nausea tightening her stomach. There had to be *something*.

A single tear slid from one of her eyes, rolling down her cheek, and at that exact moment Thanos Stathakis appeared in the door frame of his office, looking out at her, his expression as forbidding and handsome as it had been the day before.

He opened his mouth to speak, then saw her expression and closed it. His eyes roamed her face quite freely, and Alice stood completely still, so overwhelmed that she didn't even think to wipe away her tear.

'Did you need something?' Her voice was a little wobbly, but there was pride in her question, because she wasn't going to let things get any worse by acting unprofessionally.

His lips tugged downwards at the corner. 'Yes. Come in.' He waved a hand in the direction of his office and Alice sucked in a breath, moving quickly to her desk and sliding her credit-card statement under her keyboard before doing as he'd said and stepping into his massive workspace.

'Please, have a seat.' He gestured to the boardroom table.

She shook her head. Alice didn't feel like sitting down.

'You're upset?'

She blinked, shaking her head, lifting her fingers to her cheeks now and wiping her tears. 'No,' she lied—badly. 'I'm fine. What did you need?'

His eyes narrowed but he turned away from her, apparently accepting her statement, pouring a cool glass of water and carrying it across the room. When he passed it to her, their fingers brushed and a jolt of electricity travelled the length of Alice's arm, burning brightly into her chest cavity.

'You may feel better if you speak about what is troubling you,' he invited.

Alice's eyes flew wide, this kindness completely unexpected. 'I… It's my problem,' she demurred.

Thanos nodded slowly, assimilating this information. 'And you like to solve your problems yourself,' he surmised.

Alice nodded. 'As, I think, do you.'

His smile lacked humour; in fact, his smile had the look of someone who'd almost forgotten how. 'Wherever possible, certainly.' He crossed his arms over his broad chest, a gesture that drew her attention to his muscled abdomen in a way that sparked heat in her cheeks.

'But you're inviting me to pour my heart out to you?' she prompted, to which he pulled a face, as if it was actually the last thing he'd been expecting. Alice laughed, despite her enormous worries.

'I'm saying… I don't like tears.' The words were uneasy. 'If talking would help…'

Her heart lurched a little inside her chest. Alice didn't want to think about how long it had been since she'd had anyone she could speak to. It felt like an eternity.

'It's hard to explain,' she said, sipping the water with hands that were still unsteady.

He was quiet. Watchful. Some might have said calculating, but Alice didn't know Thanos well enough to see that glint in his eye, nor was she looking for it. She paced towards the boardroom table, placing her water down, her eyes focussed on the stunning view of Manhattan. Somehow, it was easier to speak without looking at him.

'It's my mom,' she said, shaking her head, because that wasn't, strictly speaking, the truth. 'I mean, it is and it isn't. She's…not well. And looking after her is hard, and expensive, and it's been years now, and no matter what I do, I can't seem to get on top of it, and I have no idea what to do or how I can make this any easier.' She ground her teeth together, but it didn't help; a sob bubbled up and out of her chest. She looked at him apologetically. 'I'm never like this at work, I swear.'

'I know that.' His voice was carefully blanked of emotion.

'I mean, I work really hard, because I can't risk getting a bad reference, because I need the next job, and at the moment I'm one of the top-rated temps at the agency, so I work hard to make sure I don't lose that.'

Thanos considered this. 'Would permanent employment not suit you better? You'd get a steadier salary.'

'True.' Alice nodded. 'But the pay is way less, and I need some flexibility. There are times when I have to be off work for two or three weeks to help with mom, and if I'm a temp, that's a lot easier to arrange.'

'So you support your mother?'

'Yes.' She nodded. 'She had a stroke. She's in a coma. I can't afford a bed in a home so she lives with me, and the cost of home nursing—which she needs through the day—is astronomical. I'm basically working to cover her medical bills and then there's food and rent and…' A tear slid down her cheek. 'I'm sorry.'

'What for?' He surprised her then, pulling a tissue from the drawer of his desk and striding across to her. Instead of handing the tissue to her, he dabbed at her cheeks. It was a gesture of such kindness that it somehow made her feel worse, rather than better.

She wasn't used to anyone helping her. Listening to her. And it was as if a crack had formed into which she wanted to pour all her grief, all her worries. But he was her boss, and this was a job, and she'd already created a bad enough impression without making it worse.

'Thank you.' She spoke firmly, taking a step back, away from him, away from sympathy. 'I don't know what came over me. It's just been one of those days.'

She lifted the water glass from the table, intending to take it to the kitchen to wash it, but he put a hand on her wrist, stilling her. Only it didn't still *all* of her. Alice's blood thundered at the light, innocent touch.

'I also have a problem, Alice,' he said, his eyes boring into hers with an intensity that sent a shiver down her spine. It was easy to see in that moment how he had, side by side with his brother, turned a crumbling business into a global behemoth. She felt strength slamming into her from every single pore of his body.

But his words didn't quite make sense. Did he wish to unburden himself? Did he want a sympathetic ear? It didn't exactly fit with the character profile she had of Thanos but Alice found herself listening intently.

'And it occurs to me that we could be of use to one another.'

Her eyes flared wide at this idea. Without knowing any details, she knew she shouldn't get her hopes up. And yet, it felt like…a light in the dark.

'How so?'

'My brother suggested last night that I should give Kosta Carinedes exactly what he wants.'

'You're going to stop getting photographed by paparazzi?' Alice prompted, a hint of scepticism in her words, because the media loved Thanos and his antics like bees loved nectar.

'I'm not sure that's possible.' He echoed her unspoken doubts. 'But I'm going to give them the right thing to photograph.'

'What do you mean?'

'If Kosta wants me to settle down, then I'll do just that. I'll get married.'

It was so absurd that Alice laughed. 'You're getting married?'

'That depends.'

'On…?'

'On if you'll agree to be my wife.'

CHAPTER THREE

'DON'T THINK OF it as a marriage,' he added, when she hadn't spoken for several long, confused seconds of silence. 'Think of it as a job offer.'

'To be your wife?' She roused herself, finally, blinking as though that might help make sense of matters.

Thanos's eyes narrowed speculatively. 'Yes.'

'Do you feel okay? Are you drunk?'

He laughed; a hoarse sound. 'No.'

'You can't seriously be expecting me to marry you?'

'Why not?'

'Um…' She sipped her water for something to do. 'Because we just met yesterday?'

'Yes,' he agreed. 'But I already know everything I need to know to make this marriage a success.'

Alice lifted her brows in a silent entreaty for him to continue.

'You are efficient, trustworthy and intelligent. I have been very impressed with your work ethic.'

Pleasure zipped through her.

'But more than that, Alice, you need money, and this marriage would simply be a business arrangement.'

'A business arrangement?' She echoed his pronouncement, trying to make sense of that.

'Why not?'

A crease formed between her brows and she lifted a hand, tucking a loose bit of chestnut hair behind her ear. 'Is that even legal?'

His smile held a hint of derision. 'You think arranged marriages are not binding?'

'I…' She couldn't think straight. 'I'm sorry. This has come totally out of the blue. You're seriously saying you want to marry me?'

His gaze was laced with fierce determination, sharp enough to send a blade of apprehension down her spine. 'I would do anything to get Petó back. Kosta has made his terms clear. This is the only way to fulfil them.'

'I can kind of see that, I guess.' She sounded anything but convinced. 'Except I'm the last woman you'd ever marry. He's never going to believe this is genuine.'

'On the contrary, the fact that you are not like the kind of women I am attracted to makes you perfect for this ruse.'

Alice let out a soft laugh, hiding the way his pronouncement hurt. She knew she wasn't particularly beautiful, and she had no hope that a man like Thanos would ever look twice at her. Not that she wanted him to—she was done with men, done with love altogether. Still, she had a little pride left and in that moment it had been completely hollowed out. 'How do you figure?'

'Because you *are* different. It makes sense that when I do eventually settle down, it would be with someone who challenges me, who stands out compared to my usual… type.'

She resisted the urge to pull a face, even though this conversation was becoming somewhat mortifying. 'Okay, fair enough. But we just met yesterday.'

'He doesn't know that.'

'I…'

'For all he knows, you and I have been seeing one another for months.'

Alice lifted a brow. 'Well, that would hardly be a ringing endorsement of my judgement.' She lifted her hands apologetically, but continued explaining. 'I mean, you've been in the papers—recently—photographed with different women.'

He waved a hand in the air, as though it barely mattered. 'Kosta is an intelligent man, who has also done his share of living in the public eye. He knows as well as I do that papers make stuff up. I don't particularly care what is written about me. I understand the newspapers and blogs have a job to do, but only a fool would take gossip as gospel.'

Alice ignored the implication that she was a fool, given that it had never occurred to her to question what was written about him. 'I just can't see this working.'

Determination fired in Thanos's expression. 'I would not suggest it if I didn't think we could convince Kosta.'

Alice's stomach flipped and flopped. 'Marriage is a very permanent way to fix a problem like this.'

His smile was bordering on indulgent and Alice felt, suddenly, very naïve. 'Marriages frequently end in divorce; ours would be just the same.'

'Fated from the beginning,' she said, nodding slowly.

'As most are.'

She was too caught up in the complexity of this to properly note the hard cynicism to his voice.

'So how would it work?'

He expelled a breath, as though he was relieved, taking her acquiescence for granted, so she hastened to add, 'I'm not saying yes. I'm just curious as to the details.'

'I admire your prudence.'

More pleasure, this time slamming against her ribs and catching her completely unawares. 'Have you eaten lunch?'

'Lunch?' The unexpected question roused her from her

thoughts. She thought of the bare pantry at home, and her stomach grumbled betrayingly. 'No.'

'Fine. Let's go and discuss this properly.'

'It's two o'clock in the afternoon.'

'So?' He gestured towards the door with his natural authority and she found herself walking towards it.

But as she crossed the threshold, she felt the need to insist, 'I'm not agreeing to this, Thanos. I think this is one of the craziest ideas I've ever heard, actually.'

'Fine.' He nodded, brushing aside her objection with ease. 'But you are intrigued, no?'

'Yes,' she admitted, a half-smile reluctantly lifting her lips. 'I'm intrigued.'

'Good.' He grinned. 'Then this is a beginning.' He moved to the elevator, pressing the button. It opened instantly. 'I promise, I will make it impossible for you to refuse me, Alice.'

She stepped into the lift, and when it began to ascend instead of descend, she suspected the loopy feeling in her tummy had very little to do with the sudden change in altitude.

Alice knew there was a helipad on the roof of the building. She didn't know that a helicopter was parked there, nor that it was sleek and black, the sky equivalent of a private limousine. As they walked towards it, Thanos pressed something in his pocket and the door slid open.

'After you,' he prompted, as if all of this was completely normal. Alice stared at the aircraft, her mouth open in sheer awe, but after a few seconds she pulled it together, forced herself to take a breath and step up into the helicopter's interior. It was like nothing she'd ever seen before. All beige caramel and white glossy wood, pure luxury and glamour.

Thanos took the seat beside her, and, despite the generous proportions of the craft, he made it feel tiny. She was conscious of his every exhalation, conscious of the way his frame was so large that his legs were so, so close to touching hers. She kept her own pinned together, her hands in her lap.

'Clip in,' he said, turning to face her, nodding towards the seat belt.

Alice reached behind her, fumbling the seat belt as she tried to clip it into the unfamiliar lock. He reached over, his eyes holding hers, a slight smile at the edges of his face. 'May I?'

Feeling both naïve and stupid, she nodded. 'Thank you.' The words were crisp, and she was glad she'd spoken before he actually reached for the seat belt. Because the way he dragged it across her body sent a thousand volts of electricity into her nervous system, so heat pooled in her gut and spread through her limbs.

It was an innocent gesture though, and Alice had to remind herself that she was definitely not his type. That was the reason he was proposing this ridiculous marriage of convenience. Except—was it really so ridiculous? She could perfectly see the benefit to him, if it meant he could secure the purchase of P & A.

And for Alice?

Dared she hope he would offer some kind of salary to her—better than she was earning now—in order for her to go along with this? That had to be what he had in mind.

'Here.' He handed her a white headset then looped his own in place, before flicking some dials and switches and bringing the rotor blades to life. The noise was loud—too loud to speak over. He tapped the headset again, smiling as he lifted up off the rooftop.

'Where are we going?' she yelled, despite the fact she had a small microphone hooked up to the headset, so he winced a little, sending her a look of amusement.

'Sorry.' She laughed. 'Where are we going?' A whisper now.

Then he laughed, and the sound was like sun-warmed caramel, her body warmed in an instant and involuntary response.

'Lunch.'

She arched a brow. 'I thought you meant a sandwich at the deli downstairs.'

It was his turn to pull a face, his expression scandalised. 'That's not food.'

'It's…not?'

'I do not like this American way of eating while you are doing other things. Sandwiches!' He said the word as if it was an affront to good food everywhere, and she found a small smile playing about her lips.

'Sandwiches are actually very practical. Portable, tasty, filling…'

He shrugged. 'Boring.'

And she understood then, because Thanos enjoyed nice things. He enjoyed experiences. Parties. Food. Wine. The sun on his body as he sunned himself on the deck of his yacht.

'You're a hedonist.'

He turned to face her. 'Perhaps. But shouldn't we all be?'

Alice didn't say anything. She didn't want to remind Thanos that she'd spent the better part of the last few years wondering how long she could survive on just potatoes, or just bread.

'So where are we going?'

'A little place I know.'

The 'little place he knew' turned out to be a restaurant in Brooklyn, so exclusive it wasn't even signposted. He brought his helicopter down on the roof of a building that was only about ten stories tall, busying himself with the technical requirements of flying for a few moments. Moments in which Alice sat completely still and tried to get her head around this bizarre turn of events.

It only became more bizarre when they entered the restaurant through the kitchen and the chefs stopped what they were doing to basically fawn over Thanos. They all wanted to speak to him, and, to his credit, he took a moment with each of them, and seemed to know most of their names. She watched, fascinated, as he asked questions of each, managing small details—the names of their children or partners, offering condolences to one woman who, Alice gathered, had recently lost her father.

'You come here often?' she prompted as they swept into the restaurant itself—a loft space that could have accommodated a hundred diners but which had instead been converted into a room that felt almost like a penthouse lounge, all elegant sofas interspersed with enormous fiddle-leaf fig plants in copper pots. This made it possible for the dining tables to be set far apart, creating complete privacy, and suddenly Alice understood the appeal.

No one would hear their conversation; they could speak entirely unobserved.

He held a chair out for her only seconds before a waiter appeared.

'Mr Stathakis, welcome back. Would you like to see a menu?'

Thanos tilted his head towards Alice. 'I usually just eat what is served. However, you might like to take a look?'

'No, that's fine.' She shook her head. 'Whatever you have will be great, I'm sure.'

'I can ask if they will serve you sandwiches?' he teased and her heart skipped a beat.

'That would be lovely.' She winked to show she was joking.

Thanos grinned, dismissing the waiter with a few words in Greek, before taking the seat opposite her. She felt an unwelcome burst of nerves, and did her best to quell them.

In the office, his proposition had been surprising. On the helicopter, she'd been overawed by the glamour and completely unusual turn of events. But here, in a romantic, secluded restaurant, sitting across from one of the world's wealthiest men—to say nothing of his personal charms and physical appeal—Alice's pulse was trembling unstoppably.

'Relax,' he murmured, apparently intuiting her panic.

'I'm sorry, it's just not every day I get proposed to,' she said with a sardonic smile.

'But this is not a real proposal,' he reminded her smoothly, his eyes intent on hers. 'It is a business proposition.'

'You'd know more about that than I do.'

He nodded. 'Let me explain it for you,' he offered. 'Just like in business, we would have a contract to protect both of our interests.'

'A pre-nuptial agreement?'

'A divorce settlement,' he corrected. 'I would have our divorce papers confidentially drawn up and filed by my personal lawyer, on terms we will agree to now.'

'What kind of terms?' she asked quickly, her heart racing.

He examined her thoughtfully, then shrugged. 'What would you like?'

Alice's stomach swooped to her toes. 'You want me to choose?'

'In a negotiation, it is normal for one party to come in with a list of demands. You know what I need from you, so tell me, Alice, what do you need from me?'

She chewed on her lip, the possibilities endless. 'I want not to worry about my mom,' she said, simply. 'She needs to be in a home. A good one. Somewhere with kind staff where she can be as…comfortable as possible.' Alice's voice cracked. 'Somewhere I can go and see her often.'

Thanos nodded. 'Fine. What else?'

It was on the tip of Alice's tongue to say that was everything she needed, but when she thought of her overburdened credit cards, the threatened bankruptcy, she decided she might as well go for broke. 'I'd need to continue earning my temp salary,' she said, tilting her chin to show she was serious. 'I presume in order to make this seem legitimate, I wouldn't be able to work, but I'd need to continue earning so I could cover rent for as long as we were married. That way, I'll have my apartment to come back to,' she tacked on, when he didn't speak.

He remained silent, staring at her for so long and so hard that she wondered if she'd pushed it too far.

And then he laughed, a cracking sound that reverberated around the room.

'What?' Heat spread through her cheeks.

'Your old apartment? *Dio*, Alice.' He shook his head, laughter lines still creasing the corners of his eyes. 'I can see that of your many strengths, negotiating is not one of them.'

Her heart rate notched up a gear. She knew the cost of a bed in a good nursing home wasn't cheap. It would be half a million dollars, easily, to buy an ongoing position.

'So tell me what you want to pay me,' she said instead.

'I am asking you to walk away from your life, to pretend to be my wife—which is not likely to be a walk in the park, let me tell you. You would be photographed, and I would expect you to attend events with me often, in order to sell this as real. You will need to completely overhaul your way of life. And you ask for only your salary?'

Her jaw dropped. 'And my mother's care.'

He waved a hand in the air, dismissively.

'I wasn't sure what you had in mind.'

'Alice, you should not undervalue yourself like this.'

'Well, what do *you* suggest?'

'For starters, an apartment in New York. You can choose what you like. I have several, but if none of them is to your liking then feel free to contact a realtor.'

Her jaw dropped lower.

'A cash settlement. I was expecting you to ask for twenty million dollars, to which I intended to counter ten, and settle on perhaps fifteen after some back and forth. So shall we just save ourselves the trouble and say fifteen million dollars?'

'Fifteen million dollars? In cash?'

'Alice, I'm a very wealthy man, and if you marry me, you'll be enabling me to buy a business that is worth more to me than anything else. *Yes*. Fifteen million dollars.'

'And a home in New York. And my mother's care.'

'And health insurance,' he seemed to add as an afterthought. 'Starting immediately.'

Alice gaped. It was too much.

'But I could just pay for that myself with the money…'

He laughed again. 'Your negotiation skills are really quite poor.'

'I don't want to feel like I'm scamming you.'

Surprise crossed his face, but he covered it quickly. 'You're not.'

'It feels a lot like I am.'

'It's a job.'

'A ridiculously over-paid job.'

'I'm already paying above the odds for the company.' He shrugged. 'This is just another expense to factor into its reacquisition.'

'It means that much to you?'

His eyes glittered like black gemstones and in response he simply dipped his head forward.

'Petó means everything to me.'

'Because it used to be yours?'

'Because it was my grandfather's.' And despite the fact the words were delivered quietly, she felt passion in every single syllable. 'Because it was sold under duress, and because I swore I would get it back.' He closed his eyes for a moment. 'And because Kosta Carinedes will sell eventually, and I do not wish him to sell it to anyone else.'

'You think he would?'

Thanos pierced her with his gaze. 'Yes.'

'So how would this work?' she prompted, breaking off when the waiter reappeared with a bottle of wine. Alice watched as he unscrewed the cork and poured two glasses, then disappeared once more.

'We'd get married quickly. Two weeks should be enough time to organise the details. I have a hotel in the South of France that would be perfect—just the kind of place I would choose for my wedding. It's private and difficult to get to, so while we'll leak it to the press, there won't be an abundance of paparazzi hanging off the gates.'

A shiver ran down her spine at the image he created, and she fought an urge to ask him about his life—how it felt to be hounded everywhere he went. She was curious, but there were far more pressing concerns. 'Two weeks?' The words came out strangled.

'It has to be soon. The way his figures are tanking, he's going to become desperate to sell, and I would not risk him testing the market by listing his business interests.'

Alice swallowed. That made perfect sense. And yet… it was so soon.

'And your mother could be moved into a suitable facility as early as tomorrow,' he promised, making Alice's stom-

ach twist, because she would do anything for her mother—
anything—and here Thanos was promising a solution that
would finally take away their concerns.

'That's…the wedding,' she heard herself respond stiffly,
just a whisper, and her eyes dropped to the table nervously.
She reached for her wine glass, lifting it and taking a gulp
that did little to settle her frazzled nerves.

He sat opposite, waiting for her to finish, and eventually, Alice lifted her face, staring at him nervously for
several anguished beats. 'I'm talking about the marriage.'

The words emerged as barely a croak, so Thanos had
to lean forward to hear them better.

'Go on?' he prompted.

Alice's cheeks felt sun-warmed from embarrassment.
'I get that there'll be a big wedding, but what about the
marriage?'

'What about it?'

'How long would you envisage this going on for?'

He shrugged. 'A year?'

'A year!' She gulped more wine back.

'We would not have to live together that whole time,'
he back-pedalled. 'Just for the first few months, while I
was getting the deal through with Kosta.'

'Live together?' The words squeaked out, her eyes slamming shut in silent refutation of this very idea.

'Well, yes. I mean, that's kind of the point…'

Alice's blood was rushing through her so hard and fast
it was all she could hear. She gaped, her lips moving with
no sound coming out.

When she finally dared to glance at Thanos, she found
him watching her with a concentration that almost robbed
her of all breath. 'I can't… I mean… I can't live with you.'

He arched a brow. 'No?'

Her cheeks weren't pink now, they were bright red. 'I'm

not… I mean… I know you're very…erm…sophisticated, but I'm not, and I'm not interested in the kind of relationship you're…suggesting.'

He stared at her for several seconds and then burst out laughing, so she frowned, with no idea what he found so laughable.

'Relax, Alice. I'm not propositioning you for sex.'

She felt as if she were about to have a heart attack. Mortification spread through her and she lifted the wine glass once more, drinking at least half of what remained in one quick sip.

It burned all the way down her throat, the unfamiliar flavour like acid. 'You just said we were going to live together.'

'Yes,' he agreed with a shrug. 'But behind closed doors, our relationship will be as it is now. Businesslike. Professional. Courteous. In fact, we probably won't see much of each other, given how much I travel.'

'And you'd continue to travel,' she murmured, her heart rate slowing to something approaching normal.

He nodded. 'I don't see any reason to make huge changes to either of our lives, behind closed doors.'

'But you wouldn't see other women?' she blurted out, wondering why that bothered her so much. Pride, she supposed. Pride, and her experience with Clinton, and having seen what her father was capable of. She didn't want to be used by some man, made a laughing stock. Not again.

'I do not really "see" women now,' he pointed out with a lift of his shoulders.

'But you couldn't be photographed flirting with some supermodel at a party,' she insisted. 'If the whole point is to fool Mr Carinedes, then you'll need to play the part of a doting newly-wed as much as I will.'

'This is not exactly a hardship,' he said with a dip of his head. 'As you know, I am very motivated to succeed in this.'

'I know,' she whispered, gripping her wine-glass stem as though it were a lifeline.

'I spend most of my time in Greece,' he continued, as though this matter were dealt with. 'I presume once I have arranged suitable accommodation for your mother, you will be able to join me there?'

Her mouth dropped open, her tongue darting out to trace the line of her lower lip; she barely noticed the way his eyes fell to the gesture.

'Alice?'

'I…yes.' She nodded, painfully aware of the void that was her private life.

He took a moment to consider that and then smiled, relaxed, relieved. 'So?' He lifted a brow and her heart *kerthunked* hard against her chest in a vicious, imperious warning.

Because only a fool would fail to see the danger here. The danger in agreeing to marry a man like Thanos Stathakis, with more charm and sex appeal in his little finger than any man had a right to possess.

'It would be purely business,' she insisted. 'I wouldn't be marrying you for any reason except to get out of debt. And to help you,' she admitted grudgingly, because it was true.

He nodded. 'And the same could be said for me. Shall we shake on it to seal the deal?'

And while there might have been a thousand and one more traditional and romantic ways to cement a marriage proposal, shaking hands perfectly suited the sensible, commercial nature of this agreement.

Just business, not personal, and for no longer than a year.

Alice could most definitely live with that.

CHAPTER FOUR

'You could consult with a lawyer,' Thanos offered.

Alice lifted her gaze from the divorce contracts, a look of cool determination in her gaze. For the first time in a long time, she felt as if she was in control of her life, she felt as if things were going to be okay, and she desperately needed to believe that. Already, things were so much better. Two days after her agreeing to marry Thanos, a bed had been made available for Jane Smart at an upscale nursing home, only an hour's drive from Manhattan.

Thanos had flown Alice to inspect the facility in his helicopter, and she'd been completely floored by how perfect everything was. And how considerate he was, in taking her to inspect it himself.

More to the point, it had all been so *easy*. Money, apparently, opened doors, and Thanos had the kind of money that made anything possible. He'd smoothed the way to this marriage completely, paying Alice's rent for a year so she wouldn't feel rushed to move out of her own place, giving her time to think about where to store her things, what she wanted to take with her into her new life.

And now, in his Manhattan penthouse, he was taking the time to meticulously explain the divorce settlement to her.

If only she were able to give it one hundred per cent of her focus!

If only she weren't completely distracted! By the spectacularly expensive apartment—all designer furniture, black leather, polished wood, with high ceilings and glistening chandeliers, and a wrap-around balcony that showed stunning views of Manhattan and Central Park.

And beyond the apartment, there was Thanos.

Dressed casually.

In jeans and a simple T-shirt, he was undeniably handsome, but it was more than that. It was his thoughtfulness, his astuteness, his attention to detail and the rich, husky tone of his voice. She found her pulse throbbing ferociously in her veins as she toyed with the pen, so perhaps he interpreted her actions as hesitation, rather than a desire not to keep staring at his pectoral muscles.

'Do you think I need to see a lawyer?' she threw the question back to him, turning her attention to the papers once more.

'No,' he shook his head once. 'It is as we discussed. But if you doubt my word...'

'I don't.' She couldn't say why, but she trusted him. She smiled distractedly. 'It's just a big thing to do, you know.'

'Yes.' He reached over and curved his hand over hers, so heat spun through Alice. 'But it is just make-believe, and this contract proves that you have a way out.'

She nodded. 'I know.'

'At any point, either of us can file these papers and commence divorce proceedings.' His smile barely changed his expression. 'Think of it as an insurance policy.'

She nodded, lifting her hand and running it through her dark hair. It was pulled back in a bun, but suddenly her head ached and she needed to release the tension pain. She pulled the pins out on autopilot, as she did every evening, slipping them into the pocket of her battered leather handbag—which was completely incongruous with this designer space—before running her fingers through the long, dark waves. Her eyes remained on the divorce papers.

It was all exactly as he'd said on the day he'd proposed.

She skimmed the clauses, reassuring herself with growing disbelief of the amount he'd offered, and the property value cap—which was frankly exorbitant!—in the instance that none of his apartments suited her, and finally hovered the pen over the signature line at the bottom.

Her eyes lifted to his and, with the sense that she was stepping over the edge of the cliff, she added her signature.

Thanos expelled a long, steady breath, then stood up from his chair, coming to stand behind Alice and leaning forward so he could add his own signature to the papers. Only, the action brought his powerful frame so close to hers, he was almost wrapped around her, and suddenly her blood was pounding even harder and faster, making any kind of thought impossible. She swallowed to bring moisture back to her instantly dry throat.

'So, that's it?' she murmured, her eyes scanning his.

'Almost.'

'What else is there?'

He reached into his pocket, pulling out a black velvet box with a world-renowned jeweller's name emblazoned across the top in gold writing.

Alice looked at the box without making an effort to touch it.

'Your ring,' he prompted after a beat.

Only then did Alice slowly push her hand across the table, her fingers trembling as she cracked open the lid.

She couldn't have said what she'd expected. Certainly something worthy of the bride of Thanos Stathakis. But this?

It was ludicrous. She lifted the solitaire ring from its velvet enclosure. Without any real experience it was impossible for Alice to say if the diamond was ten carats or twenty, only that it was as large as two of her thumb nails put together, and so bright it almost blinded her. The setting was simple, six claws and platinum gold.

She felt Thanos's eyes on her as she slid it onto her finger, the weight of it strangely familiar, something she felt she could get used to.

'It's...lovely.' She swallowed past a sudden lump in her throat.

Thanos shrugged. 'I thought it appropriate.'

'It is.' She looked up at him, a small frown tweaking her lips. 'Is this what the women you date would generally expect?'

'A ring like that?' He lifted his shoulders once more. 'I suppose so.'

She shook her head. 'Not just the ring. The whole deal.' Her hand gestured towards the divorce settlement. Thanos's eyes followed the gesture.

'No, *agape*. If this were a real marriage, my wife would undoubtedly expect a lot more.'

Shock was reflected in Alice's expression. 'Seriously?'

'You know what I'm worth?'

Alice tilted her head to the side. 'A lot.'

His laugh was short and sharp. 'Yes.'

'So? You think that means your wife—your real wife— would be automatically entitled to a huge share of that wealth?'

His eyes narrowed imperceptibly. 'It's a moot point, Alice. This will be my only wedding, you my only wife.'

'Why?' She stood, and then regretted it, when the simple action brought her body so close to his.

'Because I,' he said slowly, his eyes boring down on hers, the air between them suddenly crackling with an awareness that Alice assured herself was completely one-sided, 'am not made for marriage.' His smile covered a deeper confession, Alice was sure of it.

'In what way?' It was curiosity that fired her to ask it.

'In every way.' His own response was teasing, and she had a feeling he was hiding himself away from her, covering a truthful response with a glib joke.

Then again, who was she to pry? This wasn't a real marriage. They weren't even friends. It was business— purely business.

'So, all that is left now is to seal the deal.'

Alarm jolted down her spine, as for a moment, out of nowhere, the image of Thanos kissing her crashed into Alice's mind. Her knees began to tremble and her pulse was thready and inconsistent. Her eyes, when they lifted to his, were half shuttered, her lips parted in a breathy, silent, invitation she had no idea she was issuing.

'Seal the deal?' she heard herself whisper.

He made a throaty noise of agreement, and then took a step backwards, away from her, a desertion that had every single one of her senses screaming with disappointment.

'I thought we would go out.'

'Out?'

'Dancing. Getting your photo in the paper is the quickest way to let news of our engagement slip to the world.'

Alice's eyes shifted—reluctantly—from Thanos's face to the boulder she now wore on her finger, then to the reflective wall panel just a little way across the room. She'd come directly from the office and still wore an ill-fitting brown suit. It was hardly the stuff of elegant nightclubs, nor the kind of thing Thanos's real fiancée would, she presumed, be caught dead in.

'Dancing.' She found herself nodding. 'I can meet you at a club…'

He frowned. 'But you're right here.'

'I need to get changed first,' she pointed out, looking down at her figure.

His eyes narrowed and a smile played about his lips. 'So you do.' Then, with a confident gesture of his tanned fingers, he motioned for her to join him as he strode through the penthouse.

Curious, she did exactly that, until he paused in the middle of a large, cream-coloured bedroom.

A dress was hanging against another door, a slinky red colour with spaghetti straps, made of silk, that she suspected would fall to mid-thigh, at best, and which looked to dip dangerously low over the cleavage.

It was the complete opposite of anything she'd ever buy for herself, and yet she found herself fascinated by its delicate construction, its beautiful design.

'This is for me?' She flicked her gaze to his in time to catch a hint of speculation in his eyes.

He nodded though, brusque and efficient. 'There are others,' he offered, 'but this is the one I liked best.' His wink did funny things to her gut. 'I'll be waiting outside.'

She nodded, not quite equal to making a verbal response, pulling the dress from the hanger a little uneasily and running her fingertips over the sensual material. A quick inspection of the wardrobe showed several other dresses, all of them designer, all somehow—mysteriously—in her size. Then again, Thanos was no doubt an expert in women's bodies—he could probably guess her measurements to within a millimetre's accuracy despite the fact he'd only ever seen her in business suits.

She scanned all of the dresses, and though there were some which were far more conservative and in keeping with her normal dress code, she found her attention continually returning to the strappy red he'd expressed a preference for. Finally, with a guttural noise of surrender, she undressed and pulled it on over her head, catching her reflection almost as soon as it had settled on her body.

And she forze.

Because Alice never wore anything revealing. She never showed more than a hint of cleavage, nor anything above the knee.

Her mother had been strict when Alice was growing up. *'Men are only ever after one thing, Alice Smart. Don't be like I was—fooled by any handsome man with a silver tongue.'*

And the one time Alice had defied her mother and gone out in a skimpy halter-neck top and miniskirt, she'd met Clinton—and everything her mother had said had been brought vividly to life.

Now, as a grown woman, and despite the fact Jane Smart was no longer able to deliver sermons on virtue and men's general failings, Alice remembered the lessons that had been drummed into her again and again, and chose to wear clothes that hid her figure completely.

This dress hid nothing.

And yet she liked it.

With a small smile on her pale pink lips, she dropped her gaze to the ring she wore and breathed out. Because she was 'engaged'. She wasn't going to fall prey to some guy who just wanted to get her into bed.

She was going out with the man she planned to marry. What did it matter that the marriage was a ruse?

Holding onto her determination, she fluffed her hair around her face, so it fell a little wild and abandoned, and pinched her cheeks until they had a pleasant flush.

Several pairs of high heels were lined up in the closet, and this time they were in different sizes, so when she settled on a pair that fitted—strappy sandals with a small heel—she felt a little like Cinderella.

Just as she began to contemplate what her own handbag would look like with this chic outfit, she spied another wardrobe. A quick inspection showed several handbags had been laid out on shelves, as well as jewellery that she knew—despite its glistening diamonds—wasn't costume.

Swallowing, she grabbed a clutch purse that matched the shoes, and turned to check her appearance one more time.

A stranger looked back at Alice.

A woman who was confident and in control. A woman who was *sexy*. The word came to Alice out of nowhere and a hive of bees seemed to take up residence in her belly, buzzing and swarming through her body.

Thanos was sexy.

He was sex appeal on a pair of very strong, long, lean legs.

She, Alice, was a fraud. A woman dressed up to play a part. And she needed to remember that; for her own sanity and emotional well-being, she couldn't let herself be suckered into this fantasy. She couldn't let herself believe, even for a moment, that this kind of thing could ever really happen to her.

It was just an act.

And soon, it would all be over.

She moved like an angel.

The discovery that his sensible, staid assistant actually had a killer figure and danced as though she'd been born with a beat inside her bones gave him the first tremor of alarm he'd felt since acquiescing to Leonidas's suggestion and proposing a marriage of convenience.

Alice had been easy to imagine as his wife.

Alice, as she'd been in the office, had been attractive in a way you'd never really notice. Nice face, nice eyes, nice smile, but there was nothing remarkable about her. He'd imagined her as the perfect bride to show Kosta how much he'd changed, without really demanding too much of Thanos's attention, once they were married.

But now, as she moved on the dance floor, her body being pushed close to his by the crush of people dancing around them, he began to see that perhaps he'd miscalculated.

She might not be anything like his usual lovers— blonde, leggy, slender and oftentimes dull as anything— but she was also nothing like he'd imagined either, and Thanos didn't generally like surprises. He dealt in known quantities and he had every reason to worry that Alice was not precisely that.

The music seemed to pulse through her, so she danced with her eyes shut, her generous lips pouted into a half-smile, half-hum, her arms moving rhythmically, and her breasts pushed against the fabric that had seemed like *such* a good idea at the time.

He moved his own body, hoping that it would distribute his blood a little more evenly throughout, rather than letting it pool in one limb only.

Her hips were mesmerising. She swayed and rolled them as if it was second nature and the very unwelcome image of her completely naked, straddling him, rolling her hips in just this manner, filled his mind so he knew he was fighting a losing battle trying to bring his blood back to his body.

Theos. What was the matter with him? He went dancing with women all the time. He could control this. He had to.

Besides, he'd brought her here to be photographed, so word could get around that he was getting married. It was hardly going to work if he spent the whole night forcibly keeping her at arm's length so she wouldn't realise that desire was flooding his body.

'Thank you for this,' she said, lifting up onto tiptoes to offer the words closer to his ear. Her breasts brushed his torso and he had to pull back a little so she wouldn't feel the force of his arousal against her gut.

'For what?'

'For everything.' Her smile was quick to spread. He stared at it, desire like a drug now. 'Mom, mainly. But also for this. I haven't been dancing in a long time. I'd forgotten how much I love it.'

Her gratitude was the last thing he'd expected. He smiled, but knew it to be dismissive, and he felt her pull away from him, a hint of hurt on her features as she put a little physical space between them and began to dance once more.

He fought an urge to apologise and explain. This was business. Even this—the dancing—was a carefully staged photo op. And his body needed to remember that.

This wasn't a normal date. He wasn't going to take Alice home to his bed, seduce her all night until she screamed his name into his apartment, nor was he going to coax pleasure and euphoria from her, syllable by syllable.

Up until three days ago, she'd been his damned assistant. Up until three days ago, he hadn't known she existed. Not outside a voice at the end of the phone, or a name at the bottom of an email.

And she was definitely not his type.

Okay, tonight she looked a lot more like his type—only better. Fascinating. Rare. Unusual.

But Alice Smart was complicated. She moved in a completely different circle from him. He didn't need to look beyond the meagre requirements she'd voiced when they'd first negotiated their marriage bargain to know that they lived in different worlds.

Besides which, Thanos wasn't interested in a real relationship.

The very idea turned his blood to ice in his veins. All his life, he'd known one thing with blinding clarity: *love stinks.*

If his own mother's decline hadn't proven that, then having a front-row seat to Dion and Maria's marriage breakup—a situation his arrival had caused—had definitely sent him the message with complete certainty.

People were born alone; they died alone. It was futile to try to live your life in a way that defied this. A marriage that would get him back a company he should never have lost seemed about the best thing Thanos could hope for.

So desiring Alice was utterly out of the question.

With the kind of discipline he'd brought to his business when it had gone completely pear-shaped, he forced his body to behave, concentrating on calming an over-excited member of his anatomy in particular, grinding his teeth until things were a little less heated, and then he smiled down at the woman he was going to marry.

The woman he'd arranged to marry purely because it made business sense. The woman he'd selected because she needed money, and money was the strongest motivator.

And he relaxed.

Because they both knew it was a commercial agreement. They both knew it was a contractual arrangement, nothing more. They both knew the terms, and were prepared to stick to them. Desire was neither here nor there in this marriage.

She was covered in a fine sheen of perspiration when they emerged from the nightclub two hours later, and she knew it made the dress cling to her even more. Knew, and didn't care. Her body was throbbing with pleasure and happiness, with a kind of light-heartedness she hadn't felt in a long time—if ever. When she was a child, they'd always been so stretched financially that their home had been tense, and Alice had borne that tension, had carried it inside her.

Then Jane had had her stroke and Alice's life had been plunged into an existence of worrying and stressing, of heartache and pain that she could rarely engage.

She couldn't remember the last time she'd simply danced. She couldn't remember the last time she'd smiled because happiness had been turning over inside her.

Everything was simple, and good, and she could relax a little.

A flash burst in her face, the light bright and blinding, and instinctively she curved her body closer to Thanos's, her expression shifting from a relaxed smile to a look of pure panic. She heard his curse, and remembered the main reason they'd come out tonight was to be photographed. They were here purely for this.

Why had she forgotten?

Fool! She should have at least checked her appearance in the cloakroom before leaving the bar.

'Got a live one, Thanos?' one of the paparazzi shouted, his accent cockney despite the fact they were in New York.

Thanos glared over Alice's head and then looked down into her face. She felt a strange, budding sense of calm despite this odd invasion of their privacy.

'You are sure about this?' he asked, quietly, his eyes roaming her face, giving her one last opportunity to pull out.

As if she could—even if this one very brief brush with his lifestyle had made her balk at what lay ahead. Thanks to his generosity, her mother was in a five-star care facility.

Thanks to Thanos, Alice would be living debt-free for the first time in years.

'I'm sure,' she agreed firmly.

'Okay, then.' He dipped his head forward and Alice had barely a second to get a grip of her emotions before his lips brushed hers. Just a quick buzz, skin on skin, an exhalation, and her pulse began to run riot in her veins, her skin prickling all over with goosebumps and anticipation.

Oh, my.

She lifted a hand to his chest, clinging to his shirt as though without his support she might topple to the ground, and unknowingly flashing her huge engagement ring for all the world to see. And see it they did, the photographers perched outside the Manhattan hotspot snapping furiously as they stayed clinging to one another, his body hard like a rock, hers soft and pliant. His hand curved around her back, resting just above the indentation of her spine, and his own breathing seemed ragged and out of control.

He was an excellent actor, because even as the moment threatened to drag every inch of sanity from her, there was still a small part of her that knew how run-of-the-mill this was for Thanos. How un-scintillating. How ordinary. This was a man who socialised with some of the most beautiful women in the world, who threw parties that Hollywood A-listers fought to attend.

He was hardly going to be truly moved by something as simple as a brushing of lips—and definitely not with someone like her.

If it weren't for the fact he was paying her handsomely, she'd have pulled away and put some distance between them. But this was an act, a charade, and she'd agreed to play her part.

So she moved her hand a little higher, curving it over his shoulder to make sure the photographers behind them

got a chance to glimpse the diamond. Only the act brought
her body even closer, and as her flesh moulded to his she
felt for herself all the proof she needed that he wasn't entirely unmoved by this.

His arousal was like a rock against her belly and her
harsh intake of breath was evidence that she'd felt it. Her
eyes slid to his and her heart began to churn, because a
drum was beating, slow and steady but unstoppably, and
it was pulling Alice towards it, demanding she listen, and
then that she answer.

'Let's go home.' The throaty command came to her as
if on delay. She heard his words, struggled to compute
them, and finally nodded.

Home.

With her fiancé.

Her body trembled as he put a hand in the small of her
back and guided her to a waiting limousine, opening the
rear door for her and using his own body to cover hers as
she stepped into the car in a dress that was too small to
accomplish such a manoeuvre easily.

A second later, he was in the space with her, and the
air seemed to crackle as though lightning were whipping
between them.

Ten minutes ago, this had seemed simple. And then
he'd kissed her, and her brain had fired up and her body
had begun to feel things it had no business feeling and
Alice could have sworn she was tipping right off the edge
of the earth.

CHAPTER FIVE

HE SHOULDN'T HAVE kissed her.

Thanos lay in his bed, on his back, staring at the ceiling, unable to sleep, unable to get Alice Smart from his mind.

The kiss had been a mistake.

Sure, he'd wanted to get papped. He'd wanted a photo of them in all the papers and on all the blogs in the morning. He'd wanted to hit Kosta with a one-two-surprised-you when next they spoke.

But kissing Alice?

Hell.

He'd opened a can of worms.

Dancing with her had been bad enough, but feeling her body pressed to his, capturing her lips, feeling her rush of warm breath, tasting her sweetness. Every single nuance of that interaction replayed in his mind now.

The feel of her body, warm and moist from dancing, her hair—the way it had smelled, like wildflowers on a sunny field. The way her fingers had knotted in his shirt, clinging to him as if she were drowning, the way her eyes had flown to his, filled with a surge of desire powerful enough to rob them both of breath.

It had taken every ounce of his legendary self-control to have his driver take Alice to her own home, to walk her to the door without going anywhere near enough to touch her—even by mistake.

Come home with me.

The words had rushed through his brain, demanding to be spoken, but thank *Christós* his tongue had obeyed him, refusing to offer an invitation that would only serve to complicate matters.

He groaned as his body tightened, growing hard beneath the sheet, so he thrust the thought away, pushing out of bed and striding to the windows that overlooked Manhattan.

This had the potential to be a total disaster if he didn't control it.

He had no intention of really marrying a woman— ever—and that was why this marriage would work so well! It was business. Business, business, business.

Except it wasn't.

Or rather, it wouldn't be, if he didn't take very great care to keep a lid on his desire for her, and to ensure she did the same.

With a roll of his eyes and a guttural moan, he wondered if it was too late to insert a non-consummation clause in their marriage contracts. A threat that she'd void everything if they slept together.

It wasn't exactly unreasonable, but the second the thought occurred to him, he dismissed it. And that alone should have given him a mountain of doubt.

Because he wasn't fighting hard enough to control this—and Thanos always fought for what he wanted.

Sydney Harbour glistened before him. He kicked back on his yacht, staring out at the world-famous skyline, glad he'd had business here in Australia to take him away from Alice. After the night at the club, he'd needed some space. The kind of space he couldn't get in a city like Manhattan. True, it was teeming with more than one and a half million people, but there was one who kept drawing his focus, distracting him when he could really do without it.

And so, Sydney.

He'd always loved this city for its mix of old and new, for its air of entrepreneurialism and elitism, its egalitarian spirit. And he loved it now for being a port in the storm.

A reprieve.

A bolthole.

Yes, he'd run away.

He'd had an envelope delivered to Alice at home the morning after the club, containing his credit card and a list of things he suggested she buy. Clothes, shoes, bags, jewels, all the things his wife would be required to have on hand, as well as some things she might not think of, which only she could deal with, such as updating her passport.

And then, he'd left the country without daring to see her again.

It was too risky.

He didn't want to complicate this.

Their arrangement had been perfect, and it still would be. They both just needed to get used to what they'd agreed to, to remember the reasons it made sense to keep things on a certain level, and everything would be fine.

Alice stroked her mother's hand, wondering when her skin had become so papery, and tears cloyed her throat.

'I bought my wedding dress today, Mom.' She lifted her gaze to her mother's face, as always, looking for a hint of recognition, anything that might suggest Jane had heard a word of what was being said. 'It's beautiful. You'd love it. Or maybe you'd hate it,' Alice said in a voice that was half apology, half amusement.

The dress had cost a fortune, but once she'd started looking on the Internet for inspiration, scouring the weddings of people 'like' Thanos—not that there were many—she'd realised she'd have to up her game and buy something a little more luxurious than the chain-store gown she'd been eyeing.

Besides, these wedding photos would be printed in huge publications. She needed to look as if she'd gone to an appropriate degree of effort.

'It's so nice.' Nice? What a bland word for the stunning creation. A spectacular bodice fitted to her torso, sculpting her breasts in a way that even Alice had to admit was flattering, flaring into a big tulle skirt that was like something out of a fairy tale. The front was all Cinderella but the back was next-level sexy.

So much so, she'd almost resisted trying it on, but the stylist had been insistent and the second Alice had been buttoned into it, she'd gasped, because the stylist was right: it was perfect. Completely backless, it showed Alice's elegant figure to advantage, her creamy skin just the right shade to complement the crisp white of the dress.

'I wish you could be at the wedding,' she said honestly, thinking of how strange it would be to get married without her mother there. How utterly surreal to stand up in front of hundreds of people and say her vows to a man she'd only met a week or so ago, a man who most women would give their eye-teeth to marry.

Jane Smart lay completely still, as she had done ever since her stroke, and Alice sat beside her, gently padding a thumb over her mother's hand, knowing, without any reason to believe it, that being there meant something to Jane. That her mother *knew* Alice was with her and was glad.

'It's not too late to pull out of this,' Leonidas, murmured out of the side of his mouth.

Thanos looked around the packed marquee at the four

hundred guests who'd travelled deep into the Provençal countryside on incredibly short notice to attend the nuptials of Europe's most famous and established bachelor.

'You don't think?'

Leonidas grinned, shrugging his shoulders. 'You're Thanos Stathakis. You can do whatever the hell you want.'

Thanos discounted the idea immediately. This made sense. Almost two weeks apart from Alice had reminded him of the professionalism required by this arrangement. She'd worked for him in one capacity for six months; this wasn't really hugely different. It was a business arrangement, pure and simple.

'What I want is to buy Petó,' he reminded Leonidas softly, turning his gaze on his brother's face. 'And Alice is the key to that.'

'Speaking of which, Kosta Carinedes is here. Did you see?'

Thanos lifted a brow, a smile quirking his lips. 'This whole thing is for his benefit. Did you think I would not invite him?'

Leonidas shook his head ruefully. 'You really are too good at this.'

Thanos shrugged, his expression like steel as the purpose for this marriage firmed in his mind. 'I've spent way too much time on P & A to lose it now.'

'After this, I imagine it is in the bag.'

'Let's hope so.'

'What's she like, anyway?'

Alice.

He frowned, trying to think of the words to describe his one-time assistant. Efficient. Pragmatic. No nonsense. And yet, she wasn't really, was she?

All it had taken was a few hours' dancing, the quickest kiss, and they'd both gone up in flames.

CLARE CONNELLY   69

His pulse lifted now, his body temperature climbing in anticipation of seeing his bride, and he had to work double time to tamp down on the response. 'She's…unusual.'

'Unusual? Does she have three heads?'

Thanos bared his teeth in an imitation of a smile. 'I mean, she's not my usual type.'

'Naturally. This isn't your usual wedding though, is it?'

'No,' Thanos was quick to agree.

'You like her, though?'

Thanos shook his head, desperate to refute that suggestion. 'It's just business.'

'Are you sure?' Leonidas's eyes rested on his brother's profile thoughtfully.

'Absolutely certain. As soon as I have the contract for P & A, this marriage is over and I'll likely never see my "wife" again.'

'And she's okay with that?'

'Okay with it? She's thrilled. We both are. That's the deal we've struck.'

Remembering the deal was important. He invoked it now as a talisman to the purpose for this wedding, smiling with an air of relaxation that he didn't completely feel.

The eleven members of the French Philharmonic Orchestra, who'd been instructed to play pre-ceremony music, brought their piece softly to a close, and silence began to descend upon the marquee.

It reigned for only a moment before the famous strains of the wedding march began to play, the music robust and beautiful.

Thanos's eyes moved with a sort of desperate fatalism towards the entrance, his whole body on alert for this moment. He reminded himself he was supposed to look like a man in love, a man waiting to see a woman he adored, and he pasted a look on his face that he hoped passed for doting—and tried not to think how much genuine anticipation there was in his body at that moment.

The instant Alice appeared, he found it almost impossible to conceal his true reaction. Several things hit him all at once.

She was walking down the aisle alone. This he had expected. He knew from their conversations that her mother was obviously bedridden, and, from the light background check Leonidas had insisted Thanos run, that her father was a mystery. No one was named on her birth certificate, no one had shared legal custody of Alice, certainly there was no one in her life who'd acted the part of father.

And there were no siblings.

He hadn't expected, therefore, that she would be accompanied down the aisle, and yet the sight of her on her own did something strange to his gut, pulling at it mercilessly, so he fought an impulse to push a hand against the wall of his stomach.

She was alone.

Just like him.

They were born alone, they died alone, and they were marrying—alone.

It wasn't just the sight of her stepping slowly towards him, with no other human to keep her company, that made his breath labour in his lungs.

As she walked purposefully up the aisle, he couldn't help but realise how little she resembled the no-nonsense assistant he'd propositioned.

Just like the night at the club, Alice Smart had transformed into something and someone completely different. This time, she was less sex siren and more Princess-in-Waiting. The dress was utterly spectacular, though he suspected on its hanger, or on another woman, it would barely catch his eye. But worn by Alice, it was a piece of mastery, flattering her body, teasing with every shift of fabric, making him want to touch it, to touch her, to feel every single inch of the fabric, and what was beneath.

Then there was the veil. While the dress was beautifully crafted and made him ache to examine it in greater detail, the veil was like something other-worldly. Made of tulle, it had a fine lace edging and on closer inspection he saw that flowers had been etched into the fabric, and, at each edge, a very fine cluster of diamonds was stitched into it. He stared at her through the gauze, the lurching in his gut entirely unwelcome and inappropriate.

'Hi.'

Her softly voiced word had sanity surge back inside him, because he heard her trepidation and nervousness and realised what a jerk he was being to be focussing on the fact she looked impossibly, tantalisingly beautiful. This was a *huge* deal for Alice. Sure, it was a fake wedding, but that didn't change the fact that the world's elite had flown in to watch them say their vows; it didn't change the fact there were television helicopters buzzing overhead, that the media had camped at the end of the private road that led to this hotel estate.

It didn't change the fact that this was her wedding day and she was way out of her comfort zone. As was he, come to think of it, but he stood to gain immensely from this wedding.

He smiled—reassuringly, he hoped—and put a hand out for her. She placed her own in it, her fingertips trembling, so he squeezed and tucked her hand in his.

'You ready?' he asked quietly, leaning towards her. And as with outside the nightclub, she blinked her eyes up to him and nodded. Fearless, even when he suspected she truly was afraid.

The ceremony was short enough—just the vows, the

legal stuff, and finally, the invitation that he may now kiss his bride.

His bride.

He looked towards Alice and studied her face in profile, wondering at the wisdom of this, simultaneously knowing it was too late to change a thing.

Remembering their audience, and one man in particular, he put an arm around her waist and drew her close enough to whisper so only Alice could hear, 'It's show time, Mrs Stathakis.'

The words were teasing, intended to be light-hearted, but there was nothing light-hearted about being close to Alice. Nothing light-hearted about the way passion soared through him, desire hammering against his body like a call he must answer.

He had just a moment to see her eyes widen and surprise flare in their depths before he kissed her.

It was a performance, an act. Except, it wasn't.

True, Kosta Carinedes was there watching, as well as four hundred other interested people, but Thanos pulled Alice into his arms and kissed her as though he was picking up right where they'd left off outside the nightclub.

He kissed her as if there were no one else in the marquee, he kissed her with all the desire that had been firing between them since he'd walked into his office in New York and come face to face with the woman who'd reorganised his life and dealt with every possible query he could throw at her.

He kissed her and his arms came around her bare back, so he groaned when he felt her naked flesh beneath his fingertips, holding her tight to his body, his kiss deepening even when he knew he ought to pull back, to lift his head, to give them both space to breathe. Right when he was about to do so, she pushed her own body closer, as though she too couldn't get enough of this, her hips shifting a little from one side to the other, just as they had in the club, moving so perfectly, so sweetly, that he ached for her in a way he recognised as pure white-hot desire, and from which he knew he needed to run a thousand miles.

Except this felt so good. So right.

He couldn't help but surrender to it, for just a little longer.

Besides, if Kosta Carinedes had any doubts whatsoever about the veracity of this hastily arranged marriage, then he imagined they were quickly fading into nothing.

Telling himself it was purely for the older man's benefit, he gave up trying to fight the kiss and he gave into it entirely. His tongue duelled with hers, his chest moved in time with Alice's, their breathing in unison as they exploded—simultaneously—in a moment of passion that could only have been better if there had been a bed within easy reach.

'You used to work for him, didn't you?'

Alice blinked up, her eyes chasing the question. The wedding reception was taking place in the grand ballroom of the Stathakis hotel, and there were at least twice the guests in attendance as had been at the ceremony itself. Trays of locally produced champagne were circulating in cut-crystal glasses and the hors d'oeuvres had all been exceptional. An enormous oyster bar stood in the corner, brimming with the crustacean, which could be enjoyed *au natural* or with any number of additions—beluga caviar, sour cream and smoked salmon, bacon and Worcestershire sauce.

Alice turned away from the incredible display to regard the woman who'd approached her, who was asking how she knew Thanos. She was tall, skinnier than a beanpole, dressed in silky couture with perfect make-up, perfect nails, and long blonde hair that had been curled into loose waves, which now hung with artful elegance around her face.

'Yes,' Alice responded, hiding her uneasiness with a look that could freeze ice. She didn't bother smiling—she didn't need to move in these social circles to see the way these women were looking at her.

As if she didn't belong. As if she'd come in and taken some kind of prize from their laps.

Of their own accord, her eyes skipped across the room, not stopping until they found him in the crowd. Despite her repeated mental reminders that this was just a job, a performance, her stomach did a funny little lurch at the sight he made.

There, in the middle of the polished marble floor, he was dancing, but not with any one of the glamorous women making eyes at him. Thanos had a little girl in his arms, and he was twirling her around the room, his eyes crinkled in the corners with laughter, as she held on tight and giggled.

She'd been introduced to Leonidas's wife Hannah and their eighteen-month-old Isabella earlier in the day. She'd never really thought of Thanos as someone with family—even though she knew the bare details. His father was in prison, and of course his brother was his business partner; they owned their enterprise together.

But seeing Thanos with these people humanised him in a dangerous way, in a way she didn't welcome. It made her want to know more about him. To ask him questions about his life growing up, about his relationship with his brother and sister-in-law, to know more than the bare facts of his father's imprisonment, and more than she could find on the Internet. She wanted to know how Thanos had *felt*. How he had survived such an awful phase of his life.

It was easier for Alice to think of him as a billionaire tycoon—successful, arrogant, fiercely intelligent and determined. It was easier for her to think of him as the 'playboy prince of Europe', to remember he had a reputation for taking women to bed with the same kind of regularity with which most people changed underwear.

Seeing him play with a little girl, though, added another dimension to his personality. One Alice wasn't entirely sure she wanted to recognise.

'It's strange,' the blonde beside her continued. 'I was with him only a few weeks ago and he never mentioned you.'

'I'm not surprised,' Alice murmured, figuring there wasn't much more she could say.

'You must be pregnant,' the woman continued thoughtfully. 'That would make sense.' She dragged her gaze over Alice's body questioningly.

'If I am, it would be news to me.'

'I just think it's weird that he never spoke about you.'

Alice's gut lurched at the lie they were perpetuating. This woman's confusion was easy to understand. This wedding had come out of the blue—for all of them.

'We wanted to keep it private,' she murmured. 'The media can be such a pain.'

'Don't I know it,' the blonde agreed, and Alice found herself softening towards the other woman a little. 'You get used to it eventually. Sort of.'

Alice nodded, even though she knew there'd be no need to get used to it. Not in the long term. Sooner rather than later, this marriage would be ended, and Alice would go back to her real life, her real self. As much as possible, anyway, given that she'd be a millionaire.

At that moment, Thanos tilted his head and his eyes caught Alice, and everything inside her went completely off-balance. Anticipation was a tsunami inside her and it was dragging her forward and sucking her under. She was losing all of herself in that moment, losing everything she knew about herself, everything she'd ever thought. She stared at him, powerless to look away, even when the blonde began speaking again.

'You'll have to come away with us next time we sail.'

'Oh?' Alice was going through the motions of the conversation now. Her body was pulling her forward, onto the dance floor, begging her to move to her groom's side.

He hadn't looked away and Alice was drowning in the depths of his eyes.

'A big group of us go a few times a year. It's fine. Lots of champagne. Sunshine. Too much food.' The woman— about the size of a pencil—grimaced, but Alice didn't see the gesture.

'Sounds fun,' she said, wondering in the back of her mind if she'd even be around when the next trip took place.

'He's a real catch, you know,' the woman said on a small sigh. Alice nodded, and in that moment she rather suspected he might be.

For someone else.

The words rushed through her body, jolting her back to reality.

Not for Alice.

Never for Alice.

He had laid all his cards out on the table. This was just business. Nothing personal. He didn't want this to be anything more than a business transaction.

Whatever desire was zapping between them simply had to be controlled.

And it was more than just Thanos's wishes. Alice had

learned her lesson at her mother's side and then again when she'd briefly let her own guard down, she'd paid the price with a heart that had been shattered well beyond repair. At least, well beyond a point that would allow her to trust again.

He lifted a hand, beckoning her slowly towards him, and she straightened, schooling her breath into a soft, gentle pattern, telling herself this was just a performance and that she must, as he'd said during the ceremony, play her part.

'Excuse me,' she murmured, turning a vague smile in the direction of the wedding guest she'd been speaking to. 'I'm going to dance with my husband.'

CHAPTER SIX

IT WAS EVERY bit as troubling as dancing with her in the nightclub had been. More so, because now Alice was his wife. Mrs Stathakis. And despite all the promises he'd made himself over the years, his utter certainty he would never do anything so foolish as marry, he felt an odd puffing of his chest when he thought of Alice in those terms.

She moved in his arms so perfectly, her body moulded to his, and his hands roamed her back distractedly, feeling the smoothness of her skin, the ridges of her spine.

'Do you actually know all these people?' she murmured, looking up at him so he tilted his head down to hers. Their eyes locked and for a moment his dancing slowed.

He started moving again, swirling her around gently. 'Most of them. Why?'

Her smile was self-deprecating. 'It's just so many people. It's kind of overwhelming.'

'I don't know many of them well,' he amended honestly.

'So they're mostly business associates?'

Thanos considered that. 'Many are, yes. But I suppose a few hundred are people I socialise with.'

'But aren't actually friends with?' she prompted, a teasing smile on her face, a divot between her brows that he had an irrational urge to drop his lips to and kiss.

'What's your definition of a friend?'

'Someone you could call at any time, day or night, who'd have your back when you needed support.'

He lifted a brow, his stomach churning a little. 'In that case, I have only one friend.'

'Oh?'

He swivelled his head, moving his gaze across the room. 'My brother, Leonidas.'

'Ah.' Her smile was just a lift at the corners. 'I think that's cheating.'

He laughed, a sound that ruffled through his broad chest. 'Is it?'

'Yep. And I can't compete because I have no siblings, so it's not really fair.'

'You didn't invite any of your friends?'

She pulled her mouth to the side a bit, as she thought about that. 'I don't really have any friends.'

He saw regret cross her face followed swiftly by confusion, almost as though she'd said more than she'd intended, and wanted to draw the words back in. But he wouldn't let her. Her admission fascinated him.

'Why not?'

'Honestly?'

'Yeah.'

'It's complicated.'

He arched a brow. 'I'm your husband, remember.'

She pulled a face and lowered her voice, lifting up onto the tips of her toes so he alone would hear her. 'In name only.'

'Ah.' He grinned. 'Don't hold that against me.'

Alice lowered her body back, staying close to him, her brow furrowed thoughtfully. 'I'll try not to.'

'So? Friends?'

She expelled a soft sigh. 'We moved around a lot when I was growing up. It was hard to meet friends, and once I did, we'd leave town again. I used to email a few, but after about my sixth school, I stopped even trying to learn the names.' She grimaced. 'Work is no different. I mean, I'm a temp, so by the very nature of my job, I'm never in the same place for long. And when I am, and I do by chance come across someone I click with socially, I can't really catch up with them because I care for Mom so much of the time.'

Thanos hadn't been born with the proverbial silver spoon in his mouth. True, he'd known excessive wealth and comfort during his childhood, but he'd also known a corresponding degree of pain and emotional distance, of loss and hardship, and yet he found it hard to think of a single thing he'd gone through that could compare to the sheer loneliness of what Alice had experienced.

'I'm only twenty-four but I don't really do the stuff people my age are into. I can't afford it.'

He smiled but it was completely without humour.

'There wasn't anyone I could think of to invite,' she said with a lift of her shoulders.

'I'm sorry.'

'Please don't be,' she said with a shake of her head and a slightly tremulous smile. 'If you're going to feel sorry for me, feel sorry for me because my dad never wanted to know me or because my mom is in a coma, or because I had a credit-card debt the size of Mount Everest until you entered the picture. I can live without friends.'

He slowed his dancing once more, thinking again how similar they were, how independent, how determined to show that they were okay with being on their own.

'I'm sorry for those things, too.' He stared down at her, wondering at the twists and turns life had served this woman, at the reality she'd been forced to live, and sympathy tore through him.

But she smiled, and even if it didn't reach her eyes, it totally changed her face.

'It's our wedding day,' she reminded him. 'We should look happy, not glum.'

Before he could reply, they were interrupted by the arrival of Kosta Carinedes.

'Thanos,' he said with a nod, his eyes shifting to Alice's with obvious interest. 'Miss Smart.'

'Mrs Stathakis,' Alice corrected without missing a beat, tilting her face towards Thanos's and smiling in a way that was now a perfect imitation of a woman madly in love. And even though she was simply pretending, something like warmth spread through Thanos, starting at his chest and radiating out through his body in waves.

'Of course.' Kosta still seemed as if he was waiting for the punchline. He looked from one to the other with a sense of bemusement.

'We're so glad you could join us,' Alice enthused, going over the top of his doubts with a truly gifted performance. 'I felt quite bad the other day, when you came to the office and we didn't confess the truth.'

Thanos's eyes narrowed.

'So this was going on then?'

Alice arched a brow teasingly. 'We just got married,' she pointed out. 'Of course it was going on then.'

'So you've been an item for some time?'

Thanos stroked Alice's side without realising he was doing it. 'We wanted to keep things quiet for as long as possible. You know, privacy concerns.'

'Naturally.' Kosta's eyes narrowed. 'How long have you been dating?' he prompted, like a dog with a bone, refusing to give up on his inquisition.

Thanos ground his teeth together, pushing his impatience aside. 'It feels like a very long time ago that I first saw Alice and lost my heart.'

Alice's expression showed surprise as she looked at him, so he stroked her side, and slowly she smiled, turning back to Kosta. 'I understand your concerns about my husband, Mr Carinedes. But it's important to remember that newspapers will write a story about just about anything.'

Kosta considered this for a moment. 'That is true, m'dear. Very true.'

They were quiet for a moment, and Thanos had to bite back an impulse to ask the older man when he intended to sign the company over to him—surely his last objection had been dealt with?

'You're having a honeymoon?' Kosta asked, and Thanos could tell he'd surprised Alice when he nodded in the affirmative.

'That is the norm, is it not?' Thanos prompted.

'Of course. Where will you go?'

Thanos turned to Alice, a smile on his face. 'It's a surprise, for my bride.'

'Ah.' This appeared to please the old man. He clapped his hands together and offered the first genuine smile Thanos had seen from him in a long time. 'Well, when it's over, why don't you two join me in Port D'Angelo for an evening?'

'Port D'Angelo?' Alice prompted.

'A small town on the southern coast of Kalatheros— my home is there. Come—see the ocean, eat *galaktoboureko* and drink wine. I would enjoy getting to know you better, Alice.'

Thanos smiled, but he read the subtext. This would be a test. A 'throwing down of the gauntlet' to make sure their marriage was the real deal. He couldn't blame the older man for taking the precaution. The circumstances were highly suspicious—and with good reason.

'Fine.' Alice's smile was completely relaxed. She was clearly an excellent actress—better even than he'd suspected. 'I'd like that. Thanos?'

'We'll come as soon as we can,' Thanos murmured.

'Shall we say a week?'

'A week?' Thanos balked at that, for no reason he could think of. 'Make it three.'

Beside him Alice stiffened, and lifted her face to his. 'Don't be silly, Thanos. A week is fine.' Her smile was encouraging, and he couldn't have said why but he felt annoyed. Impatient.

'Good,' Kosta rolled on, their acquiescence now apparently something he took for granted. But he sobered, his expression growing serious as he looked up at Thanos. 'She is your family now. All that you do is for her.'

The wedding dress *on* Alice had been bad enough. But it was somehow so much worse when he stepped into the luxurious bathroom of the hotel penthouse to see it carefully arranged over a coat hanger, suspended from the gold frame of the shower screen.

He ran his fingers over the lace bodice, as he'd been aching to do all day, his gut tightening with memories of how Alice had looked *in* the dress. And imagining how she looked *out* of it.

He stifled a groan, washing his face and unbuttoning his own shirt, discarding it considerably less carefully, in a pile on the floor. He braced his palms on the marble counter and stared at his reflection, a haunted look in his eyes as he noted the detail of the gold band on his wedding finger.

He was married.

And it didn't matter that it was just a sham, he felt a

panicking constriction in his chest, rising to his throat, making breathing momentarily difficult.

Married.

Just as he'd sworn he'd never be.

He swept his eyes shut for a moment, inhaling, exhaling, ignoring the panic, focussing on the end result of this.

Petó. The company that would be his.

It didn't matter that he'd got way more than he'd bargained for with Alice Smart. It didn't matter that he'd suggested this when he'd thought her efficiency outstripped any other quality she possessed, when he'd thought she'd be a convenient bride—convenient in that he'd barely notice she was around.

How wrong he'd been!

He was noticing her, noticing her in all the ways he didn't want to.

The brief kiss at the nightclub had been bad, but he'd been able to tame it. The kiss at their wedding? It had pulled at every single one of his senses and even now his body was on fire, wanting to know how that kiss would end if they gave it free rein.

A noise from beyond the bathroom had him moving to the door, and when he stepped out, it was to see Alice in the kitchen, filling a kettle with water.

And desire throbbed low in his abdomen, refusing to be quelled. Because the wedding dress had been impressive, but even now, with her face wiped of make-up, her dark hair loose around her face, dressed in a simple T-shirt and pants that looked to be stretchy yoga tights, she was working her way into his mind, so he couldn't look away, and couldn't think of anything else.

He must have made a noise without realising it, because she lifted her face, her eyes locking to his in surprise, her lips parting a little.

'I didn't know you were in here.'

The kiss had been fascinating.

He hadn't expected such a depth of response from her, nor had he expected to want her in a way that had robbed him of any common sense.

Thanos stood on a precipice now. Common sense and safety were on one side, and on the other, something far more dangerous and infinitely more pleasing.

'I…' A furrow developed between her brows. 'I thought I'd go to bed. With a cup of tea. And a book.' Her breath moved quickly, her chest lifting with each huff, so her nipples strained against the flimsy cotton material of her shirt and he wondered what she'd feel like. If he reached his hands out and curved them over her breasts…

He banished the thought from his mind and waited for her to make her tea and leave.

Except she didn't. She poured the water into a cup and stayed right where she was, her eyes roaming his face slowly, hungrily, as though she too was reluctant to put distance and sleep between them. As if this day—their wedding day—was somehow magical and apart from regular time.

'So…' She let the word hang between them, a little puff of air, a question, an answer, an invitation.

'So.' His smile was slow to spread across his face.

'A honeymoon?' she prompted, lifting her tea to her lips and sipping it, cupping it with both hands. Her wedding ring shone like a beacon of light.

'Isn't that traditional?'

'For real couples,' she said with a note to her voice that could have been wistful, and could have been teasing.

'This has to look like a real marriage,' he reminded her. 'The world will expect us to be revelling in our "happy couple" life.'

She pulled a face, and pushed up from the bench at the same time, coming around to stand beside him. 'You don't really seem like someone who'd care what the world thinks.'

His laugh was just a harsh sound of agreement. 'Generally I don't.' He didn't add that more often than not he lived to defy expectations, not to meet them.

'So this is all for Kosta's sake?'

He tilted his head towards hers, unable to explain why he wanted to deny that. He fought the temptation, and nodded instead. 'Yes, *agape*.'

'This company—'

'Petó.'

She nodded. 'It obviously means a lot to you.'

'Yes.'

'But you have lots of other companies.'

'This was my grandfather's.'

She tilted her head to the side, a gesture he now knew to mean she was considering something. Only it put sensible thought right out of his mind, so all he could do was look at the delicate curve of her neck, the creaminess of her skin. Desire kicked up a notch and he felt as though the air between them were crackling with heat and fire.

He had to fight it.

Didn't he?

'He had a lot of businesses?'

'Yes. But not like Petó.'

'Why not?'

'It was his favourite.' He made light of the question, lifting a hand and rubbing it across the back of his neck. 'It was his father's before him. When I first came to live with Dion, it was our grandfather who spent time with us. With me.' His voice deepened on the admission. 'I think perhaps he saw what no one else did.'

'What's that?'

He forced a smile to his face to compensate for the maudlin response. 'I was alone. Completely alone. And terrified.'

'You?' she teased, but she was faking it too, he could tell. Sympathy softened her eyes, and she lifted a hand to his chest, so he drew in a deep breath as she pressed her palm over his heart. 'Surely you were never afraid of anything?'

'Only a fool lives without fear,' he commented softly.

She bit down on her lip. 'That's very true.'

He lifted his hand, laying it over hers, his eyes locked to hers, daring her to say something, to do something, to pull away and put a stop to this. She didn't.

His heart was pounding, slamming against his ribs, and the pull of his desire refused to be ignored. He pushed his body up, just enough to bring them into contact, and with his spare hand he removed her teacup, reaching behind him and placing it on the bench.

'You were going to bed,' he said quietly, not sure if he was suggesting she leave, or angling for an invitation to join her.

She nodded, her eyes locked to his. 'I know.' And she lifted up onto the tips of her toes once more, her body—so soft with gentle curves in all the most fascinating places—pressing against him so he wanted to lift her up and lay her down on the kitchen bench, to take her then and there. Except that felt completely wrong, even more so than just wanting to take her to bed.

Hadn't he sworn this wouldn't be a real marriage?

And it still wouldn't be. Even if they were to succumb to this, they both knew what was on offer—and, more importantly, what wasn't.

This was a business relationship, first and foremost.

Nothing that happened between them would alter the parameters of that.

'How did your grandfather help you?'

The question surprised him. He ignored it, at first. He no longer wanted to think about his family. Nor to talk about them. All his focus was on this moment, and the woman pressed against him.

A voice from the back of his mind was shouting at him to put an end to this, but it was being swamped by other, more desirable inclinations. Inclinations that were so much easier and more pleasurable to obey.

Her hand ran across his naked chest and he closed his eyes for a moment, inhaling deeply, breathing in her fragrance, the sweetness of it, the innocence, and his gut rolled.

'Thanos?'

He didn't know if she was prompting him about her earlier question, or asking him what the hell was happening.

He jerked his eyes open and stared down at her, and a roll of something like dissatisfaction went through him, a roll of betrayal, because it hadn't been supposed to happen like this. Their wedding was meant to be rational and sensible—their marriage easy to control. They'd both said as much when they'd agreed to enter into this.

Now? He wanted to shift the goalposts, and he needed her to agree to that.

'I know we said this would be a business arrangement...' He curved his hands around her hips, lifting her shirt a little so he could feel her bare flesh. Her eyes swept shut, her lashes forming two perfect, dark crescents against the creamy pale of her cheeks.

'We did.' Her words were so throaty they were almost impossible to discern.

He lifted a hand to her cheek, holding it in his palm, staring down at her.

'This doesn't feel businesslike.'

He padded his thumb to her lip, anguish torturing him, the wait an agony. 'I have no interest in relationships.'

Her eyes flared a little wider, but she was still. Watchful. Listening.

'I don't ever lie about that. I do not believe in leading anyone on.'

She nodded, swallowing, darting her tongue out to lick the corner of her mouth. His arousal strained hard against his pants.

'Nothing that happens between us will change what I want from you. Our marriage is a construct to enable me to buy a company that I consider to be my birthright. That's all.'

She nodded slowly and made no effort to move away from him.

'But, *agape mou*, I am full of longing for you, and all I can think about is making you mine. Just for this night. Just once.'

A strangled noise escaped her throat, a sound of acquiescence, he thought, but he needed to be sure. He dropped his hands to his sides, holding his body completely still, his nostrils flaring with the strength of his breathing as he stared at her, waiting, impatient, desperately hungry. 'Tell me you understand,' he commanded. 'No.' He shook his head. 'Tell me you want what I want.'

Silence crackled between them, and he waited, each second like a torturous beat in time that was hammering against him.

'I want...' She paused, and he had no idea if she was intentionally torturing him, or if it was by accident, but, either way, he felt impatience burst through him like a physical force, strong enough to threaten the very fabric of his soul. 'This one night,' she continued shakily, and before he could respond she lifted a finger to his lips, keeping him silent. 'One night, no strings, no questions, no promises.'

And if those limitations sounded a little bit sad, the brightness of her smile contradicted that sentiment. She dropped her hand and looked up at Thanos as though he were everything she'd been waiting for.

And for that night, he really, really wanted to be.

CHAPTER SEVEN

His hands on her body were gentle, roaming her flesh slowly, so slowly, feeling every little bit of her. Her arms, where his touch sparked a torrent of nerve endings and goosebumps, her shoulders, his fingers splayed wide, his thumbs moving to the base of her neck, his eyes locked to hers, always watching, examining, seeing the way she responded.

Reading her, as though she were a book. And she stood there, looking up at him, her eyes huge in her face, her expression stricken—not with panic, so much as a sense of wild longing, and surprise that she could feel that. Surprise that he could invoke that.

She'd thought Clinton had inured her to sexual attraction.

She'd thought she'd learned how stupid it was to let your body guide you like this.

But standing there with Thanos Stathakis lifting her shirt higher up her body, she felt only relief.

'You're trembling.' His hands grazed her sides, the fabric soft against her oversensitive skin.

'I know.' She nodded, and when he pushed her shirt over her breasts, his palms grazing the sensitive flesh of her nipples, she moaned softly, the feeling like nothing she'd ever known before.

He pushed it over her head and dropped it to the floor at their feet then returned his hands to her breasts, cupping them lightly while dropping his head, his lips seeking hers, kissing her with a slow inquiry.

It was like lighting a fuse.

Desire exploded inside Alice, a spark igniting to a firework, so she was pushing up onto the bench, sitting against it, her legs wrapped around his waist, her hands desperately running over his chest and back, seeking skin, needing to feel it beneath her fingertips, to feel *him* beneath her.

'I didn't expect this.' She kissed the admission into his mouth, wondering in the back of her mind if it was true. Hadn't she looked at Thanos from that first morning and felt a kick of longing? Still, their wedding was supposed to be a means to an end—and not this end.

In response he kissed her harder, his mouth crushing hers, his fingers weaving through her hair, cupping her scalp, holding her in place for his total domination, his body weight easing her back, so she was lying on the cold marble bench top, his hair-roughened torso a torture against her sensitive nipples. She arched her back, lifting her hips in a silent, age-old invitation, and he laid a line of kisses from her lips to her throat, flicking her décolletage with his tongue, so she moaned into the night air, the word 'please' tripping out of her mouth again and again.

Ancient, primal urges drove her and she answered their call, her body wild, her breathing ragged. She dug her heels into his back, drawing him closer to her feminine heart, and his hands dropped to the yoga pants she wore, pushing inside the elastic and cupping her bottom,. He lifted her, pulling her from the bench, so she wrapped her arms around his neck and kissed him as he carried her through the palatial lounge towards a large leather ottoman.

It was jet black outside the windows—vineyards rolled away from the hotel and in the distance there was the ocean, waves relentlessly pounding against the shoreline, just as need was slashing against her heart, demanding she answer it.

He removed her pants quickly, easily, and dispensed with his own while he stood above her, his chest moving hard and fast as he came down over her, his eyes glittering in his handsome face. But the separation was too much to bear. She pushed up on her elbows, her body lifting to find his, her eyes seeking, looking, hunting, her hands pulling for him.

There was no room for self-consciousness, no room for doubt, no room for worrying about how she'd feel in the morning. A fire was raging out of control and the only way to put it out was to indulge it completely. His hands on her thighs were strong, insistent, spreading her legs wider, his arousal poised to take her, and she held her breath, desire arcing inside her in a kind of mania.

Her nails scraped down his back, urging him forward, and he laughed gruffly, but it was a sound that was as deranged as she felt.

She bucked her hips as he thrust into her—and it was not a possession of slow, lazy intent; this was a sheer, blinding thrust of need, hard and desperate. He drove into her and she cried out because it was *everything* she'd ever thought she could want in life.

She tilted her head backwards and his stubbled jaw ran across her décolletage then lower, his mouth, warm and moist, curving around one of her nipples, his tongue lashing it until she was in a state of delirium. His hard arousal thrust into her again and again, his hands lifting her bottom, holding her higher so he could reach all of her, and then one hand was moving around to her womanhood, his fingers tormenting her most sensitive cluster of nerves until she was whimpering with the sheer agony of her desire.

'I feel like I'm on fire,' she groaned, and he smiled against her breast, but it was a smile of tension, because the same agonising want was throbbing through him, churning his gut, making him impatient for a release that he wanted to stave off as long as possible.

'I like being on fire,' she said, not even sure the words made any sense; her mind was no longer a part of her body. There was only this: feeling, pleasure, desperate yearning. He moved rhythmically, his body stoking hers, and she pushed up on her elbows as a tidal wave of need she couldn't fight, didn't want to fight, dragged at her and she let it pull her out to sea. It crashed against her, pleasure a rush of awakening that made breathing almost impossible.

She cried his name out, tasting it as she exploded in his arms, oblivious to the way he stilled, watching her, his eyes intent on her pleasure-creased face as she fell apart at the seams and slowly breathed herself back together again. He watched her and just as her breathing slowed he began to move again, so her eyes flared wide, locking to his, shock in them because her needs were already back, desire shifting inside her, greedily seeking more. He spoke to her in Greek, hushed words she neither recognised nor understood, words that filled her with pleasure just the same, words that were perfect in that moment, as he drove her to the heights of her pleasure anew.

This time, when the wave dragged her under, it dragged him with it, and she held onto him for dear life, as though everything she was depended on being close to him. They were adrift at sea, but adrift together.

Just that moment, just that night.

* * *

Alice stretched in bed, the silk sheets like gossamer against her well-kissed skin. She smiled at Thanos, not at all self-conscious in her naked state. How could she be? After they'd made love on the ottoman, he'd lifted her up and carried her to this sumptuous bedroom, laying her on the bed where he'd continued to pleasure and delight her body, kissing her most intimate flesh, tasting her, inviting her to explore his body, to look and learn, and she'd lost herself down the rabbit hole of sensual awakening, a hazy fog of lust pummelling her from the inside out.

It was now somewhere near dawn, but she wasn't tired. Not even a little. She lifted her fingertips to his chest, tracing a line down the centre, her eyes following the gesture lazily. He was bronzed all over. She liked looking at his skin. She liked looking at him.

'You know,' she said, pushing up on one elbow so she could look at him properly, 'you're very, very good at that.'

Her fingers pushed lower, trailing the line of hair that arrowed down his abdomen.

'My ego is glad you think so.'

Her lips twisted in a half-smile.

'I didn't really know it could be so…*whoa*…'

'Whoa?' he teased, his eyes shuttered so she couldn't discern emotion in their depths.

'So mind-blowing,' she clarified, swirling her fingers in figures of eight, just below his navel.

'Ah.' He made a sound of comprehension, swiftly followed by a knitting together of his brows. 'And that's… different for you?'

His accent was thicker in this snatch of time, before daylight danced across the horizon, pulling out of the ocean's depths.

Alice's fingers moved lower, slowly, so slowly, until her

fingertips brushed against the base of his erection. She felt his swift intake of breath and smiled at the raw rush of feminine power.

'I don't really have much experience.' Her eyes flicked upwards and now there *was* self-consciousness there. 'Definitely nothing compared to you.'

She didn't see the frown that etched across his face.

'You were not a virgin?'

'No.' Her smile was wistful. She wished, in that moment, she had been. It was ridiculous, but the only thing that could have made what they'd shared more meaningful was if he'd been her first. She could make her peace with the fact this was a very temporary affair, she could make her peace with the fact that soon—in a matter of months—their marriage would be dissolved and they'd go their separate ways. But somehow, that didn't detract from the specialness and uniqueness of what they'd just shared.

'But you haven't found sex "mind-blowing" to date?'

She bit down on her lip, shaking her head. 'I mean, I was only with one guy.' Her eyes lifted to his. 'Once.'

He was very still then, and not because her fingers were continuing their exploration of his erection. 'You have only had sex *once* before?'

'Well, now I've had sex a lot,' she teased, sobering at his look of absolute disbelief.

'I know that must seem ridiculous to someone like you,' she said quietly. 'But it wasn't really…a great experience. Definitely not one I was rushing to repeat.'

Thanos reached beneath the sheets and captured her hand, pulling it away from his member with a warning look. 'I cannot think when you do that.'

'Good.' She blinked at him with mock innocence.

'I want you to explain to me,' he insisted, lifting her

hand to his lips and pressing a kiss against her fingertips so her heart jolted inside her.

Alice sighed, her eyes shuttering a little, her gaze focussed on his lips. He was sort of like a conversational solar eclipse; there was such an intensity in his eyes that it was hard to concentrate when she looked directly at him.

'There's not really much to explain. I learned my lesson,' she said quietly.

'What lesson is that?'

She forced her eyes to his then, burnt sugar holding glowing amber. She aimed for light-hearted; it came out strangled. 'That handsome men who promise you the world aren't to be trusted.' She flicked her lips into a smile for good measure; Thanos didn't return it. Nor did he relinquish his hold on her gaze.

'It's funny. All my life my mom drummed it into me again and again that men weren't to be trusted.' Her smile was wistful. 'It wasn't her fault. My dad burned her pretty badly and we both had to live with the consequences of that for a long time.'

'What did he do?'

She shook her head. 'It's a long story. The point is, he broke her heart and she made sure I grew up knowing there's no such thing as Prince Charming or saccharine happy endings. She was trying to protect me, and I guess she really did have a point.'

He frowned; she didn't notice.

'But then I met Clinton, and despite being a walking cautionary tale, everything I knew to be true, everything Mom had always said, flew out of the window as I fell head over heels in love with his smooth lines.'

'He was your contemporary?'

'A few years older,' she corrected. 'Twenty—which to

an impressionable sixteen-year-old meant the world.' She shook her head with disbelief. 'I was such an idiot.'

'You were sixteen?'

'And foolish.'

'What happened?'

She expelled a soft sigh. 'I slept with him and I thought it was the beginning of something amazing and special and incredible.'

'But it wasn't?'

She shook her head, her expression unknowingly haunted.

'So what?' His voice was impatient, but not with her. 'He what? Broke up with you once you'd slept together?'

Alice swept her eyes shut, the awful, horrible fallout from that weekend something she tried to forget. 'More or less.'

'Meaning?'

'Oh, he was a bastard,' she groaned, blinking her gaze to Thanos's. 'He made sure all of his friends knew he'd been my first, that I was bad in bed, inexperienced.' She shook her head. 'I thought I loved him, and he... It was a pretty horrifying experience.'

'Men like that are overcompensating for some personal deficiency.' The words were snapped from his mouth, disapproval zinging around the room.

'Undoubtedly.'

'You are not bad in bed.'

It was so not what she'd expected him to say that Alice laughed, a soft sound, and when she looked at Thanos, she found him staring at her in a way that made her body tremble a little.

'Anyway, it was an eternity ago. I'm definitely not the same girl I was then.' She tilted her chin defiantly, remembering how true that was, the leaps and bounds she'd come on since then. 'He taught me a lesson that I shouldn't have needed to be taught, but it's one I've never forgotten.'

'And what lesson is that, Kyria Stathakis?'

Her lips pulled a little to the side. 'Not to be such a gullible fool.' The mood between them had shifted; there was an intensity between them and a vulnerability within her that she didn't entirely like. She pulled her hand away from him, teasing it down his body once more, her eyes holding a silent challenge as they connected to his.

'I wouldn't have slept with you tonight if it weren't for the fact we both know what the boundaries of this are.'

He didn't move; didn't speak.

'I like that you've been honest with me. I like that we both have our reasons for knowing this will run its course and we'll go our own way. I've learned not to trust anyone but, somehow, I do trust you, Thanos.' Her hands curved around his arousal and a throaty breath pushed out of him, lifting his chest.

Thanos wasn't sure he'd ever had anyone say those words to him. It did something completely foreign to his chest. 'Why?' The question was grated out of him, as his ability to think and process were lost in a fog of uncertainty.

'Because you're not making any promises.' She flicked her gaze to his and then pushed up at the same time she pulled the sheet off his body. 'You've been honest with me from the start, and the reason I know you're telling me the truth is because nothing you've said has been designed to get me into bed.'

She straddled his legs and brought her face closer to his arousal, her eyes holding his. 'I'm here because I want to be.' It was the last thing she said before she curved her lips over the tip of his arousal, and Thanos lost any ability whatsoever to speak, think or worry.

* * *

As dawn began to crest over the ocean, spreading light and newness into the valley of vines, Thanos pushed out of bed, taking a moment to look back at a sleeping Alice before pulling on some briefs.

Her eyelids moved frantically—a sign of deep sleep and busy dreams—and he smiled a little, wondering if he was in her dreams.

But his smile shifted from his face as he moved from the bedroom back into the lounge area, his eyes falling first to the ottoman, his body hardening as he remembered the frantic, animalistic passion of their coming together, the feeling of absolute, sheer need driving him to her as though everything he was depended on that possession.

But Thanos was no stranger to sexual passion. He liked women. He liked being with women. He made no apologies for his appetite, nor did he need to. Alice was right—Thanos never lied in order to seduce a woman. In fact, he was always at great pains to be blindingly honest with any woman he was interested in.

Thanos wasn't the kind of man to offer 'more'—the elusive promise of something beyond the physical. He had no interest in anything other than sex, and never had done. It was one of the reasons he generally kept his 'relationships' to a one-time affair. It was a lot harder to hurt someone if you only spent a night in each other's company.

And that had worked for him—it had been easy. Guilt-free.

But there was danger here, so much danger. Because everything was different with Alice. The intensity of his need for her was unlike anything he'd ever known. The sex had been mind-blowing, just as she'd said, so he'd been insatiable for her, wanting more and more and more. Even now, after knowing the pleasures of her body, her hands, her mouth all night, he was still filled with a hunger for her, a desperate craving that wouldn't quit.

But by far the biggest danger they faced was that he couldn't simply walk away from this. He couldn't kiss her on the lips and fly off in his helicopter, back into his real world. He couldn't turn his back on her and never see her again, as he ordinarily might.

She was his wife, and, even though they both knew their wedding was practicality at its finest, they were inescapably bound.

Sex complicated that. It complicated it in a way that meant he couldn't make his peace with it, and yet he already knew he couldn't walk away from it either. What he needed was to regain a sense of control; to put some boundaries in place. Because she was right. He hadn't lied to her, and he didn't intend to. Not with words, certainly, but not with actions either. He owed it to both of them to show he could control the passion that flared between them. It was a delight to be carefully enjoyed, not a need that should be allowed to overtake them.

He wouldn't allow it, and he was Thanos Stathakis so naturally he didn't, for one moment, doubt his chance of success.

CHAPTER EIGHT

'WHAT HAPPENED WITH your father?'

He lifted his gaze from the newspaper he was reading to find Alice watching him with undisguised curiosity.

The yacht had been a bad idea. A very bad idea. If he'd been wanting to prove to himself that he could control this flame of desire, suggesting they take his yacht out onto the Balearic Sea had been foolhardy in the extreme.

From the minute Alice had appeared in a floaty sundress with a huge wide-brimmed hat, he'd felt a pulsing of warmth in his body that had had less to do with admiration than it did amusement—a sentiment he feared was just as dangerous.

She'd brought a huge bag with her, packed with books of all things, and a big bottle of water, as though she didn't realise his yacht had a commercial-grade kitchen on board as well as an army of staff to keep them fed and serve them drinks of any variety.

But it was when she'd removed her sundress to reveal a bright red bikini that he'd known it was going to be harder than he'd banked on to control his need for her.

Alice Smart—no, Alice Stathakis—had the most tantalisingly creamy skin he'd ever seen. Flawless and pale, with golden undertones, and toes that had been painted a surprising black matte in colour. She'd wiggled them as she'd read, and he'd found the sight of that infuriatingly erotic.

He'd had to fight an urge to ask her what she was reading. To ask her if she read often. What her favourite books were. To ask her anything and everything. Because asking, he feared, would lead to knowing her better, and, more than that, it would lead to looking at her and wanting to strip that scrap of Lycra from her body and make love to her right here on the deck of his yacht, with not a care in the world for the possibility of drone cameras overhead or long lenses on shore.

'You don't have to talk about it if you don't want to,' she offered, an apologetic heat creeping into her cheeks.

He frowned, not perfectly able to recall what she'd asked.

'I guess it was pretty hard for you. Having him be sent away.' She turned back to her book, her dark hair plaited in a single braid, which she'd pulled over her shoulder. The tasselled ends landed against her breast; a breast he'd touched and tasted and was hungry to feel again now. Her skin would be sun-warmed and salty from the ocean.

'It wasn't hard.' The admission surprised them both. Him, because he rarely spoke of Dion Stathakis to anyone. Even he and Leonidas, by unspoken yet mutual consent, had formed a silence when it came to their father and his wrongdoing. Of course, Leonidas had so much more to resent the man for than Thanos did—Leonidas who had lost his wife and child in a madman's revenge against Dion. But Thanos had still lost enough to hate his father with all his soul.

'No?' She pressed a finger into the pages of her book and placed it on her lap. His eyes followed the gesture.

'I wish he'd received a life sentence. No, sometimes I've wished he'd been put to death.'

Her breath made an audible gasp as she processed this.

'You may think that's harsh,' he said softly. 'But you have to understand the damage he did, the life he took.'

'Whose life?'

Thanos let out a laugh—but not one of amusement. 'Mine, my brother's, my grandparents' legacy, and theirs before them.' He shook his head in disapproval. 'He ruined everything and not because he needed money, but because he wanted power. Not the kind of power you can have when you own half the hotels in Europe,' Thanos pointed out with a wry shift of his lips. 'He wanted people to fear him. He wanted them to tremble when he entered a room.'

Alice was quiet for a moment and Thanos wondered if she was regretting asking the question. But after a moment, she shifted her body weight, pushing onto her side so she could face him properly. And even in the midst of recounting a time in his past he loved to forget, his eyes were drawn to the sway of her breasts, and desire offered a very welcome reprieve from the darkness of his thoughts.

'Were you afraid of him?'

The question was not at all what he'd expected.

'No.'

Alice frowned. 'Did you know he was involved in the mob?'

'No.' His nostrils flared as he breathed out, and he reached a hand towards her, running his fingers over her plait, flicking the tail distractedly. 'I am not being intentionally vague.'

'I know that.' She grimaced. 'I guess it's not exactly your favourite topic.'

His eyes flew to hers, cinnamon clashing with burnt butter. 'I never speak about him.'

'I didn't mean to be invasive.'

He frowned, because, strangely, he hadn't felt that she was. 'It's fine.' He flipped onto his back, staring at the sky. 'If we are to convince Kosta that I am a changed and happily married man, it's important we know each other well. We have no way of knowing what conversations will come up when we are at Kalatheros.'

He didn't see the small frown that crossed Alice's face, so couldn't have guessed the reason for it.

'I was not afraid of him, but nor did I feel affection for him. I suppose, if anything, I was wary of him.'

'Wary of your own father?'

Thanos nodded, a muscle jerking in his jaw. 'He was… erratic, at best. And I think he didn't like me, so what time we spent together was shaped by that dislike.'

'That would have been very hard to live with.'

He appreciated that she didn't try to argue with him. He could have imagined an outsider might have insisted that *of course* Dion had liked him. But Thanos was no fool, and his father's sentiments had been made abundantly clear over the years.

'I didn't particularly like him either,' Thanos quipped, in a futile attempt to lighten the mood. 'Leonidas—my half-brother—is only three months older. When my mother left me on Dion's doorstep, it heralded the end of my father's marriage.'

'Because you were…'

'Proof he'd cheated,' Thanos finished for Alice. 'Though I'm sure Leonidas's mother must have known even before I showed up. My mother was not the only mistress Dion spent time with.'

He looked at Alice in time to catch the sympathy in her expression. Strangely, he didn't resent it in the way he usually might. Thanos never welcomed sympathy or pity. Even as a child, he'd pushed back against those emotions.

'That's not your fault, though. How could he dislike you, because of it?'

Thanos let out a soft laugh. 'I was also a pretty unlovable child.'

Alice didn't laugh in response. 'How can you say that about yourself?'

'It's true. Even my own mother couldn't bear to be with me.'

'Why do you say that?'

'Because it is honest.' He reached a finger out, tracing the line of her lower lip. 'The last thing she said to me, before leaving me at Dion's—a man I didn't even know existed—was that she couldn't handle being my mother any more.'

Alice's sharp intake of breath did something to his gut. The wall of cement he kept locked in place to shield those memories from prying minds and fingers developed a crack. He welded over it, plastering a dismissive smile on his face.

'I was a handful. I don't blame her.'

'Well, I do!' she snapped. 'How could she say that to you? At eight years old!'

'I probably deserved it.'

Alice glared at him. 'No eight-year-old deserves that.'

'I was stubborn, sullen, demanding, and difficult.'

'So are all kids. In different measure, admittedly,' she said, a little frown forming on her face. 'But if she really felt like that, then there had to have been other options besides just depositing you with a father you didn't know you had.'

'It was a strange reality to find myself in,' he said truthfully, remembering that first afternoon, walking around the mansion, the servants' whispers filling his young ears, Leonidas's mother's shrieks burning them.

The knowledge, weeks later, that he was responsible for breaking up their family.

He turned away from her, his expression suddenly stony.

'Do you ever speak to her now?'

'No.'

'God.' Alice reached a hand out and curved her fingers over his forearm. 'That's a really awful thing to have gone through.'

He shrugged. 'I guess so. But you know what?'

'What?' Her voice was thick with emotion.

'It gave me Leonidas.' He turned to face her. 'I don't have much of a mom or a dad, but I have a brother who also happens to be my best friend. And I think sometimes the war zone we grew up in—parents who were always fighting, our dad going through a string of wives who were all destined to be disposed of within a year or two of the marriage—meant we grew even closer. You know?'

'Sure, like a shared trauma,' she agreed. 'I can definitely see that.'

'So when we realised the extent of his criminal activities, it was sort of easy to just emotionally detach from the mess he'd made. We cut him out of our lives and focussed on what really mattered.'

'Rebuilding your wealth?'

'The wealth, sure, but, more importantly, our grandfather's legacy. We spent a lot of time with him. He was the one who really raised us. We both felt we owed it to him to fix what our father had done.'

There was silence except for the gentle lapping of salt water against the side of the yacht.

'I think what you did is amazing.'

He jerked his gaze to hers.

'I mean it,' she insisted, perhaps intuiting his surprise. 'To come out of the scandal and shock of what your father did, to put it behind you, to focus on making good from bad—that's not something everyone has the strength to do.'

'But you do,' he said, after a moment, making the connection easily.

'You think?'

'Sure. Look at how you're caring for your mom. You're a young woman who's put her mother ahead of everything else, who's doing all that is good and right because you love her. What's that if not layering good over bad?'

Alice shook her head softly. 'What else could I do?'

'You've given up just about everything for her.'

'She gave up everything for me.'

'How so?'

Alice gnawed on her lip. He lifted a thumb and padded it over her lip, so she stopped, her eyes huge when they met his. 'We were really poor.' Her cheeks flushed with pink as she made the admission and he wondered, for a moment, if she was embarrassed to admit that to him. 'And Mom was incredibly bright. She should have had a dream career before her, but instead she got pregnant with me and had to work really hard just to keep her head above water.'

'What about your father?'

Alice closed her book, placing it on the deck beside her. The sunshine bounced off the cover, making it sparkle.

'I never knew him.'

'They weren't married?'

'No.'

'And he wasn't in your life?'

'Not at all.'

Thanos frowned, wondering if this was why she hadn't questioned his assertion that Dion simply hadn't liked him. She understood, apparently better than most, that the bonds of parenthood didn't necessarily guarantee love and loyalty of the life-laying-down variety. Unless… 'Is he dead?'

Her smile was genuinely amused. 'No. You think a guy has to be dead to be a deadbeat dad?'

'Of course not.'

Alice sighed softly, her breath brushing his temples, so he felt a kick of desire that almost overwhelmed him with an urge to act on it.

'My mother was only nineteen when she met him. She thought they were in love. He seduced her, promised her the world, slept with her and then vanished into thin air.' She cleared her throat. 'It's part of the reason I couldn't believe I'd been so stupid with Clinton, you know? I was so determined I wouldn't become my mother and then I walked right into the exact same situation. It's almost like all her warning me off men somehow tempted fate and led me right to the same kind of douche who'd broken her heart.'

Thanos nodded thoughtfully. 'There are some men out there who get a kick out of hurting women.'

She shrugged. 'I don't know if that's what it was with either of them. Clinton was immature and, yes, he did hurt me. But my father was so much worse. He made a calculated and determined effort to seduce my mom. He really did promise her so much, and he fought for her to fall in love with him. He set out to hurt her, I think.'

'Why?'

'I don't know. Sport? A game? Power? I can't fathom it. But it's irrefutable that he went out of his way to make her love him and then vanished.'

Thanos frowned. 'When she discovered she was pregnant, did she contact him?'

'Yeah.' Alice's voice was hoarse. 'Even then, she wanted to believe it had all been some kind of mistake, that he'd been called away on urgent family business or something. She loved him. She thought it was a dream come true.'

Alice reached her hand out, grabbing the soda that was at her side, and took a sip, replacing it with a little frown on her pink lips. 'He did everything he could to evade her, and when she finally caught up with him, she discovered he was engaged to someone else. Her world came crashing down around her that afternoon.'

'And she told you this?'

'She told me enough. She wanted to warn me off men like my father.' Alice's grimace was loaded with grief. 'And to warn me off men in general, I think. My mother, once bitten, was definitely twice shy. She couldn't even accept that, while my father had been an out-and-out cheat, there might be a man out there who would love her and accept her and do everything he could not to hurt her.'

Thanos lifted a brow, his eyes skimming Alice's face thoughtfully.

'What?'

'Nothing.' He shook his head.

'I'm serious. What?'

And despite the tone of their conversation, a little laugh escaped him. 'It's just…do you think either you or I are in a position to judge her for that?'

Alice regarded him inquisitively.

'You don't think you push men away because you're traumatised by what she went through? And what you then went through with Clinton?'

Alice's expression tightened. 'No.'

'Alice.' He reached a hand out, lacing his fingers through hers. 'That's not a criticism.'

'Isn't it?'

'No. I happen to think pushing people away is an excellent life choice.' His voice was layered with light sarcasm. 'I only mean it's understandable that your mother didn't feel like she wanted to jump back into dating some-one after all of that.'

Alice was quiet, but the column of her throat shifted as she swallowed. 'She also worked. A lot. We were pretty broke, so she had to work long hours and I don't think a love life really fit into that.' She expelled a soft, impatient breath. 'The thing is, when you said you hated your dad, I understood. I understand. Because I hate mine, even though I've never met him.' She fixed him with a steady stare, her eyes swirling with ice. 'I've made my peace with the fact he didn't want to be a parent. That he never wanted to know me.' The husk of her voice, though, betrayed her—she hadn't really made her peace with it.

Who could?

'But he's a wealthy man, Thanos. I know because I looked into him, when I was old enough to do a search on the Internet. He's wealthy and married with other children. I have no idea how many women he treated as he did my mother, but I do know he was in a position to help us and he never did.'

Thanos's eyes glittered in his handsome face and he was, temporarily, at a loss for words.

'She wrote to him, begging for some kind of financial assistance. When I was eleven, I earned a place at a pres-tigious selection school. It was a scholarship but didn't cover the cost of boarding and uniforms—which were out of Mom's reach. She wrote to him. He flat out refused.'

Anger shot through Thanos. 'How could he refuse? Surely there was some legal obligation, setting aside his obvious moral obligation.'

Her eyes were awash with memory, as though she'd been sucked back in time. 'No. He's British, and the Amer-ican courts couldn't enforce anything. Despite the fact he's incredibly wealthy, he had no interest in helping my mom with frivolities such as, you know, food, let alone a private education for me. Besides, she couldn't really afford a good lawyer, so...' Her voice trailed off.

'She did try to get him to at least contribute something.' Alice shrugged as though it hadn't mattered. 'But he sent nothing except lawyer's letters, all of which took more money to respond to.'

Thanos stared at her, no idea what he could say to make this better.

'I hate him,' she said simply.

Thanos's eyes showed his own feelings quite clearly. 'So do I.'

And at that Alice laughed, and it was as if the sun were bursting out from behind a storm cloud. Everything tilted a little, shifting and reshaping, and Thanos's breath burned in his lungs as he stared at her and wondered how the hell he hadn't noticed how beautiful she was the first moment he saw her. How come it had taken him days to recognise the danger here? To see not only that she was attractive, but also that he was obsessively attracted to her?

He'd already spent more time with her than he ever had with a woman he was sleeping with. Shared more of himself. Cared more for her stories.

But he didn't panic—too much. Because he was controlling this; he had rules and boundaries, and every intention of abiding by them.

'Tell me about this bikini,' he said, his tone completely different, lighter, teasing, a relief from the emotional heaviness of their previous conversation.

'What would you like to know about it?'

'A great many things, Kyria Stathakis,' he drawled slowly.

Did you buy it with me in mind?

The question was on the tip of his tongue but it created

an impression of dependence he didn't wish to encourage, so he pushed it aside.

Alice, though, shifted her attention to her body, her cheeks heating pink, as though she was just realising that she was practically naked beside him.

'I had no idea what I would need for this…job,' she said quietly.

'Job?'

'Our marriage.' She lifted her fingers to mime inverted commas, which shouldn't have bothered Thanos at all. It certainly shouldn't have made him feel a rolling of nausea in his gut.

'I mean, this is *so* far outside of my wheelhouse,' she said with a self-deprecating laugh, gesturing around the boat. 'I live in suits at work and yoga pants at home.' Her shoulders lifted in a shrug. 'And I wanted to fit in. To make this seem realistic.'

'You do fit in.'

She pulled a face. 'Only because I did my research.'

'Research?'

'Uh-huh. And Kosta was right about one thing, Thanos. There are a *lot* of pictures of you on the Internet.'

Something inside Thanos tightened painfully over his chest, like a metal arm being pressed hard to his sides.

'So?' The word came out harsher than he'd intended.

Alice didn't appear to notice. 'I needed to see how your usual, um, friends…' her cheeks heated pink and he wondered how he hadn't realised her degree of inexperience earlier '…dressed. The kinds of clothes they wore. This bikini seemed pretty standard.'

Thanos stared at her, unable to pinpoint why he was so annoyed at that revelation, unable to explain why he felt frustrated and…something else. Only that her casually delivered explanation filled him with a sense of being weighted down.

When he didn't speak, Alice grew quiet and a lift of his eyes to her face showed that she was anxious now. 'Is it…okay?'

More frustration. It roared through him. He was being a self-obsessed idiot. She'd done the right thing. She'd approached this marriage with professionalism, just as he would have expected. This was a marriage conceived of for one purpose, and the better she played her part, the more likely it was to succeed.

'It's perfect,' he assured her, his voice throaty, his eyes clouded with the intensity of his thoughts.

'So what else were you wondering?' she prompted, her eyes lightly teasing now.

His body hardened, and he pushed every thought from his mind with great care, acting purely on instinct as he stared at her intently. 'Just how easy it is to remove.'

She smiled sweetly as she stood, straddling him, her legs on either side of his body, her head blotting out the sun.

'Pull on the string, and find out for yourself.'

CHAPTER NINE

'KALIMÉRA, KYRIA STATHAKIS.'

The words, spoken in his native tongue, were like little beads of sunshine rolling over her skin. Alice stretched, muscles that were not used to being so well used flexing in her body. She stifled a yawn, shifting a little in the enormous bed. Beyond the window, the vines of France were a heady, vibrant green. She shifted to face him, wondering at what point they'd decided she'd join him in his room, rather than keeping to the terms of their agreement—that she would have her own space; that they'd hardly see each other. In fact, in the five days since their wedding, they'd barely been apart.

Alice might have found that troublesome, except for the certainty that their essential terms weren't changing. So they'd blurred the lines a little. So what? That was just wiggle room. Lots of wiggle room.

Neither of them was being silly about this. They both knew there were divorce papers signed in a lawyer's drawer somewhere, waiting for Thanos to make the call to have them filed.

She shifted a little, her gaze lifting to his handsome face.

'I like it when you speak Greek.'

He arched a brow. '*Tóte tha to káno sychná*. Then I will do it often.'

She smiled and placed her head flat against his chest once more, her fingertips chasing invisible circles over his taut flesh.

'I could teach you.'

'Greek?'

'Mmm.' She heard the agreement rumble through his chest.

'I'm already learning Italian.'

The fingers exploring her spine stilled. 'Are you?'

'*Sì. Ma non posso parlare bene.* But I can't speak it very well. *E molto difficile.*'

'Why are you studying Italian?' he asked in that tongue.

It took Alice a moment to put her answer into the right words. 'So that I can speak like a native when I go there.'

His hand began to move up and down her spine once more. 'You want to go to Italy?' He was back to English.

'*Sì,*' she said, a wistful smile on her lips.

'Italy's beautiful, but it is no Greece.'

Alice laughed softly. 'And you wouldn't be at all biased?'

He shrugged, the action dislodging her head a little so she lifted her face to his, pressing her chin into his chest. 'You will decide for yourself when we go there.' His hand lifted to her hair, running through it, curling behind her head. 'Why Italy?'

The past pulled at her like a string attached to her soul that she could never snip.

'Beyond the fact it's meant to be one of the most beautiful places on earth?'

'Yes.'

She smothered a smile, knowing he wouldn't let it go now he'd decided he was interested.

'For a year, we lived in Massachusetts. Mom got a job working in a call centre for a phone company and she had a friend with a spare room so we packed up and moved.' The description neatly glossed over how hard that time had been in Alice's life. She'd been twelve, and had started to put down roots, to make tentative, hesitant friendships that she'd bitterly resented having to leave.

'It was cold and dark and I hated it,' Alice said with a wry smile. 'To be fair to Massachusetts, I was a miserable pre-teen determined to hate the world and everyone in it. I'm pretty sure my perception was altered by that veil.'

'You were a miserable pre-teen?' he said with obvious disbelief.

Alice nodded sagely. 'Oh, yes. I was an *excellent* adolescent.' She shook her head then reached for his hand, lacing her fingers through it distractedly—and as though it were the most natural thing in the world.

'We had a neighbour, Signora Verde. She used to see me come home from school and I guess she worried about me—Mom worked late and the friend of hers we were living with was a nurse who had shifts all sorts of hours. I was home alone a lot. Signora Verde would bring me plates of *biscotti* and hazelnut *bomboloni* fresh from the stove. She'd sit with me a while, and tell me about her town in Tuscany—Trefiumi Nord.'

Alice shook her head wistfully, remembering Signora Verde so clearly. 'The way she described it…a hue of autumn colours all year round, walls that were golden and ochre with red-tiled roofs, buildings that nestled close together along streets that were ancient, lined with little uneven stones, roads that curved gently uphill, perfect for little Vespas to scoot along, window boxes overflowing with fragrant flowers—their pops of colour in the summer enough to take your breath away. The sound of old women sitting on plastic seats by their front doors, talking about their grandchildren as though each was a *maestro* in the making. The smell of garlic thick in the air, the noise of children running, clutching *gelato* in their sun-bronzed hands.' Alice's stomach clenched with the same sense of longing she'd felt then.

'Signor Verde got transferred to North Dakota about six months after we moved to Massachusetts. I never saw her again. But the memories of Italy formed a part of me, and, no matter how hard things got, no matter how hungry I felt, I always remembered three things because of Signora Verde.'

'And these things are?'

Alice smiled, with no idea of how the morning light caught in her eyes and turned them to pools of liquid gold—nor the effect this had on her husband. 'That Italy is heaven on earth,' she said with a wink. 'That kindness—when you expect nothing in return—is the most important gift you can give anyone.' The words were whispered because, truly, Signora Verde had come into Alice's life at a time when her heart had been heavy and she had been so full of angst and sadness, a displaced, angry teenager.

'And the third?' His question was heavy with feeling.

'The taste of freshly cooked *bomboloni* on a frigid winter's afternoon.' She smiled up at him, and her tummy rumbled on cue.

Thanos laughed. 'I can see Greece has a lot to live up to.'

'It does.' She looked towards the window, the ocean glistening in the distant background.

Thanos's smile was distracted and he was quiet for a moment. 'Would you like to go to Italy today, Alice?'

She laughed, shaking her head. 'You can't be serious?'

'Why not? Italy is only a two-hour flight. We could go for lunch.'

Alice laughed at the very idea. 'And then what? Paris for dinner?'

'If you'd like.' He shrugged, but Alice's heart turned over in her chest at the image he was painting. It was all too much. Even with all the evidence to the contrary, she found it almost impossible to believe this was her life—albeit temporarily.

'Thanos.' She laughed again, pushing up so she could see him more clearly. 'You can't just suggest we get on your private jet and fly to Italy for *lunch*!'

'Why not?'

'Because it's… I mean…it's just so…'

'Yes?'

What? So exactly what she wanted? So completely as if her dreams were coming true?

'So perfect,' she said seriously now, her eyes filling unexpectedly with moisture. 'Thank you. I'd like that. A lot.'

His smile released a thousand butterflies in her tummy.

'So, Alice? Which would you prefer? Venice, Rome, or Florence?'

She weighed those choices and then shrugged. 'Surprise me.'

His grin was relaxed. '*Tóte as páme.* Then, let's go.'

Her heart turned over in her chest as she pushed out of bed. The sun was shining on a brand-new day and Alice was going to Italy. For the first time in a very long time, Alice felt truly, utterly happy.

In the end, they went to none of the cities of Italy. Alice described Signora Verde's town Trefiumi Nord to Thanos and, with a little Internet searching on the flight over, they touched down in Florence and slipped into a limousine at the base of the aeroplane. Local time was an hour behind Port D'Angelo.

'How far away is it?' she asked, leaning forward and looking out of the window.

'Not far. Half an hour.'

Alice bit down on her lip, excitement coursing through her veins. She couldn't believe she was here in Italy—the place she'd wanted to go all her life.

And because of the man beside her.

'It's beautiful,' she murmured to herself as the car sliced through the countryside. Enormous pine trees formed a forest over rolling green hills to the left of the car, and to the right gentle undulations in a patchwork of yellows gave way to a distant view of a stone castle.

As the car drove nearer to the castle, it came alongside a bubbling river, which glistened in the early afternoon sun.

'Another river.' She pointed to a fast-flowing body of water, crossing the first at a right angle.

Beside her, Thanos nodded. 'Trefiumi Nord literally means Three Rivers to the North. I imagine the town is named for this.'

Alice turned to face him, her eyes sparkling, a smile on her lips.

'I think Signora Verde said something along those lines.' She sat back in the seat, contenting herself with watching the vista as it scrolled past their windows, with no concept of how Thanos watched her, his dark-rimmed eyes roaming over her face, seeing every flicker of delight, every roll of excitement.

'Thanos, look!' she squealed, as the car rounded a bend and a small town appeared almost out of nowhere. Nestled in the base of several rolling hills, it was crammed full of yellow and golden terracotta homes, a castle in the centre with a renaissance church and cupola beside it, pencil pines poking up between some of the homes.

'Oh, Thanos.' She spun to face him. Alice was alive—and breathtaking. 'I had no idea it would be even prettier than I'd imagined.'

The car drew to a stop on a narrow, cobbled street, and Thanos's chauffeur, Ryan, was there, opening the door. Alice stepped out, emotions flooding her as she breathed in the fragrance and atmosphere of the place—a place which had always lived in her imagination but which was now a part of her reality.

'Thank you. For bringing me here.'

His eyes were heavy on her face, his expression impossible to interpret. 'You are very beautiful when you're excited.'

An instinctive habit of knocking away the compliment filled her but she ignored it. When Thanos looked at her, she *felt* beautiful, and it had very little to do with looks.

'*Grazie,*' she whispered softly, smiling up at him.

They stood like that for a moment and to all the world, to any outsider, they must have looked like a perfectly normal pair of newly-weds. Completely besotted, in love, enamoured of one another.

Which was just as well, because a flash went off a moment later with an audible 'click' sound of a cell-phone camera.

Alice turned in that direction to find a woman holding her phone towards them. At being recognised, the cell-phone photographer quickly spun and walked away.

Alice frowned. 'Did she just take our photo?'

Thanos's expression was grim. 'It happens.'

'You're serious? People actually just…take your picture?'

He nodded, putting a hand in the small of Alice's back

and guiding her away from the limousine. 'Let's keep moving.'

Alice went with him, but she couldn't get the invasiveness of the press in his life out of her mind. 'That really happens to you?' she asked with a small shake of her head.

He tilted a wry smile at her. 'I am somewhat recognisable.'

Alice stopped walking and looked up at him, frowning. True. Thanos Stathakis was instantly identifiable— not least because he was frequently in the tabloids. The idea of living such an exposed life didn't sit well with her.

'You must hate that.'

He considered that for a moment. 'I don't particularly enjoy it.'

They weaved through a narrow street with cobbles underfoot and as they walked Thanos reached down and took Alice's hand in his and she didn't even question it. The intimacy felt normal. She liked the way it felt to hold his hand, their fingers weaved together, his thumb lightly stroking the back of her hand.

Alice couldn't take her eyes off the streetscape. It was everything Signora Verde had described, and more. The residents were vivid in her imagination and the reality was just like it. The smells, the sounds, the tiny little boutiques—clothing shops, book stores, restaurants, cafes, it was all so quintessentially Italian, she felt as if she'd stepped onto the set of a movie.

'Here.' Thanos slowed as they approached a pair of ancient timber doors nestled at the base of a stone building. Alice paused, looking up, running her eyes over the place.

The sign above the door read Ristorante Vecchio Città.

'Old City Restaurant?'

Thanos grinned. 'You're fluent already.'

Alice laughed. 'Barely. I've got a long way to go.'

'Do you take lessons?'

'No, I couldn't afford that, and I don't have the time.' She didn't see the way Thanos's expression darkened. 'I use free apps. They're good. They keep me distracted on the subway.'

He guided her towards the doors, which, on their approach, were opened inwards by an older man with silver-grey hair and dark black eyes. He was tall and wiry and wore a black apron with white stripes over a crisp white shirt and black pants.

'Signor.' He nodded curtly, gesturing into the restaurant. 'Welcome.'

'Thank you. We'd like a table for two. Something with a view.'

'Of course.' The waiter nodded and his eyes seemed to linger on Thanos for a few seconds—moments in which Alice surmised he recognised the billionaire tycoon, because within seconds the best table in the restaurant was made available and a bottle of champagne brought over, compliments of the house.

Alice took the seat offered, so distracted by the view that for a moment she said nothing. From the street it had been impossible to identify this building's location but she saw now it was right on the edge of one of the three rivers that ran through the heart of this town. A little way down there was what looked to be a medieval bridge, like a miniature version of the Ponte Vecchio, with shops built along either side of it and fairy lights strung across the roof.

The water ran quickly and children were sitting at its edge, one holding a fishing line, the other reading a book. In the distance, a family sat on a blanket, drinking wine and eating sandwiches.

It was idyllic and breathtaking.

The champagne was poured and they were left in peace with a menu that was all in Italian.

'What do you feel like eating?' Thanos asked.

She scanned the menu, picking out the words she could recognise.

'What do you think looks good?'

'Would you like me to translate?'

She nodded. 'I can read some of it.'

'Show me what you recognise.'

She lifted her eyes to his, a hint of embarrassment in her expression. 'Really only the simple ones. Bread, chicken, ham, pizza, pasta.'

'That's half the menu,' he pointed out with a grin.

Emboldened, she focussed her gaze on the words and slowed it down. '*Carne*…meat…with green beans. Potatoes.'

'*Perfetto,*' he complimented.

Her heart warmed. 'Truffle *fettucine*.'

'You know more than you think.'

Pride swelled inside her. 'Thank you.'

'*Piacere.*'

The waiter returned. 'My wife will order,' Thanos said with an encouraging nod of his head.

'What would you like?' she whispered.

He reached across and pointed to the steak on the menu.

Alice, in halting Italian, with the server waiting patiently, listed a few dishes. The waiter asked questions, speaking slowly, and Alice gave the full force of her concentration to him, so she didn't see the way Thanos was regarding her, his expression a mix of admiration and pleasure.

When the ordering was done, and the waiter had disappeared, Alice's cheeks were glowing pink with happiness.

'Wow. I think he actually understood me.'

Thanos nodded. 'You spoke well, and have a good accent.'

More pleasure. 'I'm not sure about that. But it's my first time attempting to use my Italian with a native speaker.'

'I think if you spent more time here, you'd be fluent in no time.'

'Maybe.' She sipped her champagne, the bubbles popping against the sides of her mouth. 'How many languages do you speak?'

He considered that a moment. 'Greek, English and Italian fluently, passable French and German, conversational Spanish and Cantonese.'

Alice's jaw dropped. 'Whoa.'

'Whoa?'

'Yeah. How did you learn? I'm struggling just to become passably good at Italian.'

He shrugged. 'I had the advantage of travelling, often, living in many of these places. And our piano teacher was Chinese—an exceptional musician with barely any English, so we learned how to speak casually with her.'

'I'm impressed.'

'Languages are just communication, and communication is inherent to all people.'

She sipped her champagne, considering that. 'It must make your business easier, that you can communicate all over the world.'

He dipped his head in silent concession.

He was an incredibly intelligent man, focussed, dedicated, successful. That took a fire and aptitude that was incredibly rare. Yet he was renowned for being a playboy, a party animal, someone who was more comfortable with a glass of Scotch in his hand than a billion-dollar business deal in his grip.

Alice ran her fingertip around the rim of her champagne glass, lost in thought, and a moment later, the waiter appeared with plates of food.

'I got it right,' she joked, as exactly what she'd ordered appeared. 'I was half worried ox tongue might appear.'

Thanos's wink was purely friendly, but it fired desire deep in her gut, and suddenly she didn't particularly feel like eating, she wanted to be alone with him, somewhere with a bed and a lockable door.

The food was sublime. Traditional Italian, rustic, fresh, flavoursome, and Alice found herself wishing she hadn't lost contact with Signora Verde, so she could tell her that she'd been here, that she'd eaten on the edge of one of the rivers that wended its way through Trefiumi Nord.

'When you are distracted, you get a lovely little line right here,' he murmured, reaching across the table and running a finger between her eyebrows.

Alice made an effort to straighten her face. 'I'm not distracted.'

'No?'

She pulled a face, her heart pulling as though caught on the end of a fishing line when she contemplated how well he suddenly knew her. 'It's just…'

'Yes?' he prompted, when her words trailed off into nothingness.

'You're not at all like what I would have thought.'

He set his fork down, leaning back in his chair, carefully watchful. 'No?'

She shook her head. 'You have this reputation as the playboy prince of Europe.'

He shrugged and she knew she wasn't imagining a defensive tightening of his features. 'Apparently.'

'But you're not… I don't know. I can't really see that.'

'Why not?'

'Well, you're fiercely focussed, for one.'

His lips lifted in what was almost a smile. 'You think that precludes me from enjoying an active social life?'

She pursed her lips. 'No. But I don't think you do *enjoy* that kind of lifestyle. It doesn't gel.'

'Gel?' He repeated the colloquialism with a small tug of his lips.

'Suit you.'

'Ah.' He kept his eyes on hers as he sipped his drink.

'I'm serious. I just can't imagine you going from this—' she waved her hand towards him '—to some kind of bachelor on a yacht surrounded by drunk supermodels.'

He didn't smile. His expression was unreadable.

'It got me wondering about which version of you is real?'

He expelled a breath, turning to look out of the windows. 'Can't they both be real?'

She frowned. 'I don't think so.' Alice leaned forward on the table a little, her heart running a bit faster. Despite the intimacies they'd shared, she wondered if she'd overstepped the mark in some way.

'It doesn't matter,' she offered quietly, when several moments passed without him speaking.

'I'm not ignoring you,' he said, finally. 'I was just trying to frame an answer.'

Her stomach flipped.

'I like the noise that a lot of people together make.'

And despite the seriousness of their conversation, a small laugh escaped her. 'That's your answer?'

His owns lips twisted in a smile. 'I don't know. It's hard to explain, I suppose.'

Alice thought about this. 'I've never liked crowds, myself. Nor parties. I find that kind of shallow social interaction so meaningless. Making conversation with someone you don't really know, who you don't care to know.' She studied him thoughtfully. 'I suppose parties are a great way to surround yourself with people without really forging deep relationships.'

Thanos was very still, watching her. 'Do you think that is what I do?'

The little line formed between Alice's brows. 'I don't know. What do you think?'

He expelled a breath, a grim set to his jaw. *'Forse,'* he responded—perhaps, in Italian. 'Parties became a habit some time in my teens. It grew to be a way of life I didn't question.'

She sipped her champagne, surprised to see the glass was almost empty. A waiter appeared almost instantly, topping it up. 'And now?'

He waited for her to expand.

'When you've bought P & A, and our divorce gets filed?' The words lined the insides of her mouth with acid. She swallowed to clear it. 'Will I see your photo in the tabloids again, a different woman by your side every night?'

Thanos's angular face was very still. 'Would that bother you?' The air around them was like mud; so thick, so stymying.

Alice dipped her eyes forward, shielding them from his inquisitive attention.

'It's not my business,' she pointed out slowly. 'We both know this is temporary. What you do when our marriage is over is up to you. I'm only asking if you still feel a pull towards that lifestyle.'

'We've only been married a week,' he pointed out.

Alice lifted her eyes to his, seeking something in the depths of his eyes. 'Yes,' she heard herself agree. 'It's only been a week.'

A week or a year, it didn't much matter to Alice. Something had shifted inside her, pieces of her soul were changing shape and morphing into something else, something unrecognisable.

Confusion was threatening to pull her into a dark vortex, so she pushed the thoughts aside and plastered an over-bright smile to her face. 'The calamari looks delicious.' She speared a piece and forced herself not to think of anything beyond this moment. Who or what he became beyond their marriage wasn't her concern—there was a reason she didn't want to think about it.

CHAPTER TEN

'YOU HAVE NOT forgotten my invitation?'

Thanos leaned back in the wide leather seat of his private jet, Kosta's words crackling a little through the distance of altitude.

'Of course not.'

'You'll bring your wife to Kalatheros soon?'

'Alice,' Thanos inserted, a smile playing about his lips as he thought of his convenient bride. Their marriage had been born of a desire to secure a company—a business merger with a little matrimony on the side—but he'd never expected to find himself married to someone he found so distractingly pleasing.

Thanos had never been interested in a relationship, but playing the part of a loving husband to Alice wasn't really a stretch. She was easy to get along with and the sexiest woman he'd ever known. He was still reassured to know he had the divorce documents sitting in a drawer in his lawyer's office, to know that they could put an end to this and get back to normal once he had P & A in his control, but he acknowledged now what he hadn't thought possible when he'd suggested this ruse: he'd miss her.

In his bed, in his life.

'Alice,' Thanos repeated.

Impatience cracked across his spine now. He wanted

the company. He'd jumped through all the hoops. Enough was enough.

'How's Friday?'

Kosta was quiet for a beat. 'Good, good. Come for the weekend. I look forward to it.'

'As do I.' Thanos disconnected the call, an unknowingly brooding expression on his face as he turned to look out of the window. The sky beyond them was dark, the plane cutting through the night, delivering them to Greece, to home. And he was looking forward to showing it to Alice, though he couldn't say why.

Two days later, the waves lapped gently against the shoreline of Statherá Prásino, Thanos's private island in the Aegean Sea, and Alice sat cross-legged on the grass in the shade of an impressive pomegranate tree, simply listening.

In and out, regularly, faithfully, tirelessly, the ocean kissed the sand, washing over it, spilling secrets into the tiny little gaps of crushed shell.

The sun on her skin was perfect—warm without burning, a light breeze lifting off the ocean to keep her feeling fresh. She blinked her eyes open, fixing her gaze on the expanse of green water that surrounded the white sand beach.

She'd learned, on the helicopter flight over from Athens, that the island's name roughly translated to 'never-ending green', and she had to say how well it had been named. The ocean was a rich shade of turquoise, but it was more than that. The island itself was incredibly verdant, filled with olive groves, vineyards, a full citrus orchard that included several rows of pomegranates, and an eighteen-hole golf course to the eastern side.

As if Alice hadn't already been impressed by Thanos's obvious wealth, it was this island that encapsulated how successful he'd been in his quest to rebuild his family's empire. The house on the island was not so much a mansion as a palace. She knew from one of the housekeepers—there were three!—who took care of different aspects of the running of the place that the house boasted twenty-seven bedrooms, each with their own bathroom and sitting area attached,

'Mr Stathakis likes to entertain,' the woman had explained with a smile.

Alice hadn't really wanted to think about that.

Ever since their conversation in Italy, she'd found it hard not to think of what Thanos's life had been like before their marriage, or what it would be like afterwards.

It really wasn't any of her business, and yet she'd come to hate the idea of him picking up where he'd left off, throwing lavish, decadent parties for all of Europe's elite, for film stars and rock gods. It wasn't because she was *jealous*. She wasn't.

But she'd come to care about Thanos and she wanted him to be happy. And the more she thought about it, the more she felt as if that wasn't making him happy at all. If anything, it was simply a way to hide from the real world—to make enough noise that no one noticed you weren't saying anything.

He sought shallow interactions.

But why?

He was an intelligent, interesting man, and the more she'd got to know him, the more she could see how worth knowing he was. Did he realise that? Had anyone ever told him how worthwhile he was?

She frowned, the thought incongruous in some way. Thanos Stathakis could hardly be suspected of lacking confidence or ego. After all, look at the life he'd made for himself! All that he'd achieved, his latent power and appeal, his strength and charisma…

'There you are.' She shifted her gaze over her shoulder in time to catch Thanos striding towards her. He was casually dressed in shorts and a shirt and his already deep tan had been burnished by the amount of time they'd spent outdoors during their honeymoon.

'I'm admiring the view,' she said, her breath a little shallow as he approached. They'd never agreed, at any point, that their marriage would be real, in the sense of intimacy. They'd never so much as had that conversation. It had been completely organic, but, one way or another, Alice was spending every night in Thanos's bed, and every day by his side. Despite that, the sight of him still had the power to make her body tremble with anticipation and longing.

As though they hadn't seen each other in a decade, not a few hours.

'It's quite the view,' he teased, coming to stand at her side, his frame providing a little shadow.

'I like it here,' she said with a wistful smile, turning back to the ocean. 'I feel like I could be anywhere in the world, at any point in history.'

He sat down beside her. 'We will be back soon.'

'Just a weekend?' she prompted, turning to face him, a hint of worry playing about the corners of her eyes.

'Two nights,' he agreed with a nod.

'So.' Alice expelled a soft breath. 'It's show time?'

He shifted his head to show his agreement. 'You're nervous?'

Alice thought about that. 'Not really.' She reached down and plucked a blade of grass between her fingers, feeling its smoothness slowly. 'I'm sorry your business acumen alone isn't enough for him.'

'I think it has less to do with my proficiency in the corporate world and more to do with the scandal that trails the name Stathakis.'

Alice lifted her knees to her chest and propped her cheek on them, angling her face to his. 'It's in your power to change your reputation, even without the drastic step of getting married.'

His eyes swirled with emotions. 'I wasn't referring to my lifestyle, so much as my father's crimes.'

'Ah.' Alice made a noise of comprehension. 'But you're nothing like him.'

Thanos laughed. 'That doesn't particularly matter. His name is my name. Leonidas and I will live in the shadow of what he did for ever, no matter how we pull away from his choices.'

Alice's heart constricted with pain for him, for how limiting that knowledge must make him feel.

She reached her hand out, laying it gently over his shoulder.

'You have made a name for yourself outside his acts. Your father is an aberration. What he did is deplorable, but you're not him. Nor is your brother. You have made it clear with your business choices that you are legitimate and law-abiding.'

'You are in the minority, I think.'

'I don't believe that.'

Thanos pierced her with the intensity of his stare. 'Playboy reputation or not, do you not think Kosta would have sold P & A to me a long time ago, were it not for my father's criminality?'

'I don't know,' she said quietly.

'Of course he would have. He doesn't approve of how I live my life, but what he really fears is the stain of illegality attaching itself to his legacy.'

Alice mulled this over thoughtfully. 'In which case, does marrying me do anything to change his mind?'

Thanos lifted his shoulders. 'It shows him how much I

want the company. It shows him I want to be the kind of man he thinks of as respectable and wholesome.' He said the last two words with disdain.

Alice's heart worked overtime to keep her blood pumping.

'I think,' she said, eventually, 'that you are, and always would have been, more than enough for him. His hang-ups are his problem, not yours.'

Thanos's jaw tightened as her words landed around him. 'Perhaps.' He lifted his hand to hers, curving his fingers over it. 'But one way or another, in two days I intend to have his agreement to sell the company back to me.'

A swooping feeling dropped through Alice's stomach. 'And I'll do whatever I can to help you.'

Kalatheros was only a short flight from Thanos's private island. Alice thought, as they lifted up, how accustomed she was becoming to flying in helicopters. The first time they'd lifted off, she'd been a little uncertain about how to buckle herself in, but now, she managed it all like a pro. She even knew which levers and knobs Thanos had to turn to get the big bird into the sky.

The scenery was utterly sublime, and Alice spent much of the short flight with her forehead pressed to her window, staring down at the sparkling ocean and the hundreds of tiny islands that dotted their way across its depths. There was something *magical* about the Mediterranean.

The helicopter dipped a little lower as they approached the tip of the mainland, which was shaped like an arrow, and a few minutes later, a clearing came into view. He brought the helicopter lower, and lower, so Alice could see the tops of the trees, and then the house in the distance, and, finally, Thanos cut the engines. Alice disconnected her headset and put her hand on the door.

Only, Thanos reached across, stilling her, so she turned back to face him.

'I have something for you.'

The words surprised her. She smiled, in silent invitation for him to continue.

'Here.'

He reached into his pocket and pulled out a velvet pouch. With a look of curiosity, Alice took it and slipped her finger into the drawstring, opening the mouth and up-ending it into her palm.

'Oh.' She blinked, the necklace the last thing she'd expected. It was simple, and very beautiful, a single diamond solitaire, almost as large as her engagement ring, suspended on a fine platinum chain. 'It's…stunning,' she said, honestly. 'But you didn't have to get me that. It's too much.'

Thanos reached for the necklace, shaking his head as he did so. 'You are Mrs Thanos Stathakis now, remember. Kosta will expect you to be adorned with jewels such as this.'

'Oh, of course.' Heat spread through Alice's cheeks at the fact she'd almost forgotten that she'd need props for this play-acting. That it *was* play-acting. 'I'll give it back to you once we're—when this is over,' she said.

It was the first time since their wedding that either of them had really referred to the end point of their marriage so pointedly. In the midst of their easy interaction, the reminder that it was temporary sat like a jagged rock.

'That's not necessary. I bought it for you.'

Alice's smile was just a lift of her lips and she chose to make light of the situation rather than go down the rabbit hole of how she was feeling and why. 'You don't have to buy me jewels, Thanos. When we're divorced, I can buy my own ridiculously huge diamond necklaces.'

He didn't laugh, at first. He simply stared at her almost as though he hadn't heard, and when finally he spoke, his voice was gravelled and deep. 'It suits you.'

He came around to her side of the helicopter, opening the door at the same time she stepped out, so their bodies were brought close together, and desire throbbed low in her abdomen.

Thanos's hand lifted to her cheek, his thumb stroking her flesh there. 'Alice?'

Her heart skipped a beat. Then another. She waited, her breath held, not sure what he was going to say, not sure what she wanted him to say, knowing only that she had a very familiar feeling of standing on the edge of a precipice, wondering if she should jump or not.

'Yes?' A whisper.

'Whatever happens today, this weekend, thank you.'

Alice's heart squeezed, her stomach churned. 'What for?'

'For this. For your help. For understanding how much this means to me and why.'

Her smile felt heavy on her face—there was a pervasive sadness clouding her heart, one she didn't fully comprehend. 'It's your company,' she said, gently. 'And you're the right man to run it.'

When the marriage had first been suggested, Alice had felt a little anxious about the idea of performing her role for Kosta Carinedes. After all, pretending to be a joyously happy newly-wed was one thing, but doing so in the man's home, under his scrutiny, would require a whole new level of attention to detail.

Except, in reality, it didn't.

Nothing about it felt forced or unnatural.

In fact, as she and Thanos walked, hand in hand, towards Kosta's Greek paradise, Alice found it difficult to process how bizarrely *right* it felt.

'Don't be nervous,' he said, *sotto voce*, as they reached the wide timber door and pressed a button on the buzzer. 'It will be easier than you think.'

Alice lifted her gaze to his. 'I'm fine. This will be fine.'

The door was drawn inwards and Kosta stood there, a man Alice had now met three times in the space of a month.

'Ah, the happy couple.' He beamed, and the greeting sounded genuine enough.

She smiled easily, and when he wrapped her in a warm embrace and kissed both her cheeks, Alice returned the greeting. Thanos shook his hand, his manner a little more reserved, so she reached down and laced her fingers through his, squeezing them with a smile on her lips.

It was a beautiful day—blue sky, warm sun and a sea breeze—and Kosta enjoyed providing them with a leisurely tour first of his house and then the gardens that surrounded it. Despite the fact he must have been in his eighties, he moved with alacrity, spry and confident as he strode up the steep steps towards a cave that provided shelter and incredible views of the sea.

'We used to come up here for the sunsets,' he said nostalgically.

'We?' Alice prompted, quite naturally.

'Helen. My wife.'

Alice didn't need to ask if she was still with Kosta—his grief was evident in the lines of his face. Within the space of seconds he'd gone from an athletic, confident older man to someone who appeared completely broken by sadness.

But he made an effort to cover it, pasting a heavy smile on his face. 'She loved it here.'

'In the cave?'

'Yes, and on the island.' He waved his hand around the wide space. 'We had many homes, but this was our favourite.'

'I can see why,' Alice said, sincerely.

'She grew up in the slums of Barcelona. She'd never seen anywhere so open and untamed.'

He blinked, as if clearing the memory. 'There are rock pools down there.' He nodded towards the other side of the cave, where a clearing gave way to another set of steps. 'You might enjoy a swim.'

'Definitely,' Alice agreed, lifting her face to Thanos's and startling silently. Because the man beside her was Thanos Stathakis—her pretend husband—but he was now, also, the formidable businessman tycoon, and she felt his determination emanating from him in tidal waves.

And in that moment, his worries were hers, his desires hers, and she wanted to do everything she could to help him get whatever he wanted in life. She wanted him to have P & A.

And impressing Kosta with how completely she'd changed Thanos was part of that, so she sucked in a breath and swore to herself she would play this part to absolute perfection—and that they wouldn't leave until Thanos had peace of mind about his company's future.

When they returned to the mansion, Alice faked a yawn. Thanos's eyes shifted to her face.

'Excuse me.' She smiled apologetically. 'I'm a little worn out. Do you mind if I have a rest?'

'Of course.' Kosta nodded, calling for a servant to show Alice to the room that would be hers and Thanos's. She slipped away from them, glad that Kosta and Thanos would have a chance to be alone together, knowing that all Thanos needed was a little time to bring the older man around to selling the property.

* * *

Alice woke to a feather-light touch on the tip of her nose. She lifted her hand to bat away what she thought must be a bug or a stray hair, and connected instead with Thanos's finger. Alice's eyes blinked open, a ready smile on her face. She was disoriented though, looking towards the window to see that the sun was lower in the sky, the day's brightness fading into evening.

'I fell asleep.'

Thanos grinned. 'Apparently.'

She lifted her hand to his chest, not questioning the easy intimacy that had developed between them. 'How did your afternoon go? Did you talk to him?'

Thanos made a noise of agreement.

'And?' She sat up in the bed so her eyes were level with his. 'Did he agree to sell it to you?'

Thanos's laugh was throaty. 'You are as impatient as I am.'

Impatient? Alice wasn't. In fact, there was a part of her that hoped Kosta would stretch this out, making Thanos take months and months to convince him, months and months of pretending to be married, just like this.

'He's close,' Thanos agreed, shifting his head forward a little, his eyes locked to hers as he brushed her lips. It was such a small gesture, and it reminded Alice of the night in front of the club, the night she'd agreed to marry him, but it was different too, because now he was familiar and she knew that the kiss could and would lead to so much more.

'We have an hour before dinner,' he said, his lips hovering just above hers.

'An hour?' Her eyes were heavy; she dropped them, breathing in as she pushed her body forward. A teasing smile flickered over her lips. 'That sounds like just enough time for a swim in those rock pools.'

'Exactly what I had in mind,' Thanos joked, as he found the bottom of her shirt and lifted it over her head.

His fingers moved with urgency, trailing over her body, finding her breasts, teasing her nipples, plucking them between his thumb and forefinger, his kiss deepening as he pushed her back against the bed, so every fibre of her being was vibrating with this total, desperate, all-consuming rushing of desire.

'I'm going to miss this,' he groaned, the throwaway comment said without thought, without meaning, but it drove a stake into Alice, splintering her pleasure for a moment, making it almost impossible for her to set aside the pain and feel only pleasure.

But then his mouth claimed one of her nipples and he shifted a hand to between her legs, his fingertips tormenting the sensitive cluster of nerves there, so she was totally lost to thought and feeling and was simply existing for this, for him, and for whatever it was their marriage had become.

CHAPTER ELEVEN

THANOS MEANT WHAT he'd said. He was going to miss this. He was going to miss Alice. The realisation landed against his side with a thud and he did everything he could to vanquish the thought. Casual sex was nothing new to him.

He was the playboy prince of Europe, wasn't he?

He dragged his mouth lower down her body as his hands removed her underpants, his tongue tormenting her flat stomach before finding the hair at the apex of her thighs, delighting in her responsiveness, her little sounds of pleasure that broke through the room.

He would never tire of this. Her body was like an instrument and he wanted to be its maestro. Anger soared in him whenever he thought of the man she'd once loved, who'd made her care for him, made her trust him, and had taken her virginity then discarded Alice as though she meant nothing.

Hypocrite, a little voice inside him whispered, as he brought his hands to her thighs, spreading her legs wider, allowing him greater access. Her hands threaded through his hair, her movements urgent, her heavy, impassioned voice begging him not to stop.

He didn't intend to.

But he wasn't a hypocrite. He was nothing like Clinton,

who'd hurt her. Clinton who'd promised her the world and turned his back on her.

Thanos hadn't promised Alice anything. He'd been very careful about that. He'd purposely made sure he was painstakingly honest with her every step of the way. They'd slept together out of mutual need—both had wanted this, and both had agreed to it, knowing their marriage would end one day and this would all be over.

Over.

He didn't much want to think about that.

He kicked out of his clothes, then brought his mouth back to her womanhood, savouring the sounds she made as she moved closer and closer to climax, her body writhing on the bed, her hands digging through his hair faster, her desperation and insanity palpable. Right as she tipped over the edge, her orgasm claiming her, he brought his body higher up hers and thrust inside her, feeling her wet muscles contract almost painfully around his arousal, feeling all of her wrap around him until he was completely in her hands, utterly under her control.

But he wasn't ready to end this—he wanted more of Alice, more of this. They had time, and, for as long as they did, he was going to make the absolute most of every single second.

'You remind me a little of us,' Kosta said, a glass of Scotch in his hand, his long legs sprawled in front of him.

Two days ago, they'd arrived at Kosta's house, and he'd been an acquaintance to her then. But after a weekend in his company, exploring his home, wandering the beaches he'd enjoyed for most of his life, she felt a growing affinity to the man. She liked him.

'Of Helen and me,' he explained. 'We were like you and Thanos, you know.'

'Were you?' Alice prompted, sipping her own ice-cold glass of wine in an attempt to wash a hint of guilt from her mouth. She didn't much like lying to Kosta, now that she knew him. The only saving grace was that the end justified the means. Kosta wanted to sell P & A and she had no question that Thanos was absolutely the best person to take it over.

'We met and married within one month. The second I saw her, I knew I could not live without her.'

It was just how her mother had described meeting Alice's father in all those letters. And it hadn't worked out for Jane, because Henry Jennings had been a lying bastard. But love existed, love at first sight was real, and Kosta was living proof of that.

'When did she…?'

Kosta grimaced. 'Five years ago.' He shook his head, turning to look towards the ocean. The moon shone a silvery line down its centre, broken occasionally by the rolling waves. 'It was quick. Death, that is, not grief, not mourning. That I will do for the rest of my life.'

Alice's features were loaded with sympathy. 'I'm sorry. You don't have children?'

Kosta's smile was nostalgic. 'We had a son. He died when he was four. My wife could not fall pregnant again.'

Tears filled Alice's eyes. She blinked to dispel them. 'What a tragedy.'

'Yes.' His own eyes showed emotion. He lifted his Scotch to his lips, sipping it slowly, his fingers trembling a little as he replaced it on the tabletop.

'My business is a family legacy. I have no one to leave it to. No one who will carry it on in my name.'

Alice lifted her gaze to Thanos unconsciously. His expression was unreadable. 'I want to sell it, but not because I need the money.' He waved a hand around them, showing the terrace, and the beautiful home beyond it. 'I need to sell it so I can see it go to someone who will treat it as I do. Who will value it as a family business, who will build it and pass it to their children and their children, as my grandparents intended.'

She swallowed past the lump in her throat. 'You know Thanos is the right man, don't you?'

He turned to face her, studying her intently. 'You love him?'

The question floored Alice. She knew what she needed to say, because she was playing the part of the doting, loving wife, but the question still had the power to detonate a bomb right beneath her ribcage. 'I…of course.' She jerked her head to cover the stutter.

'I can see that you do,' Kosta said quietly. 'And I hope he will make you happy. For many years I have wondered if he was capable of making anyone happy, himself included.'

Something like alarm was drumming against Alice's chest. 'Why do you say that?'

'I knew Nicholas—his grandfather—quite well. And through him, I met Thanos, when he first came to live with Dion.' He shook his head sadly.

Curiosity spurted inside Alice. 'Did you?'

'Oh, yes. He was a troubled child, driven by emotion, and I think quite insecure.'

Alice frowned, this description pulling on all her heart strings, even as she felt a desire to contradict it. Thanos wasn't insecure. Was he?

'You cannot blame him for that,' Kosta continued. 'His mother broke his heart, and his *father* was not worthy of that word.' He spat that indictment with obvious disgust. 'After the trial, Thanos began to spiral out of control,' Kosta continued, shaking his head.

Alice's heart squeezed tight. 'In what way?'

'Partying, drinking, anger. Leonidas held him together, just, but Thanos was on a dangerous downward trajectory.'

Alice wanted to do something, to say something. She clutched her own glass tighter, wondering why she couldn't simply reach back through time and make everything okay for the scared little boy Thanos had once been.

'I bought Petó because I truly believed Thanos would destroy it if he remained at the helm.'

This was news to Alice. She jerked her face to Kosta's to find him watching her shrewdly. 'I knew what it meant to him, what it had meant to my friend. I wanted to safeguard it from Thanos's ability to obliterate it.'

Alice let out a little noise, a murmur, of sympathy.

'You think that was wrong of me?'

Alice frowned so a divot formed between her brows. 'I can't say.'

'I like him,' Kosta surprised her by offering. 'I always have. When he came to live with Dion, I remember feeling disbelief and rage—rage that a man like Dion Stathakis could be awarded two such fine sons when...' He grimaced. 'He had two fine sons, and he appreciated neither. He wanted neither.'

Alice frowned, pity shifting inside her. 'He sounds like a fool.'

Kosta laughed, a crackly sound. 'Yes, and then some.'

'Thanos isn't like you think,' she said, after a moment. 'He won't do anything to hurt Petó, or P & A. In fact, I think he's the best person to run both.'

Kosta's eyes were on hers, a dark grey gaze loaded with intelligence. 'I don't worry he'll hurt the company. I worry he'll hurt himself. His lifestyle...' Kosta shook his head slowly from side to side. 'I understand how tempting it is to run from yourself. When our son died...' his fingers dug into the arms of the seat, as though it would somehow alleviate the pain '… I drank solidly for at least a year. Numbing myself—or trying to.' He fixed her with an intense gaze. 'But Helen saved me. Just like you have saved Thanos.'

Alice stared out at the water that surrounded Stathéra Prásino, a serious expression on her pretty features. One of Thanos's yachts bobbed in the distance, immaculate and enormous, and—she knew from experience—staffed with a small army, all ready to take the boat out on Thanos's whim.

In the two days since they'd returned from Kosta's home, a sense of uneasiness had followed Alice everywhere. She couldn't understand it, but she was waking up in the middle of the night with a curdling feeling of dread, the likes of which she hadn't known since Thanos had taken away her every single stress. She was no longer worried about bankruptcy or how she was to pay the rent, her credit cards were clear as a whistle, and her mother was in one of the top facilities in the world.

So why did she have a sudden and intense sense of foreboding?

She looked over her shoulder, scanning the lounge area. It was empty. Thanos was working.

The day was warm, though, the water inviting, and suddenly Alice craved the freedom of lying on her back in the sea, staring at the sky, imagining herself to be truly weightless.

She didn't bother to grab a towel or to change into her bathers. It was a private beach, a private island and she knew she'd dry off again by the time she reached the house. Something was driving her, pushing her to the ocean. At its edge, she stripped out of her dress, standing in only the designer briefs and bra that had been part of the wardrobe she'd bought to prepare for being Thanos's wife. Of course, she'd had no idea when she'd bought them that he'd ever see them. She hadn't even imagined that it might become physical between them.

She waded into the water, closing her eyes as she felt its salty balm against her sides, going deep enough to flip onto her back, just as she'd wanted, and stare up at the sky.

It was the perfect shade of blue, like something out of a fantasy. She lay on her back, breathing in and out, staying afloat as long as she could before she twisted onto her stomach and began paddling to shore. Her eyes scanned the house on autopilot, the enormous mansion so beautiful and breathtaking, and perfectly situated.

Alice hadn't been able to imagine what her life would be like, married to Thanos. If she'd tried to imagine it, she wouldn't have foreseen anything like the reality had been. And she struggled now to imagine her life in a post-Thanos world.

She'd have money, financial security, certainty for her mother's healthcare for the rest of her life. But no Thanos.

A gulf opened in her chest, as wide and expansive as the ocean she was swimming in. She tried to imagine waking up without him in bed, going to sleep on her own, not sharing a meal with him, not talking to him, not laughing with him, and the panic was back, gripping her tighter.

Because she was about to be completely and utterly alone.

But more alone than before, because for a brief while she'd known companionship and compatibility and it was all about to be stripped away from her.

Alice straightened her spine as she emerged from the water. She'd fallen in love with Clinton a long time ago, and he'd hurt her. He'd broken her heart, yet she'd recovered. She'd moved beyond it.

Whatever she was feeling now, she'd be able to beat that, too, when the time came. And until then, she was going to just enjoy being with Thanos, not dwell on a future that loomed, uncertain and all kinds of wrong.

Her fingers were toying with the necklace, sliding the diamond from side to side, a little line between her brows, the frown line he'd seen a lot these last few days. Something had shifted between them, at Kosta's place. He couldn't say what, only he felt an air of seriousness, of urgency, when they touched and kissed. He felt a sense of desperation, and he didn't know if it was coming from Alice or from him.

He had precisely zero experience with women to know what he could say to make her smile again. At least, not beyond one night. One night, he was fine with. But this kind of thing—something longer, something more meaningful—just didn't suit him.

And it *was* meaningful with Alice. He'd expected he could marry her, and even sleep with her, and somehow still abide by his usual behaviour with women, but nothing about Alice was like what he'd experienced before.

But that didn't change the fact that this thing was running its course. Not just because they'd agreed it would, but because Thanos had no hope of knowing how to maintain a relationship.

There was a reason he'd always avoided anything like commitment.

He was terrible at it.

And he didn't see a need to change that aspect of his personality. Still, he didn't like seeing Alice frown.

'You're going to break the chain,' he said, aiming for teasing and light-hearted. Her fingers immediately snapped away from it, her features apologetic.

'I didn't realise I was doing it.'

He bit back an impatient sigh. 'It doesn't matter.'

The stars of the night sky sparkled brightly, the isolation of his island ensuring complete clarity in the atmosphere.

'Kosta said something interesting about you,' she said slowly, her eyes roaming his face as though whatever it was might have an answer in his features.

'Did he?'

She sipped her wine, perhaps buying time. 'He said you were on a dangerous downward spiral, after your father's conviction.'

Thanos felt as if a knife were being sliced along the side of his heart. 'Oh?'

She nodded, somewhat self-consciously. 'He said your brother held you together.'

Thanos's smile was a self-deprecating acknowledgement of this. 'I think Kosta was right.'

'You're very close to him?'

'To Kosta?' Thanos joked, deliberately misunderstanding, looking for a smile any way he could get it.

She offered him a half-hearted lift of her lips.

'Leo and I were pretty much raised as twins from the time I came to live with him.'

'He didn't resent you?'

Thanos's lips were a grim line in his face. 'Perhaps.'

'I don't mean he should have,' she said quietly, reaching out and putting her hand over Thanos's, her comfort and perceptiveness qualities that made something sharpen against his insides. 'Only that he was a young boy himself, and his world must also have felt a bit like a bomb had been exploded into it.'

'I'm sure.'

Alice bit down on her lower lip. 'But you're close now?'

'Yes.' He smiled, because he wanted her to smile back at him, and she did, so his stomach rolled and all his breath threatened to explode from his lungs. Her smile was every bit as beautiful as the stars overhead.

'He seemed nice,' Alice said. 'And I liked his wife.'

'Hannah? She has been good for him.'

Alice was quiet a moment. 'In what way?'

'You know his first wife died?'

Alice nodded. She'd read about it at the time, and had heard of it again once she'd started temping at Stathakis. Murdered, along with Leonidas's son Brax, in a vendetta against Dion and his criminal connections. A shiver ran down Alice's spine.

'Leonidas closed himself off after that. He just took himself out of life; he became a shadow of his usual self. It was hard to watch.'

'But understandable,' Alice murmured.

'Perhaps at first. But after four years, I was worried he would never wake up again.'

'And she woke him up?'

Thanos's smile was spontaneous. 'Yes. She fell pregnant—unexpectedly—and Leonidas had no choice. If he wanted to be a part of their baby's life, he had to open himself up to Hannah.'

'Their little girl looked adorable.'

'She is.' His smile turned to something more serious as he studied Alice's face. 'I cannot imagine what was going through your father's mind, to choose not to be a part of your life.'

Alice shook her head. 'Nor yours.'

'But I was a nightmare,' he said, his voice light-hearted despite his pronouncement. 'And you were, I'm sure, a delight.'

She pulled a face. 'Hardly.' Then she leaned forward, so her legs brushed his beneath the table and her fingers could lace through his. 'And you don't really think there's any justification for choosing not to be a part of your child's life, do you?'

His eyes glittered but he didn't answer.

'I came to accept, a long time ago, that my father was a person lacking in moral fibre. That his choices weren't a reflection on me. You must see the same is true of you and Dion?'

'I think I was not an easy child to love,' he said carefully, no longer wishing to continue the conversation. He pulled his hand away with an apologetic smile, and lifted his drink. He angled his face towards the ocean, wondering at the way his heart was slamming hard against his ribcage.

'I'm sorry you feel that way.'

He shrugged. 'Don't be. I became used to being completely alone in the world a long time ago. I like being alone, Alice. It's how I'm meant to be.'

CHAPTER TWELVE

WHEN ALICE WOKE with a start that night, she knew exactly why. The panic attack that was roaring through her was intense and impossible to ignore. A fine bead of perspiration had broken out on her brow, and her breathing was ragged. She shifted a little, casting a glance over Thanos before pushing the covers back and slipping from the bed. The silk negligee she wore moulded to her skin as she moved from their bedroom, down the wide, curving staircase and into the kitchen.

It was the middle of the night, the witching hour, when dark thoughts were at their zenith and hope seemed to have ceased to exist. The view through the kitchen windows was all black, save for a milky line of moonlight that trembled across the ocean.

'I like being alone, Alice.'

His words had woken her. They'd been rushing through her, jamming her sleep, blocking her dreams, filling her with a sense of desperation, because they were *wrong*. They had to be.

He'd chosen to be alone to protect himself, and more than anyone she understood that. She'd done the same thing, hadn't she? Sure, she'd moved around a lot, but choosing not to make friends was a way of staving off hurt. Loss was something Alice had seen as a way of life, a necessity, and so she'd closed herself off to any hope of happiness and friendship.

The one time she'd let herself believe that maybe there was someone out there who would choose to love her, she'd been forcibly reminded of how completely unlikely that seemed.

So she'd gone back to choosing solitude, loneliness, and a lack not just of companionship, but of everything.

She'd fallen into a track of being on her own and it had taken this sham marriage to pull her out of it, to realise how incredible it felt to let yourself share with someone, to be vulnerable with them, to enjoy their company and crave more of it.

Her heart gave a funny thump and she sat down on one of the kitchen stools with a little gasp of understanding.

Because she hadn't just come to rely on Thanos.

She'd come to think of him as a part of her, or maybe that she was a part of him. Just that they were wound together, woven as if made of cloth, and no divorce could dissolve that. And this marriage wasn't the reason this had happened. It was something much bigger and more important than that.

She'd fallen in love with him.

She loved him.

She loved him in a way that made her unable to bear the thought of leaving him. She loved him in a way that made it impossible for her to think that he might not feel the same way—that he might be anxiously waiting on Kosta to sell P &A so he could walk away from this.

Worse, to get back to the life he'd led before they'd met.

At that, a genuine wave of nausea exploded inside her, the idea of seeing him with another woman, of seeing him with some glamorous model or actress draped over his frame, was as painful to her as if she'd cut off a limb.

She loved him. The more she thought about it, the more it exploded in her brain, the realisation as clear and plain as day. Why hadn't she seen it earlier? It was in every single moment they'd shared. She definitely hadn't realised it at the time, but from the first meal they'd shared—in that incredible restaurant tucked away in New York—something had been happening inside her. Something huge and powerful and all-important.

She had to tell him.

But what if he didn't love her? What if he didn't feel the same way?

Uncertainty shimmered on the edges of her brain because she knew from experience that there was every possibility of that.

Her own father hadn't loved her.

And Clinton had walked away from her—had derided her and humiliated her.

What if Thanos did the same?

Oh, he'd never hurt her, she knew that, but what if he looked at her with sympathy swirling in the depths of his beautiful eyes and shook his head, explained that he simply didn't love her? That she was living in a fantasy world to even *hope* he might?

Then she'd live.

Somehow.

She'd coped with heartbreak before. True, never like this had the potential to be, but it had been bad. Soul-destroying. Ugly. Unpleasant. And yet, she'd coped then; she'd cope again.

What she'd never make her peace with was pretending she didn't feel the way she did—pretending she didn't feel as though her heart were going to burst from inside her chest, to explode all the way through her.

She could live with loss.

But never, ever with not knowing.

'Thanos. Are you awake?'

He flung an arm over his eyes, squinting into the complete blackness of their bedroom. When had it become 'theirs'? He didn't even frown as the word slipped through his mind.

It was just for now. He could deal with that.

'No.'

She made an impatient noise and then Alice's fingers were prodding him in the shoulder. 'I'm serious. I need to speak to you.'

He wanted to go back to sleep. He'd never needed much—a few hours a night—but those few hours he generally liked to sleep deeply and undisturbed. Still, there was something in Alice's tone that penetrated his fog, so he sat up, his eyes scanning her face.

'Is something wrong?'

'No. Yes.' She let out a tremulous laugh. 'I don't know.'

His expression shifted, worry slipped inside him. 'What is it, *agape*?'

The column of her throat shifted visibly as she swallowed. 'I… I couldn't sleep.'

He laughed. 'So you thought you'd wake me to suffer in insomnia with you?'

She bit down on her lower lip and it wasn't light enough to see her properly, so Thanos reached out and switched on the bedside lamp. Both squinted a little as they adjusted to the brightness.

'I need to speak to you.'

'Okay.' The word was a prompt, an invitation.

But Alice didn't speak. She seemed to be choosing her words carefully, but she also seemed to be anxious about something. Stressed. Nervous.

He hadn't seen her like this since that first day in the office when she'd been staring at the stack of overdue bills and her face had been ashen and her eyes bleak.

'Tell me,' he prompted, knowing that whatever it was, he'd fix it. Money, health, her mother? 'Alice?' Impatience zipped through him. Still, she didn't speak. 'I can't help you if I don't know.'

'I'm trying,' she said, her eyes beseeching.

But it wasn't good enough. Concern was slashing through him as a whip would butter. 'Try harder.'

Her voice shook when she spoke. 'What are we doing?'

It wasn't at all what he'd expected her to say. 'Huh?'

'This. You, me.' She pointed from him to her. 'What is this?'

Something shifted inside him, an emotion he couldn't quite grasp. Guilt. Annoyance. Frustration. 'I don't understand.' His voice was guarded.

She breathed out softly, shifting a clump of her dark brown hair so he reached a hand out and caught it, smoothing it behind her ear.

'This. Our marriage. I—can't make sense of it.'

He placed his hand on her arm, gently stroking her smooth flesh. Goosebumps trailed in the wake of his touch. 'What's to make sense of?' he prompted, trying to join the dots and unable to connect them. He looked around for his phone, to check the time.

'Alice, it's two in the morning. Three hours ago we were making love and now you look as though you've seen ten ghosts. What's happened?'

A strangled noise erupted from her chest, a pained noise, and his worry grew.

'I couldn't sleep.'

'You said that.'

She nodded jerkily, standing then, pacing towards the window and staring out of it. She wore a flimsy silk negligee and even then he ached to draw her into his arms, to pull her to his body and pleasure away whatever was worrying her.

'I keep having this premonition of disaster,' she said. 'Like a blade of panic that comes out of nowhere. And I had no idea why; I couldn't understand it because everything's so good. Perfect, actually.'

She turned around to look at him, her expression haunted, her eyes pleading.

'And this is a problem?'

She nodded slowly, her expression stricken. 'Yeah, I think it might be.'

His laugh was just a short, sharp sound of confusion. 'Why?'

'Because it's the kind of perfect I want to hold onto.' She bit down on her lip, allowing her words to sink in. 'It's the kind of perfect I want to last for ever.'

For ever. Her words slammed into him, and on a cellular level he rejected each one instantly. There was no such thing as for ever. No such thing as happily-ever-after and a perfection that didn't disappear.

'I fell in love with you, Thanos.' Her voice cracked, and then there was silence, as if she was waiting for him to speak. But he couldn't because panic was strangling him, just as she'd described, wrapping around him, making his eyes a little blurry, and his brain squeal.

'I didn't mean to.' Now she was whispering, wrapping her arms around her torso so she looked both ethereally beautiful and fragile all at once. 'I swore I wouldn't ever get involved with a guy again. I was done with men.' The words were laced with self-directed anger. 'And then you came along and you were so different.'

She drew in a shaking breath. 'Different from anyone I've ever met and so different from what I expected.'

She crossed to where he sat—mute, and like stone—and kneeled before him. She had no choice—it was the only way to meet his eyes.

'I couldn't work out why I've been experiencing this growing sense of unease, but then when you said last night that you like being alone, that it's how you're meant to be, it made me see everything clearly. I don't want to be alone.' She shook her head. 'I mean, I don't want to be with anyone else either. I want to be with you.'

It was like grating his feet on boiling bitumen. He shook his head in a silent, visceral rejection of her words. He could imagine a future just as she painted it, with no end point on this marriage, with Alice by his side day in, day out, for no purpose other than that they enjoyed being together, and, damn, so much of him wanted to agree, to admit this had changed completely from what he'd expected, too.

But the thing was, there was *always* an end point. To every relationship in life, there was a cessation, and he'd rather know when and why than be blindsided. He needed those boundaries in place.

His eyes met hers and pain opened up inside him, because he felt her upset, he felt it pulling at him.

'Alice.' He had to think of what to say. She stared at him, almost as though she were holding her breath. 'What do you want from me?'

She opened her mouth, apparently not sure of that. 'I want to know how you feel.'

'How I feel?' His response was unintentionally scathing.

'Yes.' Her eyes sparked with courage. 'Because I don't think I'm the only one who's been falling in love here.'

He ground his teeth together, rejecting her implication whole-heartedly. Love was a minefield he had no intention of getting involved with.

The very idea filled him with the sense he was falling off the edge of a very tall building.

'Not once—' he spoke slowly, clearly, choosing his words with great care '—have I given you any reason to think love was on offer.'

He heard her shocked intake of breath and, a second later, tears sparkled on her lashes, tears that might as well have been made of acid, being dripped onto his flesh. 'You don't think?'

'I know. I have been very careful on that score.'

'Liar,' she whispered, her own anger obvious now.

'From the beginning, we have both been absolutely clear about the parameters of this.'

'We said one thing,' she muttered, 'and did another.'

His heart careened into his ribcage as he acknowledged that there was potentially some truth in that.

He'd been careless and stupid. His own rule of thumb—of never getting involved with anyone—had served him well all his life. And the one time he'd let his guard down, he ended up in this mess.

And it was a total mess. Because he didn't want Alice to be upset. He didn't want her to be hurt. And he sure as hell didn't want her to go, and he had a sneaking suspicion that she would, if he didn't play his cards very, very carefully.

'I like being with you.' His voice was gentle. 'Isn't that enough?'

Her eyes lifted to his and she was quiet, which he took as a very encouraging sign. Carefully, he continued. 'You think you're in love with me.' He ignored the way her eyes narrowed and her lips tightened. 'But I think maybe it's just sexual infatuation. This has been pretty amazing.' He smiled, to show how much he meant that. 'I think that we should just keep going as we are. Enjoy what we have. But not get too invested in what comes next.'

The second she stood, he knew he'd said the wrong thing. She hadn't been listening with an open mind, she'd been listening with obvious disbelief.

'What comes next is already here.' She bit down on her lip and he had the most awful feeling that she was trying not to cry. 'I don't "think" I'm in love with you. I know I am. And knowing that, there's no way I can keep pretending to be your wife, making love with you—' her voice cracked '—if it doesn't mean anything to you.'

He stood up, rejecting those words, pulling her into his arms. 'I didn't say it means nothing,' he growled, the words almost primal, coming from somewhere deep inside him. 'I just don't want you to think sex equates to love.'

'It's not just sex,' she said, not facing him, pressing her cheek to his chest. 'It's everything I feel when we're together. At dinner. Waking up beside you. I love you. I love your mind, your ideas, your passion, your determination. I'm head over heels in love with every single part of you and it will suffocate me if I have to stay here with you pretending I don't feel that way, or knowing that you don't feel that for me—I can't do it. I just can't.'

He groaned, stepping back from her just enough to see her face. He pressed a finger beneath her chin, tilting her face up to his. 'So what do you want?'

She opened her mouth, her eyes laced with disbelief, and every cell in his body was compelling him to say something, to beg her to stay anyway, to promise her just enough to keep her with him. Hell, to lie to her, if that was what it took.

But he couldn't do that.

He couldn't say he loved her when he didn't.

He felt as if he was losing his mind; nothing made sense.

'I want to go home.' Her voice was hoarse. 'I know we had a deal. I can try to pay you back what you've already spent on Mom. It will take me time but I can—'

'Seriously,' he interrupted, staying completely still. 'Don't. You think I care about *money*?'

She jerked her face away from his. 'I think you're paying me a lot of money for a marriage that I'm walking out of.'

'You did your part,' he muttered, dragging a hand through his hair. 'You saw Kosta, so, as far as I'm concerned, your obligations to me are at an end.'

She swept her eyes shut for a moment. 'Then there's no reason for me to stay here.'

He was eight years old again, having the rug pulled out from under him, having all the boundaries of his world shift brightly and unexpectedly. He was eight years old and losing someone important and valuable and unique in his life. Except this was different, because he was making this decision; he was in control, just like always.

The thought didn't reassure him at all.

But there was no way he could offer Alice what she needed—no way he'd even try. He knew what she'd been through with Clinton; he wasn't going to be another asshole who broke her heart.

'I'm sorry,' he said, simply. 'I was careless with you. I should have guarded against this better.'

A tear rolled down her cheek and his gut clenched hard and fast.

He didn't touch her. He no longer felt he had any right.

She swallowed, her face so pale, so pinched. 'What next?'

The question caught him by surprise and, briefly, hope

flared in his chest, because that sounded like there was the opening to change her mind.

'I can't get off the island without you,' she whispered. Logistics.

Ice trickled down his spine. Damn it, he didn't want her to get off the island.

He jerked his head once more. 'Do you want to stay the night?' Hope was back, his body crying out for just one last time, one last night holding her, breathing her in, one more morning of waking up with her in his arms.

She shook her head, fear in her expression, and he realised she was drowning in panic and heartbreak—because of him—and he couldn't fix this. The one thing that would make it all better wasn't in his power to give.

Desperation gnawed at him.

All he could do was to make this smoother and easier. He had to help her leave, had to stop fighting, stop thinking about what he wanted and help her get home. Help her forget him.

The insides of his gut clenched.

'I'll fly you to my hotel in Athens,' he said firmly, not a hint of emotion in the words. 'You'll stay the rest of the night in a room there, and in the morning, if you still feel you want to return to America, my plane will take you.'

She nodded, blinking away from him. 'Thank you.'

Thank you?

For what?

Thanos Stathakis felt like just about the worst human on the face of the planet. He sure as hell didn't deserve her thanks.

CHAPTER THIRTEEN

'SHE'S DOING WELL.'

Alice looked up at the nurse without hearing what she'd said.

'Your mother. She's looking well.'

Alice turned back to Jane Smart, looking at her through fresh eyes. It was true. She looked much better than she had in a long time. The facility was state-of-the-art, but it offered incredible extras. Every day, Jane was wheeled into a beautiful garden, custom-designed for comatose patients. 'The latest research suggests many of our patients are still capable of absorbing external stimuli—sunshine, warmth, a light breeze, the sound of birds chirping,' the director of the hospital had explained. 'Besides, it can't do any harm.'

Alice had smiled and nodded, acted as she'd thought she should act, when really she felt exactly as she had done in the two months since leaving Stathará Prásino.

Like a ghost, living a half-life, going through the motions instead of actually feeling anything.

She had been wrong on the island. Wrong the night she'd told Thanos how she felt. Wrong in a thousand and one ways.

Wrong to tell him how she felt, because nothing could have been worse than this. Continuing to be with him, even knowing she loved him and he didn't love her, would have been preferable to this never-ending state of loss.

She'd been wrong to think she'd get over this. Wrong to think this pain was on any playing field even remotely near what she'd felt when Clinton had humiliated her. Even the lifelong knowledge that her father had no interest in her paled in comparison to the all-consuming sense of absolute grief that stalked her daily.

Daily?

Every minute.

It had been two months.

Two months since they'd flown in complete silence over the Aegean, down low into Athens. Two months since he'd accompanied her into his six-star hotel, arranged for a penthouse suite, escorted her to the door, wheeling the luxury suitcase that was stuffed with designer clothes, two months since he'd stood back as she'd pushed open the door and prepared to walk away from him.

He'd kicked his toe in, leaving the door ajar, his eyes holding hers. 'If you change your mind,' he'd said quietly, letting the implication fade away.

But she'd known she would never act on that. Even if she did—which she had, many times—change her mind, and decide she would take any pain for the promise of a few more nights of Thanos.

The one thing she was glad for, and proud of, was that she'd stayed strong. She'd returned to New York, and, only a week or so later, had dropped her wedding ring and the enormous necklace into his lawyer's office, needing any souvenir of their marriage to disappear.

He hadn't acknowledged that, but the following week she'd received the title deed and keys to a place on the Upper East Side. When she'd caught a cab to look at it, she'd felt as if she were living in some kind of macabre fairy tale.

It was beyond anything she could ever imagine. An enormous four-bedroom apartment with two separate living spaces, decorated and furnished in a manner that would please a queen, with a pool on the wide terrace that boasted sensational views over Central Park in one direction and the city in another.

She hadn't stayed there yet.

She couldn't bring herself to.

Not without knowing if it had once been Thanos's. Or if he'd bought it with her in mind. Neither option was okay. Neither option made her feel good.

'I think she likes the sunshine.' The nurse was still talking.

Alice dropped back into the present with a thud, pasting a weak smile on her face.

'She always did.' Tears filled her eyes, but they were tears for Thanos, for Jane, for Alice, for her dad, tears that had come so easily since she'd left Greece.

'I'll leave you alone,' the nurse said softly, excusing herself with a little squeeze of Alice's shoulder.

She nodded, and when she was alone, she put a hand on her mom's. 'You got through it,' Alice whispered. 'I wish I knew how.'

And she wondered then if it would have felt different, if she'd had a child.

Thanos's baby. The very idea made her groan, because having just a piece of him would have kept love warm in her heart, would have filled her with something, at least, to focus on.

But then what?

Would he have insisted they stay married? And she'd have been trapped in a marriage with a man who didn't love her, who couldn't love anyone, who would no doubt come to resent her?

She groaned again, and put her head on her mom's hand, closing her eyes. She breathed in, and told herself it would be okay, even when she really suspected it wouldn't be.

She went to see her mother every day. She needed routine and rhythm, something to do that might distract her, and seeing her mom at least reminded her that she wasn't entirely alone in the world.

Two months became three.

She still felt no better, but surely one day that would come?

'You said it was just for show,' Leonidas said quietly, looking around Thanos's office with an expression of disbelief.

And Thanos could see why.

The space that was usually kept immaculately ordered more closely resembled a pigsty.

'It was.'

'Pséftis,' Leonidas drawled. 'If it was just for show, you wouldn't be existing on alcohol and coffee three months after she walked out on you.'

'I have told you a thousand times,' Thanos snapped harshly, reaching for his Scotch glass—which was disappointingly empty, 'she didn't walk out on me. We came to a mutual decision that it was time to end the sham of our marriage. It served its purpose. Kosta is having papers drawn up even now, as we speak.'

Leonidas nodded, his eyes glinting as he studied his brother. 'Yes? So why are you not celebrating?'

'How do you know I'm not?'

Leonidas laughed, a sharp sound of rejection. 'You are wallowing. It is the exact opposite.'

Thanos ground his teeth together, reaching for his Scotch decanter and refilling the glass. He held the bottle towards Leonidas, who curled his lips in a derisive negative.

'Do you know what I think of, when I look at Isabella?' Leonidas asked urgently, moving a step closer to his brother's desk.

'What?' A snarl.

'I think about what a responsibility it is to be a parent, to be a father. I think about our childhoods, about the way our father let us down time and time again. I think about the way my parents fought constantly, so I knew only acrimony in relationships. I think about the fact I almost let Hannah—the best thing to ever happen to me—walk away because I had no idea how to love someone.' He lowered his voice, calming his tone a little. 'I think about you, and how it must have felt to have your mother literally give up on you.'

Thanos's spine stiffened and he took a glug of Scotch, wincing as it hit his palate.

'I think about how impossible that should be—to turn your back on your own child. The idea of never seeing Isabella again makes my body ache all over.' He shook his head. 'Your mother deserted you, she chose not to love you, and you have spent the rest of your life feeling unlovable.'

Thanos finished his Scotch and stared into the empty glass, wanting everyone to go away, wanting to be alone. Particularly, not wanting to hear these words.

'You live with a chip on your shoulder the size of this island because it's easier than accepting your mother failed you and your father failed you and that you deserved better. They failed you, but now you're taking it one step further and failing yourself.'

Thanos ground his teeth together. 'You don't know what you're talking about.'

'You love her, don't you?'

Thanos glared at his brother with a rising phoenix of white-hot fury. 'For the last time, no! I don't! I don't love her, okay!' And he threw the Scotch glass across the room, until it landed with a burst against the wall and shattered into a thousand tiny shards.

'You're screwing everything up,' Leonidas said, with the kind of honesty only a sibling could offer.

'Oh, go to hell.'

Thanos hadn't had a drink in two weeks but he sure as hell could have used one. He sat opposite Kosta on the deck he would always remember from the last visit, when he had sat beside Alice, his arm around her shoulders, her body curved into his side, her fragrance, her sweetness, her willingness to help him in this ruse setting him on fire. Now he sat on the deck in a thoroughly different mindset, in a thoroughly different mood. Even the weather was different. The sky was grey today, clouds low, so the ocean was moody and unimpressed.

'I'm sorry Alice could not be here today,' Kosta murmured.

Did Thanos imagine the way the older man's eyes shifted a little, sympathy swirling in their depths?

'The contracts are ready?' Thanos barrelled past the statement, beyond caring that he was being rude.

Kosta nodded slowly.

'She's not well?'

Someone, somewhere, had offered this small lie to Kosta, when the trip was being prepared. Perhaps his assistant? He didn't know.

Kosta shifted his gaze out to the murky sea, his expression grim.

She's not well?

It was such a simple enquiry, and Thanos had no way of answering. Was Alice well? Was she happy? His chest ached as if he'd been punched.

He had no way of knowing.

They didn't speak, they didn't communicate at all. He couldn't have even said if she was still in America.

Despair groaned through him, as it often had these past three and a half months.

The whole idea had been stupid.

Pretend to be married to buy a company he was paying more than market value for from a man who was desperate to sell. Thanos should never have indulged in such a childish game. It had been foolish, foolish, foolish.

And for the first time in over a decade, he no longer cared if he reacquired Petó. It was not the most important thing in his mind or heart. In fact, the acquisition felt trivial and banal.

'She left me,' he said instead, turning back to Kosta. 'We only got married to fool you.'

Kosta didn't react for several seconds and Thanos dropped his head, running his fingers through his hair.

'At the time, I thought I wanted Petó badly enough to do anything to get it.'

Kosta remained silent and watchful, in a way that unnerved Thanos because it reminded him so strongly of his grandfather.

'It seemed easy enough,' Thanos continued. 'You wanted me to settle down, so I did. Or at least pretended to.'

'You didn't change your lifestyle?'

Thanos shook his head. 'That's not what I meant.'

'So you are still making being a bachelor a championship sport?'

Thanos locked his jaw.

'Because I have not seen you in the papers once since your marriage.'

Thanos swallowed. The idea of living the way he had before Alice was something he couldn't contemplate. He shook his head. 'I'm not here to discuss my marriage.'

'Your marriage only existed because of my ultimatum,' Kosta pointed out shrewdly. 'You think I don't have a right to understand?'

'There's nothing to understand. It's over. It was all a lie.'

Kosta shook his head slowly, his features laced with pity. 'No, it wasn't.'

'You don't know what you're talking about.'

'I know more than most.' He leaned forward a little. 'Thanos?'

He lifted his head.

'I like you.'

Thanos grimaced, feeling somehow even worse than he had before. Because Kosta was a good and kind person to whom Thanos had wilfully lied. What the hell had come over him?

'I have always liked you, more than I let on. Your grandfather told me a story about you, once. We were at a party in Europe and a princess was there. She made a speech, remarking on how her son had built the most amazing tower out of Lego. It was two feet high, she said, with windows and a door, turrets that climbed inches higher. Nicholas leaned towards me, a proud smile on his face, and told me that you'd decided, one summer, to create a house using rocks from down near the beach. According to him, you went down every day with a canvas bag, loaded it up and returned to the garden, where you set to work. It took you months, but, rock by rock, you did it. I didn't really believe it at the time—grandfathers exaggerate, in my experience—but a year or so later, I went to his island and there it was, still standing, this small house you'd made, all because you'd set your mind to it.'

Thanos remembered. He remembered the weight of the rocks, the feeling of the sun baking his back, the cuts on his hands as he locked each piece into position.

He ground his teeth together. 'What's your point?'

'I knew then that you were a young man who would achieve whatever he wanted in life. You have a rare talent that disposes you to success. When you form an intention, there is nothing that will get in your way. I knew what I was doing the day I told you I wouldn't sell you P & A unless you settled down.'

Thanos had the distinctly unpleasant feeling he was being manipulated.

'You knew? That it wasn't real?'

He shrugged unapologetically. 'I suspected.'

'Damn it.' Thanos shook his head. 'Why didn't you say something?'

'Because I couldn't be sure.' He leaned forward. 'You're the best person to run P & A, just like you've said time and again. I bought the company to keep it safe; I've never really considered Petó mine. As for P & A, there's no one else I'd rather pass it to.'

Thanos's breath hissed out of him with impatient frustration. 'All of this could have been avoided…'

'And you would have missed out on learning a very valuable lesson.'

'Oh, yeah? What's that? How to hurt innocent, beautiful, generous women?'

'On love,' Kosta corrected gently.

Thanos stood up with disbelief. 'You were, what? Trying to play matchmaker?'

Kosta's laugh was in complete contrast to the darkness swirling through Thanos. 'I expected you would marry one of the party girls you're usually seen with,' Kosta corrected. 'I thought it would at least slow you down, that it might give you a wake-up call to stop partying, if not to show you how meaningful it can be to share your life with someone.'

'You were wrong on all counts!'

'Yes, because you chose Alice, and she loves you, and I do not think for one moment her feelings aren't mutual.'

'How do you know she loves me?' he muttered, wondering if they'd had some communication beyond what they'd shared on the island.

'Only a fool wouldn't have seen that,' Kosta said softly.

Thanos's heart was churning inside him, because the older man had a fair point. Only a fool wouldn't have seen... Had he realised and just refused to do anything about it?

'I came here to sign those contracts,' Thanos ground out, his heart banging so hard he thought it might burst right out of his chest.

'And we will,' Kosta promised. 'But let me say this, first.'

'I'm sick of talking about Alice,' Thanos groaned.

'Fine. This will be the end of it. Only, indulge an old man who liked and respected your grandfather; indulge an old man who likes you, Thanos, and doesn't want you to throw your life away because of stupid, stubborn fear.'

'Fear?' Thanos shook his head in silent dispute of that.

Kosta's voice came out gently. 'I know what it's like to live without the person you love. I lost my son.' His voice was just a hoarse whisper now, almost indiscernible above the distant rumbling of thunder and the crashing of the waves. 'I lost my wife. Neither of these things I had a choice in, but *you* do. Alice is out there, and she loves you, and you love her. All you have to do is reach out and grab her with both hands, and you're too damned afraid.'

Thanos stopped fighting the truth. He stopped fighting. He turned to face Kosta, his skin pale beneath his caramel tan. 'And what happens when she decides she doesn't love me after all?'

'And what happens if she doesn't?' Kosta threw back. 'What happens if you are a man like me in fifty years' time, staring out at the ocean and looking back on a lifetime of happiness and memories that you wouldn't trade an entire fortune for?'

Thanos listened to these words, his heart in his throat, Alice in his mind, and suddenly he felt it imperative to sign the papers and leave Kalatheros that had nothing to do with P & A and everything to do with somewhere else he desperately needed to be.

Running helped.

Alice had never been much of an athlete.

But after the grief and the depression and the desire to wallow had come a strange restlessness she hadn't been able to burn off. It made her legs twitch at night, while lying in bed, and her brain run like a freight train at all hours, so she would wake up in the middle of the night and be wide awake with no hope of sleep or rest.

She had a restlessness with nowhere to put her energy and so she'd taken up running. And not just running a little bit, either. She tried to do five miles morning and night.

It helped.

She didn't sleep better but her body was weary, so that she could lie on the sofa with mind-numbing television on in the background and try not to think about what her life would be like if she hadn't told Thanos how she felt.

Would they still be married? Sleeping together every night, her body wrapped around his, the sound of the waves that surrounded Statherá Prásino whispering in her ear, filling her soul with the beats of happiness?

Maybe.

Maybe not.

Maybe he would have sealed the deal with Kosta and put an end to things, finishing it because their marriage served no practical purpose.

Her chest felt heavy and strange at the very idea of that, and she knew she'd done the right thing. It was so much better to have left rather than to have been asked to leave.

She ran, one foot in front of the other, through Central Park then onto the busy streets surrounding it, weaving through people and bikes and cars and horse-drawn carriages stuffed with loud tourists; she ran with her head bent and her hair pulled into a plait, her earphones blocking out all the noise of the city she didn't care to hear.

And when she reached the foyer to the apartment he'd bought for her, which she'd eventually stopped fighting and accepted as a part of her life, she stopped running and pressed her hands to her knees, letting herself catch her breath for a few moments before she had to dredge up a smile and offer it to the doorman.

After just a moment she straightened and nodded in his direction as he held the glass doors open for her. The foyer was a testament to white marble and glass. Even in her rubber-soled sport shoes, she couldn't cross the space silently.

She pulled her earphones out as she approached the lift, jabbing the button with more anger than it deserved. Her breathing was still rushed. The doors opened and she stepped inside. The doors slid shut, except right as they were almost closed, just an inch or so from meeting in the middle, a hand slid between them, to hold them open. Alice fumbled, reaching behind her for the panel, looking for the 'door open' button.

It wasn't necessary. The hand succeeded. The doors opened and seconds later, as if her dreams and mind and hopes and heart had conjured him, Thanos swept into the lift.

CHAPTER FOURTEEN

SHE COULDN'T SPEAK.

There were a thousand words rushing through her, begging to be spoken, but she couldn't fumble her brain towards a single one of them in that second. She stared at him hungrily, her eyes refusing to obey and look away, her brain forgetting that he'd broken her heart and ceased to exist in her life, her heart chugging like a bouncing ball in her torso.

And he stared right back, his expression, his beautiful eyes moving with urgency over her face, as though he could somehow catalogue everything she'd done and said and felt in the three and a half months since she'd left the island.

She was in a state of shock, which was the only explanation for why it occurred to her to mind that she was wearing running gear, no make-up, and was covered in a sheen of perspiration from her exercise.

The lift began to cruise upwards and it was just the jolt Alice needed.

'Why are you here?'

His eyes glittered with determination. 'Isn't it obvious?'

Alice shook her head. 'Not to me.'

'I came to see you.'

Her heart lurched. 'Why?'

There was a brief hesitation. 'I have a favour to ask you.'

Alice groaned. 'A favour? Seriously?'

He nodded. The lift doors opened and Alice glared at him, contemplating telling him to get lost. But she didn't. She'd spent three and a half months wishing she could go back in time and eat her confession, wishing she could have just a bit more time with him.

She was furious with him. Furious with him for turning up in her apartment three and a half months after they'd last seen one another, blithely asking her for a favour.

But she was also human, and completely in love with Thanos, and desperate for whatever crumb of time she could steal. Even knowing it was just a temporary reprieve, that her grief would be waiting for her, that her reality wasn't any different.

He cast an eye about the apartment as he entered. She didn't offer him any refreshments. 'What do you want?'

Her tone was far from friendly.

He didn't react. 'Kosta and I have signed the papers. He's in New York and asked if you were free to meet for a drink tonight, to celebrate. Champagne at the Stathakis hotel.'

Alice's heart dropped into her toes. 'Thanos,' she whispered, shaking her head as tears filled her eyes. 'You can't be serious?'

His expression was the most determined she'd ever seen it. 'I don't think I've ever been more serious about anything in my entire life.'

She spun away from him, swallowed desperately. 'Why?'

'Because you agreed to this, and it's not quite finished yet.'

Alice groaned, shaking her head. 'You said it was done.'

'I was wrong.'

Pain slashed through her.

'It's one hour,' he promised softly.

'One hour,' she said with disbelief. He couldn't understand her heartache, nor what he was asking of her. And yet…she thought of her mother and how well she was looking, of how her own life had changed since meeting Thanos, and she thought of the most important thing: none of this was his fault.

He'd been honest with her, even when she'd fallen in love with him, he'd tried to establish boundaries to make that impossible.

He hadn't set out to hurt her.

And she didn't want to hurt him. He needed one last favour.

With a sinking heart, and knowing how much this one hour would cost her, she found herself nodding. 'Fine.' Her voice was tremulous. 'But then, that's it. You go away again and forget I exist.'

His eyes glittered. 'Come to the hotel at six.' He reached into the breast pocket of his suit, pulling out a plastic key card. 'You remember the penthouse?'

Reluctance was awash through her central nervous system. 'Can't we meet in the bar?'

'No.' His eyes flared. 'You don't think that might tip Kosta off? Besides, I have your ring and necklace. You should wear them.'

This was a mistake.

Alice stared at her reflection in the mirrors outside the door to his penthouse, her body flashing with adrenaline as she studied her reflection.

She'd chosen a simple black dress, knee-length, figure-hugging, modest yet flattering, and teamed it with shiny black stilettos, the red sole a perfect match for the lipstick she'd chosen. Her dark hair had been brushed until it shone and left loose, if only because she knew he loved it that way.

Her fingers shook as she pulled the key card from her handbag. But before she could insert it into the door, she knocked, preferring not to just let herself in.

When no one answered, she pressed the buzzer for the apartment and continued to wait.

Still no answer.

With a frown, she used the key card, and her frown didn't lessen when she stepped into the suite to find it in complete darkness.

'Thanos?' she called out, reaching around for a light switch. When she flicked it on, she made an audible sound of surprise that ricocheted off the walls.

'What the heck?'

The entire apartment was blanketed in red rose petals.

The *entire* apartment. It was like a red carpet, thick and luscious. She shook her head as she waded through them, her heart beating harder and faster, her mind unable to make any sense of it.

'Thanos?' Her voice was curt.

And she understood why she felt annoyed.

Because this didn't make sense.

And he shouldn't be here.

And this was too much.

And, and, and… Her body's defence mechanisms were firing to life, boarding up her too-soft heart, protecting her from the kinds of vulnerability that had led to her being hurt so badly.

A noise sounded and she shifted her focus, gasping once more when she saw what was beyond the balcony doors.

Candles.

Hundreds of candles.

Her heart slammed against her chest. She moved that way, closing her eyes as she stepped outside. Because there were roses there too, but long-stemmed red roses, so beautiful, so fragrant. She moved to one, feeling the petals, swallowing hard to clear the lump in her throat.

She spun around, her eyes searching for Thanos, and finally she found him. Standing on the deck, wearing a dark suit with no tie and a button undone at his neck, his eyes on her with such an intensity that a trail of heat pooled in her abdomen and ran all the way through her.

'I told Kosta the truth.'

The words didn't make sense. 'What?'

'I told him about us.'

'Why?' She shook her head. 'I thought you wanted P & A?'

'He's selling it to me anyway.'

'Oh.' She exhaled. 'Then why does he want to see me?'

Thanos's smile was just a twist of his lips. 'He doesn't.'

'What?' Nothing made sense and her blood was pounding so hard in her ears she could barely hear anything above it.

'He's not in New York. I made it up.'

'Why?'

'I wanted to see you.'

She shook her head. 'You saw me earlier.'

'I wanted to see you properly. And for you to see me. Here. Like this.' He waved a hand around, gesturing to the roses and candles.

'What?'

She grimaced, knowing she sounded as if she had about two active brain cells and barely able to care. 'I don't get it.'

'I made a mistake.'

'When?'

He strode towards her and she clamped her mouth together, crossing her arms over her chest.

'I made a mistake when I let you go. I made a mistake every day I didn't look deep inside myself and see what was holding me back from you. I should never have let you leave.'

Alice was completely shocked. 'What?'

'I made a—'

'No.' She lifted a finger to his lips, silencing him, her eyes huge and beseeching. 'Don't you dare.'

Now it was Thanos's turn to look confused.

'Don't you dare think you can turn up after all this time—over three months—and say anything that's going to make this okay.' She glared at him, anger—the sweet relief of anger—everything she needed. 'Don't you dare think you can ever say or do anything that will make this all right.'

He lifted his hands and cupped her face, holding her still, holding her gently. 'I'm so sorry I hurt you.'

Except that.

His words were like treacle on her spine. 'Damn it.' She bit down on her lip, closing her eyes, but it did nothing to stop the tears from squeezing out of the corners.

'I'm sorry I didn't understand what we were. I'm sorry that you left and I felt like I'd been ripped into a thousand pieces and I *still* didn't see why. I'm sorry that I have been missing you and pining for you and thinking of you every day and it still didn't occur to me to realise that you have taken over my mind and soul in a way that is rare and beautiful and special.'

She sobbed, shaking her head and not really even knowing why.

'I'm sorry that I got so fixated on needing to control every single thing about us that I ruined it. I'm sorry that

I hurt you, not once, but every single day that I stayed away. I'm sorry that I left you here thinking I don't love you when the truth is you are every breath in my body.'

She could barely breathe now, and her small sobs were little explosions firing from her.

'I'm sorry,' he continued, his own voice heavy with emotion, 'that I didn't understand what love was, what true love is, because I have never felt it before. But I get it now. I see how it is the way we fit together, the way we are together, the way I feel because of you—the fact you make me want to be a better man, a better person, you make me want to deserve you. You make me happier than I've ever known possible. I am so head over heels in love with you, *Kyria* Stathakis, and all I want is to tell you this.'

She blinked, her stomach rolling.

'That's not true,' he amended quickly. 'What I want is to make you my wife again, properly and for real. Not for show but because I do not want to go another day without you. What I want is to bring you back to the island, to have you at my side, not because we had a deal to fool a kind old man, or because I'm paying you, not because you are desperate for financial help and I offered that, but because you love me and I love you, and there is no way we should be anything other than together.'

Alice sobbed, her shaking head turning into a nod and then nothing as she tried to compute what was happening.

'I love you,' he said simply, his hands framing her cheeks. 'And if you tell me I have ruined this beyond repair, I will try to prove you wrong. I will do whatever I can to fix this, for as long as it takes. I will be here, waiting, hoping, needing you but knowing I lost any right to expect you could possibly love me the day I let you walk out of my life.'

'Please don't,' she groaned, finally, tears in her voice. 'Please, just…'

'What?' His voice was gravelled. 'Tell me what I can do.'

She lifted her hands to his chest, staring at her splayed fingers, her eyes wide. 'I don't understand.' And she didn't, but it didn't stop her from believing and knowing. It didn't stop her from trusting.

'What do you not understand, *agape*?'

'What happened? Why are you here?' And then, softly, with a hint of accusation, 'It's been so long.'

'I know.' He pressed his forehead to hers. 'Too long. I was a fool, Alice Stathakis. Determined not to love you.' His eyes held hers, the truth in every fleck of them. 'I learned the flip side of loving someone at a young age, and I never forgot that pain.'

Alice's heart broke for the little boy he'd been, abandoned by his mother, made to feel unlovable, made to feel disposable.

'She was wrong to leave you,' Alice murmured. 'Wrong to let her little boy think he wasn't worthy of love; wrong to let you become a grown man who still believes that.'

And then his smile was blinding. 'But I don't believe it any more, Alice. Look what you did for me—look how you've loved me. Even tonight, after I broke your heart, you cared enough for me to come to my aid, to put your own pain aside because I asked it of you. There is no doubt in my heart that you love me, and that you will always love me.'

Alice blinked up at him, his words so beautiful, so perfect and all she wanted to do was reinforce that, to agree with him.

'And there is no doubt in my heart that I love you, and will always love you.' He brushed his lips over hers, just as he had the first time they'd kissed, and it sealed something inside her, filling her heart with all the joy she could possibly feel—and more, because she knew it was just the beginning.

'It was Kosta, you know,' Thanos murmured, stroking Alice's naked back, his fingertips revelling in the ability to touch her again so easily, his heart at peace for the first time in three and a half months.

Alice shifted a little in bed, the smile on her lips that he would work the rest of his life to preserve, to earn. 'What was?'

'Who helped me see what an imbecile I was being.' He grimaced, but it was a grimace that was full of the fears that had gripped him—and the realisation of how close he'd come to ruining this for good.

'Did he, now?'

'Mmm…' It was a throaty noise of acknowledgement. 'He reminded me how lucky I am to have a chance to be with the person I love. Losing his wife hit him hard, and I think he looked at me, a man who was grieving the loss of someone I didn't have to lose, and he wanted to shake me.'

His smile was rueful.

'I'm glad.'

'Me too. Though I have to believe I would have woken up eventually. But who knows if you would have still been here by the time I saw things clearly?'

'I would have been,' she promised, entirely serious, no smile on her lips now. 'Thanos, I'm not going anywhere. Love isn't like that. When I told you I loved you, I meant it in a for-ever kind of way.' Heat flushed her cheeks. 'I gave you my heart with no expectation of ever getting it back.'

His eyes flared at her sweetness and he kissed her, slowly, hungrily, his whole body rejoicing in their closeness.

Later, over a pancake breakfast, he reached for Alice's

hand, not liking how strange it was to see her finger without the engagement ring.

'I've been thinking,' he said quietly, 'about your mother.'

Alice's eyebrows shot up.

'Wherever we live, it should be near enough for us to see her often. I've made enquiries about having a space built on the island—fully staffed with nurses, of course—but I wanted to be sure you were happy with that. If you want to stay in New York, we can.'

Alice felt more love than she'd known possible burst through her. 'I think she—and I—would like nothing more than to live on your beautiful, sun-filled island, Thanos.'

He beamed. 'And so we shall.'

It took six months for construction to be completed, six months for world-class hospital staff to be recruited, and then they were back amongst the rolling green hills of Statherrá Prásino.

'The builders did a great job,' Alice said quietly, as they regarded the structure from a distance.

'Yes,' he agreed. 'It's close enough to the house, yet each building feels isolated and private.'

Alice tilted her head to the side, her pulse racing at the secret she'd been holding for just over a week. 'Do they do renovations as well? Or only new builds?'

'Why?' Thanos teased, wrapping his arms around his wife's waist. 'Do you fancy a remodelling project?'

'Only one room,' she said with a small smile.

'Yes?'

'I mean, it's not one hundred per cent necessary, but I thought a nursery would make it easier. You know, when the baby comes.'

'Whose baby?'

She burst out laughing. 'Ours, Thanos.'

'Our baby?'

She nodded, her eyes locked to his, her smile radiant on her face.

'Alice, do you mean…?'

She nodded, joy like a beacon glowing across the island. 'I'm pregnant!'

Thanos lifted her off the ground, spinning her around, momentarily lost for words. But when he put Alice's feet back on the sand, he knew just what he wanted to say. 'Thank you.'

She wrinkled her nose. 'What for?'

'For making me happier than I ever knew possible. Thank you for everything.'

The sun slipped into the ocean, the day drew to a close, but their lives lay before them: full of love, happiness, family and hope.

* * * * *

MILLS & BOON

Coming next month

PROOF OF THEIR ONE-NIGHT PASSION
Louise Fuller

The coffee shop was still busy enough that they had to queue for their drinks, but they managed to find a table.

'Thank you.' He gestured towards his *espresso*.

His wallet had been in his hand, but she had sidestepped neatly in front of him, her soft brown eyes defying him to argue with her. Now, though, those same brown eyes were busily avoiding his, and for the first time since she'd called out his name he wondered why she had tracked him down.

He drank his coffee, relishing the heat and the way the caffeine started to block the tension in his back.

'So, I'm all yours,' he said quietly.

She stiffened. 'Hardly.'

He sighed. 'Is that what this is about? Me giving you the wrong name.'

Her eyes narrowed. 'No, of course not. I'm not—' She stopped, frowning. 'Actually, I wasn't just passing, and I'm not here for myself.' She took a breath. 'I'm here for Sóley.'

Her face softened into a smile and he felt a sudden urge to reach out and caress the curve of her lip, to trigger such a smile for himself.

'It's a pretty name.'

She nodded, her smile freezing.

It *was* a pretty name—one he'd always liked. One you didn't hear much outside of Iceland. Only what had it got to do with him?

Watching her fingers tremble against her cup, he felt his ribs tighten. 'Who's Sóley?'

She was quiet for less than a minute, only it felt much longer—long enough for his brain to click through all the possible answers to the impossible one. The one he already knew.

He watched her posture change from defensive to resolute.

'She's your daughter. Our daughter.'

He stared at her in silence, but a cacophony of questions was ricocheting inside his head.

Not the how or the when or the where, but the *why*. Why had he not been more careful? Why had he allowed the heat of their encounter to blot out his normally ice-cold logic?

But the answers to those questions would have to wait.

'Okay...'

Shifting in her seat, she frowned. '"Okay"?' she repeated. 'Do you understand what I just said?'

'Yes.' He nodded. 'You're saying I got you pregnant.'

'You don't seem surprised,' she said slowly.

He shrugged. 'These things happen.'

To his siblings and half-siblings, even to his mother. But not to him. Never to him.

Until now.

'And you believe me?' She seemed confused, disappointed?

Tilting his head, he held her gaze. 'Honest answer?'

He was going to ask her what she would gain by lying. But before he could open his mouth her lip curled.

'On past performance I'm not sure I can expect that. I mean, you lied about your name. And the hotel you were staying at. And you lied about wanting to spend the day with me.'

'I didn't plan on lying to you,' he said quietly.

Her mouth thinned. 'No, I'm sure it comes very naturally to you.'

'You're twisting my words.'

She shook her head. 'You mean like saying Steinn instead of Stone?'

Pressing his spine into the wall behind him, he felt a tick of anger begin to pulse beneath his skin.

'Okay, I was wrong to lie to you—but if you care about the truth so much then why have you waited so long to tell me that I have a daughter? I mean, she must be what...?' He did a quick mental calculation. 'Ten, eleven months?'

Continue reading
PROOF OF THEIR ONE-NIGHT PASSION
Louise Fuller

Available next month
www.millsandboon.co.uk

Copyright ©2019 Louise Fuller

COMING SOON!

We really hope you enjoyed reading this book. If you're looking for more romance, be sure to head to the shops when new books are available on

Thursday 14th November

To see which titles are coming soon, please visit

millsandboon.co.uk/nextmonth

MILLS & BOON

MILLS & BOON
DARE

Sexy. Passionate. Bold.

Sensual love stories featuring smart, sassy heroines you'd want as a best friend, and compelling intense heroes who are worthy of them.

Four DARE stories published every month, find them all at:

millsandboon.co.uk/DARE

MILLS & BOON
A ROMANCE FOR EVERY READER

- **FREE** delivery direct to your door

- **EXCLUSIVE** offers every month

- **SAVE** up to 25% on pre-paid subscriptions

SUBSCRIBE AND SAVE

millsandboon.co.uk/Subscribe

WANT EVEN MORE

ROMANCE?

SUBSCRIBE AND SAVE TODAY!

'Mills & Boon books, the perfect way to escape for an hour or so.'

MISS W. DYER

'Excellent service, promptly delivered and very good subscription choices.'

MISS A. PEARSON

'You get fantastic special offers and the chance to get books before they hit the shops.'

MRS V. HALL

Visit millsandboon.co.uk/Subscribe and save on brand new books.

LET'S TALK

Romance

For exclusive extracts, competitions
and special offers, find us online:

facebook.com/millsandboon

@MillsandBoon

@MillsandBoonUK

Get in touch on 01413 063232

For all the latest titles coming soon, visit
millsandboon.co.uk/nextmonth

MILLS & BOON

THE HEART OF ROMANCE

A ROMANCE FOR EVERY KIND OF READER

MODERN

Prepare to be swept off your feet by sophisticated, sexy and seductive heroes, in some of the world's most glamourous and romantic locations, where power and passion collide.
8 stories per month.

HISTORICAL

Escape with historical heroes from time gone by. Whether your passion is for wicked Regency Rakes, muscled Vikings or rugged Highlanders, awaken the romance of the past.
6 stories per month.

MEDICAL

Set your pulse racing with dedicated, delectable doctors in the high-pressure world of medicine, where emotions run high and passion, comfort and love are the best medicine.
6 stories per month.

True Love

Celebrate true love with tender stories of heartfelt romance, from the rush of falling in love to the joy a new baby can bring, and focus on the emotional heart of a relationship.
8 stories per month.

Desire

Indulge in secrets and scandal, intense drama and plenty of sizzling hot action with powerful and passionate heroes who have it all: wealth, status, good looks…everything but the right woman.
6 stories per month.

HEROES

Experience all the excitement of a gripping thriller, with an intense romance at its heart. Resourceful, true-to-life women and strong, fearless men face danger and desire - a killer combination!
8 stories per month.

DARE

Sensual love stories featuring smart, sassy heroines you'd want as a best friend, and compelling intense heroes who are worthy of them.
4 stories per month.

To see which titles are coming soon, please visit

millsandboon.co.uk/nextmonth